NEBULA AWARDS
SHOWCASE 2014

ALSO FROM PYR®:

NEBULA AWARDS SHOWCASE 2014

EDITED BY
KIJ JOHNSON

THE YEAR'S BEST SCIENCE FICTION AND FANTASY
Selected by the Science Fiction and Fantasy Writers of America

STORIES, EXCERPTS & ESSAYS BY

Neil Gaiman · Gene Wolfe · Nancy Kress · Kim Stanley Robinson
Aliette de Bodard · Andy Duncan · E. C. Myers · Ken Liu
Cat Rambo · Michael Dirda
and others

an imprint of Prometheus Books
Amherst, NY

Cover illustration © 2014 Raoul Vitale
Cover design by Grace M. Conti-Zilsberger

Inquiries should be addressed to

Pyr
59 John Glenn Drive
Amherst, New York 14228
VOICE: 716–691–0133
FAX: 716–691–0137
WWW.PYRSF.COM

18 17 16 15 14   5 4 3 2 1

Library of Congress Cataloging-in-Publication Data

Nebula Awards Showcase 2014 / edited by Kij Johnson.
        pages cm
    ISBN 978-1-61614-901-7 (pbk.)
    ISBN 978-1-61614-902-4 (ebook)
    1. Science fiction, American. 2. Fantasy fiction, American. I. Johnson, Kij, editor of compilation.

PS648.S3N385 2014
813'.0876208—dc23

2013045243

Printed in the United States of America

For James Gunn

PERMISSIONS

CONTENTS

CONTENTS

Nebula Award Finalist, Best Short Story

Andre Norton Award
for Young Adult Science Fiction
and Fantasy

Nebula Award Finalist, Best Short Story

Damon Knight Memorial Grand Master: Gene Wolfe

CONTENTS

INTRODUCTION

KIJ JOHNSON

On the day I started writing this introduction, I learned that Frederik Pohl had died at the age of ninety-three. Pohl's career in science fiction spanned most of seven decades and nearly every job title: fan, long- and short-form editor, agent, award juror, author, and coauthor. His first Nebula nomination came in 1966, and, in later years, he won twice. One of those works, the brilliant novel *Gateway*, won Hugo and Nebula both, as well as the John W. Campbell Memorial Award, among others. In fact, he was nominated for awards in this field a staggering 126 times. His importance to speculative fiction was recognized by the Science Fiction Writers of America (SFWA) when he won the Damon Knight Memorial Grand Master Award back in 1993; in the nearly twenty years since then, he continued to write, winning his final major award, a Hugo, in 2010. He is irreplaceable.

Frederik Pohl's death had a powerful impact on me, but he was, of course, not the only person our field has lost recently. Joanna Russ was a unique voice; Jack Vance was another. The list goes on and on, back into history: there will never be another Andre Norton, Ray Bradbury, Octavia Butler, Theodore Sturgeon, C. L. Moore.

One piece of conventional wisdom is that our field is a graying field. The writers and the readers at its heart grow older; the *In Memoriam* lists at each year's Nebula Awards banquet lengthens. And it is hard not to stare backward, ticking each loss from a roster of living greats.

There is a second conventional wisdom that pulls contrary to this current; that is, that the field is not graying but growing. In recent years, speculative-fiction storytelling has exploded across modes and media to fuel one-hundred-thousand-person conventions and rule the theatres. Even the cloistered garden that written SF sometimes seems to be is immeasurably vaster than it was fifty years ago, as *millions* of copies of speculative-fiction books are sold, generally categorized as young adult books regardless of their sophistication.

And all the new writers. A handful of this year's nominees and recipients in the fiction categories have been nominated for Nebulas one or more decades ago, members of what might be considered an old guard; but the majority have appeared here only in the last few years. Ten of the fiction nominees were on the ballot for the first time; another seven have received multiple nominations, but only within the last four years. The writers and director of this year's winner of the Ray Bradbury Award for Outstanding Dramatic Presentation had not worked on a feature-length film before. This year's Andre Norton Award–winner is a debut novel for its author.

Judging by this year's ballot, there is no dearth of new talent.

Will these works become part of speculative fiction's canon? Will any of these authors have the profound effect on the genre that Fred Pohl did? We won't know for decades—or longer—but my guess is yes. Fred Pohl and all the other writers, editors, publishers, and agents we have lost are irreplaceable, but that does not mean they will not be joined in the canon by others. The new writers of our field will evolve and find or perfect their voices, their visions; some will become, in their turn, irreplaceable.

We are a literature of change. It's exciting to be reading speculative fiction at a time when the field seems to be looking at itself as much as the world and saying, "What now?"

The *Nebula Awards Showcase 2014* reprints the winners of the short-story, novelette, and novella awards. It also includes excerpts from this year's winning novel and this year's winner of the Andre Norton Award for Young Adult Science Fiction and Fantasy. In recognition of the new Damon Knight Memorial Grand Master, Gene Wolfe, the *Showcase* reprints a classic short story he has selected. Finally, it includes the three winners of the 2011 Rhysling Awards for speculative poetry. I hope you enjoy it all as much as I did.

ABOUT THE SCIENCE FICTION AND FANTASY WRITERS OF AMERICA

The Science Fiction and Fantasy Writers of America, Inc. (formerly known as the Science Fiction Writers of America; the original acronym "SFWA" was retained), includes among its members many active writers of science fiction and fantasy. According to the bylaws of the organization, its purpose "shall be to promote the furtherance of the writing of science fiction, fantasy, and related genres as a profession." SFWA informs writers on professional matters, protects their interests, and helps them in dealings with agents, editors, anthologists, and producers of nonprint media. It also strives to encourage public interest in and appreciation of science fiction and fantasy.

Anyone may become an active member of SFWA after the acceptance of and payment for one professionally published novel, one professionally produced dramatic script, or three professionally published pieces of short fiction. Only science fiction, fantasy, horror, or other prose fiction of a related genre, in English, shall be considered as qualifying for active membership. Beginning writers who do not yet qualify for active membership but have published some qualifying professional work may join as associate members; other classes of membership include affiliate members (editors, agents, reviewers, and anthologists), estate members (representatives of the estates of active members who have died), and institutional members (high schools, colleges, universities, libraries, broadcasters, film producers, futurist groups, and individuals associated with such an institution).

Readers are invited to visit the SFWA website on the Internet at www.sfwa.org.

ABOUT THE NEBULA AWARDS

Shortly after the founding of SFWA in 1965, its first secretary-treasurer, Lloyd Biggle Jr., proposed that the organization periodically select and publish the year's best stories. This notion evolved into an elaborate balloting process, an annual awards banquet, and a series of Nebula Awards anthologies.

Throughout every calendar year, members of SFWA read and recommend novels and stories for the Nebula Awards. The editor of the *Nebula Awards Report* (NAR) collects the recommendations and publishes them in the *SFWA Forum* and on the SFWA members' private web page. At the end of the year, the *NAR* editor tallies the endorsements, draws up a preliminary ballot containing ten or more recommendations for each category, and sends it to all active SFWA members. Under the current rules, each work enjoys a one-year eligibility period from its date of publication in the United States. If a work fails to receive ten recommendations during the one-year interval, it is dropped from further Nebula Award consideration.

The *NAR* editor processes the results of the preliminary ballot and then compiles a final ballot listing the five most popular novels, novellas, novelettes, and short stories. For purposes of the award, a novel is determined to be 40,000 words or more; a novella is 17,500 to 39,999 words; a novelette is 7,500 to 17,499 words; and a short story is 7,499 words or fewer. Additionally, each year SFWA impanels a member jury, which is empowered to supplement the five nominees with a sixth choice in cases where it feels a worthy title was neglected by the membership at large. Thus, the appearance of more than five finalists in a category reflects two distinct processes: jury discretion and ties.

A complete set of Nebula rules can be found at www.sfwa.org/awards/rules.htm.

THE RAY BRADBURY AWARD FOR OUTSTANDING DRAMATIC PRESENTATION

The Ray Bradbury Award for Outstanding Dramatic Presentation is not a Nebula Award, but it follows Nebula nomination, voting, and award rules and guidelines, and it is given each year at the annual awards banquet. Founded in 2009, it replaces the earlier Nebula Award for Best Script. It was named in honor of science fiction and fantasy author Ray Bradbury, whose work appeared frequently in movies and on television.

ANDRE NORTON AWARD FOR YOUNG ADULT SCIENCE FICTION AND FANTASY

The Andre Norton Award for Young Adult Science Fiction and Fantasy is an annual award presented by SFWA to the author of the best young adult or middle-grade science fiction or fantasy book published in the United States in the preceding year.

The Andre Norton Award is not a Nebula Award, but it follows Nebula nomination, voting, and award rules and guidelines. It was founded in 2005 to honor popular science fiction and fantasy author Andre Norton.

2012 NEBULA AWARDS
FINAL BALLOT

NOVEL

Winner: *2312* by Kim Stanley Robinson (Orbit US; Orbit UK)
Nominees:
> *Throne of the Crescent Moon* by Saladin Ahmed (DAW Books; Gollancz)
> *Ironskin* by Tina Connolly (Tor)
> *The Killing Moon* by N. K. Jemisin (Orbit US; Orbit UK)
> *The Drowning Girl* by Caitlín R. Kiernan (Roc)
> *Glamour in Glass* by Mary Robinette Kowal (Tor)

NOVELLA

Winner: "After the Fall, Before the Fall, During the Fall" by Nancy Kress
> (Tachyon Press)
Nominees:
> "On a Red Station, Drifting" by Aliette de Bodard (Immersion Press)
> "The Stars Do Not Lie" by Jay Lake (*Asimov's Science Fiction*, October–
> November 2012)
> "All the Flavors" by Ken Liu (*GigaNotoSaurus*, February 1, 2012)
> "Katabasis" by Robert Reed (*The Magazine of Fantasy & Science Fiction*,
> November–December 2012)
> "Barry's Tale" by Lawrence M. Schoen (*Buffalito Buffet*)

NOVELETTE

Winner: "Close Encounters" by Andy Duncan (*The Pottawatomie Giant & Other Stories*, PS Publishing)
Nominees:
   "The Pyre of New Day," Catherine Asaro (*The Mammoth Book of SF Wars*, Running Press)
   "The Waves" by Ken Liu (*Asimov's Science Fiction*, December 2012)
   "The Finite Canvas" by Brit Mandelo (*Tor.com*, December 5, 2012)
   "Swift, Brutal Retaliation" by Meghan McCarron (*Tor.com*, January 4, 2012)
   "Portrait of Lisane da Patagnia," Rachel Swirsky (*Tor.com*, August 22, 2012)
   "Fade to White" by Catherynne M. Valente (*Clarkesworld*, August 2012)

SHORT STORY

Winner: "Immersion" by Aliette de Bodard (*Clarkesworld*, June 2012)
Nominees:
   "Robot" by Helena Bell (*Clarkesworld*, September 2012)
   "Fragmentation, or Ten Thousand Goodbyes" by Tom Crosshill (*Clarkesworld*, April 2012)
   "Nanny's Day" by Leah Cypess (*Asimov's Science Fiction*, March 2012)
   "Give Her Honey When You Hear Her Scream" by Maria Dahvana Headley (*Lightspeed*, July 2012)
   "The Bookmaking Habits of Select Species" by Ken Liu (*Lightspeed*, August 2012)
   "Five Ways to Fall in Love on Planet Porcelain" by Cat Rambo (*Near + Far*, Hydra House)

RAY BRADBURY AWARD FOR OUTSTANDING DRAMATIC PRESENTATION

Winner: *Beasts of the Southern Wild*, Benh Zeitlin (director); Benh Zeitlin and Lucy Abilar (writers) (Journeyman/Cinereach/Court 13/Fox Searchlight)
Nominees:

The Avengers, Joss Whedon (director); Joss Whedon and Zak Penn (writers) (Marvel/Disney)

The Cabin in the Woods, Drew Goddard (director); Joss Whedon and Drew Goddard (writers) (Mutant Enemy/Lionsgate)

The Hunger Games, Gary Ross (director); Gary Ross, Suzanne Collins, and Billy Ray (writers) (Lionsgate)

John Carter, Andrew Stanton (director); Michael Chabon, Mark Andrews, and Andrew Stanton (writers) (Disney)

Looper, Rian Johnson (director); Rian Johnson (writer) (FilmDistrict/TriStar)

ANDRE NORTON AWARD FOR YOUNG ADULT SCIENCE FICTION AND FANTASY

Winner: *Fair Coin* by E. C. Myers (Pyr)
Nominees:

Iron Hearted Violet by Kelly Barnhill (Little, Brown)

Black Heart by Holly Black (Simon & Schuster/McElderry; Gollancz)

Above by Leah Bobet (Levine)

The Diviners by Libba Bray (Little, Brown; Atom)

Vessel by Sarah Beth Durst (Simon & Schuster/McElderry)

Seraphina by Rachel Hartman (Random House; Doubleday UK)

Enchanted by Alethea Kontis (Harcourt)

Every Day by David Levithan (Alice A. Knopf Books for Young Readers)

Summer of the Mariposas by Guadalupe Garcia McCall (Tu Books)

Railsea by China Miéville (Del Rey; Macmillan)

Above World by Jenn Reese (Candlewick)

NEBULA AWARD, BEST SHORT STORY

"IMMERSION"

ALIETTE DE BODARD

Aliette de Bodard has also won a Locus Award, a British Science Fiction Association Award, and Writers of the Future. "Immersion" was first published in Clarkesworld *Magazine.*

In the morning, you're no longer quite sure who you are.

You stand in front of the mirror—it shifts and trembles, reflecting only what you want to see—eyes that feel too wide, skin that feels too pale, an odd, distant smell wafting from the compartment's ambient system that is neither incense nor garlic, but something else, something elusive that you once knew.

You're dressed, already—not on your skin, but outside, where it matters, your avatar sporting blue and black and gold, the stylish clothes of a well-travelled, well-connected woman. For a moment, as you turn away from the mirror, the glass shimmers out of focus; and another woman in a dull silk gown stares back at you: smaller, squatter and in every way diminished—a stranger, a distant memory that has ceased to have any meaning.

Quy was on the docks, watching the spaceships arrive. She could, of course, have been anywhere on Longevity Station, and requested the feed from the network to be patched to her router—and watched, superimposed on her field of vision, the slow dance of ships slipping into their pod cradles like births watched in reverse. But there was something about standing on the spaceport's concourse—a feeling of closeness that she just couldn't replicate by standing in Golden Carp Gardens or Azure Dragon Temple. Because here—here, separated by only a few measures of sheet metal from the cradle pods, she could feel herself teetering on the edge of the vacuum, submerged in cold and breathing in neither air nor oxygen. She could almost imagine herself rootless, finally returned to the source of everything.

Most ships those days were Galactic—you'd have thought Longevity's ex-masters would have been unhappy about the station's independence, but now that the war was over Longevity was a tidy source of profit. The ships came; and disgorged a steady stream of tourists—their eyes too round and straight, their jaws too square; their faces an unhealthy shade of pink, like undercooked meat left too long in the sun. They walked with the easy confidence of people with immersers: pausing to admire the suggested highlights for a second or so before moving on to the transport station, where they haggled in schoolbook Rong for a ride to their recommended hotels—a sickeningly familiar ballet Quy had been seeing most of her life, a unison of foreigners descending on the station like a plague of centipedes or leeches.

Still, Quy watched them. They reminded her of her own time on Prime, her heady schooldays filled with raucous bars and wild weekends, and late-minute revisions for exams, a carefree time she'd never have again in her life. She both longed for those days back, and hated herself for her weakness. Her education on Prime, which should have been her path into the higher strata of the station's society, had brought her nothing but a sense of disconnection from her family; a growing solitude, and a dissatisfaction, an aimlessness she couldn't put in words.

She might not have moved all day—had a sign not blinked, superimposed by her router on the edge of her field of vision. A message from Second Uncle.

"Child." His face was pale and worn, his eyes underlined by dark circles, as if he hadn't slept. He probably hadn't—the last Quy had seen of him, he had been closeted with Quy's sister Tam, trying to organise a delivery for a wedding—five hundred winter melons, and six barrels of Prosper Station's best fish sauce. "Come back to the restaurant."

"I'm on my day of rest," Quy said; it came out as more peevish and childish than she'd intended.

Second Uncle's face twisted, in what might have been a smile, though he had very little sense of humour. The scar he'd got in the Independence War shone white against the grainy background—twisting back and forth, as if it still pained him. "I know, but I need you. We have an important customer."

"Galactic," Quy said. That was the only reason he'd be calling her, and not one of her brothers or cousins. Because the family somehow thought that her studies on Prime gave her insight into the Galactics' way of thought—something useful, if not the success they'd hoped for.

"Yes. An important man, head of a local trading company." Second Uncle did not move on her field of vision. Quy could *see* the ships moving through his face, slowly aligning themselves in front of their pods, the hole in front of them opening like an orchid flower. And she knew everything there was to know about Grandmother's restaurant; she was Tam's sister, after all; and she'd seen the accounts, the slow decline of their clientele as their more genteel clients moved to better areas of the station; the influx of tourists on a budget, with little time for expensive dishes prepared with the best ingredients.

"Fine," she said. "I'll come."

At breakfast, you stare at the food spread out on the table: bread and jam and some coloured liquid—you come up blank for a moment, before your immerser kicks in, reminding you that it's coffee, served strong and black, just as you always take it.

Yes. Coffee.

You raise the cup to your lips—your immerser gently prompts you, reminding you of where to grasp, how to lift, how to be in every possible way graceful and elegant, always an effortless model.

"It's a bit strong," your husband says, apologetically. He watches you from the other end of the table, an expression you can't interpret on his face—and isn't this odd, because shouldn't you know all there is to know about expressions—shouldn't the immerser have everything about Galactic culture recorded into its database, shouldn't it prompt you? But it's strangely silent, and this scares you, more than anything. Immersers never fail.

"Shall we go?" your husband says—and, for a moment, you come up blank on

NEBULA AWARDS SHOWCASE 2014

his name, before you remember—Galen, it's Galen, named after some physician on Old Earth. He's tall, with dark hair and pale skin—his immerser avatar isn't much different from his real self, Galactic avatars seldom are. It's people like you who have to work the hardest to adjust, because so much about you draws attention to itself—the stretched eyes that crinkle in the shape of moths, the darker skin, the smaller, squatter shape more reminiscent of jackfruits than swaying fronds. But no matter: you can be made perfect; you can put on the immerser and become someone else, someone pale-skinned and tall and beautiful.

Though, really, it's been such a long time since you took off the immerser, isn't it? It's just a thought—a suspended moment that is soon erased by the immerser's flow of information, the little arrows drawing your attention to the bread and the kitchen, and the polished metal of the table—giving you context about everything, opening up the universe like a lotus flower.

"Yes," you say. "Let's go." Your tongue trips over the word—there's a structure you should have used, a pronoun you should have said instead of the lapidary Galactic sentence. But nothing will come, and you feel like a field of sugar canes after the harvest—burnt out, all cutting edges with no sweetness left inside.

Of course, Second Uncle insisted on Quy getting her immerser for the interview—just in case, he said, soothingly and diplomatically as always. Trouble was, it wasn't where Quy had last left it. After putting out a message to the rest of the family, the best information Quy got was from Cousin Khanh, who thought he'd seen Tam sweep through the living quarters, gathering every piece of Galactic tech she could get her hands on. Third Aunt, who caught Khanh's message on the family's communication channel, tutted disapprovingly. "Tam. Always with her mind lost in the mountains, that girl. Dreams have never husked rice."

Quy said nothing. Her own dreams had shrivelled and died after she came back from Prime and failed Longevity's mandarin exams; but it was good to have Tam around—to have someone who saw beyond the restaurant, beyond the narrow circle of family interests. Besides, if she didn't stick with her sister, who would?

Tam wasn't in the communal areas on the upper floors; Quy threw a glance towards the lift to Grandmother's closeted rooms, but she was doubtful Tam would have gathered Galactic tech just so she could pay her respects to Grandmother. Instead, she went straight to the lower floor, the one she and Tam shared with the children of their generation.

It was right next to the kitchen, and the smells of garlic and fish sauce seemed to be everywhere—of course, the youngest generation always got the lower floor, the one with all the smells and the noises of a legion of waitresses bringing food over to the dining room.

Tam was there, sitting in the little compartment that served as the floor's communal area. She'd spread out the tech on the floor—two immersers (Tam and Quy were possibly the only family members who cared so little about immersers they left them lying around), a remote entertainment set that was busy broadcasting some stories of children running on terraformed planets, and something Quy couldn't quite identify, because Tam had taken it apart into small components: it lay on the table like a gutted fish, all metals and optical parts.

But, at some point, Tam had obviously got bored with the entire process, because she was currently finishing her breakfast, slurping noodles from her soup bowl. She must have got it from the kitchen's leftovers, because Quy knew the smell, could taste the spiciness of the broth on her tongue—Mother's cooking, enough to make her stomach growl although she'd had rolled rice cakes for breakfast.

"You're at it again," Quy said with a sigh. "Could you not take my immerser for your experiments, please?"

Tam didn't even look surprised. "You don't seem very keen on using it, big sis."

"That I don't use it doesn't mean it's yours," Quy said, though that wasn't a real reason. She didn't mind Tam borrowing her stuff, and actually would have been glad to never put on an immerser again—she hated the feeling they gave her, the vague sensation of the system rooting around in her brain to find the best body cues to give her. But there were times when she was expected to wear an immerser: whenever dealing with customers, whether she was waiting at tables or in preparation meetings for large occasions.

Tam, of course, didn't wait at tables—she'd made herself so good at logistics and anything to do with the station's system that she spent most of her time in front of a screen, or connected to the station's network.

"Lil' sis?" Quy said.

Tam set her chopsticks by the side of the bowl, and made an expansive gesture with her hands. "Fine. Have it back. I can always use mine."

Quy stared at the things spread on the table, and asked the inevitable question. "How's progress?"

Tam's work was network connections and network maintenance within the restaurant; her hobby was tech. Galactic tech. She took things apart to see what made them tick; and rebuilt them. Her foray into entertainment units had helped the restaurant set up ambient sounds—old-fashioned Rong music for Galactic customers, recitation of the newest poems for locals.

But immersers had her stumped: the things had nasty safeguards to them. You could open them in half, to replace the battery; but you went no further. Tam's previous attempt had almost lost her the use of her hands.

By Tam's face, she didn't feel ready to try again. "It's got to be the same logic."

"As what?" Quy couldn't help asking. She picked up her own immerser from the table, briefly checking that it did indeed bear her serial number.

Tam gestured to the splayed components on the table. "Artificial Literature Writer. Little gadget that composes light entertainment novels."

"That's not the same—" Quy checked herself, and waited for Tam to explain.

"Takes existing cultural norms, and puts them into a cohesive, satisfying narrative. Like people forging their own path and fighting aliens for possession of a planet, that sort of stuff that barely speaks to us on Longevity. I mean, we've never even seen a planet." Tam exhaled, sharply—her eyes half on the dismembered Artificial Literature Writer, half on some overlay of her vision. "Just like immersers take a given culture and parcel it out to you in a form you can relate to—language, gestures, customs, the whole package. They've got to have the same architecture."

"I'm still not sure what you want to do with it." Quy put on her immerser, adjusting the thin metal mesh around her head until it fitted. She winced as the interface synched with her brain. She moved her hands, adjusting some settings lower than the factory ones—darn thing always reset itself to factory, which she suspected was no accident. A shimmering lattice surrounded her: her avatar, slowly taking shape around her. She could still see the room—the lattice was only faintly opaque—but ancestors, how she hated the feeling of not quite being there. "How do I look?"

"Horrible. Your avatar looks like it's died or something."

"Ha ha ha," Quy said. Her avatar was paler than her, and taller: it made her look beautiful, most customers agreed. In those moments, Quy was glad she had an avatar, so they wouldn't see the anger on her face. "You haven't answered my question."

Tam's eyes glinted. "Just think of the things we couldn't do. This is the best piece of tech Galactics have ever brought us."

Which wasn't much, but Quy didn't need to say it aloud. Tam knew exactly how Quy felt about Galactics and their hollow promises.

"It's their weapon, too." Tam pushed at the entertainment unit. "Just like their books and their holos and their live games. It's fine for them—they put the immersers on tourist settings, they get just what they need to navigate a foreign environment from whatever idiot's written the Rong script for that thing. But we—we worship them. We wear the immersers on Galactic all the time. We make ourselves like them, because they push, and because we're naive enough to give in."

"And you think you can make this better?" Quy couldn't help it. It wasn't that she needed to be convinced: on Prime, she'd never seen immersers. They were tourist stuff, and even while travelling from one city to another, the citizens just assumed they'd know enough to get by. But the stations, their ex-colonies, were flooded with immersers.

Tam's eyes glinted, as savage as those of the rebels in the history holos. "If I can take them apart, I can rebuild them and disconnect the logical circuits. I can give us the language and the tools to deal with them without being swallowed by them."

Mind lost in the mountains, Third Aunt said. No one had ever accused Tam of thinking small. Or of not achieving what she set her mind on, come to think of it. And every revolution had to start somewhere—hadn't Longevity's

War of Independence started over a single poem, and the unfair imprisonment of the poet who'd written it?

Quy nodded. She believed Tam, though she didn't know how far. "Fair point. Have to go now, or Second Uncle will skin me. See you later, lil' sis."

As you walk under the wide arch of the restaurant with your husband, you glance upwards, at the calligraphy that forms its sign. The immerser translates it for you into "Sister Hai's Kitchen," and starts giving you a detailed background of the place: the menu and the most recommended dishes—as you walk past the various tables, it highlights items it thinks you would like, from rolled-up rice dumplings to fried shrimps. It warns you about the more exotic dishes, like the pickled pig's ears, the fermented meat (you have to be careful about that one, because its name changes depending on which station dialect you order in), or the reeking durian fruit that the natives so love.

It feels . . . not quite right, you think, as you struggle to follow Galen, who is already far away, striding ahead with the same confidence he always exudes in life. People part before him; a waitress with a young, pretty avatar bows before him, though Galen himself takes no notice. You know that such obsequiousness unnerves him; he always rants about the outdated customs aboard Longevity, the inequalities and the lack of democratic government—he thinks it's only a matter of time before they change, adapt themselves to fit into Galactic society. You—you have a faint memory of arguing with him, a long time ago, but now you can't find the words, anymore, or even the reason why—it makes sense, it all makes sense. The Galactics rose against the tyranny of Old Earth and overthrew their shackles, and won the right to determine their own destiny; and every other station and planet will do the same, eventually, rise against the dictatorships that hold them away from progress. It's right; it's always been right.

Unbidden, you stop at a table, and watch two young women pick at a dish of chicken with chopsticks—the smell of fish sauce and lemongrass rises in the air, as pungent and as unbearable as rotten meat—no, no, that's not it, you have an image of a dark-skinned woman, bringing a dish of steamed rice to the table, her hands filled with that same smell, and your mouth watering in anticipation . . .

The young women are looking at you: they both wear standard-issue avatars, the bottom-of-the-line kind—their clothes are a garish mix of red and yellow, with the odd, uneasy cut of cheap designers; and their faces waver, letting you glimpse a hint of darker skin beneath the red flush of their cheeks. Cheap and tawdry, and altogether inappropriate; and you're glad you're not one of them.

"Can I help you, older sister?" one of them asks.

Older sister. A pronoun you were looking for, earlier; one of the things that seem to have vanished from your mind. You struggle for words; but all the immerser seems to suggest to you is a neutral and impersonal pronoun, one that you instinctively know is wrong—it's one only foreigners and out-siders would use in those circumstances. "Older sister," you repeat, finally, because you can't think of anything else.

"Agnes!"

Galen's voice, calling from far away—for a brief moment the immerser seems to fail you again, because you *know* that you have many names, that Agnes is the one they gave you in Galactic school, the one neither Galen nor his friends can mangle when they pronounce it. You remember the Rong names your mother gave you on Longevity, the childhood endearments and your adult style name.

Be-Nho, Be-Yeu. Thu—Autumn, like a memory of red maple leaves on a planet you never knew.

You pull away from the table, disguising the tremor in your hands.

Second Uncle was already waiting when Quy arrived; and so were the customers.

"You're late," Second Uncle sent on the private channel, though he made the comment half-heartedly, as if he'd expected it all along. As if he'd never really believed he could rely on her—that stung.

"Let me introduce my niece Quy to you," Second Uncle said, in Galactic, to the man beside him.

"Quy," the man said, his immerser perfectly taking up the nuances of her name in Rong. He was everything she'd expected; tall, with only a thin layer of avatar, a little something that narrowed his chin and eyes, and made his chest slightly larger. Cosmetic enhancements: he was good-looking for a Galactic, all things considered. He went on, in Galactic, "My name is Galen Santos. Pleased to meet you. This is my wife, Agnes."

Agnes. Quy turned, and looked at the woman for the first time—and flinched. There was no one here: just a thick layer of avatar, so dense and so complex that she couldn't even guess at the body hidden within.

"Pleased to meet you." On a hunch, Quy bowed, from younger to elder, with both hands brought together—Rong-style, not Galactic—and saw a shudder run through Agnes' body, barely perceptible; but Quy was observant, she'd always been. Her immerser was screaming at her, telling her to hold out both hands, palms up, in the Galactic fashion. She tuned it out: she was still at the stage where she could tell the difference between her thoughts and the immerser's thoughts.

Second Uncle was talking again—his own avatar was light, a paler version of him. "I understand you're looking for a venue for a banquet."

"We are, yes." Galen pulled a chair to him, sank into it. They all followed suit, though not with the same fluid, arrogant ease. When Agnes sat, Quy saw her flinch, as though she'd just remembered something unpleasant. "We'll be celebrating our fifth marriage anniversary, and we both felt we wanted to mark the occasion with something suitable."

Second Uncle nodded. "I see," he said, scratching his chin. "My congratulations to you."

Galen nodded. "We thought—" he paused, threw a glance at his wife that Quy couldn't quite interpret—her immerser came up blank, but there was something oddly familiar about it, something she ought to have been able to name. "Something Rong," he said at last. "A large banquet for a hundred people, with the traditional dishes."

Quy could almost feel Second Uncle's satisfaction. A banquet of that size would be awful logistics, but it would keep the restaurant afloat for a year or more, if they could get the price right. But something was wrong—something—

"What did you have in mind?" Quy asked, not to Galen, but to his wife. The wife—Agnes, which probably wasn't the name she'd been born with—

who wore a thick avatar, and didn't seem to be answering or ever speaking up. An awful picture was coming together in Quy's mind.

Agnes didn't answer. Predictable.

Second Uncle took over, smoothing over the moment of awkwardness with expansive hand gestures. "The whole hog, yes?" Second Uncle said. He rubbed his hands, an odd gesture that Quy had never seen from him—a Galactic expression of satisfaction. "Bitter melon soup, Dragon-Phoenix plates, Roast Pig, Jade Under the Mountain . . ." He was citing all the traditional dishes for a wedding banquet—unsure of how far the foreigner wanted to take it. He left out the odder stuff, like Shark Fin or Sweet Red Bean Soup.

"Yes, that's what we would like. Wouldn't we, darling?" Galen's wife neither moved nor spoke. Galen's head turned towards her, and Quy caught his expression at last. She'd thought it would be contempt, or hatred; but no; it was anguish. He genuinely loved her, and he couldn't understand what was going on.

Galactics. Couldn't he recognise an immerser junkie when he saw one? But then Galactics, as Tam said, seldom had the problem—they didn't put on the immersers for more than a few days on low settings, if they ever went that far. Most were flat-out convinced Galactic would get them anywhere.

Second Uncle and Galen were haggling, arguing prices and features; Second Uncle sounding more and more like a Galactic tourist as the conversation went on, more and more aggressive for lower and lower gains. Quy didn't care anymore: she watched Agnes. Watched the impenetrable avatar—a red-headed woman in the latest style from Prime, with freckles on her skin and a hint of a star-tan on her face. But that wasn't what she was, inside; what the immerser had dug deep into.

Wasn't who she was at all. Tam was right; all immersers should be taken apart, and did it matter if they exploded? They'd done enough harm as it was.

Quy wanted to get up, to tear away her own immerser, but she couldn't, not in the middle of the negotiation. Instead, she rose, and walked closer to Agnes; the two men barely glanced at her, too busy agreeing on a price. "You're not alone," she said, in Rong, low enough that it didn't carry.

Again, that odd, disjointed flash. "You have to take it off." Quy said, but got no further response. As an impulse, she grabbed the other woman's arm—felt her hands go right through the immerser's avatar, connect with warm, solid flesh.

You hear them negotiating, in the background—it's tough going, because the Rong man sticks to his guns stubbornly, refusing to give ground to Galen's onslaught. It's all very distant, a subject of intellectual study; the immerser reminds you from time to time, interpreting this and this body cue, nudging you this way and that—you must sit straight and silent, and support your husband—and so you smile through a mouth that feels gummed together.

You feel, all the while, the Rong girl's gaze on you, burning like ice water, like the gaze of a dragon. She won't move away from you; and her hand rests on you, gripping your arm with a strength you didn't think she had in her body. Her avatar is but a thin layer, and you can see her beneath it: a round, moon-shaped face with skin the colour of cinnamon—no, not spices, not chocolate, but simply a colour you've seen all your life.

"You have to take it off," she says. You don't move; but you wonder what she's talking about.

Take it off. Take it off. Take what off?

The immerser.

Abruptly, you remember—a dinner with Galen's friends, when they laughed at jokes that had gone by too fast for you to understand. You came home battling tears; and found yourself reaching for the immerser on your bedside table, feeling its cool weight in your hands. You thought it would please Galen if you spoke his language; that he would be less ashamed of how uncultured you sounded to his friends. And then you found out that everything was fine, as long as you kept the settings on maximum and didn't remove it. And then . . . and then you walked with it and slept with it, and showed the world nothing but the avatar it had designed—saw nothing it hadn't tagged and labelled for you. Then . . .

Then it all slid down, didn't it? You couldn't program the network anymore, couldn't look at the guts of machines; you lost your job with the tech company, and came to Galen's compartment, wandering in the room like a hollow shell, a ghost of yourself—as if you'd already died, far away from home and all that it means to you. Then—then the immerser wouldn't come off, anymore.

"What do you think you're doing, young woman?"

Second Uncle had risen, turning towards Quy—his avatar flushed with anger, the pale skin mottled with an unsightly red. "We adults are in the middle of negotiating something very important, if you don't mind." It might have made Quy quail in other circumstances, but his voice and his body language were wholly Galactic; and he sounded like a stranger to her—an angry foreigner whose food order she'd misunderstood—whom she'd mock later, sitting in Tam's room with a cup of tea in her lap, and the familiar patter of her sister's musings.

"I apologise," Quy said, meaning none of it.

"That's all right," Galen said. "I didn't mean to—" he paused, looked at his wife. "I shouldn't have brought her here."

"You should take her to see a physician," Quy said, surprised at her own boldness.

"Do you think I haven't tried?" His voice was bitter. "I've even taken her to the best hospitals on Prime. They look at her, and say they can't take it off. That the shock of it would kill her. And even if it didn't . . ." He spread his hands, letting air fall between them like specks of dust. "Who knows if she'd come back?"

Quy felt herself blush. "I'm sorry." And she meant it this time.

Galen waved her away, negligently, airily, but she could see the pain he was struggling to hide. Galactics didn't think tears were manly, she remembered. "So we're agreed?" Galen asked Second Uncle. "For a million credits?"

Quy thought of the banquet; of the food on the tables, of Galen thinking it would remind Agnes of home. Of how, in the end, it was doomed to fail, because everything would be filtered through the immerser, leaving Agnes with nothing but an exotic feast of unfamiliar flavours. "I'm sorry," she said, again, but no one was listening; and she turned away from Agnes with rage in her heart—with the growing feeling that it had all been for nothing in the end.

*   *   *

"I'm sorry," the girl says—she stands, removing her hand from your arm, and you feel like a tearing inside, as if something within you was struggling to claw free from your body. Don't go, you want to say. Please don't go. Please don't leave me here.

But they're all shaking hands; smiling, pleased at a deal they've struck—like sharks, you think, like tigers. Even the Rong girl has turned away from you; giving you up as hopeless. She and her uncle are walking away, taking separate paths back to the inner areas of the restaurant, back to their home.

Please don't go.

It's as if something else were taking control of your body; a strength that you didn't know you possessed. As Galen walks back into the restaurant's main room, back into the hubbub and the tantalising smells of food—of lemongrass chicken and steamed rice, just as your mother used to make—you turn away from your husband, and follow the girl. Slowly, and from a distance; and then running, so that no one will stop you. She's walking fast—you see her tear her immerser away from her face, and slam it down onto a side table with disgust. You see her enter a room; and you follow her inside.

They're watching you, both girls, the one you followed in; and another, younger one, rising from the table she was sitting at—both terribly alien and terribly familiar at once. Their mouths are open, but no sound comes out.

In that one moment—staring at each other, suspended in time—you see the guts of Galactic machines spread on the table. You see the mass of tools; the dismantled machines; and the immerser, half spread-out before them, its two halves open like a cracked egg. And you understand that they've been trying to open them and reverse-engineer them; and you know that they'll never, ever succeed. Not because of the safeguards, of the Galactic encryptions to preserve their fabled intellectual property; but rather, because of something far more fundamental.

This is a Galactic toy, conceived by a Galactic mind—every layer of it, every logical connection within it exudes a mindset that might as well be alien to these girls. It takes a Galactic to believe that you can take a whole culture and reduce it to algorithms; that language and customs can be boiled to just a simple set of rules. For these girls, things are so much more complex than this; and they will never understand how an immerser works, because they can't think like a Galactic, they'll never ever think like that. You can't think like a Galactic unless you've been born in the culture.

Or drugged yourself, senseless, into it, year after year.

You raise a hand—it feels like moving through honey. You speak— struggling to shape words through layer after layer of immerser thoughts.

"I know about this," you say, and your voice comes out hoarse, and the words fall into place one by one like a laser stroke, and they feel right, in a way that nothing else has for five years. "Let me help you, younger sisters."

To Rochita Loenen-Ruiz, for the conversations that inspired this.

NEBULA AWARD, BEST NOVELETTE

"CLOSE ENCOUNTERS"

ANDY DUNCAN

Andy Duncan's fiction has also won two World Fantasy Awards and the Theodore Sturgeon Award. "Close Encounters" was published in Asimov's Magazine *and in his collection,* The Pottawatomie Giant and Other Stories.

She knocked on my front door at midday on Holly Eve, so I was in no mood to answer, in that season of tricks. An old man expects more tricks than treats in this world. I let that knocker knock on. *Blim, blam!* Knock, knock! It hurt my concentration, and filling old hulls with powder and shot warn't no easy task to start with, not as palsied as my hands had got, in my eightieth-odd year.

"All right, damn your eyes," I hollered as I hitched up from the table. I knocked against it, and a shaker tipped over: pepper, so I let it go. My maw wouldn't have approved of such language as that, but we all get old doing things our maws wouldn't approve. We can't help it, not in this disposition, on this sphere down below.

I sidled up on the door, trying to see between the edges of the curtain and the pane, but all I saw there was the screen-filtered light of the sun, which wouldn't set in my hollow till nearbouts three in the day. Through the curtains was a shadow-shape like the top of a person's head, but low, like a child. Probably one of those Holton boys toting an orange coin carton with a photo of some spindleshanked African child eating hominy with its fingers. Some said those Holtons was like the Johnny Cash song, so heavenly minded they're no earthly good.

"What you want?" I called, one hand on the deadbolt and one feeling for starving-baby quarters in my pocket.

"Mr. Nelson, right? Mr. Buck Nelson? I'd like to talk a bit, if you don't mind. Inside or on the porch, your call."

A female, and no child, neither. I twitched back the curtain, saw a fair pretty face under a fool hat like a sideways saucer, lips painted the same black-red as her hair. I shot the bolt and opened the wood door but kept the screen latched. When I saw her full length I felt a rush of fool vanity and was sorry I hadn't traded my overalls for fresh that morning. Her boots reached her knees but nowhere near the hem of her tight green dress. She was a little thing, hardly up to my collarbone, but a blind man would know she was full growed. I wondered what my hair was doing in back, and I felt one hand reach around to slick it down, without my really telling it to. Steady on, son.

"I been answering every soul else calling Buck Nelson since 1894, so I reckon I should answer you, too. What you want to talk about, Miss —?"

"Miss Hanes," she said, "and I'm a wire reporter, stringing for Associated Press."

"A reporter," I repeated. My jaw tightened up. My hand reached back for the doorknob as natural as it had fussed my hair. "You must have got the wrong man," I said.

I'd eaten biscuits bigger than her tee-ninchy pocketbook, but she reached out of it a little spiral pad that she flipped open to squint at. Looked to be full of secretary-scratch, not schoolhouse writing at all. "But you, sir, are indeed Buck Nelson, Route Six, Mountain View, Missouri? Writer of a book about your travels to the Moon, and Mars, and Venus?"

By the time she fetched up at Venus her voice was muffled by the wood door I had slammed in her face. I bolted it, cursing my rusty slow reflexes. How long had it been, since fool reporters come using around? Not long enough. I limped as quick as I could to the back door, which was right quick, even at my age. It's a small house. I shut that bolt, too, and yanked all the curtains to. I turned on the Zenith and dialed the sound up as far as it would go to drown out her blamed knocking and calling. Ever since the roof aerial blew cockeyed in the last whippoorwill storm, watching my set was like trying to read a road sign in a blizzard, but the sound blared out well enough. One of the stories was on as I settled back at the table with my shotgun hulls. I didn't really follow those women's stories, but I could hear Stu and Jo were having coffee again at the Hartford House and still talking about poor dead Eunice and that crazy gal what shot her because a ghost told her to. That blonde Jennifer was slap crazy, all right, but she was a looker, too, and the story hadn't been half so interesting since she'd been packed off to the sanitarium. I was spilling powder everywhere now, what with all the racket and distraction, and hearing the story was on reminded me it was past my dinnertime anyways, and me hungry. I went into the kitchen, hooked down my grease-pan and set it on the big burner, dug some lard out of the stand I kept in the icebox and threw that in to melt, then fisted some fresh-picked whitefish mushrooms out of their bin, rinjed them off in the sink, and rolled them in a bowl of cornmeal while I half-listened to the TV and half-listened to the city girl banging and hollering, at the back door this time. I could hear her boot heels a-thunking all hollow-like on the back porch, over the old dog bed where Teddy used to lie, where the other dog, Bo, used to try to squeeze, big as he was. She'd probably want to talk about poor old Bo, too, ask to see his grave, as if that would prove something. She had her some stick-to-it-iveness, Miss Associated Press did, I'd give her that much. Now she was sliding something under the door, I could hear it, like a field mouse gnawing its way in: a little card, like the one that Methodist preacher always leaves, only shinier. I didn't bother to pick it up. I didn't need nothing down there on that floor. I slid the whitefish into the hot oil without a splash. My hands had about lost their grip on gun and tool work, but in the kitchen I was as surefingered as an old woman. Well, eating didn't mean shooting anymore, not since the power line come in, and the supermarket down the highway. Once the whitefish got to sizzling good, I didn't hear Miss Press no more.

"This portion of *Search for Tomorrow* has been brought to you by . . . Spic and Span, the all-purpose cleaner. And by . . . Joy dishwashing liquid. From grease to shine in half the time, with Joy. Our story will continue in just a moment."

* * *

I was up by times the next morning. Hadn't kept milk cows in years. The last was Molly, she with the wet-weather horn, a funny-looking old gal but as calm and sweet as could be. But if you've milked cows for seventy years, it's hard to give in and let the sun start beating you to the day. By first light I'd had my Cream of Wheat, a child's meal I'd developed a taste for, with a little jerp of honey, and was out in the back field, bee hunting.

I had three sugar-dipped corncobs in a croker sack, and I laid one out on a hickory stump, notched one into the top of a fencepost, and set the third atop the boulder at the start of the path that drops down to the creek, past the old lick-log where the salt still keeps the grass from growing. Then I settled down on an old milkstool to wait. I gave up snuff a while ago because I couldn't taste it no more and the price got so high with taxes that I purely hated putting all that government in my mouth, but I still carry some little brushes to chew on in dipping moments, and I chewed on one while I watched those three corncobs do nothing. I'd set down where I could see all three without moving my head, just by darting my eyes from one to the other. My eyes may not see *Search for Tomorrow* so good anymore, even before the aerial got bent, but they still can sight a honeybee coming in to sip the bait.

The cob on the stump got the first business, but that bee just smelled around and then buzzed off straightaway, so I stayed set where I was. Same thing happened to the post cob and to the rock cob, three bees come and gone. But then a big bastard, one I could hear coming in like an airplane twenty feet away, zoomed down on the fence cob and stayed there a long time, filling his hands. He rose up all lazy-like, just like a man who's lifted the jug too many times in a sitting, and then made one, two, three slow circles in the air, marking the position. When he flew off, I was right behind him, legging it into the woods.

Mister Big Bee led me a ways straight up the slope, toward the well of the old McQuarry place, but then he crossed the bramble patch, and by the time I had worked my way anti-goddlin around that, I had lost sight of him. So I listened for a spell, holding my breath, and heard a murmur like a branch in a direction where there warn't no branch. Sure enough, over thataway was a big hollow oak with a bee highway a-coming and a-going through a seam in the lowest fork. Tell the truth, I wasn't rightly on my own land any more.

The McQuarry place belonged to a bank in Cape Girardeau, if it belonged to anybody. But no one had blazed this tree yet, so my claim would be good enough for any bee hunter. I sidled around to just below the fork and notched an X where any fool could see it, even me, because I had been known to miss my own signs some days, or rummage the bureau for a sock that was already on my foot. Something about the way I'd slunk toward the hive the way I'd slunk toward the door the day before made me remember Miss Press, whom I'd plump forgotten about. And when I turned back toward home, in the act of folding my pocketknife, there she was sitting on the lumpy leavings of the McQuarry chimney, a-kicking her feet and waving at me, just like I had wished her out of the ground. I'd have to go past her to get home, as I didn't relish turning my back on her and heading around the mountain, down the long way to the macadam and back around. Besides, she'd just follow me anyway, the way she followed me out here. I unfolded my knife again and snatched up a walnut stick to whittle on as I stomped along to where she sat.

"Hello, Mr. Nelson," she said. "Can we start over?"

"I ain't a-talking to *you*," I said as I passed, pointing at her with my blade. "I ain't even a-*walking* with you," I added, as she slid off the rockpile and walked along beside. "I'm taking the directedest path home, is all, and where you choose to walk is your own lookout. Fall in a hole, and I'll just keep a-going, I swear I will. I've done it before, left reporters in the woods to die."

"Aw, I don't believe you have," she said, in a happy singsongy way. At least she was dressed for a tramp through the woods, in denim jeans and mannish boots with no heels to them, but wearing the same face-paint and fool hat, and in a red sweater that fit as close as her dress had. "But I'm not walking with you, either," she went on. "I'm walking alone, just behind you. You can't even see me, without turning your head. We're both walking alone, together."

I didn't say nothing.

"Are we near where it landed?" she asked.

I didn't say nothing.

"You haven't had one of your picnics lately, have you?"

I didn't say nothing.

"You ought to have another one."

I didn't say nothing.

"I'm writing a story," she said, "about *Close Encounters*. You know, the new movie? With Richard Dreyfuss? He was in *The Goodbye Girl*, and *Jaws*, about the shark? Did you see those? Do you go to any movies?" Some critter we had spooked, maybe a turkey, went thrashing off through the brush, and I heard her catch her breath. "I bet you saw *Deliverance*," she said.

I didn't say nothing.

"My editor thought it'd be interesting to talk to people who really have, you know, claimed their own close encounters, to have met people from outer space. Contactees, that's the word, right? You were one of the first contactees, weren't you, Mr. Nelson? When was it, 1956?"

I didn't say nothing.

"Aw, come on, Mr. Nelson. Don't be so mean. They all talked to me out in California. Mr. Bethurum talked to me."

I bet he did, I thought. Truman Bethurum always was a plumb fool for a skirt.

"I talked to Mr. Fry, and to Mr. King, and Mr. Owens. I talked to Mr. Angelucci."

Orfeo Angelucci, I thought, now there was one of the world's original liars, as bad as Adamski. "Those names don't mean nothing to me," I said.

"They told similar stories to yours, in the fifties and sixties. Meeting the Space Brothers, and being taken up, and shown wonders, and coming back to the Earth, with wisdom and all."

"If you talked to all them folks," I said, "you ought to be brim full of wisdom yourself. Full of something. Why you need to hound an old man through the woods?"

"You're different," she said. "You know lots of things the others don't."

"Lots of things, uh-huh. Like what?"

"You know how to hunt bees, don't you?"

I snorted. "Hunt bees. You won't never need to hunt no bees, Miss Press. Priss. You can buy your honey at the A and the P. Hell, if you don't feel like going to the store, you could just ask, and some damn fool would bring it to you for free on a silver tray."

"Well, thank you," she said.

"That warn't no compliment," I said. "That was a clear-eyed statement of danger, like a sign saying, 'Bridge out,' or a label saying, 'Poison.' Write what you please, Miss Priss, but don't expect me to give you none of the words. You know all the words you need already."

"But you used to be so open about your experiences, Mr. Nelson. I've read that to anyone who found their way here off the highway, you'd tell about the alien Bob Solomon, and how that beam from the saucer cured your lumbago, and all that good pasture land on Mars. Why, you had all those three-day picnics, right here on your farm, for anyone who wanted to come talk about the Space Brothers. You'd even hand out little Baggies with samples of hair from your four-hundred-pound Venusian dog."

I stopped and whirled on her, and she hopped back a step, nearly fell down. "He warn't never no four hundred pounds," I said. "You reporters sure do believe some stretchers. You must swallow whole eggs for practice like a snake. I'll have you know, Miss Priss, that Bo just barely tipped three hundred and eighty-five pounds at his heaviest, and that was on the truck scales behind the Union 76 in June 1960, the day he ate all the silage, and Clay Rector, who ran all their inspections back then, told me those scales would register the difference if you took the Rand McNally atlas out of the cab, so that figure ain't no guesswork." When I paused for breath, I kinda shook myself, turned away from her gaping face and walked on. "From that day," I said, "I put old Bo on a science diet, one I got from the Extension, and I measured his rations, and I hitched him ever day to a sledge of felled trees and boulders and such, because dogs, you know, they're happier with a little exercise, and he settled down to around, oh, three-ten, three-twenty, and got downright frisky again. He'd romp around and change direction and jerk that sledge around, and that's why those three boulders are a-sitting in the middle of yonder pasture today, right where he slung them out of the sledge. Four hundred pounds, my foot. You don't know much, if that's what you know, and that's a fact."

I was warmed up by the walk and the spreading day and my own strong talk, and I set a smart pace, but she loped along beside me, writing in her notebook with a silver pen that flashed as it caught the sun. "I stand corrected," she said. "So what happened? Why'd you stop the picnics, and start running visitors off with a shotgun, and quit answering your mail?"

"You can see your own self what happened," I said. "Woman, I got old. You'll see what it's like, when you get there. All the people who believed in me died, and then the ones who humored me died, and now even the ones who feel obligated to sort of tolerate me are starting to go. Bo died, and Teddy, that was my Earth-born dog, he died, and them government boys went to the Moon and said they didn't see no mining operations or colony domes or big Space Brother dogs, or nothing else old Buck had seen up there. And in place of my story, what story did they come up with? I ask you. Dust and rocks and craters as far as you can see, and when you walk as far as that, there's another sight of dust and rocks and craters, and so on all around till you're back where you started, and that's it, boys, wash your hands, that's the Moon done. Excepting for some spots where the dust is so deep a body trying to land would just be swallowed up, sink to the bottom, and at the bottom find what? Praise Jesus, more dust, just what we needed. They didn't see nothing that anybody would care about going to see. No floating cars, no lakes of dia-monds, no topless Moon gals, just dumb dull nothing. Hell, they might as well a been in Arkansas. You at least can cast a line there, catch you a bream. Besides, my lumbago come back," I said, easing myself down into the rocker, because we was back on my front porch by then. "It always comes back, my doctor says. Doctors plural, I should say. I'm on the third one now. The first two died on me. That's something, ain't it? For a man to outlive two of his own doctors?"

Her pen kept a-scratching as she wrote. She said, "Maybe Bob Solomon's light beam is still doing you some good, even after all this time."

"Least it didn't do me no harm. From what all they say now about the space people, I'm lucky old Bob didn't jam a post-hole digger up my ass and send me home with the screaming meemies and three hours of my life missing. That's the only aliens anybody cares about nowadays, big-eyed boogers with long cold fingers in your drawers. Doctors from space. Well, if they want to take three hours of my life, they're welcome to my last trip to the urologist. I reckon it was right at three hours, and I wish them joy of it."

"Not so," she said. "What about *Star Wars?* It's already made more money than any other movie ever made, more than *Gone With the Wind*, more than *The Sound of Music*. That shows people are still interested in space, and in friendly aliens. And this new Richard Dreyfuss movie I was telling you about is based on actual UFO case files. Dr. Hynek helped with it. That'll spark more interest in past visits to Earth."

"I been to ever doctor in the country, seems like," I told her, "but I don't recall ever seeing Dr. Hynek."

"How about Dr. Rutledge?"

"Is he the toenail man?"

She swatted me with her notebook. "Now you're just being a pain," she said. "Dr. Harley Rutledge, the scientist, the physicist. Over at Southeast Missouri State. That's no piece from here. He's been doing serious UFO research for years, right here in the Ozarks. You really ought to know him. He's been documenting the spooklights. Like the one at Hornet, near Neosho?"

"I've heard tell of that light," I told her, "but I didn't know no scientist cared about it."

"See?" she said, almost a squeal, like she'd opened a present, like she'd proved something. "A lot has happened since you went home and locked the door. More people care about UFOs and flying saucers and aliens today than they did in the 1950s, even. You should have you another picnic."

Once I got started talking, I found her right easy to be with, and it was pleasant a-sitting in the sun talking friendly with a pretty gal, or with anyone. It's true, I'd been powerful lonesome, and I had missed those picnics, all those different types of folks on the farm who wouldn't have been brought together no other way, in no other place, by nobody else. I was prideful of them. But I was beginning to notice something funny. To begin with, Miss Priss, whose real name I'd forgot by now, had acted like someone citified and paper-educated and standoffish. Now, the longer she sat on my porch a-jawing with me, the more easeful she got, and the more country she sounded, as if she'd lived in the hollow her whole life. It sorta put me off. Was this how Mike Wallace did it on *60 Minutes*, pretending to be just regular folks, until you forgot yourself, and were found out?

"Where'd you say you were from?" I asked.

"Mars," she told me. Then she laughed. "Don't get excited," she said. "It's a town in Pennsylvania, north of Pittsburgh. I'm based out of Chicago, though." She cocked her head, pulled a frown, stuck out her bottom lip. "You didn't look at my card," she said. "I pushed it under your door yesterday, when you were being so all-fired rude."

"I didn't see it," I said, which warn't quite a lie because I hadn't bothered to pick it up off the floor this morning, either. In fact, I'd plumb forgot to look for it.

"You ought to come out to Clearwater Lake tonight. Dr. Rutledge and his students will be set up all night, ready for whatever. He said I'm welcome. That means you're welcome, too. See? You have friends in high places. They'll be set up at the overlook, off the highway. Do you know it?"

"I know it," I told her.

"Can you drive at night? You need me to come get you?" She blinked and chewed her lip, like a thought had just struck. "That might be difficult," she said.

"Don't exercise yourself," I told her. "I reckon I still can drive as good as I ever did, and my pickup still gets the job done, too. Not that I aim to drive all that ways, just to look at the sky. I can do that right here on my porch."

"Yes," she said, "alone. But there's something to be said for looking up in groups, wouldn't you agree?"

When I didn't say nothing, she stuck her writing-pad back in her pocketbook and stood up, dusting her butt with both hands. You'd think I never swept the porch. "I appreciate the interview, Mr. Nelson."

"Warn't no interview," I told her. "We was just talking, is all."

"I appreciate the talking, then," she said. She set off across the yard, toward the gap in the rhododendron bushes that marked the start of the driveway. "I hope you can make it tonight, Mr. Nelson. I hope you don't miss the show."

I watched her sashay off around the bush, and I heard her boots crunching the gravel for a few steps, and then she was gone, footsteps and all. I went back in the house, latched the screen door and locked the wood, and took one last look through the front curtains, to make sure. Some folks, I had heard, remembered only long afterward they'd been kidnapped by spacemen, a "retrieved memory" they called it, like finding a ball on the roof in the fall that went up there in the spring. Those folks needed a doctor to jog them, but this reporter had jogged me. All that happy talk had loosened something inside me, and things I hadn't thought about in years were welling up like a flash flood, like a sickness. If I was going to be memory-sick, I wanted powerfully to do it alone, as if alone was something new and urgent, and not what I did ever day.

I closed the junk-room door behind me as I yanked the light on. The swaying bulb on its chain rocked the shadows back and forth as I dragged from beneath a shelf a crate of cheap splinter wood, so big it could have held two men if they was dead. Once I drove my pickup to the plant to pick up a bulk of dog food straight off the dock, cheaper that way, and this was one of the crates it come in. It still had that faint high smell. As it slid, one corner snagged and ripped the carpet, laid open the orange shag to show the knotty pine beneath. The shag was threadbare, but why bother now buying a twenty-year rug? Three tackle boxes rattled and jiggled on top of the crate, two yawning open and one rusted shut, and I set all three onto the floor. I lifted the lid of the crate, pushed aside the top layer, a fuzzy blue blanket, and started lifting things out one at a time. I just glanced at some, spent more time with others. I warn't looking for anything in particular, just wanting to touch them and weigh them in my hands, and stack the memories up all around, in a back room under a bare bulb.

A crimpled flier with a dry mud footprint across it and a torn place up top, like someone yanked it off a staple on a bulletin board or a telephone pole:

SPACECRAFT
CONVENTION
Hear speakers who have contacted our Space Brothers
PICNIC
Lots of music—Astronomical telescope, see the craters on the Moon, etc.
Public invited—Spread the word
Admission—50c and $1.00 donation
Children under school age free
FREE CAMPING

Bring your own tent, house car or camping outfit, folding chairs, sleeping
bags, etc.
CAFETERIA on the grounds—fried chicken, sandwiches, coffee, cold
drinks, etc.
Conventions held every year on the last Saturday, Sunday and Monday of
the month of June
at
BUCK'S MOUNTAIN VIEW RANCH
Buck Nelson, Route 1
Mountain View, Missouri

A headline from a local paper: "Spacecraft Picnic at Buck's Ranch Attracts
2000 People."

An old Life magazine in a see-through envelope, Marilyn Monroe all puck-
ered up to the plastic. April 7, 1952. The headline: "There Is A Case For Inter-
planetary Saucers." I slid out the magazine and flipped through the article. I read:
"These objects cannot be explained by present science as natural phenomena—
but solely as artificial devices created and operated by a high intelligence."

A Baggie of three or four dog hairs, with a sticker showing the outline of
a flying saucer and the words HAIR FROM BUCK'S ALIEN DOG "BO."

Teddy hadn't minded, when I took the scissors to him to get the burrs off,
and to snip a little extra for the Bo trade. Bo was months dead by then, but
the folks demanded something. Some of my neighbors I do believe would have
pulled down my house and barn a-looking for him, if they thought there was a
body to be had. Some people won't believe in nothing that ain't a corpse, and
I couldn't bear letting the science men get at him with their saws and jars, to
jibble him up. Just the thought put me in mind of that old song:

> *The old horse died with the whooping cough*
> *The old cow died in the fork of the branch*
> *The buzzards had them a public dance.*

No, sir. No public dance this time. I hid Bo's body in a shallow cave, and
I nearabouts crawled in after him, cause it liked to have killed me, too, even

48

with the tractor's front arms to lift him and push him and drop him. Then I walled him up so good with scree and stones lying around that even I warn't sure any more where it was, along that long rock face.

I didn't let on that he was gone, neither. Already people were getting shirty about me not showing him off like a circus mule, bringing him out where people could gawk at him and poke him and ride him. I told them he was vicious around strangers, and that was a bald lie. He was a sweet old thing for his size, knocking me down with his licking tongue, and what was I but a stranger, at the beginning? We was all strangers. Those Baggies of Teddy hair was a bald lie, too, and so was some of the other parts I told through the years, when my story sort of got away from itself, or when I couldn't exactly remember what had happened in between this and that, so I had to fill in, the same way I filled the chinks between the rocks I stacked between me and Bo, to keep out the buzzards, hoping it'd be strong enough to last forever.

But a story ain't like a wall. The more stuff you add onto a wall, spackle and timber and flat stones, the harder it is to push down. The more stuff you add to a story through the years, the weaker it gets. Add a piece here and add a piece there, and in time you can't remember your own self how the pieces was supposed to fit together, and every piece is a chance for some fool to ask more questions, and confuse you more, and poke another hole or two, to make you wedge in something else, and there is no end to it. So finally you just don't want to tell no part of the story no more, except to yourself, because yourself is the only one who really believes in it. In some of it, anyway. The other folks, the ones who just want to laugh, to make fun, you run off or cuss out or turn your back on, until no one much asks anymore, or remembers, or cares. You're just that tetched old dirt farmer off of Route One, withered and sick and sitting on the floor of his junk room and crying, snot hanging from his nose, sneezing in the dust.

It warn't all a lie, though.

No, sir. Not by a long shot.

And that was the worst thing.

Because the reporters always came, ever year at the end of June, and so did the duck hunters who saw something funny in the sky above the blind one frosty morning and was looking for it ever since, and the retired military fellas who talked about "protocols" and "incident reports" and "security breaches," and the powdery old ladies who said they'd walked around the rosebush one afternoon and found themselves on the rings of Saturn, and the beatniks from the college, and the tourists with their Polaroids and short pants, and the women selling funnel cakes and glow-in-the-dark space Frisbees, and the younguns with the waving antennas on their heads, and the neighbors who just wanted to snoop around and see whether old Buck had finally let the place go to rack and ruin, or whether he was holding it together for one more year, they all showed up on time, just like the mockingbirds. But the one person who never came, not one damn time since the year of our Lord nineteen and fifty-six, was the alien Bob Solomon himself. The whole point of the damn picnics, the Man of the Hour, had never showed his face. And that was the real reason I give up on the picnics, turned sour on the whole flying-saucer industry, and kept close to the willows ever since. It warn't my damn lumbago or the Mothman or Barney and Betty Hill and their Romper Room boogeymen, or those dull dumb rocks hauled back from the Moon and thrown in my face like coal in a Christmas stocking. It was Bob Solomon, who said he'd come back, stay in touch, continue to shine down his blue-white healing light, because he loved the Earth people, because he loved me, and who done none of them things.

What had happened, to keep Bob Solomon away? He hadn't died. Death was a stranger, out where Bob Solomon lived. Bo would be frisky yet, if he'd a stayed home. No, something had come between Mountain View and Bob Solomon, to keep him away. What had I done? What had I not done? Was it something I knew, that I wasn't supposed to know? Or was it something I forgot, or cast aside, something I should have held onto, and treasured? And now, if Bob Solomon was to look for Mountain View, could he find it? Would he know me? The Earth goes a far ways in twenty-odd years, and we go with it.

I wiped my nose on my hand and slid Marilyn back in her plastic and reached for the chain and clicked off the light and sat in the chilly dark, making like it was the cold clear peace of space.

*   *   *

I knew well the turnoff to the Clearwater Lake overlook, and I still like to have missed it that night, so black dark was the road through the woods. The sign with the arrow had deep-cut letters filled with white reflecting paint, and only the flash of the letters in the headlights made me stand on the brakes and kept me from missing the left turn. I sat and waited, turn signal on, flashing green against the pine boughs overhead, even though there was no sign of cars a-coming from either direction. Ka-chunk, ka-chunk, flashed the pine trees, and then I turned off with a grumble of rubber as the tires left the asphalt and bit into the gravel of the overlook road. The stone-walled overlook had been built by the CCC in the 1930s, and the road the relief campers had built hadn't been improved much since, so I went up the hill slow on that narrow, straight road, away back in the jillikens. Once I saw the eyes of some critter as it dashed across my path, but nary a soul else, and when I reached the pullaround, and that low-slung wall all along the ridgetop, I thought maybe I had the wrong place. But then I saw two cars and a panel truck parked at the far end where younguns park when they go a-sparking, and I could see dark-people shapes a-milling about. I parked a ways away, shut off my engine and cut my lights. This helped me see a little better, and I could make out flashlight beams trained on the ground here and there, as people walked from the cars to where some big black shapes were set up, taller than a man. In the silence after I slammed my door I could hear low voices, too, and as I walked nearer, the murmurs resolved themselves and became words:

"Gravimeter checks out."

"Thank you, Isabel. Wallace, how about that spectrum analyzer?"

"Powering up, Doc. Have to give it a minute."

"We may not have a minute, or we may have ten hours. Who knows?" I steered toward this voice, which was older than the others. "Our visitors are unpredictable," he continued.

"Visitors?" the girl asked.

"No, you're right. I've broken my own rule. We don't know they're sentient, and even if they are, we don't know they're *visitors*. They may be local, native to the place, certainly more so than Wallace here. Georgia-born, aren't you, Wallace?"

"Company, Doc," said the boy.

"Yes, I see him, barely. Hello, sir. May I help you? Wallace, please. Mind your manners." The flashlight beam in my face had blinded me, but the professor grabbed it out of the boy's hand and turned it up to shine beneath his chin, like a youngun making a scary face, so I could see a shadow version of his lumpy jowls, his big nose, his bushy mustache. "I'm Harley Rutledge," he said. "Might you be Mr. Nelson?"

"That's me," I said, and as I stuck out a hand, the flashlight beam moved to locate it. Then a big hand came into view and shook mine. The knuckles were dry and cracked and red-flaked.

"How do you do," Rutledge said, and switched off the flashlight. "Our mutual friend explained what we're doing out here, I presume? Forgive the darkness, but we've learned that too much brightness on our part rather spoils the seeing, skews the experiment."

"Scares 'em off?" I asked.

"Mmm," Rutledge said. "No, not quite that. Besides the lack of evidence for any *them* that *could* be frightened, we have some evidence that these, uh, luminous phenomena are . . . responsive to our lights. If we wave ours around too much, they wave around in response. We shine ours into the water, they descend into the water as well. All fascinating, but it does suggest a possibility of reflection, of visual echo, which we are at some pains to rule out. Besides which, we'd like to observe, insofar as possible, what these lights do when *not* observed. Though they seem difficult to fool. Some, perhaps fancifully, have suggested they can read investigators' minds. Ah, Wallace, are we up and running, then? Very good, very good." Something hard and plastic was nudging my arm, and I thought for a second Rutledge was offering me a drink. "Binoculars, Mr. Nelson? We always carry spares, and you're welcome to help us look."

The girl's voice piped up. "We're told you've seen the spooklights all your life," she said. "Is that true?"

"I reckon you could say that," I said, squinting into the binoculars. Seeing the darkness up close made it even darker.

"That is so cool," Isobel said. "I'm going to write my thesis on low-level nocturnal lights of apparent volition. I call them linnalavs for short. Will-o-the-wisps, spooklights, treasure lights, corpse lights, ball lightning, fireships, jack o'lanterns, the *feu follet*. I'd love to interview you sometime. Just think, if you had been recording your observations all these years."

I did record some, I almost said, but Rutledge interrupted us. "Now, Isobel, don't crowd the man on short acquaintance. Why don't you help Wallace with the tape recorders? Your hands are steadier, and we don't want him cutting himself again." She stomped off, and I found something to focus on with the binoculars: the winking red light atop the Taum Sauk Mountain fire tower. "You'll have to excuse Isobel, Mr. Nelson. She has the enthusiasm of youth, and she's just determined to get ball lightning in there somehow, though I keep explaining that's an entirely separate phenomenon."

"Is that what our friend, that reporter gal, told you?" I asked. "That I seen the spooklights in these parts, since I was a tad?"

"Yes, and that you were curious about our researches, to compare your folk knowledge to our somewhat more scientific investigations. And as I told her, you're welcome to join us tonight, as long as you don't touch any of our equipment, and as long as you stay out of our way should anything, uh, happen. Rather irregular, having an untrained local observer present—but frankly, Mr. Nelson, everything about Project Identification is irregular, at least as far as the U.S. Geological Survey is concerned. So we'll both be irregular together, heh." A round green glow appeared and disappeared at chest level: Rutledge checking his watch. "I frankly thought Miss Rains would be coming with you. She'll be along presently, I take it?"

"Don't ask me," I said, trying to see the tower itself beneath the light. Black metal against black sky. I'd heard her name as *Hanes*, but I let it go. "Maybe she got a better offer."

"Oh, I doubt that, not given her evident interest. Know Miss Rains well, do you, Mr. Nelson?"

"Can't say as I do. Never seen her before this morning. No, wait. Before yesterday."

"Lovely girl," Rutledge said. "And so energized."

"Sort of wears me out," I told him.

"Yes, well, pleased to meet you, again. I'd better see how Isobel and Wallace are getting along. There are drinks and snacks in the truck, and some folding chairs and blankets. We're here all night, so please make yourself at home."

I am home, I thought, fiddling with the focus on the binoculars as Rutledge trotted away, his little steps sounding like a spooked quail. I hadn't let myself look at the night sky for anything but quick glances for so long, just to make sure the Moon and Venus and Old Rion and the Milky Way was still there, that I was feeling sort of giddy to have nothing else to look at. I was like a man who took the cure years ago but now finds himself locked in a saloon. That brighter patch over yonder, was that the lights of Piedmont? And those two, no, three, airplanes, was they heading for St. Louis? I reckon I couldn't blame Miss Priss for not telling the professor the whole truth about me, else he would have had the law out here, to keep that old crazy man away. I wondered where Miss Priss had got to. Rutledge and I both had the inkle she would be joining us out here, but where had I got that? Had she quite said it, or had I just assumed?

I focused again on the tower light, which warn't flashing no more. Instead it was getting stronger and weaker and stronger again, like a heartbeat, and never turning full off. It seemed to be growing, too, taking up more of the view, as if it was coming closer. I was so interested in what the fire watchers might be up to—testing the equipment? signaling rangers on patrol?—that when the light moved sideways toward the north, I turned, too, and swung the binoculars around to keep it in view, and didn't think nothing odd about a fire tower going for a little walk until the boy Wallace said, "There's one now, making its move."

The college folks all talked at once: "Movie camera on." "Tape recorder on." "Gravimeter negative." I heard the click-whirr, click-whirr of someone taking Polaroids just as fast as he could go. For my part, I kept following the spooklight as it bobbled along the far ridge, bouncing like a slow ball or a balloon, and pulsing as it went. After the burst of talking, everyone was silent, watching the light and fooling with the equipment. Then the professor whispered in my ear: "Look familiar to you, Mr. Nelson?"

It sure warn't a patch on Bob Solomon's spaceship, but I knew Rutledge didn't have Bob Solomon in mind. "The spooklights I've seen was down lower," I told him, "below the tops of the trees, most times hugging the ground. This one moves the same, but it must be up fifty feet in the air."

"Maybe," he whispered, "and maybe not. Appearances can be deceiving. Hey!" He cried aloud as the slow bouncy light shot straight up in the air. It hung there, then fell down to the ridgeline again and kept a-going, bobbing down the far slope, between us and the ridge, heading toward the lake and toward us.

The professor asked, "Gravitational field?"

"No change," the girl said.

"Keep monitoring."

The light split in two, then in three. All three lights come toward us.

"Here they come! Here they come!"

I couldn't keep all three in view, so I stuck with the one making the straightest shot downhill. Underneath it, treetops come into view as the light passed over, just as if it was a helicopter with a spotlight. But there warn't no engine sound at all, just the sound of a little zephyr a-stirring the leaves, and the clicks of someone snapping pictures. Even Bob Solomon's craft had made a little racket: It whirred as it moved, and turned on and off with a *whunt* like the fans in a chickenhouse. It was hard to tell the light's shape. It just faded out at the edges, as the pulsing came and went. It was blue-white in motion but flickered red when it paused. I watched the light bounce down to the far shore of the lake. Then in flashed real bright, and was gone. I lowered the binoculars in time to see the other two hit the water and flash out, too—but one sent a smaller fireball rolling across the water toward us. When it slowed down, it sank, just like a rock a child sends a-skipping across a pond. The water didn't kick up at all, but the light could be seen below for a few seconds, until it sank out of sight.

"Awesome!" Isobel said.

"Yeah, that was something," Wallace said. "Wish we had a boat. Can we bring a boat next time, Doc? Hey, why is it so light?"

"Moonrise," Isobel said. "See our moonshadows?"

We did all have long shadows, reaching over the wall and toward the lake.

I always heard that to stand in your own moonshadow means good luck, but I didn't get the chance to act on it before the professor said: "That's not the moon."

The professor was facing away from the water, toward the source of light. Behind us a big bright light moved through the trees, big as a house. The beams shined out separately between the trunks but then they closed up together again as the light moved out onto the surface of the gravel pull-around. It was like a giant glowing upside-down bowl, twenty-five feet high, a hundred or more across, sliding across the ground. You could see everything lit up inside, clear as a bell, like in a tabletop aquarium in a dark room. But it warn't attached to nothing. Above the light dome was no spotlight, no air-craft, nothing but the night sky and stars.

"Wallace, get that camera turned around, for God's sake!"

"Instruments read nothing, Doc. It's as if it weren't there."

"Maybe it's not. No, Mr. Nelson! Please, stay back!"

But I'd already stepped forward to meet it, binoculars hanging by their strap at my side, bouncing against my leg as I walked into the light. Inside I didn't feel nothing physical—no tingling, and no warmth, no more than turning on a desk lamp warms a room. But in my mind I felt different, pow-erful different. Standing there in that light, I felt more calm and easeful than I'd felt in years—like I was someplace I belonged, more so than on my own farm. As the edge of the light crept toward me, about at the speed of a slow walk, I slow-walked in the same direction as it was going, just to keep in the light as long as I could.

The others, outside the light, did the opposite. They scattered back toward the wall of the overlook, trying to stay in the dark ahead of it, but they didn't have no place to go, and in a few seconds they was all in the light, too, the three of them and their standing telescopes and all their equipment on folding tables and sawhorses all around. I got my first good look at the three of them in that crawling glow. Wallace had hippie hair down in his eyes and a beaky nose, and was bowlegged. The professor was older than I expected, but not nearly so old as me, and had a great big belly—what mountain folks would call an *investment*, as he'd been putting into it for years. Isobel had long stringy hair that needed a wash, and a wide butt, and black-rimmed glasses so thick a welder could have worn them, but she was right cute for all that. None of us cast a shadow inside the light.

I looked up and could see the night sky and even pick out the stars, but it was like looking through a soap film or a skiff of snow. Something I couldn't feel or rightly see was in the way, between me and the sky. Still I walked until the thigh-high stone wall stopped me. The dome kept moving, of course, and as I went through its back edge—because it was just that clear-cut, either you was in the light or you warn't—why, I almost swung my legs over the wall to follow it. The hill, though, dropped off steep on the other side, and the undergrowth was all tangled and snaky. So I held up for a few seconds, dithering, and then the light had left me behind, and I was in the dark again, pressed up against that wall like something drowned and found in a drain after a flood. I now could feel the breeze of the lake, so air warn't moving easy through the light dome, neither.

The dome kept moving over the folks from the college, slid over the wall and down the slope, staying about 25 feet tall the whole way. It moved out onto the water—which stayed as still as could be, not roiled at all—then faded, slow at first and then faster, until I warn't sure I was looking at anything anymore, and then it was gone.

The professor slapped himself on the cheeks and neck, like he was putting on aftershave. "No sunburn, thank God," he said. "How do the rest of you feel?"

The other two slapped themselves just the same.

"I'm fine."

"I'm fine, too," Isobel said. "The Geiger counter never triggered, either."

What did I feel like? Like I wanted to dance, to skip and cut capers, to holler out loud. My eyes were full like I might cry. I stared at that dark lake like I could stare a hole in it, like I could will that dome to rise again. I whispered, "Thank you," and it warn't a prayer, not directed *at* anybody, just an acknowledgment of something that had passed, like tearing off a calendar page, or plowing under a field of cornstalks.

I turned to the others, glad I finally had someone to talk to, someone I could share all these feelings with, but to my surprise they was all running

from gadget to gadget, talking at once about phosphorescence and gas erup-
tions and electromagnetic fields, I couldn't follow half of it. Where had they
been? Had they plumb missed it? For the first time in years, I felt I had to tell
them what I had seen, what I had felt and known, the whole story. It would
help them. It would be a comfort to them.

I walked over to them, my hands held out. I wanted to calm them down,
get their attention.

"Oh, thank you, Mr. Nelson," said the professor. He reached out and
unhooked from my hand the strap of the binoculars. "I'll take those. Well, I'd
say you brought us luck, wouldn't you agree, Isobel, Wallace? Quite a remark-
able display, that second one especially. Like the Bahia Kino Light of the Gulf
of California, but in motion! Ionization of the air, perhaps, but no Geiger
activity, mmm. A lower voltage, perhaps?" He patted his pockets. "Need a
shopping list for our next vigil. A portable Curran counter, perhaps—"

I grabbed at his sleeve. "I saw it."

"Yes? Well, we all saw it, Mr. Nelson. Really a tremendous phenomenon—if the distant lights and the close light are related, that is, and their
joint appearance cannot be coincidental. I'll have Isobel take your statement
before we go, but now, if you'll excuse me."

"I don't mean tonight," I said, "and I don't mean no spooklights. I seen
the real thing, an honest-to-God flying saucer, in 1956. At my farm outside
Mountain View, west of here. Thataway." I pointed. "It shot out a beam of
light, and after I was in that light, I felt better, not so many aches and pains.
And listen: I saw it more than once, the saucer. It kept coming back."

He was backing away from me. "Mr. Nelson, really, I must—"

"And I met the crew," I told him. "The pilot stepped out of the saucer to
talk with me. That's right, with me. He looked human, just like you and me,
only better-looking. He looked like that boy in *Battle Cry*, Tab Hunter. But
he said his name was—"

"Mr. Nelson." The early morning light was all around by now, giving
everything a gray glow, and I could see Rutledge was frowning. "Please.
You've had a very long night, and a stressful one. You're tired, and I'm sorry to
say that you're no longer young. What you're saying no longer makes sense."

"Don't make sense!" I cried. "You think what we just saw makes sense?"

"I concede that I have no ready explanations, but what we saw were lights, Mr. Nelson, only lights. No sign of intelligence, nor of aircraft. Certainly not of crew members. No little green men. No grays. No Tab Hunter from the Moon."

"He lived on Mars," I said, "and his name was Bob Solomon."

The professor stared at me. The boy behind him, Wallace, stared at me, too, nearabouts tripping over his own feet as he bustled back and forth toting things to the truck. The girl just shook her head, and turned and walked into the woods.

"I wrote it up in a little book," I told the professor. "Well, I say I wrote it. Really, I talked it out, and I paid a woman at the library to copy it down and type it. I got a copy in the pickup. Let me get it. Won't take a sec."

"Mr. Nelson," he said again. "I'm sorry, I truly am. If you write me at the college, and enclose your address, I'll see you get a copy of our article, should it appear. We welcome interest in our work from the layman. But for now, here, today, I must ask you to leave."

"Leave? But the gal here said I could help."

"That was before you expressed these . . . delusions," Rutledge said. "Please realize what I'm trying to do. Like Hynek, like Vallee and Maccabee, I am trying to establish these researches as a serious scientific discipline. I am trying to create a field where none exists, where Isobel and her peers can work and publish without fear of ridicule. And here you are, spouting nonsense about a hunky spaceman named Bob! You must realize how that sounds. Why, you'd make the poor girl a laughing stock."

"She don't want to interview me?"

"Interview you! My God, man, aren't you listening? It would be career suicide for her to be *seen* with you! Please, before the sun is full up, Mr. Nelson, please, do the decent thing, and get back into your truck, and go."

I felt myself getting madder and madder. My hands had turned into fists. I turned from the professor, pointed at the back-and-forth boy and hollered, "You!"

He froze, like I had pulled a gun on him.

I called: "You take any Polaroids of them things?"

"Some, yes, sir," he said, at the exact same time the professor said, "Don't answer that."

"Where are they?" I asked. "I want to see 'em."

Behind the boy was a card table covered with notebooks and Mountain Dew bottles and the Polaroid camera, too, with a stack of picture squares next to it. I walked toward the table, and the professor stepped into my path, crouched, arms outstretched, like we was gonna wrestle.

"Keep away from the equipment," Rutledge said.

The boy ran back to the table and snatched up the pictures as I feinted sideways, and the professor lunged to block me again.

"I want to see them pictures, boy," I said.

"Mr. Nelson, go home! Wallace, secure those photos."

Wallace looked around like he didn't know what secure meant, in the open air overlooking a mountain lake, then he started stuffing the photos into his pockets, until they poked out all around, sort of comical. Two fell out on the ground. Then Wallace picked up a folding chair and held it out in front of him like a lion tamer. Stenciled across the bottom of the chair was PROP. CUMBEE FUNERAL HOME.

I stooped and picked up a rock and cocked my hand back like I was going to fling it. The boy flinched backward, and I felt right bad about scaring him. I turned and made like to throw it at the professor instead, and when he flinched, I felt some better. Then I turned and made like to throw it at the biggest telescope, and that felt best of all, for both boy and professor hollered then, no words but just a wail from the boy and a bark from the man, so loud that I nearly dropped the rock.

"Pictures, pictures," I said. "All folks want is pictures. People didn't believe nothing I told 'em, because during the first visits I didn't have no camera, and then when I rented a Brownie to take to Venus with me, didn't none of the pictures turn out! All of 'em overexposed, the man at the Rexall said. I ain't fooled with no pictures since, but I'm gonna have one of these, or so help me, I'm gonna bust out the eyes of this here spyglass, you see if I won't. Don't you come no closer with that chair, boy! You set that thing down." I picked up a second rock, so I had one heavy weight in each hand, and felt good. I knocked them together with a *clop* like hooves, and I walked around to the business end of the telescope, where the eyepiece and all those tiny adjustable thingies was, because that looked like the thing's underbelly. I held the rocks up to either side, like I was gonna knock them together and smash the instruments in between. I bared my teeth and tried to look scary, which warn't easy because now that it was good daylight, I suddenly had to pee something fierce. It must have worked, though, because Wallace set down the chair, just about the time the girl Isobel stepped out of the woods.

She was tucking in her shirttail, like she'd answered her own call of nature. She saw us all three standing there froze, and she got still, too, one hand down the back of her britches. Her darting eyes all magnified in her glasses looked quick and smart.

"What's going on?" she asked. Her front teeth stuck out like a chipmunk's.

"I want to see them pictures," I said.

"Isobel," the professor said, "drive down to the bait shop and call the police." He picked up an oak branch, hefted it, and started stripping off the little branches, like that would accomplish anything. "Run along, there's a good girl. Wallace and I have things well in hand."

"The heck we do," Wallace said. "I bring back a wrecked telescope, and I kiss my work-study goodbye."

"Jesus wept," Isobel said, and walked down the slope, tucking in the rest of her shirttail. She rummaged on the table, didn't find them, then saw the two stray pictures lying on the ground at Wallace's feet. She picked one up, walked over to me, held it out.

The professor said, "Isabel, don't! That's university property."

"Here, Mr. Nelson," she said. "Just take it and go, OK?"

I was afraid to move, for fear I'd wet my pants. My eyeballs was swimming already. I finally let fall one of my rocks and took the photo in that free hand, stuck it in my overalls pocket without looking at it. "Preciate it," I said. For no reason, I handed her the other rock, and for no reason, she took it. I turned and walked herky-jerky toward my truck, hoping I could hold it till I got into the woods at least, but no, I gave up halfway there, and with my back to the others I unzipped and groaned and let fly a racehorse stream of pee that spattered the tape-recorder case.

I heard the professor moan behind me, "Oh, Mr. Nelson! This is really too bad!"

"I'm sorry!" I cried. "It ain't on purpose, I swear! I was about to bust." But I probably would have tried to aim it, at that, to hit some of that damned equipment square on, but I hadn't had no force nor distance on my pee for years. It just poured out, like pulling a plug. I peed and peed, my eyes rolling back, lost in the good feeling ("You go, Mr. Nelson!" Isobel yelled), and as it puddled and coursed in little rills around the rocks at my feet, I saw a fisherman in a distant rowboat in the middle of the lake, his line in the water just where that corpse light had submerged the night before. I couldn't see him good, but I could tell he was watching us, as his boat drifted along. The sparkling water looked like it was moving fast past him, the way still water in the sun always does, even though the boat hardly moved at all.

"You wouldn't eat no fish from there," I hollered at him, "if you knew what was underneath."

His only answer was a pop and a hiss that carried across the water loud as a firework. He lifted the can he had opened, raised it high toward us as if to say, Cheers, and took a long drink.

Finally done, I didn't even zip up as I shuffled to the pickup. Without all that pee I felt lightheaded and hollow and plumb worn out. I wondered whether I'd make it home before I fell asleep.

"Isobel," the professor said behind me, "I asked you to go call the police."

"Oh, for God's sake, let it go," she said. "You really *would* look like an asshole then. Wallace, give me a hand."

I crawled into the pickup, slammed the door, dropped the window—it didn't crank down anymore, just fell into the door, so that I had to raise it two-handed—cranked the engine and drove off without looking at the bucktoothed girl, the bowlegged boy, the professor holding a club in his bloody-knuckled hands, the fisherman drinking his breakfast over a spook hole. I caught one last sparkle of the morning sun on the surface of the lake as I swung the truck into the shade of the woods, on the road headed down to the highway. Light through the branches dappled my rusty hood, my cracked dashboard, my baggy overalls. Some light is easy to explain. I fished the Polaroid picture out of my pocket and held it up at eye level while I drove. All you could see was a bright white nothing, like the boy had aimed the lens at the glare of a hundred-watt bulb from an inch away. I tossed the picture out the window. Another dud, just like Venus. A funny thing: The cardboard square bounced to a standstill in the middle of the road and caught the light just enough to be visible in my rear-view mirror, like a little bright window in the ground, until I reached the highway, signaled ka-chunk, ka-chunk, and turned to the right, toward home.

Later that morning I sat on the porch, waiting for her. Staring at the lake had done me no good, no more than staring at the night sky over the barn had done, all those years, but staring at the rhododendron called her forth, sure enough. She stepped around the bush with a little wave. She looked sprightly as ever, for all that long walk up the steep driveway, but I didn't blame her for not scraping her car past all those close bushes. One day they'd grow together and intertwine their limbs like clasped hands, and I'd be cut off from the world like in a fairy-tale. But I wasn't cut off yet, because here came Miss Priss, with boots up over her knees and dress hiked up to yonder, practically. Her colors were red and black today, even that fool saucer hat was red with a black button in the center. She was sipping out of a box with a straw in it.

"I purely love orange juice," she told me. "Whenever I'm traveling, I can't get enough of it. Here, I brought you one." I reached out and took the box offered, and she showed me how to peel off the straw and poke a hole with it, and we sat side by side sipping awhile. I didn't say nothing, just sipped and looked into Donald Duck's eyes and sipped some more. Finally she emptied her juice-box with a long low gurgle and turned to me and asked, "Did you make it out to the lake last night?"

"I did that thing, yes ma'am."

"See anything?"

The juice was brassy-tasting and thin, but it was growing on me, and I kept a-working that straw. "Didn't see a damn thing," I said. I cut my eyes at her. "Didn't see *you*, neither."

"Yes, well, I'm sorry about that," she said. "My supervisors called me away. When I'm on assignment, my time is not my own." Now she cut *her* eyes at *me*. "You *sure* you didn't see anything?"

I shook my head, gurgled out the last of my juice. "Nothing Dr. Rutledge can't explain away," I said. "Nothing you could have a conversation with."

"How'd you like Dr. Rutledge?"

"We got along just fine," I said, "when he warn't hunting up a club to beat me with, and I warn't pissing into his machinery. He asked after *you*, though. You was the one he wanted along on his camping trip, out there in the dark."

"I'll try to call on him, before I go."

"Go where?"

She fussed with her hat. "Back home. My assignment's over."

"Got everthing you needed, did you?"

"Yes, I think so. Thanks to you."

"Well, I ain't," I said. I turned and looked her in the face. "I ain't got everthing I need, myself. What I need ain't here on this Earth. It's up yonder, someplace I can't get to no more. Ain't that a bitch? And yet I was right satisfied until two days ago, when you come along and stirred me all up again. I never even went to bed last night, and I ain't sleepy even now. All I can think about is night coming on again, and what I might see up there this time."

"But that's a *good* thing," she said. "You keep your eyes peeled, Mr. Nelson. You've seen things already, and you haven't seen the last of them." She tapped my arm with her juice-box straw. "I have faith in you," she said. "I wasn't sure at first. That's why I came to visit, to see if you were keeping the faith. And I see now that you are—in your own way."

"I ain't got no faith," I said. "I done aged out of it."

She stood up. "Oh, pish tosh," she said. "You proved otherwise last night. The others tried to stay *out* of the light, but not you, Mr. Nelson. Not you." She set her juice box on the step beside mine. "Throw that away for me, will you? I got to be going." She stuck out her hand. It felt hot to the touch, and powerful. Holding it gave me the strength to stand up, look into her eyes, and say:

"I made it all up. The dog Bo, and the trips to Venus and Mars, and the cured lumbago. It was a made-up story, ever single Lord God speck of it."

And I said that sincerely. Bob Solomon forgive me: As I said it, I believed it was true.

She looked at me for a spell, her eyes big. She looked for a few seconds like a child I'd told Santa warn't coming, ever again. Then she grew back up, and with a sad little smile she stepped toward me, pressed her hands flat to the chest bib of my overalls, stood on tippytoes, and kissed me on the cheek, the way she would her grandpap, and as she slid something into my side pocket she whispered in my ear, "That's not what I hear on Enceladus." She patted my pocket. "That's how to reach me, if you need me. But you won't need me." She stepped into the yard and walked away, swinging her pocketbook, and called back over her shoulder: "You know what you need, Mr. Nelson? You need a dog. A dog is good help around a farm. A dog will sit up with you, late at night, and lie beside you, and keep you warm. You ought to keep your eye out. You never know when a stray will turn up."

She walked around the bush, and was gone. I picked up the empty Donald Ducks, because it was something to do, and I was turning to go in when a man's voice called:

"Mr. Buck Nelson?"

A young man in a skinny tie and horn-rimmed glasses stood at the edge of the driveway where Miss Priss—no, Miss *Rains*, she deserved her true name—had stood a few moments before. He walked forward, one hand outstretched and the other reaching into the pocket of his denim jacket. He pulled out a long flat notebook.

"My name's Matt Ketchum," he said, "and I'm pleased to find you, Mr. Nelson. I'm a reporter with The Associated Press, and I'm writing a story on the surviving flying-saucer contactees of the 1950s."

I caught him up short when I said, "Aw, not again! Damn it all, I just told all that to Miss Rains. She works for the A&P, too."

He withdrew his hand, looked blank.

I pointed to the driveway. "Hello, you must have walked past her in the drive, not two minutes ago! Pretty girl in a red-and-black dress, boots up to here. Miss Rains, or Hanes, or something like that."

"Mr. Nelson, I'm not following you. I don't work with anyone named Rains or Hanes, and no one else has been sent out here but me. And that driveway was deserted. No other cars parked down at the highway, either." He cocked his head, gave me a pitying look. "Are you sure you're not thinking of some other day, sir?"

"But she," I said, hand raised toward my bib pocket—but something kept me from saying *gave me her card*. That pocket felt strangely warm, like there was a live coal in it.

"Maybe she worked for someone else, Mr. Nelson, like UPI, or maybe the Post-Dispatch? I hope I'm not scooped again. I wouldn't be surprised, with the Spielberg picture coming out and all."

I turned to focus on him for the first time. "Where is Enceladus, anyway?"

"I beg your pardon?"

I said it again, moving my lips all cartoony, like he was deaf.

"I, well, I don't know, sir. I'm not familiar with it."

I thought a spell. "I do believe," I said, half to myself, "it's one a them Saturn moons." To jog my memory, I made a fist of my right hand and held it up—that was Saturn—and held up my left thumb a ways from it, and moved it back and forth, sighting along it. "It's out a ways, where the ring gets sparse. Thirteenth? Fourteenth, maybe?"

He just goggled at me. I gave him a sad look and shook my head and said, "You don't know much, if that's what you know, and that's a fact."

He cleared his throat. "Anyway, Mr. Nelson, as I was saying, I'm interviewing all the contactees I can find, like George Van Tassel, and Orfeo Angelucci—"

"Yes, yes, and Truman Bethurum, and them," I said. "She talked to all them, too."

"Bethurum?" he repeated. He flipped through his notebook. "Wasn't he the asphalt spreader, the one who met the aliens atop a mesa in Nevada?"

"Yeah, that's the one."

He looked worried now. "Um, Mr. Nelson, you must have misunderstood her. Truman Bethurum died in 1969. He's been dead eight years, sir."

I stood there looking at the rhododendron and seeing the pretty face and round hat, hearing the singsong voice, like she had learned English from a book.

I turned and went into the house, let the screen bang shut behind, didn't bother to shut the wood door.

"Mr. Nelson?"

My chest was plumb hot, now. I went straight to the junk room, yanked on the light. Everything was spread out on the floor where I left it. I shoved aside Marilyn, all the newspapers, pawed through the books.

"Mr. Nelson?" The voice was coming closer, moving through the house like a spooklight.

There it was: *Aboard a Flying Saucer*, by Truman Bethurum. I flipped through it, looking only at the pictures, until I found her: dark hair, big dark eyes, sharp chin, round hat. It was old Truman's drawing of Captain Aura Rhanes, the sexy Space Sister from the planet Clarion who visited him eleven times in her little red-and-black uniform, come right into his bedroom, so often that Mrs. Bethurum got jealous and divorced him. I had heard that old Truman, toward the end, went out and hired girl assistants to answer his mail and take messages just because they sort of looked like Aura Rhanes.

"Mr. Nelson?" said young Ketchum, standing in the door. "Are you OK?"

I let drop the book, stood, and said, "Doing just fine, son. If you'll excuse me? I got to be someplace." I closed the door in his face, dragged a bookcase across the doorway to block it, and pulled out Miss Rhanes' card, which was almost too hot to touch. No writing on it, neither, only a shiny silver surface that reflected my face like a mirror—and there was something behind my face, something aways back inside the card, a moving silvery blackness like a field of stars rushing toward me, and as I stared into that card, trying to see, my reflection slid out of the way and the edges of the card flew out and the card was a window, a big window, and now a door that I moved through without stepping, and someone out there was playing a single fiddle, no dance tune but just a-scraping along slow and sad as the stars whirled around me, and a ringed planet was swimming into view, the rings on edge at first but now tilting toward me and thickening as I dived down, the rings getting closer dividing into bands like layers in a rock face, and then into a field of rocks like that no-earthly-good south pasture, only there was so many rocks, so close together, and then I fell between them like an ant between the rocks in a gravel driveway, and now I was speeding toward a pinpoint of light, and as I moved toward it faster and faster, it grew and resolved itself and reshaped into a pear, a bulb, with a long sparkling line extending out, like a space elevator, like a chain, and at the end of the chain the moon became a glowing light bulb. I was staring into the bulb in my junk room, dazzled, my eyes flashing, my head achy, and the card dropped from my fingers with no sound, and my feet were still shuffling though the fiddle had faded away. I couldn't hear nothing over the knocking and the barking and young Ketchum calling: "Hey, Mr. Nelson? Is this your dog?"

NEBULA AWARD, BEST NOVELLA

"AFTER THE FALL, BEFORE THE FALL, DURING THE FALL"

NANCY KRESS

Nancy Kress's fiction has also won four previous Nebulas, as well as the Sturgeon Award, the John W. Campbell Memorial Award, and two Hugos. "After the Fall, Before the Fall, During the Fall" was published as a stand-alone book by Tachyon Publications.

NOVEMBER 2013

It wasn't dark, and it wasn't light. It wasn't anything except cold. *I'm dead*, Pete thought, but of course he wasn't. Every time he thought that, all the way back to his first time when McAllister had warned him: *"The transition may seem to last forever."*

Forever was twenty seconds on Pete's wrister.

Light returned, light the rosy pink of baby toes, and then Pete stood in a misty dawn. And gasped.

It was so *beautiful*. A calm ocean, smooth and shiny as the floor of the Shell. A beach of white sand, rising in dunes dotted with clumps of grasses. Birds wheeled overhead. Their sharp, indignant cries grew louder as one of them dove into the waves and came up with a fish. Just like that. A fresh breeze tingled Pete's nose with salt.

This. All this. He hadn't landed near the ocean before, although he'd seen pictures of it in one of Caity's books. *This*—all destroyed by the Tesslies, gone forever.

No time for hatred, not even old hatred grown fat and ripe as soy plants on the farm. McAllister's instructions, repeated endlessly to all of them, echoed in Pete's mind: "You have only ten minutes. Don't linger anywhere."

The sand slipped under his shoes and got into the holes. He had to leave them, even though shoes were so hard to come by. Cursing, he ran clumsy and barefoot along the shoreline, his weak knee already aching and head bobbing on his spindly neck, toward the lone house emerging from the mist. The cold air seeped into his lungs and hurt them. He could see his breath.

Seven minutes on his wrister.

The house stood on a little rocky ridge rising from the dunes and jutting into the water. No lights in the windows. The back door was locked but McAllister had put their precious laser saw onto the wrister. (*"If you lose it, I will kill you."*) Pete cut a neat, silent hole, reached in, and released the deadbolt.

Five minutes.

Dark stairs. A night light in the hallway. A bedroom with two sleeping forms, his arm thrown over her body, the window open to the sweet night air. Another bedroom with a single bed, the blanketed figure too long, shadowy clothes all over the floor. And at the end of the hallway, a bonanza.

Two of them.

Four minutes.

The baby lay on its back, eyes closed in its bald head, little pink mouth sucking away on dreams. It had thrown off its blanket to expose a band of impossibly smooth skin between the plastic diaper and tiny shirt. Pete took precious seconds to unfasten a corner of the diaper, but he was already in love with the little hairless creature and would have been devastated if it were male. It was a girl. Carefully he hoisted her out of the crib and onto his shoulder, painfully holding her with one crooked arm. She didn't wake.

No doubt that the toddler was a girl. Glossy brown ringlets, pink pajamas printed with bunnies, a doll clutched in one chubby fist. When Pete reached for her, she woke, blinked, and shrieked.

"No! Mommy! Dada! Cooommme! No!"

Little brat!

Pete grabbed her by the hand and dragged her off the low bed. That wrenched his misshapen shoulder and he nearly screamed. The child resisted, wailing like a typhoon. The baby woke and also screamed. Footsteps pounded down the hall.

Ninety seconds.

"McAllister!" Pete cried, although of course that did no good. McAllister couldn't hear him. And ten minutes was fixed by the Tesslie machinery: no more, no less. McAllister couldn't hurry the Grab.

The parents pounded into the room. Pete couldn't let go of either child. Pete shrieked louder than both of them—his only real strength was in his voice, did they but know it—the words Darlene had taught him: "Stop! I have a bomb!"

They halted just inside the bedroom door, crashing into each other. She gasped: perhaps at the situation, perhaps at Pete. He knew what he must look like to them, a deformed fifteen-year-old with bobbly head.

"Moommmeeeee!" the toddler wailed.

"Bomb! Bomb!" Pete cried.

Forty-five seconds.

The father was a hero. He leaped forward. Pete staggered sideways with his burden of damp baby, but he didn't let go of the toddler's hand. Her father grabbed at her torso and Pete's wrister shot a laser beam at him. The man was moving; the beam caught the side of his arm. The air sizzled with burning flesh and the father let go of his child.

But for only a few precious seconds.

Now the mother rushed forward. Pete dodged behind the low bed, nearly slipping on a pillow that had fallen to the floor. Both of them sprang again, the man's face contorted with pain, and clutched at their children. Pete fired the laser but his hold on the child had knocked the wrister slightly sideways and he missed. Frantically he began firing, the beams hitting the wall and then Pete's own foot. The pain was astonishing. He screamed; the children screamed; the mother screamed and lunged.

Five seconds.

The father tore the little girl from Pete. Pete jerked out his bad arm, now in as much pain as his foot, as much pain as the man's must be, and twined his fingers in the child's hair. The mother slipped on a throw rug patterned with princesses and went down. But the father held on to the toddler and so did Pete, and—

Grab.

All four of them went through in a blaze of noise, of light, of stinking diapers and roasted flesh, of shoulder pain so intense that Pete had to struggle to stay conscious. He did, but not for long. Once under the Shell, he collapsed to the metal floor. The father, of course, was dead. The last thing Pete heard was both children, still wailing as if their world had ended.

It had. From now on, they were with him and McAllister and the others. From now on, poor little devastated parentless miracles.

MARCH 2014

On the high plateau of the Brazilian state of Paraná, the arabica trees rustled in a gentle rain. Drops pattered off dark green, lance-shaped leaves, cascading down until they touched the soil. The coffee berries were small, not ready for harvest until the dry season, months away. At the far edge of the vast field, a fertilizer drove slowly among the rows of short, bushy trees, some of them fifty years old. A rabbit raced ahead of the advancing machinery.

Deep underground, something happened.

Non-motile, rod-shaped bacteria clung to the roots of the coffee trees, as they had for millennia. The bacteria stuck to the roots by exuding a slime layer, where it fed on and decomposed plant matter into nutrients. In the surrounding soil other bacteria also flourished, carrying on their usual life processes. One of these was mitosis. During the reproductive division, plasmids were swapped between organisms, as widely promiscuous as all of their kind.

A new bacterium appeared.

Eventually it, too, began to divide, not too rapidly in the dry soil. By and by, another plasmid exchange took place, with a different bacterium. And so on, in an intricate chain, ending up with a plasmid swap with the non-motile, rod-shaped root dweller. A mutation now existed that had never existed before. Such a thing happened all the time in nature—but not like this.

Above ground, thunder rumbled, and the rain began to fall harder.

NOVEMBER 2013

The woman was hysterical. *As she had every right to be*, Julie thought. Julie laid her hand across her own belly, caught herself doing it, and removed the hand. Quickly she glanced around. No one had noticed. They all watched the woman, and all of them, even the female uniform, had the expressions that cops wore in the presence of hysterical victims: a mixture of stern pity and impatient disgust.

"Ma'am . . . ma'am . . . if you could just calm down enough to tell us what happened. . . ."

"I told you! I told you!" The woman's voice rose to a shriek. She wore a gaping bathrobe over a flimsy white nightdress, and her hair was so wild it looked as if she had torn out patches by the roots, like some grieving Biblical figure. Perhaps she had. A verse from Julie's unwilling Temple childhood rose, unbidden, in her mind: *"In Rama was there a voice heard, lamentation, and weeping, and great mourning, Rachel weeping for her children, and would not be comforted, because they were no more."*

"Ma'am . . . shit. Get a doctor here with a sedative," the "detective" said. He was a captain in this seaside town's police. Julie had picked up from Gordon an FBI agent's contempt for local law enforcement; she would have to rid herself of that, or else turn into as much of a machine as Gordon could be. She stepped forward.

"May I try?"

"No." The captain glared; he hadn't wanted her along in the first place. They never did. Julie stepped back into the shadows. Gordon would be here soon.

The woman continued to wail and tear her hair. A uniform phoned for a doctor. In the bedroom the forensics team worked busily, and through the window Julie could see men fanning out across the beach, looking for clues. Had this mother drowned her infants? Buried them? Hidden them safe in baskets of bulrushes, a crazy latter-day Jochebed with two female versions of Moses? Julie knew better. She studied the room around her.

Simple, classic North Atlantic beach cottage: white duck covers on the wicker furniture, sisal mats on the floor, light wood and pale colors. But the house had central heating and storm windows already in place; evidently the family lived here year-round. Bright toys spilled from a colorful box. Beside the sofa, a basket of magazines, *Time* shouting CAN THE PRESIDENT CONTROL CONGRESS? and THE DESERTIFICATION OF AFRICA. On the counter separating the kitchen from the living area, a homemade pie under a glass dome, next to a pile of fresh tomatoes, onions, zucchini. Everything orderly, prosperous, caring.

Gordon strode through the door and went unerringly to the detective. "Captain Parsons? I'm Special Agent in Charge Gordon Fairford. We spoke on the phone."

Parsons said sourly, "No change from what I told." On the sofa, the woman let out another air-splitting wail.

"What do you think happened, Captain?" Gordon said. Whatever his private opinion, Gordon was always outwardly tactful with locals, who always resented both the tact and the FBI involvement. The eternal verities.

Parsons said, "The husband took the kids, of course. Or they disposed of them together and he took a powder."

"Any signs of his leaving, with or without them?"

"No," Parsons said, with dislike.

Nor would there be, Julie thought. Gordon went on extracting as much information from Parsons as he could, simultaneously smoothing over as much as possible of the inevitable turf war. Julie stopped listening. She waited until Parsons moved off and Gordon turned to her.

He said, "This time your location forecast was closer."

"Not close enough." If it had been, Gordon would have been at the beach house before the kids' disappearance happened. As it was, he and she had only managed to be in the next town over. Not enough, not nearly enough.

74

The woman on the couch had quieted slightly. Gordon said softly to Julie, "Go."

This was never supposed to be part of her job. She was the math wizard, the creator of algorithms, the transformer of raw data into useful predictions. But she and Gordon had been working closely together for over six months now, and he had discovered her other uses.

No, no, not what I meant!

Julie sat next to the sobbing woman, without touching her. "Mrs. Carter, I'm Julie Kahn. And I know you're telling the truth about what happened to your husband and children."

The woman jerked as if she had been shot and fastened both hands on Julie's arm. Her nails dug in, and her eyes bored silently into Julie's face, wider and wilder than any eyes Julie had ever seen. She tried not to flinch.

Julie said, "There was a flash of light when they were taken, wasn't there? Very bright. Almost blinding."

"Yes!"

"Tell me everything, from the beginning."

"Can you get them back? Can you? Can you?"

No. "I don't know."

"You must get them back!"

"We'll do what we can. Was it a short teenage boy with a wobbling head, as if the head were too big for his neck? Or was it a girl?"

Mrs. Carter shuddered. "It was a demon!"

Oh. It was going to be like that.

"A demon from Hell and he has Jenny and Kara!" She began to wail again and tear her hair.

Slowly, painfully, Julie extracted the story. It wasn't much different from the others, except that this time there had been two children, and the husband had disappeared, too. Apparently he had been hanging onto one of the kids. Was that significant?

How did you know what was significant when it was all unthinkable?

Eight other children in the last year, all vanished without a trace, each taken from a different town on the Atlantic coast. Only three of the abductions had been witnessed, however, and one of those had not succeeded. The mother had beaten off the kidnapper—a young girl—before the perp vanished in a dazzlingly bright light. Or so the mother said. But children disappeared all the time, which is why the press had not yet gotten the larger story. But even the unwitnessed disappearances followed a pattern, and patterns were what Julie did. There were other incidents, too: mostly thefts from locked stores. She was less sure those fitted, and her algorithms had to weight for that. But the geographical pattern was there, if bizarrely non-linear, and what kind of kidnapper was both smart enough to plan ten flawless abductions and stupid enough to leave any signature at all in their geography?

Julie was not law enforcement. Gordon was, and they had discussed the question endlessly over the last months. Gordon's answer: *A psycho who wants to be caught.*

Julie had no answers. Only terrible fears.

"It was a demon! A demon!" Mrs. Carter suddenly shrieked. "I want Ed and my kids back!" She tore out of the dune cottage, robe flapping and hair whipping around her ravaged face, as if she could find her husband and children on the cold beach. A cop leaped after her; she was of course a suspect.

Julie wiped the blood off her arm where Mrs. Carter's nails had pierced the skin. Did that mean she needed a tetanus shot? Was a tetanus shot even safe for her now?

She crossed her arms over her belly and closed her eyes. When she opened them again, Gordon stood watching her.

APRIL 2014

The sun rose above the salt marsh on the Connecticut coast. The tide flowed gently out, toward the barrier island that sheltered the land. A light breeze ruffled the cordgrass, although the breeze was not strong enough to cause waves on the pearly water. A blue heron did disturb the water, landing on a mudflat to dip its long bill, searching for breakfast. A sea-pink bloomed on a raised hummock, turning its dome-shaped cluster of flowers toward the sun.

In the mud beside the heron's long thin toes, something changed.

Bacteria sliming the roots of cordgrass swapped plasmids with another species, the result of a long and intricate chain of such exchanges. The new bacteria began to feed. Abruptly, it died, unable in this mutated form to tolerate the high salt content of brackish marsh.

The heron rose and flew away into the dawn.

2035

It took Pete days and days to recover from the laser burn on his foot, which became infected. McAllister was out of her special medicine—"antibiotics," Pete thought it was called—because one of the Grab kids had needed the last dose. Sometimes McAllister sat beside Pete, sometimes Paolo and once Caity, but usually no one tended him. No one could be spared.

He came to loathe his tiny, bare "bedroom" with no bed, just a pile of blankets on the floor and a shit bucket in the corner. Why hadn't he taped something to the wall like Caity did in her room—something, anything to look at. They still had some tape left. Caity had taped up a picture that one of the children tore out of a precious book, a girl riding a big black horse, and beside it a bright piece of patterned cloth from an old Grab. All Pete had to look at was white Tesslie-metal walls, white Tesslie-metal ceiling, white Tesslie-metal floor.

He drifted in and out of sleep that never refreshed him. When his fever rose high enough he thought he saw other rooms around him: the impossibly gorgeous, rich bedroom from which he'd taken the round-headed baby that Bridget had named Kathleen. The ugly city apartment with stained and crumbling walls where he'd found Tina, alone in her bed except for the rat attracted by the milk around her unwiped little mouth. The strange house, decorated only with bright pillows and low, silver-inlaid tables where he'd snatched dark, curly-haired Karim, whose name he knew only because his mother had screamed it just before Pete pushed her down that short flight of stairs to get away. Those other rooms rose around him, shimmered on the air like the world he'd seen only in snatches on Grabs, and then collapsed into so much rubble.

"Sleep, Pete." McAllister, a cool hand on his forehead. Or maybe not, because McAllister collapsed, too, but into a shimmer of golden sparks. Like the Tesslie that McAllister described in learning circles! Pete struggled to sit up.

"No! No . . . not you . . . Tessl . . ."

"Sleep."

When he woke for the last time from fever and delirium, he was alone.

Cautiously he got himself up off the pallet of blankets. Pete recognized them; he'd brought them back himself, from his first store Grab. They needed washing. Everything needed washing, including himself. But that could wait.

He lurched dizzily to the door. A Grab was supposed to be painless, and usually it was. But you weren't supposed to shoot your own foot! Still, everyone took risks during Grabs, or at least everyone who could still go. Look what had happened to Caity on her last Grab: that mother had beat Caity off, breaking her arm, and Caity hadn't even been strong enough to keep the child. McAllister was thinking of taking Caity off Grab duty, which would leave just Pete, Ravi, and Paolo to do them all, at least until Terrell turned twelve. Anyway, it was better than shit-bucket duty.

Pete's room opened onto the corridor that ran the whole half-mile length of the egg-shaped Shell. Each end of the corridor branched into maybe a hundred of these tiny rooms. The Survivors and the Six used some of them at the living end as bedrooms, and McAllister had designated a few more as storage or work areas. None of the rooms at the far end of the Shell were used at all. In the center was the important stuff.

Such a long way to hobble. Below Pete's halting feet, one painful enough that finally he just hopped on the other and leaned against the wall for support, stretched the same featureless white metal as his room. Above curved the ceiling of the Shell, three times his height. On either side were doors, some open and some closed, leading to more tiny rooms, white metal walls. Tesslie stuff, all of it. Stuff preserving his life. Pete hated it.

Another hundred yards to the farm, the children's room, the Grab room.

All at once he didn't want to go to any of them. The children's room, spacious and always busy, would be cheerful with toys, learning circles, babies cooing or wailing. Caity or Jenna or Terrell would be there, whoever was on duty. Someone would also be on duty with Darlene in the farm. Someone else would be watching—endlessly, boringly—the Grab machinery. Pete was sick of all of it. This time it had nearly gotten him killed. The only person he would have liked to see was McAllister, and he'd been sick so long that he'd lost track of the duty roster and had no idea where McAllister, or anybody else, might be now.

Miraculously unnoticed, Pete crept past the wide archways which opened on one side of the corridor to the children's room and on the other to the farm. From the farm came the smell of dirt and the fall of water in the disinfecting and clean-water streams. Also the clank of buckets; someone was on duty at the fertilizer machine. From the children's room came the usual babble, the playing and crying and talking of eight—no, now ten!—small children.

Head wobbling on his thin neck, he hopped past the smaller, doorless openings to the rooms holding Tesslie machinery and entered the maze of tiny, unused rooms at the far end of the Shell. His foot, wrapped in pieces of torn blanket, still hurt. "Stupid fucking foot!" McAllister had forbidden that word, but Pete—all of the Six—had learned a rich cursing vocabulary from Darlene. Her only useful contribution, in Pete's opinion, to life in the Shell. Mean old woman.

Finally he reached a small, low chamber at the very tip of the Shell. Here part of the outer wall was, for some reason, clear. Why had the Tesslies done that? But, then, why had they destroyed the world nearly twenty-one years ago and then chosen to imprison a handful of survivors? Nobody knew why the fucking bastards did anything. Pete sank to the metal floor and looked out.

There wasn't much to see: just a strip of land between him and where the ground curved abruptly away. That strip was a uniform expanse of empty black rock, once smooth but now starting to split in places. The rock had a name, and so did the thing the Shell sat on, but Pete didn't remember them. Basil? No, that was a prince in *The Illustrated Book of Fairy Tales*. Balit? Basalt? He'd never been good at learning such stuff, not like Jenna or Paolo. They were the smart ones. What Pete was good at was the Grab.

And hatred. He was terrific at hatred. So he gazed out at his tiny view of the vast dead world the Tesslies had killed, and thought about the beauty of the shore cottage where he had Grabbed the two children, and he hated.

APRIL 2014

Deep beneath the ice pack of the Canadian glacier, the earth shifted. Basalt magma flowed into a chamber heavy with silica and the two mingled. From below, more magma pushed upward, exerting pressure. Above, glacial ice tens of thousands of years old but already thinned by global warming, gleamed under a cold spring sky.

NOVEMBER 2013

Gordon stood at one end of the table that was really two tables pushed together, one moved from the bedroom of the motel "suite." Julie stood at the other end, willing him to leave. The rest of the task force had already gone to their own rooms for the night, leaving Styrofoam cups with a half-inch of cold coffee, empty pizza boxes, crumpled paper napkins, half-crushed beer cans. On the desk Julie's industrial-strength laptop, in sleep mode, glowed with a blue light.

It had been a bad idea to hold the team meeting in her room, but Gordon's wife, impelled by some marital crisis Julie wanted no part of, kept phoning his room after she'd been told not to call his cell. Maybe that was why he hadn't left yet; Deborah was a weeper. Or so Julie had been told. She didn't want to know for sure. If Gordon tried to talk personally with her now . . .

He didn't. He studied her latest printout, frowning at the equations as if he understood them. "So you think somewhere in Hingham, next Thursday?"

"That's what the algorithms say."

"God, Julie, I need a more specific location than that! Unless I can witness an actual kidnapping, maybe even have a camera set up—"

She held onto her temper. "I'm a mathematician, Gordon, not a magician. And I've given you everything I've got."

A second later, horror hit her at her own wording, but Gordon, frowning at the sheaf of papers, apparently hadn't noticed. That caused horror to give way to anger. He never had been any good at reading her feelings, had always enclosed himself in that "objective" professional shell. Well, let him.

He ran a hand over the gray stubble on his head. "I know. I didn't mean to snap. But funding for this task force is hanging by a thread. The A-Dic isn't convinced that the child abductions are linked, and he's never believed any of the witnesses, you know that."

"I know. Can't blame him, really." Two witnesses—no, three now, with Mrs. Carter—attesting that someone had invaded their homes, stolen or tried to steal a child, and then dissolved, child and all, into thin air, to the accompaniment of a burst of bright light. Twice the alleged intruder was a deformed teenage boy with a wobbly head, dressed in what was described as a blanket. Once it was a girl, who had been successfully fought off until she dematerialized. Who would believe any of that? Nor did it help that two of the women had been hysterical types; one was now in a mental institution. Some days Julie wasn't sure that she herself believed this stuff. The common M.O.s, yes. The irrefutable fact that the children were gone, yes. Above all, the algorithms that traced a non-linear but discernible mathematical path for the kidnappings.

She said, "Your Assistant Director has reason to doubt. But I think my usefulness to the task force is pretty much over, and anyway Georgetown wants me back for the spring semester. I've booked a flight back to D.C. for tomorrow."

Gordon looked up. Was that relief in his eyes? She was lying about Georgetown, but he didn't know that. He said, "Will you stay on call if we have any questions?"

"Sure." She rose, which was a mistake. The wave of nausea took her by surprise, surging up her throat so suddenly that she barely made it to the bathroom. After she threw up, she kicked the door closed behind her, then took her time rinsing her mouth and brushing her teeth. By the time she came out, he would have gone.

He hadn't. He stood at the end of the table, papers crumpled in one hand, his still handsome face as white as the print-outs. A little vein throbbed in his forehead. "My God, Julie."

"It's nothing. Something I ate at dinner."

"It's not." And then, "I have three kids, remember."

Something in her that she hadn't counted on, some streak of anger or blame, made her lash out at him. "Now you've got one more."

"Why didn't you *tell* me?"

She sat down. The motel chair creaked under her. "Let's get one thing straight, Gordon. This has nothing to do with you. I mean, it *will* have nothing to do with you. You don't need to be involved at all."

"You're keeping it?"

"Yes." She was thirty-eight, with no real relationship in sight now that the ill-thought-out thing with Gordon had ended. This might be her last chance.

"How far along are you?"

"Three and a half months." Her stocky figure meant that, with her habitually loose clothing, no one had yet noticed. They would soon. She had arranged to extend her sabbatical from Georgetown to a full year, had already bought a crib, a changing table, impossibly tiny onesies. The nausea was supposed to have stopped by now but, as her obstetrician said, every pregnancy is different.

Gordon's jaw tightened. "You weren't going to tell me at all, were you?"

"No." And then, from that same unexplored well of anger—but at what? "You have your hands full already, with Deborah and your kids."

They stared at each other for a long moment. Julie found herself studying him almost impersonally, as if he were someone she'd just met. Such a handsome man, with his deep blue eyes, firm jaw, prematurely gray hair that looked masterful rather than old. "Masterful"—that was the right word for Gordon. He liked to control situations. And yet he had been tender with her, from the conventional beginning of too-long "business dinners," through the trite progression to so much more.

Had she really ever loved him? It had felt like romance, those first few months of delicious hidden hours. And yet even then, Julie had had her doubts. Not because Gordon was married, but because of something in his character and—be honest!—in her own. Both of them wanted to make their own decisions, keep their options open. That stubborn independence was why Julie had never married, and why Gordon cheated on his wife. Neither had ever told the other "I love you." Both had wanted freedom more than the inevitable compromises and sacrifices of genuine love.

And yet now Gordon stood at his end of the littered table, running his hand through his gray hair and looking more troubled than Julie had known possible. But, then, Gordon was not one to shirk responsibilities. That wouldn't have fit with his image of himself.

"Julie, if there's anything I can do . . . money . . ."

Her anger evaporated. This situation was not his fault. Nor hers—precautions sometimes failed. Gordon would never leave drama-queen Deborah, and she didn't want him to, no matter what romantic fantasies dictated that she should want. Julie needed nothing from him.

"I'm fine," she said gently. "Truly."

"At least let me—"

"No." She went into her motel bedroom and closed the door, her back to it until she heard him leave.

APRIL 2014

The sheep pasture high in New Zealand hills lay thick in white clover. One corner of the pasture had been planted with chicory, but the clover grew wild. Low, white-flowered, sweet-smelling, it attracted the bees buzzing above the fenced pasture. Sheep munched contentedly, flicking their tails. Beside the fence, two lambs chased each other.

The clover's root system, fibrous and fast-growing, laced itself through the soil. The original tap root extended three feet deep; branches clustered thickly near the top grew, in turn, a mass of fine rootlets. Much of the system was slimed with new bacteria, created by a long chain of plasmid swaps. There had been more than enough candidates for this gene-swapping: a teaspoon of the sheep pasture's soil contained over 600 million bacteria. The new anaerobic strain included a gene that broke down carbohydrates, producing carbon dioxide and alcohol.

The alcohol accumulated on the plant roots. In a short time the fermentation had deposited ethanol on the plant roots in a concentration of one part per million. When the concentration reached twice that, the clover began to die.

The new bacteria went on multiplying. A ewe munched up a handful of clover, jostling the root system so that it touched another. The ewe ambled on toward her lamb.

2035

McAllister didn't let Pete sit alone by the Shell wall for very long. She found him in another of the maze of unused rooms, as she always found him wherever he went, and knelt beside him. The folds of her simple long dress, made from a blue bed sheet patterned with yellow flowers, puddled on the metal floor. "Pete."

"Go away."

"No." She didn't put her arms around him; she knew better, after last time. He had hit her. From frustration, hurt, anger, hate. Never had he regretted anything so much in his short life.

"Then don't go away. I don't care."

She smiled. "Yes, you do. And I have something good to tell you."

Despite himself, he said, "What?"

"The two little girls you brought us a week ago are doing fine."

"They are?" And then, because he didn't want to look yet at anything good, "A *week* ago? I was sick for a week?"

"Yes."

"I missed a whole week of duties?"

"Yes, but don't worry about it. Your foot got infected and you were wonderful. Just kept fighting. You always do."

That was McAllister: always encouraging, always kind. She was one of the Survivors, from the time before the Tesslies destroyed the world. When that happened, McAllister had been only twenty-one, six years older than

Pete was now. The Tesslies had put her and twenty-five others in the Shell, and then—what? Kept them there to breed and. . . . Pete didn't know what the Tesslies had wanted, or wanted now. Who could understand killer aliens who destroyed a world and then for over twenty years kept a zoo going with random survivors? And when that experiment failed, having produced only six children, replaced it with another experiment involving machinery that they could have put in the Shell decades before?

Only four of the Survivors were still alive: McAllister, Eduardo, Xiaobo, and the awful Darlene. "Radiation damage created cancers and genetic damage," McAllister had said; Pete hadn't listened closely to the rest of the explanation. Jenna and Paolo, not him, were good at that science stuff. What Pete knew was that the Survivors miscarried, got weaker, eventually died. Most of them he couldn't even remember, including both his biological parents, although he was the oldest of the Six. But he remembered Seth and Hannah, Robert and Jenny, and especially kind and loving Bridget, who had died only three months ago. All the Six had loved Bridget, and so had the Grab kids.

Pete looked at McAllister. She was so beautiful. Her face was lined and her breasts sagged a little beneath her loose dress, but her body was slim and curving, her dark eyes and rich brown skin unmarred. And she was whole. Not damaged like the next generation, the Six. Not old-looking like the other three Survivors. She was the smartest of everybody, and the sweetest. Again Pete felt the love surge up in him, and the lust. The latter was completely hopeless and he knew it. The knowledge turned him sullen again.

"So who did the next Grab? Was there one?"

"The platform brightened but nobody went."

"Why didn't Paolo go? He was next in line!"

"He fell asleep and missed it."

"He's a wimp." It was their deadliest insult, learned from the Survivors. It meant you shirked your fair share of work and risk and unpleasant duties like lugging shit buckets to the fertilizer machine. It was also unfair applied to Paolo, who had always been sickly and couldn't help falling asleep. He had some disease that made him do it. Pete had forgotten the name.

"Paolo isn't really strong enough for a Grab unless it's a store, and who can predict that?" McAllister said reasonably. "I'm taking him off Grab duty. Pete, don't you want to hear about the little girls?"

"No. Caity could have gone on the Grab when Paolo fell asleep," he said, although he knew that if it wasn't her turn, she wouldn't have been anywhere near the machinery. But Pete had his own reasons for a grudge against Caity, reasons he couldn't tell McAllister. And the truth was that of the Six, Pete and Ravi were best at the Grab. Terrell wouldn't go until he turned twelve, Paolo and Jenna had gotten too sickly, Caity had her arm broken when she tried to Grab a child, which she hadn't even been able to bring back. Although, to be fair, Caity insisted on going again as soon as her arm healed. But Pete was in no mood to be fair to Caity.

Only the Six could go through the Grab machinery. Before the humans in the Shell knew that, they'd lost two Survivors, Robert and Seth. You'd think the Tesslies would have told McAllister about the age limit when they left the Grab machinery a year ago! But no one had even seen them leave the machinery (and how did they do that?) Nobody had seen a Tesslie in twenty-one years, and nobody ever had heard one speak. Maybe they couldn't.

McAllister said, still trying to cheer up Pete, "Both little girls are adjusting so much better than we'd hoped. You must come see them. The little girl said her name is Kara. She just called the infant 'Baby,' so we had to pick a name for her, and we chose 'Petra.' After you."

Petra. Despite himself, Pete rolled the name on his tongue, savoring it as once—only once—he'd savored "candy" that Paolo had Grabbed when he'd found himself sent to a store. They'd all had a piece. Reese's Peanut Butter Cups, McAllister had called them. Feeling the astounding sweetness dissolve on his tongue, Pete had hated the Tesslies all over again. This, this, *this*—he might have had a Reese's Peanut Butter Cup every day of his life! A whole Peanut Butter Cup, every day!

He might even have had a woman like McAllister.

"Come see Petra," she coaxed.

He'd been trained since birth not to indulge himself. *Don't be a wimp!* Indulgence in moods was selfish and against the restarting of humanity. Some of the others might be better at remembering that—well, *all* of the others—but Pete had his pride. He'd been indulgent enough for one day. He got painfully to his feet, his head wobbling, and followed McAllister to see Petra.

APRIL 2014

The Connecticut salt marsh had been filled in during the 1940s, restored during the 1980s, overrun with too many tourists enjoying its beauty in the 1990s, and finally declared an ecologically protected area in 2004. Although it proved impossible to completely eliminate the invasive non-native plant species, the natural floral layering of back-barrier marsh was returning. At the lowest level, where the tide brought surges of salt water twice a day, cordgrass and glassworts dominated. Higher up, it was salt hay. Higher still, on the upland border of the marsh, the ground was thick with black rush and marsh elder.

A particularly large marsh elder, nearly eight feet high, held a half-finished nest. A red-winged blackbird brought another piece of grass, laid in in the nest, and flew off. The shrub's still furled buds, which would soon become greenish-white flowers, bobbed in a wind from the sea.

Below ground, bacteria mutated again. This time it found the lower salinity much more congenial than it had the roots of cordgrass, a month ago. The bacterial slime engaged in all its metabolic processes, including mitosis and fermentation. Alcohol began to accumulate on the marsh elder's roots.

NOVEMBER 2013

Julie sat in a crowded Starbucks in D.C. across the table from her best friend, Linda Campinelli. Julie's latte and Linda's double caramel macchiato sat untouched. The women known each other since Princeton, brought together by the vagaries of the roommate-matching computer even though they were complete opposites. Linda, a large untidy woman with a large untidy husband

and three riotous sons, was an animal psychologist in Bethesda. She told long, funny stories about neurotically territorial cats or schnauzers that developed a fear of their water dishes. But not today.

"Ju . . . are you *sure?*"

"I'm four months along. Of course I'm sure."

"Gordon?"

"Of course it was Gordon! How many men do you think I was banging at once?"

"I meant what will Gordon and you *do?*"

Julie had expected this. Linda was not only a romantic, she was sociability squared. Maybe even cubed. Not even after four years of dorm living did Linda understand Julie's preference for silence and solitude. For Linda, all decisions and all endeavors were group activities.

"Linda, there is no 'Gordon and me.' And I don't want there to be. I'm having the baby, I'm keeping the baby, I'm raising the baby. Georgetown's given me a year's sabbatical, for which I was overdue anyway. I've got great medical coverage. I feel fine now that morning sickness is over. And I'm happy to be doing this alone."

"Except for me," said Linda, to whom anything else was unthinkable.

Julie smiled. "Of course. You can be my labor coach. Always good to have a coach who won all her own games."

"And your due date is—"

"May 1."

Linda sipped her caramel macchiato. Julie saw that her friend was still troubled. Linda would never understand isolates like Julie and Jake.

As if reading Julie's mind, Linda said, "And how is that gorgeous brother of yours?"

"Still monitoring mud in Wyoming." Jake was a geologist.

"What did he say about the baby?"

"I haven't told him yet."

"But he'll come here for the birth, right?"

"I'm sure he will," said Julie, who was sure of no such thing. She and Jake liked being affectionate at a distance.

"Then you'll have me and Jake, and I'm sure that Lucy Anderson will come to—"

Ah, Linda! Even parturition required a committee.

That evening Julie's cell rang just as she was tapping the lid back on a paint can in her D.C. apartment. Paint had spilled over the side of the can and flowed down its side, but fortunately she had laid down a thick wad of paper. Winterfresh Green puddled over a science article: POLLUTION FROM ASIA CONTAMINATES STRATOSPHERE. Julie's paper mask was still in place; the baby book had recommended a filter mask if a pregnant woman felt it absolutely necessary to paint something. Julie had felt it absolutely necessary to paint her mother's old chest of drawers, after which she would apply decals of bears. The ultrasound showed she was having a girl. But no Disney princesses or any of that shit; Julie's daughter would be brought up to be a strong, independent woman. Bears were a good start.

The nursery, formerly Julie's study, was very cold, since the baby book had also recommended painting with open windows. She shivered as she picked up her cell and walked into the hallway of the two-bedroom apartment, squeezing past the furniture and boxes moved from her former study. Somehow she would have to find room for all this stuff. At the moment her computer and printer sat on the dining table and her file cabinet crowded the kitchen. The baby wasn't even here yet and it had disrupted everything. "Hello. Julie Kahn speaking."

"It's Gordon."

Damn. She said neutrally, "Yes?"

"Is that really you? You sound all muffled."

She took off the filter mask and said crisply, "What is it, Gordon?"

He was direct, one of the things she'd liked about him, when she still liked things about him. "There was no kidnapping Thursday at Hingham."

That threw her. "Are you sure? Could there possibly be a child missing but the parents didn't report it, or . . . or maybe just another burglary, the algorithms used those to—"

"I know my damn job. If there were so much as a misplaced *screwdriver* in this town tonight, we'd fucking well know about it."

In his unaccustomed irritability she heard his tension over the situation. Unless his tension was over her, which she definitely did not want.

She said, "I explained to you that the burglaries complicated the algorithms, made them more than a simple linear progression. It was a judgment call which ones to include. I might have included some that were inside jobs with no forced entry, I might have missed some that—"

"I know all that. You did explain it. Several times. But the fact is that your predictive program isn't working, and you need to fix it in part because I've staked my credibility with the A-Dic on it."

Not like him to say so much. Her temper rose. "You can't blame this failure on me, Gordon. I told you when you approached me at the university that predictive algorithms with this kind of data—"

"I know what you told me. Stop talking to me like I'm an idiot. Just put this new non-data in and give me something else I can work with. If you really can."

"I'll do what is possible," she said stiffly.

"Great. Call me whenever it's done." He hung up, everything else unsaid between them.

Julie closed the door to the freezing nursery-to-be, put on a heavy sweater, and went to her computer.

APRIL 2014

From the floor of the Atlantic Ocean rose the longest mountain range in the world, separating huge tectonic plates. All at once a northern section of the African Plate moved closer to the South American Plate. The move was only an inch, and the resulting earthquake so slight it was felt by nobody. But the hydrophones set around the ocean picked up the shift from its low-frequency sonic rumbles, sending the information to monitoring stations on four continents.

"¡Mirar esto!" a technician called to his superior in Spain.

"Regardez!"

"Ei, olhar para esta!"

"*Kijk naar dit!*"
"Will you fucking take a look at that!"

2035

Kara started screaming as soon as Pete came through the archway to the children's room.

Thirteen children played or slept or learned in this large open space. Like all interior Shell rooms, it had featureless white metal walls, floor, and ceiling. There was no visible lighting but the room was suffused with a glow that brightened at "day" and dimmed at "night," although never to complete blackness. The Shell contained only those objects originally gathered by Tesslies before they destroyed the world, or else seized on Grabs with the machinery the aliens had supplied a year ago. Pallets of blankets either thin and holey or else thick and new. Pillows on the floor for the adults to sit on. Many bright plastic toys, from the time that one of Jenna's Grab had landed her in something called a "Wal-Mart." That Grab was famous. Jenna, almost as smart as her mother, had used her ten minutes to lash together three huge shopping carts and frantically fill them with everything in the closest aisles, toys and tools and clothing and "soft goods." The pillows had come from that Grab, and the sheets and blankets that made both bedding and clothes for those who didn't happen at the moment to fit into any clothes Grabbed at other stores. The shopping carts were now used to trundle things along the central corridor.

One wall held McAllister's calendar. Crayons and paint just slid off the metal walls, but McAllister had put up a large sheet with packing tape and on that she kept careful track of how long humanity had been in the Shell. As a little boy Pete had sat in front of that calendar in a learning circle and learned to count. He'd been taught to read, too, although until Jenna's Grab all the letters had to written on a blanket using burned twigs from the farm. Now the Shell had six precious books, which everyone read over and over. All the pages were smeary and torn at the edges.

The children's room—and many other rooms as well—held piles of buckets. These had been here from the beginning; evidently the Tesslies considered buckets important. The Shell contained whole rooms full of buckets, from fist-sized (these were used as bowls and cups) to big ones on the farm. The buckets could be stuck to each other with something in tubes that Jenna had brought back from her Wal-Mart Grab. A shoulder-high wall of stuck-together buckets divided the babies' corner from the rest of the children's room. And, of course, the buckets were used for pissing and shitting.

Jenna would never do another Grab. Her deformities were worse than most, and now her spine would not hold up her body for more than a few minutes of painful movement. It wouldn't be long before one of the shopping carts would have to trundle her. But despite the constant pain, she retained the sweet nature she had inherited from McAllister, and now she sat on a pillow, back against the wall beside the open door, reading to four kids sprawled on the floor. *Goodnight, Moon.* Pete knew it well.

Kara looked up, saw Pete, and shrieked. "No! No! Nooooooo!" The child threw herself on the floor and kicked her bare feet against the metal.

McAllister picked her up. "No, sweetheart, no . . . ssshhhhhh, Kara-love, ssshhhhh. . . ."

Kara went on screaming until Caity rushed over, took Kara from McAllister, and carried her away, tossing a reproachful glance over her shoulder at Pete. He'd never liked Caity, not even when they were kids themselves. *"She's too much like you,"* McAllister had said to him once, and Pete had hid from McAllister in the far end of the Shell for an entire day. He still didn't like Caity, not even when he was having sex with her.

Jenna said, "How are you, Pete?"

"Great, just great, on this great ol' day in the morning." Almost immediately he regretted saying that. Jenna loved the songs Bridget had crooned to them as kids, and she'd loved Bridget. At Bridget's funeral a few months ago, Jenna had sobbed and sobbed.

Jenna didn't react to the sarcasm. She, of all the Six, was the best at setting aside her own feelings for the common good. Terrell and Paolo were pretty good at it, too. Pete, Ravi, and Caity often failed.

Failed, failed, failed . . . That was Pete's song, unless he made hatred sing louder.

Jenna said, "I'm glad you recovered from your Grab. Kara is coming along very well—"

"Unless she sees me, of course."

"—and Petra is a darling."

"I better go Outside to give Kara a chance to adjust."

McAllister said, sharply for her, "That's enough of that talk, Pete. Come with me."

As if anyone could really get Outside!

But he followed her meekly, wishing for the hundred hundredth time that he had Jenna's patience. Ravi's physical strength and good looks. Anything that anyone else had and he didn't. Wishing he could seize McAllister's waist and take her into one of the rooms at the far end of the Shell, just the two of them and a blanket . . . His cock rose.

Not a good time! Still, he was glad he was only infertile, not impotent like Paolo. "*Pre-embryonic genetic damage is a capricious thing,*" McAllister had said. "*We were lucky you Six survived at all.*"

Lucky. Great, just great, on this great ol' day in the morning.

McAllister led Pete around the bucket-wall to the babies' corner. Three infants lay asleep on blankets, watched over by Ravi, who didn't much like babies but it was his turn for this duty. Ravi was the least deformed of the Six. His eyes were permanently crossed, but his body was strong and even though he was a year younger than Pete, he was taller and heavier. With thick dark hair and a handsome face, he looked the most like the princes in *The Illustrated Book of Fairy Tales*. Sometimes Pete hated him for that, although in general they got along well enough. Ravi was his biological half-brother, after all. Not that that counted for much; what counted was the good of all.

"Look," McAllister said to Pete, "at the treasure you brought us."

Petra lay asleep on a blanket, a square of plastic between it and the clumsy diaper made of another blanket. On top she wore a very faded yellow shirt too big for her. Her tiny pink mouth, the little curled fists with the creases at the wrists, the shape of her head . . . She was a perfect human person and of course she would be fertile. Radiation levels had subsided enough by now, McAllister had said, although Pete didn't really understand what that meant. It didn't matter. What mattered was that he had done this thing: brought back a perfect, precious boost to the restarting of humanity on Earth. Someday that restarting would move Outside, McAllister said.

If the Tesslies permitted it.

McAllister put her thin hands on either side of Pete's face and turned him toward her. "Listen to me, dear heart. I am making you this baby's father. You are now responsible for her life and, as much as possible, her happiness. Do you understand me? I put Petra's life in your hands. You are her father."

Both Pete and Ravi gaped at her. No one in the Shell was "father" or "mother" to any kid taken on a Grab! Everyone was responsible for the good of all, always. Why now, why Petra, why Pete? The questions were lost in the feel of McAllister's hands on his face.

"Why him?" Ravi blurted. "Is it because he's the oldest?"

McAllister didn't answer. She never answered anything she didn't choose to. But she gave Ravi a look that Pete couldn't read, and didn't want to. All he wanted was for her to keep on holding his face between her long slim fingers, forever and ever.

She didn't. But he could feel her hands long after she took them away, could feel his own deep blush, could feel the burden, welcome because she had given it, that McAllister had just placed on his heart. To turn his red face away from her, he gazed down at Petra.

"Hey," he said to the baby, who woke and immediately shit her diaper.

NOVEMBER 2013

Julie sat in her apartment, studying the graphs on her computer screen. Her desk was jammed against the living room window. Beyond the glass a few flakes of early snow drifted through darkness. Cars swooshed through street slush and swept ghostly patterns of light across the ceiling.

The kidnappings and mysterious store burglaries had followed an erratic path, but the rough outline was clear. The first abduction—the first they knew about and had included in the data, she corrected herself—had been in Sarasota a year ago. October 16, 2011: Tommy Candless, age six. Parents divorced, and the child basically a ping-pong ball for power struggles between them. John Candless, who did not have custody, had grabbed his son and run before, but he'd easily been caught by state troopers since he hadn't even had the sense to leave Florida. Heather Candless had one conviction for DWI. Julie wasn't even positive that Tommy wasn't squirreled away with some obscure relative or friend somewhere that Gordon's task force had failed to discover. Or the child could have been killed and the body never found. Both parents seemed to her capable of even that in their intense hatred for each other.

Drop Tommy from the data? Would that help? No, her gut said to leave him in. She did.

The path of subsequent abductions moved roughly up the East Coast, sometimes swerving inland, sometimes back-tracking. The intervals weren't even, coming in clusters that themselves weren't even. Nine children after Tommy, including Kara and Jennifer Carter. The kids ranged from ten months old to Tommy's six years. Seven girls, three boys. Two hysterical witnesses, one relatively calm one (but her baby hadn't been taken; she'd fought off the young abductress). One hysterical witness had been pushed over the slippery edge of her already advancing illness into an institutional schizophrenia, which did not help the FBI Assistant Director to trust her credibility.

The big problem with the data, as Julie had told Gordon, were the store burglaries. Here, too, the M.O. was the same: no forced entry, no money taken, seemingly random grabs of diverse merchandise, including shopping carts. Why take shopping carts, both worthless and conspicuous? Why take an entire display of Reese's Peanut Butter Cups? At Wal-Mart's why take pillows and leave untouched a display of diamond rings? And should the Baltimore Kohl's burglary be included or not? How about that earlier one in Georgia? Or the one in the New Jersey convenience store? That store had had a broken back window, which might have taken it off the list of no-forced-entry burglaries. However, a neighbor walking his dog at 3:00 a.m. thought he heard glass breaking. He shouted and saw kids ran away, empty-handed, so did that mean there were two incidents at the same store at the same night, a coincidence?

She played with the data, putting in one incident, taking out another, changing the patterns. The maddening thing was that the patterns were there, and not just in M.O.s. The numbers showed patterns, too: non-linear, closer to fractals than to conventional graphs, but nonetheless there. And the numbers should have pointed to another abduction or burglary in Hingham, Massachusetts, on Thursday. Which hadn't happened. So obviously she had included something erroneous, or left something out, or missed something altogether.

She sat far into the night, scrutinizing data.

APRIL 2014

In Xinjiang Autonomous Region of northern China, the cotton fields lay serene under the sun. Acre upon acre of the plants stretched to the horizon, dark green leaves a little dusty from lack of rain. Clouds overhead, however, promised water soon. The white boles had only just begun to open, filling the green fields with lopsided polka dots. A golden eagle coasted on an air current, a darker speck against the gray clouds. To the south lay the ancient Silk Road, and much farther south, the majestic and forbidding peaks of the Kun Lun.

On the roots of the cotton plants, bacteria mutated.

2035

The Grab machinery was Tesslie, of course. It sat in its own room in the Shell, a room without a door just down the central corridor from the farm and the children's room. Someone had to sit there day and night because no one knew when the machinery would brighten. When it did, they had only a few minutes to get someone on it. Then ten minutes in Before to make a Grab. The whole system was stupid. Pete said so to McAllister, often.

"It isn't our machinery, remember," she said. "We don't know how the Tesslies manage time, or intervals of time. We don't know how they think."

"They think it's fun to destroy the Earth, rescue a few Survivors, put them in the Shell, and watch them for twenty years."

"There's no reason to think they watch us."

"There's no reason to think they don't."

"They need machinery, Pete—they're aliens but not gods. I see no cameras here."

Pete turned away, because McAllister had just, as she so often did, gone abruptly beyond him. He didn't know what "gods" were, although some of the Survivors had babbled about them when Pete was little, and Darlene still did. She sang songs about green pastures and washing in blood and rowing boats ashore, all in her scratchy tuneless very loud voice. However, nobody listened to Darlene, who was a nasty old woman. Pete wasn't too sure about the word "camera" either, although it seemed to be a non-Tesslie machinery that made pictures. Pete didn't know how machines could draw that fast. But how could the Grab do what it did?

The machinery sat in the center of the room, looking like nothing but a gray metal platform a few inches above the floor. If climbed onto it, ordinarily nothing happened. But sometimes the platform started to glow and then it became a stupid invisible door. No, not a door. Something else. Whatever it was, if you jumped on the platform and went through it, you had ten minutes in Before.

The Grabs usually came a few close together, then long weeks of no brightening. After the Grab when Pete got Kara and Petra, while he'd been feverish with his infected foot, Paolo had fallen asleep and missed the whole thing. Even if Paolo hadn't been sick, Pete couldn't really blame him. Watching the Grab machine do nothing, with only your own thoughts to occupy you, was easily the most boring duty on the roster.

But did the Tesslies watch humanity? That was the question that now consumed Pete. Did they watch Pete and Caity when they had sex? Even though Pete didn't like Caity, she was his only choice. Jenna had grown too fragile, and the kids from the Grab were still too young. That was why they were Grabbed, of course—to have sex when they were older. The girls would be fertile. The boys would be fertile, too, but the Shell needed a lot more girls than boys. None of the Six apparently were fertile, and the four Survivors left were too old to have babies.

But they had had a lot of sex when they were young and newly in the Shell. Even way back then they had been trying to start humanity all over again. Lots of sex—Pete got hard just imagining it—and lots of babies, most of which died.

But had the fucking bastards (more of Darlene's useful words) watched while the Survivors had all that sex? Did they watch Pete and Caity? And what was a "bastard," anyway?

Pete tried to sneak across the corridor from the farm to the children's room. It had been his turn for fertilizer duty, a job he hated. The fertilizer was made from everybody's shit. You dumped it into a huge closed metal box (more Tesslie machinery!) and the box did something to it. When it fell out a hole into a bucket, it didn't smell like shit anymore and McAllister said it couldn't make you sick. But it still *looked* like shit. Pete had been collecting shit buckets from all over the Shell, trundling them along the wide central corridor on a shopping cart and dumping them into the fertilizer box. Then he had to rinse each bucket thoroughly under the disinfectant waterfall, which was a continuous rain of blue water that shot out of a wall and disappeared into a hole in the floor. Just after he'd rinsed the last bucket, the fertilizer machine delivered a load of fertilizer. Pete tried to pretend he hadn't seen the bucket fill, so that spreading the fertilizer would have to be the next person's job, but Darlene caught him.

"Ha! Don't be sneaking off before the job's done! I seen you!"

"I wasn't sneaking off!"

"Sure you was. You're bone lazy, Pete. A wild one for sure. Go spread that bucket."

When Bridget died, Pete wished it had been Darlene instead. "Where should I spread this?" He picked up the bucket of fertilizer. "On the soy?"

"Them ain't soy," she said scathingly. "Them are some concoction the Tesslies dreamed up and don't you think nothing different, boy! Them plants will probably poison us yet!"

"Yeah, right," Pete said. Darlene was crazy. The Tesslies keeping humans alive for twenty years, giving them Grab machinery to get fertile kids to make more humans, just to poison the whole lot.

Then he realized that Darlene's craziness was driving him to defend the Tesslies, and he threw the brown gunk—it still looked like shit!—harder than necessary onto the soy. Or whatever it was. "High-protein, dense-calorie plants," Jenna had told him once. McAllister was teaching Jenna and Paolo all the science she knew from Before, so it wouldn't be lost. The other Survivors had done the same, but they hadn't known nearly as much. "We must save everything we can," she always said.

Pete spread the fertilizer through the soy. There was enough for half the onion bed, too. Then he rinsed the bucket. Darlene watched him every minute.

Darlene was in charge of the farm. In a way that was weird because Eduardo was the Survivor who had been studying plants when the Tesslies put him into the Shell. "Ecobiology," McAllister had called it. But that just meant that the plants Eduardo knew about were wild ones, and he told Pete that no special knowledge was needed to grow the vegetables on the farm. Besides, nobody wanted Darlene anywhere near the Grab children. She was too mean.

The farm was the biggest room in the Shell, with rows and rows of raised beds holding various crops, crossed by long metal pipes that leaked water. The farm also housed the disinfecting waterfall and the clean-water waterfall, from which endless buckets of water were hauled for drinking, washing, cooking. Here, too, stood the raised section of the floor that could be turned hot by pressing a button. Bridget had been especially good at simmering vegetable stews on the hot box, in buckets. Now Eduardo did it, less well. The farm smelled good, of dirt and water and cooking, and it would have been a lovely place if it hadn't been for Darlene.

"Rock of ages," she sang in her tuneless, scratchy voice while Pete spread fertilizer. "'Cleft for me' . . . You spread that even, Pete, you hear me? Bone lazy!" He escaped as soon as he could and went to see Petra.

She was awake, lying on a blanket, kicking her fat little legs. Caity was on duty in the babies' corner behind its wall of buckets. At the sight of her, Pete again thought of sex, but Caity didn't seem interested, and after a moment he realized that he wasn't, either. Not with Caity.

She said, "Did you hear about Xiaobo?"

"What about him?

"He's dying."

It took Pete a moment to take it in, even though the news wasn't unexpected. "Where?"

"His room."

McAllister would be there. Pete walked back through the children's room. At the sight of him, Kara started screaming. How long was *that* going to keep on? Kara would just have to get over it. The older children, three to five years old, were clustered around Jenna in a learning circle, being taught to count buckets and read letters and sing songs. When they were older, McAllister and Eduardo would teach them about stars and atoms and the digestive system. *"We must save everything we can."*

McAllister wasn't with Xiaobo, but Eduardo and Paolo were.

Eduardo was the oldest of the Survivors, and looked it. Only a few years older than McAllister, he seemed to Pete to be older than time. Thinning gray hair straggled around a deeply lined face. Eduardo, a quiet and courteous man, had never lost his soft Spanish accent, and when Pete had been little, he'd loved to have Eduardo tell him stories. He was Paolo's father, and the two looked alike, although even now Eduardo was stronger than the sickly Paolo. The two sat one on each side of Xiaobo, who lay on a pile of blankets in the bare little room. Paolo held Xiaobo's hand. Next to these three, Pete actually felt strong and whole.

He knelt at the foot of the nest of blankets. "Xiaobo."

The dying man opened his eyes. When Pete had been very small, Xiaobo's eyes had fascinated him: small, slanted, hooded by a fold of skin. At the same time, Xiaobo had scared him because he spoke so weird. English had come slowly to him, and now that Pete was grown himself he realized how lonely Xiaobo must have been in the Shell, the only Survivor of his people, the only one who could not talk to anyone else.

"Xiaobo, are you hurting?"

"No."

"Can I get you anything?"

"Nothing. I go now, Pete."

"You don't know that you—"

"It is time. I go." He closed his eyes again, and smiled.

I will never go that quietly. The thought built itself in his mind, solid as the Shell itself. *I will not.*

He didn't know what else to say, but then there wasn't time to say anything else. Tommy, at seven the oldest of the children and the only one yet permitted to leave the children's room alone, raced into Xiaobo's room. "The Grab is bright!"

Pete leapt up. "Where's McAllister?"

"I don't know!" The boy throbbed with excitement. Unlike Kara, Tommy was one who'd adapted easily to his new life.

"It's Ravi's turn to go on the Grab," Pete said. "Where's Ravi?"

"I don't know that either! Anyway Terrell was supposed to go because McAllister said he's twelve now but Terrell got sick again and threw up and Darlene came over from the farm and told him to go lie down in his room like a useless stone."

Darlene wasn't supposed to tell Grab watchers anything. Pete, Paolo, and Eduardo looked at each other. How much longer would the platform stay bright? Paolo said, "You just went, Pete. Caity can go."

"She's on baby duty," Pete said. And he was off running down the corridor, cursing Ravi for being—where? Doing what? It was Ravi's turn, not Terrell's! And why had McAllister changed the duty roster?

Tommy raced at his heels. "Can I go, Pete? Can I, huh? Can I go, too?"

"No!"

The boy stopped cold and shouted after him, "You're selfish! You're a selfish piggy who doesn't care about the good of all! I'm telling! I am!"

Pete reached the Grab machinery and climbed onto the platform.

DECEMBER 2013

Julie sat on her new sleep sofa in her living room, which had grown smaller with the addition of her desk, smaller still with the broad sofa, and yet again smaller with the Christmas tree crowded into a corner. The scent of Douglas fir drifted through the room. She was wrapping presents in bright metallic paper. Jake was flying in from Wyoming for Christmas and although they weren't particularly close, each was the only family the other had since their parents had died in a plane crash three years ago, and it was Christmas. For Christmas you gathered family, even if half your heritage was Jewish. Jake, who would sleep on the extended sofa with his feet against the tree, was about to discover that he had one more family member than he thought.

She hadn't told him before about her pregnancy because he was going to disapprove. Not of her getting pregnant, although he would undoubtedly consider that careless, but of her having and keeping the baby. Jake, deeply ambitious, had risen rapidly through the ranks of the U.S. Geological Survey. He was proud of both her career and his own, and he would frown at the year-long sabbatical she was taking to even have the baby, due May 1, let alone the professional sacrifices that she knew perfectly well would follow. Julie did not intend to have her child raised by a succession of nannies, even if she had had room for a nanny. She would make the transition from brilliant professor to brilliant consultant and work at home, perhaps teaching one course per semester as a sideline. Already she had feelers out for potential projects with various industries and government agencies.

She taped wrapping paper around a Bunny Mine, the current hot toy for toddlers. Her daughter, now a four-and-a-half-month fetus, wouldn't be playing with a Bunny Mine for at least a year, but it would look cute on the shelves that Julie had put up in the nursery. The nursery was finished. The layette was complete. The childbirth classes began in January. It was all planned out, everything under control.

Julie had just begun to wrap a sweater for Jake when her cell rang. "Hello, Julie Kahn speaking."

"This is Gordon."

Her lips pursed. She hadn't heard from him in nearly a month, since she'd given him her best stab at the revised data on the kidnappings. Since then she'd watched the Massachusetts, Connecticut, Rhode Island, and Maine newspapers; no child had been reported as missing. Plenty of burglaries, of course—theft always picked up as Christmas approached—but without Gordon's input, Julie had no way of knowing which ones fit the M.O. that the task force had been pursuing.

"Hello, Gordon," she said neutrally, hoping this call wasn't personal.

It wasn't. He said, "I wanted you to know that the A-Dic pulled the plug on the task force. Each kidnapping has been assigned to a local Special Agent in Charge. The A-Dic just doesn't believe a connective enterprise exists."

"The mathematical pattern exists."

"Maybe. No more kidnappings since Kara and Jennifer Carter. No store burglaries with that M.O., either."

"Before this there have been long stretches between incidents."

He made a noise she recognized: the verbal equivalent of a shrug. Gordon was moving on. He was not a man to hold on to what he could not control.

She said, "The pattern exists, Gordon."

Instead of agreeing or arguing, he said, "How are you?"

"Still pregnant, if that's what you're asking."

"Can I come see you?"

"No. You're married, Gordon."

"There were two of us in those motel rooms, Julie."

"I'm not accusing you of anything. I take complete responsibility for my actions, and for this result. It doesn't involve you."

"Damn it, I'm the father!"

She drew a deep breath. "Only biologically. I don't mean that to be nasty, Gordon. You have no room for us in your life, and anyway I don't want that. I don't think you do, either, not really. Please just leave me be."

"If you need money—"

"I don't. Bye, Gordon. I'm sorry about the task force, because I still think there's something there."

"But Julie—"

Gently she pressed the disconnect button on her cell.

Within her body, the baby moved, and she put her hand on her belly and watched the lights twinkle on and off on the little Christmas tree above the festive packages.

2035

It wasn't dark, and it wasn't light. It wasn't anything. *I'm dead*, Pete thought, as usual, but of course he wasn't, as usual.

When the nothing receded, disappointment warred with relief. There would be no little girls here. But there would be no fighting or dying, either. He stood in dim light inside a store filled with objects he couldn't even identify until he saw a big doll, life-size, with no head or arms or legs, wearing some of the objects. Oh—it was *clothing*! Skimpy filmy pants, strips of fancy cloth across the breasts, racks and racks of this stuff . . . All at once he pictured Caity wearing it, and then McAllister, and his cock rose and he groaned. He couldn't bring back stuff like this!

He glanced at his wrist to see how much time he had left, but of course he wasn't wearing the wrister. Terrell still had it. Now what?

He ran past the headless dolls wearing fancy skimpy things and discovered that around the corner were other parts of the store, that in fact it was as big as the children's room, maybe even bigger than the farm. The other areas held different stuff, as well as shopping carts. He grabbed one and started throwing things into it from under a sign labeled HOMEWARES. Blankets, towels, rugs—damn this was good!—and then pots and a big red tray and boxes of spoons and—

A dog came racing down a set of metal stairs, snarling and barking.

Pete screamed and climbed on top of the shopping cart, nearly slipping on the red tray and falling back off. The dog leaped and its teeth closed on Pete's leg, although only for a moment before the animal's weight sent it crashing back to the floor. Pete screamed, grabbed the tray, and held it in front of him. With his other hand he yanked a pot free of the stuff in the shopping cart and threw it at the dog, missing it. How much time was left—*how much?* Blood streamed down his leg.

The dog leapt again, but it couldn't reach Pete on top of the cart. However, the impact of its body sent the cart skittering across the floor. Alarms sounded and lights came on. The dog barked and Pete shrieked at it.

The cart rolled past a display of DIGITAL FOTO FRAMES, heavy-looking metal squares. Pete grabbed one. Before he could throw it at the dog, the Grab took him back.

On the platform, the rolling shopping cart kept rolling. It crashed over the edge and tipped on its side. Pete fell heavily amid pots, rugs, blankets. For a moment his head rang, but nothing on him broke and he staggered up out of the debris, clutching the DIGITAL FOTO FRAME and more furious than he'd ever been in his life.

He roared at Tommy, "Where the fuck is Ravi?"

The child was not a weeper. He stared back, scared but not budging, and said, "Where did you go?"

Others rushed into the Grab room: Darlene, Paolo, Eduardo. From down the corridor Caity and Jenna, who could not leave the children, screamed, "What is it? What is it?" But no Ravi, and no McAllister.

Pete pushed past everyone and ran down the corridor to the unused far end. Behind him Darlene cackled, "Oh, lovely, an electric fryer! Just what we need!"

Paolo, unable to keep up, called, "Wait, Pete! Wait!"

Tommy, easily able to keep up, ran beside him saying, "What is it? What, Pete? What?"

He found them in the maze of rooms near the tip of the Shell. A blanket had been spread on the floor. McAllister had just slid her loose dress back onto her body, but Ravi was still naked, lying on the blanket, too drained and heavy to move. Pete recognized Ravi's sated heaviness; he'd felt it after sex with Caity. But never with McAllister: never, never, never.

She said, "Pete—"

"You fucking bastards."

Tommy gaped. "What is it? What?"

In rage and hurt and frustration, and before he knew he was going to do it, Pete threw the DIGITAL FOTO FRAME at McAllister. It grazed her on the side of the head and she cried out. Ravi leapt up and threw a punch at Pete. Pete dodged, Ravi missed, and Pete kicked him in the balls.

"Stop! That's enough!" McAllister shouted. But it wasn't her words, or even that she shouted—McAllister, who never raised her voice! It was the blood on her head, streaming down one cheek. *He had hurt McAllister.* He collapsed to the ground in tears.

Ravi was up and charging, but McAllister stopped him with a word. She bent over Pete. Now Paolo and Eduardo and Darlene were all there; Pete could see their bare feet from where he huddled on the floor. McAllister sent them all away with sharp commands, even Ravi, who snatched up his clothes as he left.

"Pete," she said, her voice soft again, "listen to me. Ravi—"

"You never would with me! You said it would cause trouble! You said for the good of all—"

"I know what I said. But listen to me, dear heart. Please listen, I know you're strong enough to listen. This *is* for the good of all. Ravi is fertile."

He stopped ranting, too desolate even for rage.

"You know I checked you boys' sperm with the little microscope Jenna got on her Wal-Mart Grab. Ravi is the only one of you who is fertile. He's had sex with both Caity and Jenna, and neither got pregnant, and now Jenna is too fragile. This is the only chance left among ourselves."

"We have the Grab kids!"

"Yes, of course. But we need every soul we can get, you know that. The Tesslies could end the Grabs at any time. And we miss some of them."

"Well, Ravi just missed his. And so did Terrell because he was throwing up—did you know that? So I just did the Grab and nearly got killed!" He tried to wrench free of her, but McAllister held on and the truth was that he didn't want to get free.

He wanted what Ravi had had.

He put a hand on her breast. When she removed it, he forced her down onto the blanket.

"No, Pete," she said, calm as ever, "I know you wouldn't do that. That's not you. Dear heart, please try to understand. You have a deep, sweet nature and I know you *can* understand. For the good of all."

He let her up, gazing bleakly at the blood on her face. "I hurt you."

"And I hurt you. I'm deeply sorry for that, but we need to survive."

He said fiercely, "Did you like it?"

She touched his eyelids, one after the other, a delicate finger-kiss.

"Because Ravi liked it! I know!"

"I love you, Pete. I love you all."

He got to his feet and seized the DIGITAL FOTO FRAME. Something had to be his, something had to be outside of the "good of all," something had to be . . . He didn't know what his confused thoughts meant. But he said defiantly, stupidly, "I'm keeping this!"

"All right," McAllister said.

"It's mine! Just mine!" Nothing ever belonged to one person, nothing.

"All right," she repeated.

He clutched it, scowling at her, hating her, loving her. The silence stretched on. She waited, but he didn't know for what. For him to say something, for him to look away.

He looked away, down at the object in his hand, and said, "What is it?"

MARCH 2014

Under the Canadian glacier, molten rock bubbled up from a fissure in the earth. When the pressure became great enough, the ground erupted. Lava met ice, which instantly boiled into steam. The magma hitting the steam exploded into miniscule fragments, sending pillar after pillar of ash billowing overhead. The magma was heavy on silica from the chamber it had breached earlier, which made it much more viscous and sticky than usual. That prevented air bubbles from escaping quickly and so pressure built relentlessly, leading to more and more explosions.

Ash blew southeast on a cold wind, toward Ontario and Québec.

MARCH 2014

Julie sat in the Starbucks on K Street. Linda had just left, full of plans for her family, Julie, and the baby to take a cottage together in August on Maryland's Eastern Shore. "The baby'll be nearly four months by then, and it'll be such fun!" Julie wasn't sure about that—two weeks with Linda's noisy kinds and noisier dogs? On the other hand, two weeks with Linda and Ted *would* be fun. Or two weeks in separate, side-by-side cottages. Or two weeks someplace else.

She frowned at the out-of-town newspaper she'd bought at World Wide News. The headlines were all about air traffic hopelessly snarled in Canada by blowing and drifting ash, but that was not what she stared at. *Was it or wasn't it?* Then, wryly: *I sound like a Clairol commercial.* And not even a current commercial. She was showing her age.

Again she read the short, not-very-informative article about the burglary in a small town in western Massachusetts, which was one of the projected paths of her original algorithm. A family-owned department store, one of the few left in the country, had been robbed of a collection of miscellaneous objects, primarily blankets, rugs, and cookware. Also a shopping cart, which was considered "an unusual theft for this kind of burglary." Julie wasn't sure what "kind of burglary" the small-town news stringer meant, but she knew what she was looking at. Shopping cart, no forced entry. This time, however, the store had had a guard dog, which had not been harmed. Drops of blood on the floor indicated that the "perpetrator" might have been harmed, but the police had as yet made no arrests.

Whose blood?

"May I sit here? There don't seem to be any free tables."

He was tall, attractive, dressed in a suit and tie. He carried the *Wall Street Journal*, folded to show the headline: FINANCIAL IMPACT OF COMING FRESH WATER SHORTAGES. Glancing at her ringless left hand, he smiled and sat down without waiting for an invitation. Julie stood, and as soon as the curve of her belly under her open coat came into view, his smile vanished.

Julie grinned. "Sure, the table's all yours."

Relief on that handsome face.

She buttoned her coat and waddled out. The OB had said she was gaining too much weight, once she'd stopped throwing up, but that otherwise everything was "progressing swimmingly," a phrase she had liked instantly. Little Alicia, swimming in her secret sea. The baby now had fully developed toenails. Her body could store calcium and phosphorus. She had begun to show the brain waves of REM sleep. What will you dream of, my darling?

Julie left Starbucks. Walking was supposed to be good for her, so she walked even though she had piles of work at home. Consulting work for a high-resolution space imagery firm, for a professor doing research on microbes, even for the Bureau, in a division different from Gordon's. Everybody, it seemed, needed well-recommended and high-priced mathematical insight. Things were working out well.

The air was crisp and cold, unusually cold for March. Julie walked briskly. Some kids who probably should have been in school ran frantically in the pocket park across the street, trying to get a kite aloft. Daffodils and tulips splotched the park with color.

Whose blood had been on the floor of that department store in western Massachusetts?

2035

The DIGITAL FOTO FRAME held pictures that moved out of the frame so the next one could come in. Pete had never imagined anything like it. It was even better than the drawings in *The Illustrated Book of Fairy Tales* or *Good Night, Moon* because these pictures looked far more real. There were three, and Pete never tired of looking at them. He wouldn't let any others of the Six look at them, and for once McAllister did not insist that he share.

One of the pictures was of two children playing with a dog. This didn't look anything like the dog that had attacked Pete in the store. This dog was reddish and happy-looking, but Pete didn't like it anyway and sometimes he closed his eyes when that picture appeared. The other two were glorious. One was a beach like the place where he'd Grabbed Petra and Kara, but with mountains across the water, colored gold by a setting sun. The other showed a forest filled with trees and flowers. Pete had never seen mountains or sunset, but on Grabs he'd seen sunrise, several trees, and some flowers, and now it was wonderful to sit and gaze at them without the fear and tension of a Grab.

"Why aren't there more pictures?" he asked Eduardo. He was avoiding McAllister. It was a complaint, not a real question, but Eduardo had a real answer.

"There could be more if we had them to upload," he said in his soft accent. "These are just demonstration photos. You understand that the battery will run out eventually?"

"Of course," Pete said scornfully. Some of the children's toys from Jenna's famous Grab had used batteries, which all died.

"The more you use it, the less long it will last."

"I know." But he couldn't stop gazing at the DIGITAL FOTO FRAME.

He held it, clutched in one hand, during Xiaobo's funeral. The funeral room, located off the central corridor across from the Grab room, was yet another featureless white-metal room. There was absolutely nothing in it except the outline of the slot on the far wall, close to the floor, and the button set high on the opposite wall, by the door. Caity, Eduardo, Terrell, McAllister, Darlene, Ravi, and Pete attended the funeral. Also Tommy, now that he was nearly eight. Jenna and Paolo stayed with the Grab children.

It was Tommy's first funeral and he held tight to McAllister's hand, although to Pete he looked more interested than scared. Tommy was tough. Well, good. He'd have an easier time of it than some of the children did. Kara still screamed every time she saw Pete.

Ravi, another tough one, stared down at Xiaobo's body, wrapped in their oldest blanket. On top of the body, as was the custom, lay one small thing that the dead person had cherished. For Xiaobo, it was a little stone statue of a fat smiling man that Xiaobo had had with him all the way back when the Tesslies put him in the Shell. Bridget had gone with a lock of hair from a baby of hers that had been stillborn.

Ravi's face remained blank. Caity and Terrell leaned against the wall, tearful. Darlene, Eduardo, and McAllister, the last of the Survivors, had so many feelings on their faces that Pete could barely look at them.

His own feelings troubled him, because there didn't seem to be enough of them. He'd known Xiaobo his whole life, had worked beside him, eaten with him, probably been diapered by him when Pete was a baby. They hadn't talked much, given Xiaobo's limited English, but he'd always been kind to Pete, to everyone. Right up until this last illness, Xiaobo had been a hard worker. And all Pete felt was that he should feel more, along with a vague curiosity about what it felt like to be dead. Darlene said that the ghosts of billions murdered by the Tesslies haunted the Shell. But Pete had never seen a ghost at all, and anyway where in the Shell could you fit billions of them? He wasn't exactly sure how much a "billion" was, but it sounded large.

Eduardo said in his musical voice, "As for man, his days are like grass. As a flower of the field, so he flourishes. For the wind passes over it, and it is gone, and its place remembers it no more." That was what he always said at funerals, and Pete always hated it. It sounded sad, and anyway it was stupid. Xiaobo wasn't grass—people were made of skin and bones and blood. There was no wind inside the Shell. And this place certainly would remember Xiaobo. Pete would, and so would the other Six and Darlene and Eduardo and, of course, McAllister.

Her words made more sense. "To the Earth we commit the body of our friend and family, Lung Xiaobo. His bones and tissues and heart will enrich the land and help to make it one to which humanity will, someday, return. Go with our gratitude, Xiaobo, and our love."

Darlene began to sing, another of her awful scratchy songs with words Pete didn't understand. There were so many things he didn't understand, starting with how McAllister could bear to have sex with Ravi. He hated him, he hated her, he hated everything. He clutched his DIGITAL FOTO FRAME tighter.

Darlene howled, "Abide with me, 'tis eventide. . . ."

When the song was finished, McAllister pressed the funeral button. A section of the wall opened, a slot near the floor three feet wide and two high. Xiaobo didn't need that much room. Some unseen force pulled him into the wall. Tommy squatted to peer inside, just as Pete had done when he was little. Now, after being present at three funerals for Survivors and six for miscarriages, Pete knew there was nothing to see. The slot opened into a small bare featureless space, and the other side wouldn't open to deposit Xiaobo's body Outside until the first wall closed up.

Darlene bawled another song, this one about the land being beautiful with spacious skies and a lot of grain, but Pete wasn't listening. He watched Ravi, who had turned his gaze to McAllister. Ravi looked the way he used to when there was a treat Grabbed from a store—oh, those Reese's Peanut Butter Cups!—and Ravi had tried to figure a way to get a bite of another child's share. Pete's hand tightened on the DIGITAL FOTO FRAME. He wanted to throw it at Ravi, to get his hands around Ravi's neck and squeeze. . . . No, he didn't. Ravi was his half-brother. Yes, he did—Ravi had sex with McAllister, he was going to have more sex with McAllister, Pete wanted to kill him—

Ravi caught Pete's look and glared back.

The funeral was over. People moved away, returning to their duties. Caity stomped off, covering whatever softer feelings she had with vague bad temper. Pete lingered, and Tommy stayed with him. When they were the only two left in the funeral room, Tommy demanded, "How does McAllister know that the fucking bastard Tesslies will really put Xiaobo's body outside to help grass to come back?"

Tommy must have been listening to Darlene. "McAllister knows."

"But how?"

Pete looked down at the intense little face. "Well, you didn't see any other bodies in there, did you? We've had a lot of funerals—you know that from learning circles. If the bodies weren't dumped out, they would just pile up in there."

Tommy considered. "Maybe the Tesslies just put them in a fertilizer machine. Like shit. And then we spread them on the farm."

Pete had never thought of this. He could see that Tommy wished he hadn't thought of it, either. He knelt beside Tommy and said firmly, "No, that doesn't happen. The Tesslies told McAllister."

"I thought she never talked to them."

"Well, then they got her to understand some other way, like they got her to understand to press the funeral button, and how the fertilizer machine works and the Grab machinery and everything else." Actually, Pete wasn't sure how any of that had happened. Maybe the Survivors just figured everything out by themselves.

"All right," Tommy said. "But why do we believe the Tesslies?"

A good question. But not one that Pete wanted troubling Tommy. "We believe McAllister. You know how smart she is, right?"

"Yeah."

"Then there you have it, laddie." One of Bridget's favorite expressions.

"Okay." And then, "But I have another question."

"Go ahead."

"Why are you and Ravi mad at each other?"

Pete stood. This he was not going to discuss with Tommy.

"It's because Ravi had sex with McAllister, right? But you have sex with Caity. And when he wasn't sick, Terrell tried to have sex with Jenna, only she said he was still too young. And—"

Was there anything the kid didn't know? Pete said, "I want privacy on this." Those were words they all learned young, and learned to respect. *A necessity in such a small, closed family*, McAllister often said.

Tommy said, "Can I see the DIGITAL FOTO FRAME? Please, Pete, please please please?"

"All right." He turned it on, let the pictures move through the frame once each. Tommy watched, rapt. He reached out one finger to touch the mountain range. When Pete turned off the DIGITAL FOTO FRAME, Tommy sighed the same way he did right after Jenna finished reading aloud a fairy tale.

"Now go back to the children's room," Pete said.

Tommy said importantly, "I have *farm duty*."

"Oh. Then go do that."

Tommy left the funeral room, said "Oh, hi," to someone in the corridor, and ran off. Pete tensed. If that was Ravi out there, waiting for him . . .

It was McAllister. "Pete, I want to talk with you."

"I want privacy on this," Pete said, with as much coldness as he could.

She smiled. "You don't even know what 'this' is yet, so how can you want privacy on it?"

He gazed sullenly at the wall behind her.

"What I wanted to say was thank you for being so good with Tommy. He's more unsure inside than he shows. Jenna says sometimes in bed he still cries for his mother. But he adores you and looks up to you, and you're such a good influence on him."

Pete glared at her. "I know what you're doing. You're trying to make me feel good so I won't fight Ravi. Well, he's the one who wants to fight me. Didn't you see him smirk at me during the funeral?"

"I saw you smirking and glaring at each other. That has to stop. Pete, there is a statement from Before, said by a very smart and wise man, that the biggest threat to any society is its own young males between the ages of fourteen and twenty-four. Do you understand what that means?"

"No."

"It means—"

"I want privacy on this," Pete said and walked away. Whether or not the words fit—who the fuck cared, anyway?

APRIL 2014

In the complex network of faults in the Pacific Seismic Network, a thrust fault two hundred miles off the shore of Japan abruptly moved, as had happened before. The seabed deformed, vertically displacing an enormous volume of water. A huge wave rose on the ocean, long and low enough that an oil tanker barely noticed when it passed beneath its hull. As the wave raced toward shore, the shallower water both slowed and raised it. By the time the tsunami broke on Tokyo, the highest wave crested at ninety-four feet of water, smashing and inundating the city as well as the country far inland.

This had been predicted for a long time as a possibility for Tokyo. Only a few years earlier, it had happened north of that ancient city, with devastating results. Not the prediction, not the unfairness of being struck twice within a few years, not Japan's excellent tsunami-warning system—none of it lessened the horrific destruction.

2035

Pete sat cross-legged in his secret room by the Shell wall, gazing out. The room wasn't all that secret anymore; McAllister knew where it was, and Tommy had followed him here. Since Xiaobo's funeral, Pete had had unhappy sex with Caity here. Twice. The second time she'd bitten his ear; she was always rougher than he was. He wasn't going to do it with her anymore. He'd just masturbate.

The DIGITAL FOTO FRAME was in his hand, but Pete wasn't looking at it. He was looking at a miracle.

Crouched against the clear impenetrable wall, head wobbling as he craned his neck as far left as it would go, Pete saw a flash of green. *A piece of grass.* Several blades of grass, or something like grass, pushed out of the ground. "Volcanic rock," McAllister had once called it: "I think we're on the collapsed lip of a caldera." Pete didn't know what that meant, but he knew what the grasses meant.

The Earth was coming back. And he was the first to see it.

He didn't want to tell anyone. Or rather he did, he wanted to speak the incredible words out loud, but he also didn't want anyone else to know the secret. Maybe Darlene was right: he was "a wild one." But that's what he wanted. He crept from the room, through the maze of tiny rooms at this end of the Shell, and along the corridor to the children's room.

It was so early that the kids lay asleep on blankets, some in diapers and some in little clothes that happened to fit at the moment. Karim, who didn't like clothes, slept naked, clutching a stuffed toy. The non-walking babies lay behind their bucket wall, with Jenna on duty. She was asleep, too. Pete knelt beside Petra and scooped her up with his good arm.

Petra didn't wake. Pete started around the bucket wall, then turned back. He didn't want to worry Jenna if she woke and found Petra gone. So he laid the DIGITAL FOTO FRAME on Petra's nest of blankets.

In the larger area, Tommy woke. Instantly he was on his feet, rubbing his eyes with his knuckles. His hair stood up in all directions. "Where are you going? Can I come, too?"

"Ssshhhh! No. You stay here."

The boy's face, still puffy with sleep, went sad. Pete whispered, "You stay here now, Tommy, and later I'll take you on a big adventure."

"Really? What?"

Pete had no idea. But he couldn't think of anything else to deter Tommy. So he just shook his head and repeated, "You'll see. Stay here."

Tommy stayed. Pete carried Petra, who grew heavier with each step, to the secret room. She woke when he put her on the floor by the window.

"See, Petra—see the grass? The Earth is coming back!"

The baby screwed up her face and whimpered.

Ridiculously disappointed, Pete gazed alone at the grasses, jiggling Petra to quiet her. This didn't work. She whimpered louder, wailed a few times, and worked herself up to full, hungry screaming. Why were babies so much trouble? There should be a better way to restart humanity!

Since there wasn't, Pete crossly scooped up Petra to return her to Jenna, who would probably want him to stay to help with the children. At least he could get his DIGITAL FOTO FRAME back. He could trust Jenna not to touch it, but maybe not Tommy.

He had just left the maze, carrying the wailing Petra, when Tommy ran toward him. "Pete, you gotta come—McAllister's sick!"

His blood froze. McAllister. One by one the Survivors had sickened and died—"badly weakened immune systems, slow-growing cancers, and a fresh influx of micro-organisms with each Grab," McAllister had said, but only Paolo and Jenna understood the words. If it was now McAllister's turn . . . They could not do without McAllister.

"She's in the farm," Tommy said. He added, "You didn't say I couldn't go there, only that I couldn't follow you!"

Pete didn't care where Tommy went. He put Petra down in the middle of the corridor and ran.

She was beside the fertilizer machine, puking into a bucket. There shouldn't have been a bucket there, unless one was being rinsed out in the disinfectant stream. McAllister must have brought a shit bucket with her and rinsed it out, but why? Today Caity was on shit-bucket duty. McAllister straightened and raised the hem of her loose homemade dress to wipe her mouth. She saw Tommy and Pete staring at her.

Tommy blurted, "Are you going to die? Like Bridget and Xiaobo?"

"No," McAllister said. She closed her eyes briefly.

"Then why are you—"

"Tommy, go to the children's room. Now."

All the children obeyed McAllister, without bribes or arguments. Tommy went, although he muttered and scowled. Pete said nothing. But when she'd raised her dress he had seen, and she knew it. As the oldest of the Six he'd seen enough bellies curved like that: Bridget's, Sarah's, Jessica's, Hannah's. But not for a long, long time.

"Pete—"

"You're pregnant."

"Yes."

"From sex with Ravi."

McAllister didn't answer; no need.

Pete said the first ugly thing that popped up from his foul-tasting hatred. "It'll die. Like all the other babies."

Something painful passed behind McAllister's eyes, but she said only, "Maybe not. You Six survived, including my Jenna. Pete, you are going to have to come to grips with this. It's reality, and not only that, it's a joyful reality for the good of all. Every additional soul expands our gene pool, gives us one more chance to restart humanity. You know that, and you're no longer a child. You must accept this. If you can, be happy for all of us as a group."

"I can't."

"I think you can. I've observed you your whole life, you know, and I've always found you strong enough to accept this life we have to live. Strong enough to make positive contributions to it. As you must now."

"But I love you!"

"And I love you. Just as I love all of you. And I'm doing the best I can to ensure a future for all of—" She turned and threw up again into the bucket.

Pete left her there. He thought of waking Jenna to help her, but Jenna was with the babies and anyway McAllister never needed help. She was that stone in Darlene's otherwise baffling song, "Rock of Ages." It was Pete who needed help, but nobody was going to give him any, that was for sure.

He thought of volunteering for the next Grab, which was supposed to be Terrell's if he wasn't sick again, and deliberately getting himself killed. Then they'd be sorry! He thought of hitting Ravi over the head with the DIGITAL FOTO FRAME until Ravi was dead and then sending his body outside through the funeral slot before anyone even knew he was missing. They'd never suspect Pete. He thought of taking water and a shit bucket and going to live in his secret room, refusing to talk to anybody, just sneaking out at night to the farm to eat raw soy.

"Pete!" Caity yelled at him. "You left Petra on the floor in the middle of the corridor! What were you *doing?*"

She held Petra, whose screaming had woken everyone. Kids cried or peered through the archway of the children's room. Terrell looked out from the Grab room, on duty to watch for brightening. Darlene bustled from her room, her bitter mouth turned down, her eyes still puffy from sleep. "You know them babies don't leave the children's room, Pete! What the hell were you doing?"

Tommy darted through the archway and wordlessly held out the DIGITAL FOTO FRAME. "Keep it," Pete snarled. Why not? Everything was shit, anyway.

Tommy looked incredulous with joy. Caity stared. Petra yelled. Darlene scolded. Pete's heart hurt so bad he thought it would burst right there in his chest, like some rotten protein-rich soy nut too spoiled to eat.

From down the hall Terrell cried, "The Grab is brightening! I'm going, everybody!"

APRIL 2014

Julie grunted and screamed on her living room floor. She lay in a pool of her waters. Her insides were trying to burst free of her body. The pain was incredible.

Jake, kneeling helplessly beside her, said, "I still think we should go to the hospital."

Between contractions, she glared at him; almost she spat at him. The hospital! She couldn't move, couldn't do anything but push. She gasped, "I'm shitting a pumpkin here!"

"But at the hospital—"

She screamed again and he shut up.

It wasn't supposed to happen like this. Last night Jake had flown in from Wyoming, arriving a full week before she was supposed to go into labor. He would drive her to the hospital and then wait decorously in the waiting room. Linda would coach Julie in the labor room. The first baby, her OB had assured her, always took a long time to come; Julie might even have false labor pains, similar to Braxton-Hicks contractions but "a little bit more intense," for several days. The baby nurse would come every day for two weeks after Julie came home from the hospital. It was all meticulously planned.

Then came these sudden, wrenching pains that woke her in the middle of the night, apparently already many more centimeters dilated than she should be because now the pumpkin was moving inexorably through her body, trying to kill her. Julie writhed and screamed, Jacob's terrified face looming over her. She would die, the baby would die, nobody could do this, *nobody*—

A final scream that brought neighbors pounding on the wall and a terrified oath from Jake. Linda, in a coat thrown over leopard-print pajamas, threw open the door and burst into the room. The pumpkin slid out and stopped torturing her, although everything on her still hurt and apparently always would. Julie burst into tears. The neighbor pounded harder. Jake cried, "What do I do now?" And the answering machine burst into life.

If the phone had been ringing, she hadn't heard it. But now she heard Gordon's voice, almost as if the relative cessation of pain had somehow created a pool of silence.

"Julie, this is Gordon. We've had another kidnapping. Three-year-old boy disappeared from his bed in southern Vermont. I remember that was on one of the projections you—"

Julie wasn't listening. Her baby had started to cry, and the sound filled the entire world, joyous and alive, leaving no room for anything else at all.

2035

Pete tried. McAllister had asked him to, so he did. He tried to be happy about her pregnancy. He tried to remember the good of all. He tried to be happy that Terrell's first Grab had brought back another child, even though it was a boy and not a girl. He tried to be pleasant to Caity while not having any more sex with her. He succeeded in none of these things, and both efforts and failure turned him very quiet.

"I like you better like this," Caity said after sex. "You don't talk."

Pete said nothing, turning his face away from her. They lay not in his secret room but in her bedroom at the other end of the Shell. Caity had taped to the wall another picture, this one torn from the box that had contained a toy. The actual toy, a doll, had been broken by some rambunctious child but the picture remained perfect: long body, tiny waist, big breasts, feet made in a permanent tip-toe. It looked nothing like any real woman Pete had ever seen, neither in the Shell nor on a Grab. Why had the Before people made dolls like that?

Terrell was disappointed that he hadn't Grabbed a girl. But McAllister said they should all be grateful that Terrell's first Grab had been so easy. Terrell had been able to get into the house, pick up the kid, and get out without waking anyone. McAllister named the boy "Keith," since he wouldn't, or couldn't, say his own name. "Never mind," Caity said. "Maybe McAllister's baby will be a girl."

"She's too old to be having a baby at all," Darlene said. "Pure foolishness. Probably we'll lose them both."

Pete stalked away, fists clenched at his side.

Caity had insisted she could handle another Grab—look how easy Terrell's was! She went and it did turn out to be easy, a store Grab in a "supermarket." Caity brought back a huge shopping cart of food and they had interesting feasts until it was gone, although the haul had not included any Reese's Peanut Butter Cups. The oversize shopping cart remained and was useful for hauling shit buckets. The next Grab would be Ravi's.

Pete spent a lot of time with Petra and Tommy, Petra because he wanted to, Tommy because he'd attached himself to Pete, pestering him about the promised "big adventure." Pete was harvesting soy in the farm, picking off the thick ripe leaves and hard nuts, when Tommy started in again. Two half-full buckets sat on the floor beside the dirt beds. The farm smelled of rich dirt, growing crops, and the disinfectant waterfall by the fertilizer machine.

Tommy said, "When are we going on the adventure?"

"I don't know."

"What will it be?"

"You have to wait and see."

"I don't want to fucking wait."

"Don't let McAllister hear you using that language of Darlene's."

Tommy looked around fearfully as if McAllister might suddenly appear, then changed direction. "Why are those new grasses growing outside the Shell?"

This was no longer Pete's secret, just like nothing else was his, not even the DIGITAL FOTO FRAME. He said, "You know that, Tommy. You had it in learning circle. The Earth was sick but it's getting better."

"Why did it get sick?"

"The Tesslies did it. They destroyed the whole Earth."

"Why?"

"Because they're bastards."

"Oh. Why don't we kill them dead?"

"Because nobody but the Survivors has ever seen one, and that was a long time ago."

"Are the Tesslies going to come back?"

"I don't know."

Tommy considered this. "They have to come back, Pete, to let us out of the Shell."

"Maybe when it's time the Shell will just melt around us. You know, like the briar hedge in the fairy tale book."

"Really? When?"

"McAllister says when the air is good to breathe again."

"Oh. When will that be?"

"I don't know, Tommy!"

Tommy said judiciously, "I don't think you know much."

Another voice behind Pete said, "You're right. He doesn't."

Ravi. Pete willed himself to not turn around. He was trying for the good of all, he was trying, he was *trying*. But Ravi these days had a cutting edge. McAllister had stopped having sex with him once she got pregnant; Pete knew this from Jenna, who'd been trying to make Pete feel better. At first Ravi swaggered and pretended that he and McAllister still did it. When Pete had smirked at him and rolled his eyes, Ravi had stalked away. After that he'd avoided Pete. Now he had come from the direction of McAllister's room, and Pete heard the dangerous note in his brother's voice, and knew that Ravi was as angry and frustrated as he was. And looking for a way to let that anger out.

Ravi repeated, "Pete doesn't know anything. He only thinks he does."

Tommy said, "Pete knows lots!"

"Really? I say he doesn't. Do you, Pete?"

Pete said nothing. Trying, trying, *trying*! Tommy, wide-eyed, looked back and forth between them.

Ravi pushed harder. "Pete doesn't know, for instance, how McAllister's breasts feel, do you, Pete?"

He knew he shouldn't. He knew a fight was what Ravi wanted, and that in giving it to him, Pete was losing. He even knew, somewhere in the back of his love-sick brain, what McAllister had said: *The biggest threat to any society is its own young males between the ages of fourteen and twenty-four.* None of it stopped him. In one fluid motion he grabbed the bucket of soy nuts and swung it at Ravi's head.

The bigger boy was unprepared. The edge of the bucket caught him in the mouth. Ravi cried out and went down, blood and teeth spurting onto the farm floor. Tommy screamed. Then Darlene was there, running from the other end of the farm, shrieking something about Cain and Abel.

Pete stared, horrified, at the writhing Ravi. "Is he dead? Is he dead?" Tommy cried, even though Ravi clearly was not. But he was hurt, badly hurt, all that blood, those *teeth* . . .

Then Pete was running down the corridor. For once Tommy didn't follow him. Pete hurled himself into the funeral room and pressed the button high on the wall; he had to jump to reach it. The slot opened, low on the opposite wall. Pete dropped to his knees and then onto his belly and crawled into it. The wall closed up behind him, and he was in darkness.

JUNE 2014

Julie walked the floor of her living room with Alicia, now six weeks old. Despite being premature, Alicia had weighed a healthy six pounds at birth and just kept on putting on weight, emptying Julie of milk as if she'd had a suction pump in her tiny pink mouth. Then, because she drank so fast, she got a tummy-ache and Julie had to walk her, steadily patting the baby's back, singing songs until Alicia burped, farted, threw up, or fell asleep. Tonight none of these things had yet happened. Julie paced up and down, caught as always in the rich stew of love, exasperation, fatigue, and joy that was motherhood. Behind her, CNN murmured softly. Sometimes the sound of the TV lulled Alicia into sleep. But not tonight.

Love, exasperation, fatigue, joy—but mostly love. Julie had never expected to feel such fierce, passionate, possessive attachment for anyone as she did for this damp, malodorous bundle on her shoulder. She'd always thought of herself as a cool person (in emotional temperature, not in hipness—she'd never been hip in her life). Certainly Gordon, nor any other man, had never ignited in her this intense love. Did he feel this way about his children? Did Linda about hers? Why hadn't anyone warned her?

". . . continues in the clean-up efforts in Tokyo. Officials say it may be months before there is anywhere near a complete list of the dead. With damage reckoned in the billions and—" And there was the video again, shot from a tourist helicopter over Tokyo when the tsunami hit. The tsunami had registered 4.2 on the Soloniev-Imamura Intensity Scale, almost as large as the 2004 one in Indonesia. A wall of water fifty feet high had crashed over Tokyo.

". . . not unexpected in that the Pacific Rim is well known for underwater faults that—"

Julie jiggled at the remote, trapped between Alicia's diaper and Julie's forearm. She got a rerun of *M*A*S*H*, then PBS: "—over 9,000 species going extinct each year, largely because of human activity. The rainforest is particularly susceptible as—" Another fumble at the remote, which fell to the floor. Unthinking, Julie bent to retrieve it. The sudden motion knocked a huge burp out of Alicia. She jerked in Julie's arms, let out a contented sigh, and went to sleep.

Don't think about the children drowned in Tokyo. There was nothing Julie could do about it. But standing there in the dim living room, she clutched her infant tight.

2035

As soon as the funeral slot closed up behind him, Pete wanted to get out again. In the complete darkness he pounded on the wall, all the walls. Nothing happened.

I always knew I would die this way, he thought, and immediately thought how stupid that was; he'd never had any such thought. He'd thought he would die on a Grab for the good of all, or from some sickness, or just old age. Or that he'd fight a Tesslie to both their deaths. But this—why didn't somebody else push the funeral button to let him out? Somebody would! Tommy would get someone tall enough, McAllister or Eduardo or Ravi . . . but Ravi lay bleeding on the farm floor with his teeth knocked out. Still, somebody must come soon. . . .

The air went out of the dark room.

Pete heard it, in a whoosh, and then he couldn't breathe. Pain invaded his chest. So he would die here, he *would*—

Air rushed back in, and light, and Pete was shot forward by a force he couldn't see. It felt like someone had pushed him hard from behind. He landed beside Xiaobo, half-glimpsed through the rotting blanket, and a pile of bones.

Pete screamed and skittered away. Xiaobo was barely recognizable, a stinking mass of rotting flesh crawled over by disgusting white things. If it hadn't been for the little statue of the naked fat-bellied man on top of the mass, Pete wouldn't have known it was a human. But that was Xiaobo. Pete started to cry, then abruptly stopped.

He was Outside, but something was wrong with the air.

He could breathe it; this wasn't like the airless funeral slot. But the air was . . . *dirty*. He didn't know what he meant except that it was somehow not clean and fresh like the air in the Shell, but clogged with stuff he could smell and taste even if he couldn't see it. Still, it was air and he was breathing it and he was Outside.

Outside.

Partly to get away from Xiaobo and the other bones—which were Bridget's? Robert's? His father's?—Pete moved along the sides of the Shell. A plan formed in his dazed mind. He would find the outside of the clear patch of wall at the end of the Shell and he would wait there until Tommy or somebody went there and saw him. Then Pete would gesture to be let back in. McAllister could open the funeral slot and Pete could crawl past Xiaobo— ugh—back inside the Shell.

Unless—

He rounded the far edge of the Shell and forgot his plan.

The Shell sat on a hill of black rock. The black rock, broken with various grasses, sloped gently and unevenly a long way down, but then it gave way to . . . what? "Fields," McAllister had called them about his pictures in the DIGITAL FOTO FRAME. Not fields of amber grain like in Darlene's song, but of low spindly bushes covered with green leaves. So many bushes that Pete felt dizzy. And none of them were soy! Beyond that were stretches of very tall grasses dotted with clumps of pink flowers and beyond those, more water than he had ever imagined still existed. It was blue water like on the beach where he had Grabbed Petra and Kara, water like Before!

He started to run down the hill, across the black rock toward the water. Pebbles and scrub crunched under his bare feet. Then something stopped him. At first he thought it was the hard-to-breathe air slowing him down, but this was more like someone had grabbed his arm from behind without him even feeling it. He turned, and there stood a Tesslie.

McAllister had described the alien over and over to the Six when they were younger: "In case you ever encounter one when I'm gone." At first Pete had thought she meant gone to use a shit bucket, or maybe to sleep, but when he grew older he knew she meant if she died. The Tesslie looked just as she had described: not a being but a hard metal case like a bucket, four feet high and squarish, with no head or mouth or anything. The bucket-case floated a few inches above the ground. Whatever the Tesslies were, they were inside. Or else this was a "robot," a machine like the battery-car from Jenna's Grab, and the Tesslie was controlling it from someplace else. McAllister had said she didn't know which, and now Pete didn't know either.

"Aaaarggghhhh!" Pete cried and tried to leap on it, knock it over, split it open as he had split Ravi's mouth. This thing had killed his world!

He couldn't move. Not even a finger.

The Tesslie said nothing. But all at once Pete found it much harder to breathe. He wasn't breathing, he wasn't doing anything. He woke inside one of the tiny featureless rooms in the far end of the Shell, and it turned out that, in their concern over Ravi's injuries, no one even realized he'd been gone.

JUNE 2014

Julie sat in front of the young professor's desk. She didn't much like him, even though she'd only met him ten minutes ago. Pompous, self-satisfied, and perhaps even a little sleazy, or how else would he have the "top secret" information he claimed to possess? He'd made her sign a non-disclosure agreement, standard for her job, but still. . . . She didn't like him.

He said, "You come with top-level recommendations from people I'm not at liberty to name. You understand why not."

"Of course." He was name-dropping by not dropping any names, and he was out to make his own reputation. Nonetheless, curiosity was rising in her about the nature of the project for which he wanted predictive algorithms. He was a researcher in biology, after all—not usually the stuff of intense secrecy unless you were involved in genetic engineering or pharmaceutical research, which he was not. She'd checked him out. Two published articles so far, both on the geographical distribution of weeds nobody ever heard of, or cared about since the weeds were not edible, threatening, invasive, or endangered. The statistical analyses in both articles struck her as sloppy. But he was old money, Harvard, Skull and Crossbones—all the things that gave one contacts in high places.

His office was the usual thing for academics just starting to climb the university ladder: small, dark, crowded with metal shelves holding messy piles of papers, binders, fodders, books. A scuffed wooden desk and two chairs. Still, he wasn't housed in the building's basement with the teaching assistants, his office had a window, and on the wall hung an expensively framed photo of young men crewing on the Charles River.

Julie shifted on her chair. Beneath her maternity bra and thick sweater, she felt her breasts begin to leak. Alicia was a hungry little milk demon. Julie tried not to be away from her for more than a few hours at a time, for both their sakes.

Dr. Geoffrey Fanshaw pursed his lips theatrically, studied her, and nodded several times, as if making a decision that clearly had been made before. With a flourish suited to a bad Shakespearean actor, he handed her a sheaf of papers, then rose to lock his office door.

Ten minutes later Julie sat in shock, staring at him.

"How did you come by this information?"

"I told you that I can't say." He puffed with importance instead of what he should have felt: fear.

"The data on the simultaneous appearance of the altered *Klebsiella planticola* on three separate continents—you're sure of its authenticity?"

"Absolutely."

"And its accuracy?"

"Yes."

"Have you personally visited any of these sites? The Connecticut one, maybe?"

Annoyance erased his habitual smirk. "No, not yet. New Zealand and Brazil, of course, would be difficult to get to. And—"

"But," she burst out, unable to restrain herself, "what is anybody *doing* about this?"

"I don't know. My concern is publishing on-line with the predictive algorithms in place as soon as the story blows in the press. Which can't be too long now—some smart journalist will get it. As soon as that happens, I want to be poised to publish in a professional journal with some prominence."

Julie heard what Fanshaw wasn't saying: He wanted to be the instant go-to guy for the news shows, talk shows, sound-bite seekers. A professor, personable, well-connected, first to publish a serious analysis—he'd be a natural. He wanted the *60 Minutes* interview and the *Today* show discussion, and to hell with the fact that in three widely separated locations around the planet—three known about now, who was to say there weren't actually more—a deadly bacterial mutation was killing the roots of plants through an alcoholic by-product. Drowning them in booze. A bacterium found on the roots of virtually every plant on Earth except those growing in or near brackish water.

Fanshaw said eagerly, "Can you do the statistical analysis?"

She managed to get out, "Yes."

"By when? I need it, like, yesterday."

"I'll start this afternoon." The statistical part wasn't hard. There must be mathematicians—not to mention biologists!—working frantically on this around the globe. Fanshaw was right—the press would get this very soon. And if—

The fuller implications hit her.

"If this isn't natural—*three* locations for a naturally occurring identical mutation just doesn't seem likely. Even an accidental release of a created genetic mutation would only happen in one place. So is this a terrorist attack?"

"I don't know." For a second he looked almost concerned, but that washed away in a fresh surge of self-obsession. "As I said, Dr. Kahn, time is of the essence, I need those algorithms."

"Yes." She stood, unable to stand him one minute more.

On her way to the parking lot, breasts leaking milk with every step, she passed summer-term students hurrying to class, chatting on a low wall, sprawled on the grass over open books or laptops. Despite herself, she stopped to gaze at a flower bed, unable to look away. Pansies, impatiens, baby's breath.

Nearly every plant on Earth.

Who? And in the name of every god she didn't believe in—*why?*

2035

McAllister and Tommy were the only ones who believed Pete had been Outside. Tommy was angry because Pete hadn't taken him along on the "adventure." McAllister was tense with hope. "Tell me again," she said.

They sat alone in her room. Pete avoided looking at the curve of her belly. Again he recited everything that had happened, too frightened at what he himself had done to leave anything out, not even the cause of the fight with Ravi. But that wasn't what she was interested in.

"You saw bushes and grasses. Trees?"

"No."

"Animals?"

"No."

"And you could breathe."

"It was a little hard."

"Like you weren't getting enough air?"

"Yeah. But not very bad." How could that be? There had been air all around him, blowing gently as it never did inside the Shell.

She guessed the question he wasn't asking. "You had trouble breathing because the air mix still isn't right out there. Maybe there's too much CO_2— the destruction of the Earth's forests would have really screwed up the oxygen-carbon dioxide balance. Maybe too many volcanic particles still, maybe toxins, maybe too much methane. I don't know. I wasn't an ecologist. But I think the atmosphere was becoming unbreathable when the Tesslies put us into the Shell. And now *you* could breathe it."

"Does that mean they'll let us out soon?"

McAllister raised both hands, let them drop, screwed up her face. Her pregnancy had made her more emotional, which everyone had observed and Pete did not understand. Was that usual? "Pure foolishness, getting herself knocked up at her age," Darlene had said. "Who does she think she is, Abraham's Sarah?" Caity bit her lip and looked away every time McAllister waddled into a room. Pete was just glad he wasn't female.

McAllister said, "How should I know what the Tesslies will do?"

Pete burst out, "I'll kill them if I can!"

She didn't answer that; they both knew it was too ridiculous. Instead she said yet again, "And you couldn't tell if the Tesslie was a living being inside a space suit or a robot."

"I don't know."

She smiled. "Neither did I, the one time I saw one."

"How did it *get* here?"

"I don't know, dear heart. Until the Grab machinery appeared, I assumed they'd all left Earth after putting us Survivors in the Shell. After all, nobody had seen one for twenty years. But either they returned or else they were observing us all along."

Pete had known they watched him! Fucking bastards—

McAllister said, "Thank you, Pete. You can go now, but later I want to talk to you and Ravi together."

"I've got Grab duty."

"Do you want someone else to take it?"

"No." He made himself ask, "Is Ravi all right?"

"He will be."

She looked very tired. Pete said awkwardly, "Are *you* all right? With . . . everything?"

"I'm fine. I'm just a little old to be doing this."

Well, you didn't have to! Pete didn't say it. He blundered out and went to the Grab room.

Staring at the inert Grab machinery, which might brighten but probably wouldn't, Pete thought about his own questions. The air outside was breathable. It wasn't really good, but it was breathable enough. What was "enough?" There were bushes and grasses and—yes, he remembered now, wrenching the picture into his mind as if yanking up a pair of pants—berries. There had been red berries on some of the bushes. Almost he turned back to tell McAllister, but he didn't want to face her again.

He had no choice. Somewhere during his Grab duty she came in with Ravi. Immediately Pete wanted to be somewhere else. He got to his feet, scowling to cover his confusion.

Ravi's mouth was all swollen. His two top front teeth were broken off into jagged stumps. Pete had a moment of panic—how would Ravi eat? Well, he still had all his other teeth. . . . But his good looks were badly marred. Even without all the puffy swelling, Ravi was never again going to look like the handsome princes in the fairy-tale book.

McAllister said, "Both of you men were at fault in this fight, but—" For a minute Pete didn't listen, caught by her referring to them as "men." Had McAllister ever done that before? When he heard her again, it was clear she was blaming him more than Ravi, because ". . . violence. Not only is it never needed to settle disputes, it damages the good of all and sets a terrible example for the children. Pete, you wouldn't want Tommy or Petra to someday behave as you did today, would you?"

Pete couldn't imagine Petra behaving any way at all except smiling or wailing or kicking her fat little legs. Too far in the future. But he saw what McAllister meant, and hung his head.

She was talking to Ravi now. "What you were doing, looking to start a fight with Pete because you were angry with me, is something all humans have to struggle against all the time. Do you understand, Ravi? Winning that struggle with ourselves will be a huge part of what lets us successfully restart humanity. Do you understand that?"

"Yes," Ravi said. Pete couldn't tell if Ravi meant it or not. His voice came out mangled through the swollen mouth.

"You two are brothers," McAllister said passionately, "and I know that your biological parents, Richard and Emily and Samir, would not have wanted you to act the way you did today. But even more than brothers, you are members of this colony, with a mission that others have already struggled and died for. You must work together no matter what for our survival, or all those other deaths are wasted."

Ravi said something. McAllister didn't understand the garbled words; she leaned forward and said, "What?" Ravi shook his head.

But Pete had heard. Ravi had said, "Kill Tesslies." That was what Ravi thought was their "mission." And Pete did, too! His head snapped up to look at Ravi, who gazed back. Something passed between them, and all Pete's animosity vanished. They had a joint mission: revenge. That was more important than who had sex with McAllister, who anyway wasn't looking very attractive with her belly swollen in pregnancy and all those tired lines around her eyes.

Ravi nodded. They understood each other. McAllister beamed.

"Good," she said. "Now shake hands."

They did, and Pete squeezed his brother's hand. They were on the same side again. They would be killers together.

McAllister said, "I'm so happy."

Both of them smiled at her.

JUNE 2014

Along the Euphrates river grew a strip of green: trees, grass, flowers. Away from the river the land turned more arid, dotted with scrub grazed on by sheep and goats. Here, not far from where Babylon had once stood, bacteria mutated on the long tap root of a plant.

2035

Pete and Ravi were now allies. Together they were going to get revenge for Earth. The first Tesslie they saw—and one had to show up eventually, after all Pete had seen one when he'd gone Outside!—they were going to kill.

A week after the fight they sat in the clear-walled room, gazing out at the growing grasses in the black rock. "Those are taller than yesterday," Ravi said.

"Yeah," Pete said, although to him the grasses looked exactly the same height. Pete felt obliged to agree with most of what Ravi said because with Ravi's swollen mouth and broken teeth, Ravi's words came out a little garbled. On the other hand, he still had his greater height and bigger muscles, which saved Pete from feeling as bad as he would otherwise. The fight had merely evened things up, he felt, the way Darlene "evened up" blankets when she folded them. The same for both sides. Still, Pete sometimes wished that he and Ravi had had the same father, not the same mother. Ravi's build came from his father Samir, whom Pete could just remember, unlike both of his own parents.

"When we find a Tesslie," Ravi mumbled—it was always *when*, not *if*—"we should have a plan. I'll grab it from behind and you—"

"Wait a minute," Pete said. "Is the Tesslie an alien inside a bucket-case or a robot?"

"Does it matter?"

"Yes! If it's a robot, then you hold it and I'll find the battery case, open it, and pull out the batteries."

"Good, good," Ravi said. "If it's an alien inside a bucket case, then I'll hold it tight, you find the place where the bucket-case opens and unbutton or unzip or pry it apart or whatever. Then we can drag the bastard out and hit it with something."

"With what?" Pete said.

Ravi considered. "We should have a weapon all ready. Hidden, but someplace where we can get at it quick when we need them. I know! Those metal-toed boots from that Grab!"

Pete nodded enthusiastically. The boots were never worn; who wanted all that weight? In the Shell everyone went barefoot. Pete had never seen the point of them. But as a weapon . . .

Ravi said, "We can kick the Tesslie with those boots and stomp on it until it's all bloody!"

Pete frowned. The vivid picture created by Ravi's words didn't look as appealing as before Ravi described it. Ravi, however, went on and on, spouting things they could do to the Tesslie.

Partly to stop him, partly because the thought had been growing in him for some time, Pete said, "Ravi, I have another idea."

"What?"

"I think it would help us if we understood more about how Tesslie machinery works. In case, you know, the Tesslies *are* machinery. We should pick one piece of it and take it apart, examine it real good, then put it back together before McAllister even knows we did it."

Ravi's mouth fell open, fully exposing his broken teeth. "Take it apart?"

"Yes. For information about the Tesslies."

"What if . . . what if we can't get the machinery back together again?"

"We'll be careful, go slow, look at each piece in great detail." They were words Jenna had used about McAllister's lesson in taking apart and cleaning McAllister's precious microscope. Pete wasn't allowed near the microscope, not since that business with the shit bucket and the broken glass slide.

Ravi said, "Well, if you're sure . . ."

"I am," said Pete, who wasn't. But all at once the project seemed the most fascinating thing he'd ever done. Find out more about the Tesslies, the better to defeat them! He was like the Little Tailor in the fairy-tale book, using his brain to triumph over evil giants.

"What machinery do we take apart?"

"Well," Pete said, thinking it out as he spoke, "there are only five Tesslie machines in the Shell. The Grab platform—"

"We can't risk *that*," Ravi said.

"—and the funeral slot and the fertilizer machine and the main waterfall and the disinfectant waterfall. I think the funeral slot."

"No, the fertilizer machine! Then if we can't get it back together, we won't have to do shit-bucket duty anymore!"

"And the shit will just pile up inside the Shell," Pete said. Sometimes Ravi didn't think things through. "The funeral slot is better. Nobody else is sick enough to die. Anyway, I don't think it will be as hard as the other machines. When I was inside the slot, I could see some pipes or something overhead before it got completely dark."

"Pete, did you really go—*look at that!*"

Pete's head snapped around. Outside the Shell, something streaked past, too fast for him to see. "What was it? What was it?"

"I don't know? Maybe . . . a cat!"

"There are no cats not in houses or stores," Pete said, with an authority he didn't feel. He'd never seen a cat except in the books. Why did Ravi and not him get to see the not-cat?

"Something like a cat, then! I don't know! But it was alive!"

They both pressed their faces to the clear part of the Shell, but the thing didn't reappear. Finally Pete said sulkily, "*Yes*, I went Outside—I told you! So let's start on that funeral slot. You go get the flashlight and some rope and . . . and a bucket. A big one."

"What for?"

"You'll see."

Ravi obeyed him, which made Pete feel a little better. Next time, *he* would see the not-cat.

In the funeral room, Pete worked slowly. It was a pleasure to not have to hurry, hurry, hurry like on a Grab. He put the bucket close to the slot, the rope in his hand, the flashlight, usually stored in the children's room for an emergency that had never come, in his teeth. Then he had to take it out again to explain to Ravi what was going to happen.

"You press the button to open the slot, and I'll go in. Then you jam the bucket in the slot so it can't close up again. I'll study the machinery above my head in the slot, and if I see something we want for a closer look, I'll tie the rope around it and use that to yank it out."

"Why do you get to go? I want to go, too! The slot is big enough for both of us if we squeeze."

It was, although just barely. Although Pete didn't like the idea of being jammed that close to Ravi.

Ravi added, "It's only fair that I get to go in the slot, too. You already had a turn! You went all the way Outside!"

"I thought you didn't even believe me about that! And stop whining!"

"I'm not whining!"

Glaring at each other, they got into position. Ravi pressed the button. Pete scooted in. Ravi jammed the bucket into the opening and then crawled past it so that he and Pete lay side by side on their backs. The flashlight was necessary because their bodies blocked nearly all the light coming from the funeral room. Pete swept the beam over the ceiling a foot above them.

The Tesslie machinery wasn't pipes after all, as he had originally thought. It was hard to say what it was. Rounded bumps, irregular indentations, two protrusions shaped vaguely like small bowls. These were easiest to tackle. Pete looped the rope around one. "I'm going to pull on this, just a little bit."

Ravi said, "I want to go Outside."

"Ravi! That's not what we're doing! Besides, I promised McAllister I wouldn't do that again."

"*I* didn't promise her that. And you had a turn Outside so it's only fair that I do. How do I get the other door to open?"

"Ravi, no, it won't open until you—"

Ravi kicked away the bucket.

Pete tried to hit him but there was no room to swing his fist. Pete took a huge gulp of air, knowing what would come next: the air whooshing out of the slot, the outer door sliding open to push him and Ravi out on top of Xiaobo's rotting body. . . . Let Ravi get his own air!

Nothing happened.

The boys lay in the glow from the flashlight. The air did not leave the chamber; Pete could hear Ravi's breathing. Finally Ravi said in a small voice, "When does it open?"

"It isn't going to, you fucker! The Tesslies must have changed the machine! We're trapped!" All at once Pete, who had never minded small spaces before (but when had he ever been in one this small?) felt his heart speed up. Sweat sprang onto his forehead, his palms. Frantically he jostled Ravi, trying to get more space, get more air, *get out*. . . .

"Ow!" Ravi said. "Stop it! Hey, everybody in the Shell, we're trapped inside the funeral slot! Terrell! Tommy! Caity! Hey!"

Pete joined him in screaming. He yelled until his throat hurt. How thick was that slot wall? What if no one ever came?

After what seemed days, weeks, Pete heard a voice on the other side of the wall: "Lord preserve us—ghosts!"

"It's Darlene," Ravi whispered hoarsely.

Darlene began to howl one of her songs. "Save us from ghosts and demons that . . ."

"Darlene! It's not ghosts or demons, it's Pete and Ravi! We're trapped in here! Let us out!"

The howling stopped. Darlene said, "Pete?"

"Yes! Press the funeral button!"

Silence. Then Darlene's voice again but closer, as if she now squatted close to the low slot. "You want to come out?"

"Yes!" Of course they wanted to come out—why did it have to be crazy Darlene that found them?

She said, "I'll let you out after you repent of your sins. You, Pete—you say you're a sinner for sassing me and for disobedience and for setting yourself above your elders!"

Pete's teeth came together so fast and hard that he bit his lip. Ravi snapped, "Do it! Or she'll never let us out!"

He could wait for someone else, anyone else. But now that escape was at hand, the thought of waiting even one unnecessary minute longer in this place was intolerable. Pete snarled, "All right! I repent of my sins!"

"Name them!" Darlene said.

"I repent of sassing you and disobedience and setting myself up above my elders!"

"Now you, Ravi. You repent of fornication with McAllister, who is another generation, and of sassing me and disobedience."

Ravi yelled, "I repent! Open the fucking slot!"

"That ain't true repentance, but I'll take it. Now both of you sing with me a cleansing hymn of—"

"What is going on here?"

McAllister's voice. Pete's heart leapt and then sank, a reversal so quick it left him gasping. Ravi yelled, "McAllister, Pete and I are in here! Let us out!"

The slot slid upwards. Pete and Ravi scuttled out on their backs. Pete felt dizzy. Blood streamed down his chin from his bitten lip. McAllister stared down at the flashlight in his hand, the rope trailing out behind him, the bucket on the floor. From this angle, her belly jutted out like a shelf. Pete had never seen that look on McAllister's face. He felt four years old again, except that no adult but Darlene ever glared like that at a four-year-old.

Ravi, the great lover, hung his head. In a tiny voice he said, "I saw a cat outside, McAllister, running past the Shell. Really. I did."

JUNE 2014

Geoffrey Fanshaw did not get the notoriety he'd hoped for.

Julie finished the analysis he wanted and sent it to him. She expected to hear back from him, but—nothing. On reflection, she decided she'd been dumb to expect acknowledgement. She had served her purpose to Fanshaw and he had discarded her; that was what narcissists did. She was left with his check and her own fears.

At night she dreamed of plants dying, all over the world.

Two more jobs came her way, and she took them both. Around the consulting work she fit a separate, obsessive routine: Wake at 5:00 a.m. Coffee, banishing the lingering night dreams with wake-up caffeine. Care for Alicia. Bundle the baby into her pram and, before the streets of D.C. got too hot, make the long walk to World Wide News to buy newspapers. The *Washington Post*, the *New York Times*: the online versions left too much out. Also a host of small-town papers. The rest of the day she stayed inside, bathed in the air conditioning that divided her and Alicia from the steaming D.C. summer. She worked and then she read, barely glancing at the wide variety of usual disasters available in the world:

FOREST FIRES OUT OF CONTROL IN BRAZIL

MAN KILLS WIFE, SELF

ECOLOGICAL BALANCE SEVERELY THREATENED BY OVER-GRAZING

ILLEGAL STRIP MINING CAUSES ARMED STAND-OFF WITH LAW

She was looking for something unusual, and she would know it when she found it. No, not "it"—"them." She searched for two things, and on the first day of July she finally found one of them. Only a small item far inside the *Times*, bland and inoffensive:

SCIENTISTS SOLVE PLANT MYSTERY

A team of scientists led by Dr. Simon Langford of the U.S. Department of Agriculture announced that the "mystery plague" affecting plants along the

Connecticut shoreline has been stopped. "It was a random, natural mutation in one specific microbe," Langford said, "but relatively easy to contain and kill off with appropriate chemicals. No mystery, really."

A section of shoreline in the Connecticut Wetlands Preserve has been closed to the public for several days while the botanical correction was carried out. Preserve officials announced that the wetlands will remain closed for the near future, "for further monitoring, as a purely precautionary measure." Disappointed tourists were turned away by Security personnel but given free passes to other local attractions.

"This sort of thing happens routinely," Langford concluded. "We're on top of it."

"Bullshit," Julie said aloud to Alicia, who gurgled back.

It was a cover-up—but why? And of what?

Julie knew, or thought she knew, but she didn't want to know. Not yet. She could be wrong, it was a fancifully dumb idea, in fact it skirted the edges of insanity. Just one of those stray ideas that crossed the mind but meant nothing. . . .

She read the bland article again, then stared out her apartment window at a tree, carefully enclosed in a little wrought-iron fence, growing where a section of city sidewalk had been meticulously removed to accommodate it.

2035

All at once the Grab machinery went crazy.

Ravi was on duty. He and Pete had been talked to by McAllister, a talk that left both of them near tears. She wasn't angry, she was disappointed. Angry would have been better. Not even Ravi's sighting of the not-cat outside had deterred McAllister from her disappointment. Pete wasn't sure that McAllister even believed Ravi. Pete wasn't sure he did, either. When McAllister was finished with them, Pete and Ravi avoided each other for a week—until Ravi was restored to puffed-up triumph by his amazing Grab.

"I was all ready," he later told everyone, although Pete had his doubts about that—why even bother to repeat it over and over unless it wasn't true? And Ravi had a history of falling asleep during Grab-room duty. But whether he had leaped onto the platform at first brightening, or had just barely caught the Grab before it went away, it was irrefutable that Ravi had gone. He had gone close-mouthed both because of McAllister's scolding and because he was embarrassed by the lack of the teeth that Pete had knocked out, but he returned smiling wide. His shout had reached both the children's room and the farm. Pete, on crop duty with Darlene, had run toward the Grab room, along with everyone else.

Ravi stood on the platform behind the biggest pile of *stuff* that Pete had ever seen. It almost hid Ravi; it spilled off the edges of the platform; it clanked and clattered as it fell. Pete couldn't even identify half of it. How could even Ravi, the strongest of them all, load all this in ten minutes? And onto what?

McAllister, running clumsily behind the bulk of her pregnancy, stopped in the doorway. She went still and white.

"Look what I got!" Ravi shouted. "Look!"

"What is it all?" Caity said. She held a child in each arm. "How did you *bring* it all?"

"The Grab stayed open for more than ten minutes—for twenty-two minutes! It was a store Grab and I got this big rolling thing—see, it's under all this—and just piled things on. There only was this kind of stuff, so that's what I took. But look how much of it!" Ravi practically swelled with pride. *Bloated*, Pete thought. Like when someone was diseased in their belly.

Why couldn't Pete have been the one to bring back the big haul? Whatever it was.

McAllister finally spoke. "Twenty-two minutes?"

"I timed it," Ravi said proudly.

Caity repeated, "What is it all? What's that thing with the skinny metal spikes coming out of it?"

"A rake," McAllister said. Then it seemed that once started talking, she couldn't stop. "A rake, several hoes, bags of seed and fertilizer, trowels, flower seeds, hoses, flower pots, wind chimes—*wind chimes*!"

Pete had never seen McAllister like this—wild-eyed, hysterical—not even when he and Ravi had gotten trapped in the funeral slot. Fear pricked him. But the next moment she had recovered herself.

"You were in a garden store, Ravi. And you did well. Let's get this stuff off the rolling cart so we can get the cart down off the platform. Caity, take Karim and Tina back to the children's room, and on your way get Darlene to help Jenna with the children. She'll have to do it because we need you here. Tommy, go wake up Eduardo. Terrell, you and Ravi and Pete start moving this stuff. We need that platform clear right away."

"Why?" Pete said.

"I don't know yet. Let's just do it."

Caity ran down the corridor with the kids. Pete leaped forward to help unload the platform. If McAllister was ordering Darlene to help with the children, then something important was going on.

They got all the stuff off the platform, including the long, heavy rolling cart. Immediately Terrell jumped on it and Ravi pushed him out the room and down the corridor. Terrell laughed delightedly. "I want a ride, too!" Caity cried, running after the cart.

The platform glowed.

Pete gaped at it. It never brightened again so soon after a Grab—never!

McAllister said, in a voice somehow not her own, "Go." She handed Pete the wrister that Ravi had turned over to her.

Pete hopped onto the platform, the laughter from the corridor still ringing in his ears.

JUNE 2014

Julie continued to read the papers obsessively: "Starvation Reaches Critical Point in Somalia." "Overpopulation Biggest Threat to Planet." But nothing more was mentioned about the mutated bacteria, not anywhere in the world. Nor could she find anything on line. If the story about *K. planticola* was being repressed, several countries must be cooperating in doing that, by every means available. The completeness of the suppression was almost as scary as the microbial mutation.

Almost.

Several times she picked up the phone to call Fanshaw's office. Each time she laid it down again. If there *was* a cover-up going on, if there really were scientists and covert organizations and high officials in several countries working to keep this from the public, then Julie did not want to call any attention to herself. Fanshaw had probably, given his narcissism, erased any trace of help from anybody else in crafting the article he never got to publish. He would, of course, have preserved her non-disclosure agreement, and Julie could only hope he had it in a safe, secret place. But he had also written her a check "For professional services," and she had cashed it.

She Googled him. Until two weeks ago he had been all over the Net. Then his posts on Facebook ceased, as did his blog.

"You seem preoccupied," Linda said. They sat under an awning in her back yard, drinking cold lemonade and watching Linda's three kids splash in the pool. Alicia lay asleep in her infant seat. The beach-cottage-in-August scheme had been dropped; Linda and Ted were taking the children to visit their grandmother in Winnipeg, where it was twenty-five degrees cooler.

"I'm sorry," Julie said.

"Everything all right? The consulting?"

"Going better than I'd dared hope. And I'm making a lot more money than I was teaching."

"Well, I can see that Alicia's all right. So . . . Ju, is it Gordon? I know he called the night Alicia was born. You were on the floor with Jake, I burst in, and Gordon's voice was coming from your answering machine."

Linda had never mentioned this before. It had been two days before Julie even listened to Gordon's message: *"We've had another kidnapping. A three-year-old boy taken from his bed in southern Vermont."*

She said to Linda, "He called about the work project. You know I can't discuss it with you."

"I know. Spook stuff. But that wasn't all he said. At the end his voice changed completely when he said, 'Are you all right?' Have you seen him since? Do you miss him? Is that why you seem so . . . not here?"

Julie put her hand, cold from the lemonade glass, over her friend's. "No,

I haven't seen him. And no, I don't miss him. Sometimes I feel guilty about that, like it proves I'm a shallow person."

Linda grinned. "You're not that. Still waters, brackish but deep."

"Thanks. I think." And then, before she knew she was going to say it, "Linda, did you ever read James Lovelock?"

"No. Who's he?"

"It doesn't matter. Do you believe . . . do you think there are things about the universe that we can't explain? Things that lie so far beyond science they're something else entirely?"

"I lapsed from Catholicism when I was fourteen," Linda said, "and never saw any reason to unlapse. Ju, have you suddenly got religion?"

"No, no, nothing like that. It's not anything, really. Just the heat."

"Yeah, I can't wait until we leave for—Colin! If you do that one more time you're getting out of the pool, do you hear me?"

Alicia woke. Colin did that one more time. Normal life, routine and mundane as precious as the propagation of plants.

JULY 2014

It wasn't dark, and it wasn't light. It wasn't anything except cold. *I'm dead*, Pete thought, but of course he wasn't. Then he was through and the ocean lay to his right, just as it had all those months ago when he'd Grabbed Petra and Kara. But this beach was smaller than the other, a strip of stony ground jammed between sea and a sort of little cliff. Big rocks jutting out of the water as well as the land. Also, the air was warmer and lighter. In fact, for the first time ever, the Grab seemed to be happening in full daylight. The sun shone brightly halfway above the horizon—so brightly that Pete blinked at it, momentarily patterning his vision with weird dots.

When they cleared, he saw the little house on the top of the cliff above him. There seemed to be no path up. Cursing, Pete climbed, hands and feet seeking holds in the rock, some of which crumbled under his grip. Once he nearly fell. But he made it to the top and stood, his back against the house, to look at his wrister.

Five minutes gone.

The sea below him lay smooth as the mirror Caity had Grabbed long ago. Sunlight reflected off it, enveloping everything in a silver-blue glow. Pete wasted precious seconds staring at the beauty; it made good fuel for his hatred. When he and Ravi eventually found Tesslies . . .

No time now for revenge pictures.

The house had long since lost all its paint to the salt winds. A window, small and too high for Pete to peer into, stood open, but he heard no sounds coming from within. Cautiously he rounded the corner of the house.

It stood on a point jutting above the ocean, and now he had a new angle on the path down to the beach below. Two figures walked there, away from the house, holding hands. They stopped briefly to kiss, then moved on. Pete moved to the front door of the cottage.

It stood open. The screen door, with a metal screen so old and soft that it felt like cloth under his hands, was unlocked. Pete slipped into a tiny hallway, cool after the bright sun outside. He could see clear through to the back of the house, which was all glass with yet another view of the sea. All the rooms were small, to fit the house on the narrow point. To his left was a kitchen, to the right a steep staircase. Pete climbed it.

Two little bedrooms, both with slanted walls and windows set into alcoves. One room held a double bed and a long, low dresser. Crowded into the other were a crib and a single bed, both occupied.

She was the most beautiful girl he'd ever seen, more beautiful even than McAllister. Pete gaped at her long red hair—he hadn't known hair could be that color!—her smooth golden skin, her sweetly curved body and long legs. She wore a thin white top and panties, and nearly everything was on display. Something about her attitude suggested that she had only recently flung herself onto the bed and had fallen instantly asleep. It was a few moments before he could even look into the crib.

When he did, he found a miniature of the girl. Not plump and smooth like Petra, this child looked delicate, graceful, like the fairies in *The Illustrated Book of Fairy Tales*. When Pete lifted her, he scarcely felt her weight, not even on his weak arm. Neither the baby nor her gorgeous sister woke.

Could he bring the older girl back, too? Pete gazed down at her. The rules of the Grab were strict, except that no one knew what they were. Everyone above a certain age died going through the Grab—but what age? Robert had died going through, at thirty-nine, Seth at forty-two. Petra's father had died, at who knew what age. Pete could still go through at fifteen. Where between fifteen and thirty-nine was the death age? How old was this girl?

Pete couldn't risk it. A lingering look at the redhead and he crept downstairs with the baby.

Twelve minutes had passed. If he had the same twenty-two minutes as Ravi, then he had to wait ten more minutes. But maybe he didn't have ten more—who knew what the Tesslies would do? Other than watch humans squirm and struggle to survive. When he and Ravi caught one—not *if*, when—they would—

Chime chime chime . . .

The doorbell! Pete looked frantically around for somewhere to hide. But it wasn't the doorbell, it was a clock sitting on a table made of tree branches painted white. *Chime chime chime . . .*

The girl upstairs screamed.

Pete looked frantically around. Nothing to hide behind, or under . . . He sprinted for the hall. Before he could reach the front door, the girl came tearing down the stairs. Pete ran into the kitchen. A door stood open and he darted inside, closing it behind him. The girl went on screaming, an incoherent mix of words; if she was calling the baby's name, Pete couldn't decipher it.

Through all of this, the baby hadn't awakened. Pete couldn't see his wrister in the darkness of the pantry. But he could smell food all around him. Cautiously he shifted the baby to his shoulder and felt around with his free hand. When it closed on a package of something, he clasped it to the baby and felt for another.

Now the door slammed; the girl had gone outside. A moment later she was back, tearing upstairs and then down again, still screaming but this time as if talking to someone. "My sister my baby sister Susie she's gone! I was asleep—I *can't* calm down don't you understand you moron Susie is gone! Taken! I was—they're walking the beach and—1437 Beachside Way and— yes I'm sure some fucking bastard took her!"

145

Pete heard McAllister's voice in his head, "Not that language, Pete. I know Darlene uses it but's not a good example for the kids." *Fucking bastard.* The beautiful, beautiful girl was talking about Pete with the same words Pete talked about Tesslies.

For the first time, he thought about the people left behind when he took their children. How they must feel.

Why hadn't he ever thought about that before? Why hadn't McAllister made him think about it? Did Caity or Ravi or Jenna or Terrell? Maybe Jenna did. But Pete had only thought about getting back home safely with the Grabbed kids, about how important it was to restart humanity.

Well, it was! And that was how McAllister always said it. Restarting humanity and saving the Grab children from the Tesslie destruction of the Earth. It was a heroic thing to do, and Pete was a hero for doing it.

The girl on the other side of the pantry door threw something hard against the kitchen wall and again slammed the screen door, screaming, "Mom! Dad! Where the fuck are you!"

Still the baby slept. Pete felt around again on the pantry shelves. He found another package of something, then yet another. Then the Grab caught him, and he was back on the platform with the slumbering baby, two packages of penne pasta, and a loaf of whole wheat bread with rosemary and dill.

"Oh!" Tommy cried. "A baby!"

Everyone clustered around the platform to greet him and take the infant, and even Caity smiled at him. Even Darlene. Pete smiled back. Jauntily he jumped down and handed the baby to McAllister.

Behind him, the Grab platform brightened again.

JULY 2014

Just past midnight Julie, seated in front of her computer, put her hands to her face and pulled at the skin hard, trying to fully wake herself up. Today—no, yesterday—was her thirty-ninth birthday. Jake had called from Wyoming. Linda, in the midst of packing her family for Winnipeg, had dashed over with a chocolate cake with a mini-forest of candles. It had been a good day and Julie should have been in bed reliving it in dreams, but instead she'd sat at her computer for four and a half hours, flipping between news sites and screens full of data.

She almost had it, the right algorithm.

She could smell it, tantalizing as apples in October. But this was not autumn and this particular apple evoked Snow White's Wicked Witch, Alan Turing's cyanide-laced fruit, the serpent in the Garden of Eden.

God, she was beyond tired, or her thoughts wouldn't turn so metaphorical. It wasn't as if there weren't enough to fear without figurative exaggeration.

Three more data points. One she felt certain about: the kidnapping in Vermont on the night Alicia was born. A three-year-old boy had vanished from his bedroom while his parents were out at a party. Local cops had his baby-sitter, a Dominican woman who barely spoke English, in custody. She swore she had been asleep on the living room sofa when the abduction occurred; undoubtedly they assumed she was lying. Julie knew she was not.

The other two data points were more uncertain. A break-in in a garden shop in Massachusetts, no forced entry, the cash box untouched. The usual bizarre collection of goods had been taken: rakes, seeds, wind chimes. And yesterday's incident, the kidnapping of a Maine infant who was supposed to be watched by her teenage sister while the parents strolled on the beach. No trace of the baby girl had been found, but the whole thing so closely resembled a set-up that even the local cops were suspicious, regarding the sister as either a suspect or a scapegoat; Julie couldn't tell which. Could be a significant, could not. The location fit with her current algorithm, but not so closely if she didn't include it as a data point to create the algorithm in the first place, which was the kind of thinking that drove mathematicians crazy. And when had she started thinking of a lost child as a "data point"?

She had to go to bed. Just one more scan of breaking news. And there it was:

SCIENTIST ARRESTED FOR SECURITY BREACH
Dr. Geoffrey Fanshaw, Biologist, Believed Connected to
Unspecified Terrorist Activity

The article said nothing much. It didn't have to. Julie, all exhaustion banished, ran into her bedroom and started packing.

2035

Two Grabs right in a row, then nothing for a few days, then another Grab for Caity.

"They're playing fucking games, ain't they," Darlene said. "With our lives!"

"Not yours," Caity answered spitefully. "*You* never have to go." She was disappointed with the results of her Grab. She'd found herself in a strange, small store for twenty-two minutes and had not known what to do. There were no shopping carts, and anyway she was afraid of this store. She hadn't said that, not even later, but then Caity didn't ever admit fear. Still, Pete knew that's what she'd felt. She hadn't wanted to touch anything, but neither did she want to come back empty-handed and anyway, she said later and in a strong temper, "Who knew what the fuck McAllister was going to want?" So she yanked some zippered carrying-bags off a shelf and made herself stuff things into them.

"Gerbils?" Eduardo said, astonished. He and Tommy happened to walk by the Grab room just as Caity returned.

"That's what they had!" Caity was near tears. "Get McAllister! Never mind, I'll go myself!"

"Wow, a puppy!" Tommy cried, unzipping a bag with mesh sides.

The Six had never seen gerbils before. Only Terrell, Jenna, and Pete had seen dogs during Grabs, and the one Pete saw had tried to kill him. He didn't much like the puppy, a small brown-and-white creature with floppy ears. It barked and shit everywhere and chewed up any shoes left on the floor. But everyone else thought it was wonderful, cute and cuddly. Tommy named it Fuzz Ball.

The gerbils were kept in their own room, with an old blanket that McAllister wearily ordered to be torn into strips. The gerbils then finished the job. Unlike the puppy, which had to be coaxed to eat mashed-up soy and only did so when it got hungry enough, the gerbils ate the vegetable crops happily. But their room smelled and had to be cleaned out every day, and Pete couldn't see the point of them.

"Wait," McAllister said. "Something is going to happen, I think."

"What?" Pete said.

"I don't know."

"Is it because of what I saw?"

"I really don't know."

She didn't seem to know much. And once, Pete had thought she knew everything!

Two of the gerbils died the day after Caity brought them back. Pete hoped the rest would die, too, and maybe even the puppy, but they didn't. The gerbils ate and smelled, the puppy raced around and barked and chewed, the babies wailed.

"A regular madhouse, this," Darlene muttered.

Ravi went on a Grab and returned with yet another large load of objects on yet another large rolling cart. "Look! Look what I got!"

Bundles of tough, heavy cloth that Pete thought would be poor blankets: too uncomfortable. However, it turned out they were not blankets at all. Eduardo let out a whoop such as Pete had never before heard the quiet man make. Eduardo sat on the floor and did things to one of the bundles and it sprang into a little cloth *room*.

"A tent!" Tommy cried, and crawled inside.

McAllister leaned against the wall, her hand on her belly, and stared at the "tent."

Eduardo said to McAllister, "Five-pole four-season Stormkings. An earlier generation of these is what we used to use on field expeditions in the mountains, when I was a grad student in botany." Pete didn't know what a botany or a grad student were, and he didn't ask. He was too jealous.

There were more tents, plus a lot of rope, a sharp "axe" that McAllister immediately took away someplace, and many metal things Pete didn't understand the use of. McAllister directed it all to be stowed back on the rolling cart—no playing with this one—and pulled into the room next to the gerbils.

But the most interesting thing, McAllister didn't see at all. Ravi said quietly to Pete, "Come with me. I want to show you something."

"I can't leave the Grab room. I'm next." Pete already wore the wrister.

"Then wait until everybody leaves."

Pete nodded, although he wasn't sure he wanted to see anything from Ravi. Pete regarded it as a private triumph that when he masturbated he no longer thought of McAllister; now he imagined the beautiful red-haired girl that had been Susie's big sister. He'd already calculated how many years before Susie herself would be ready for sex. Still, every time he saw the growing curve of McAllister's belly, the old animosity toward Ravi stirred.

At the same time, he and Ravi were now allies. Together they were going to get revenge for Earth. The first Tesslie they saw—and one had to show up eventually, after all he'd seen one when he'd gone Outside!—they were going to kill. They spent a lot of time in Pete's clear-walled secret room, gazing out at the growing grasses in the black rock and planning ways to accomplish this. If the Tesslie was an alien inside a bucket-case they could hit the case with something until it cracked open, drag the alien out, and stomp on it. If it was a robot, they would find the batteries and pull them out.

"Look," Ravi said when everyone else had left the Grab room. He reached under his tunic, made from a thick blanket folded and sewn to create pockets. Ravi pulled out something encased in leather. The leather slipped off and there was the knife, long and gleaming and, Pete knew without testing it, really sharp. Then another one.

"They had a lot of knives in the store and I put some on the rolling cart. But these two are for us."

"Yes," Pete said. He took one. Just holding it made him feel strange: powerful and bad, both. But he liked the feeling.

"Yes," he said again.

JULY 2014

Julie tried to be good at running and hiding, but most of the time she felt like a fool. After all, she didn't even know if whichever agency had arrested Fanshaw would come for her. And what if they did? All she had done was work on data he had given her.

Data that she knew had been obtained illegally, which made her at the very least an accessory to crime. Data that might, in fact, constitute a terrorist risk.

So why hadn't she reported Fanshaw? Because he must have gotten the data from some government agency, which meant they were already aware of the threat. She couldn't have helped any, and she might have endangered herself. Material witnesses could be detained by the FBI or CIA indefinitely, in secret and without filed charges. If that had happened, who would have cared for Alicia? Linda had her hands full with her job and her own family; Jake was out of the question.

It was because of Alicia that Julie was trying to plan responsibly now. At first light she packed the car carefully. She stopped at the bank as soon as it opened and withdrew $3,000 in cash. She turned off her cell phone. Then she drove north from D.C. on I-270. In Pennsylvania, just over the border from Maryland, she found a seedy motel that looked like it would accept cash. It did. The bored clerk behind a shield of bullet-proof glass didn't check the parking lot to see if the false license number she put down matched the one on her car. If the clerk was surprised to see a woman with a baby walk in to his establishment, which usually catered to an entirely different sort of trade, he didn't show it.

Locking the motel door behind her, Julie had a moment of panic. What was she doing? Her life had been going so well, had felt so sweet—

She was doing what she had to do.

After feeding Alicia, Julie drove to the nearest library and used their Internet connection until the library closed. It helped that Alicia, an unusually good baby now that the first bouts of colic were over, slept peacefully in her infant seat or stared calmly at whatever crossed her vision. Back in her motel room, Julie worked on her own laptop, which couldn't have accessed the Internet if she'd wanted to; this was not the sort of place with wi-fi.

When she couldn't go any further with the data she had, she watched the TV. It only got three channels, but that was enough. Through the thin walls came first loud music and then louder laughter, followed by a lot of sexual moaning. Sleep came late and hard. Julie upped the volume on the TV, flipping channels to find what she sought.

"Dead zones" were increasing in the world's oceans. No fish, no algae, no life. The Nile was threatened by industrial pollution. No fish, no algae, no life. CO_2 levels in the atmosphere were creeping upward.

Overfishing was causing starvation in southeast Asian islands.

The noise from adjoining rooms grew louder. A door slammed, hard. Julie's gun, a snub-nosed .38, lay on the floor beside her bed. Julie was licensed to carry, and a reasonably good shot. She didn't expect to have to use the gun, but it was comforting to know she had it.

2035

Pete sat in the Grab room, waiting for the platform to brighten. He had been there each day for a week now, relieved from duty only to sleep, and he was terrifically bored. Darlene had brought him onions and peppers to slice and chop. Eduardo had brought him sewing. Tommy popped in and out, too restless to stay very long. Caity had strolled in, nonchalantly offering sex, and had stalked out, her back stiff, when Pete said no. Jenna brought Petra, both of them trundled in on the rolling cart by Terrell. Petra was just learning to walk. Pete and Jenna sat a few paces apart and set the baby to waddling happily between them until she got tired and went to sleep.

But most of the time he was bored. Of the Shell's six books, two of them were too hard for Pete, and he'd read the others over and over. He knew all about the Cat in the Hat, the fairy tales with all the princes and horses and swords, the moon you said good-night to, and *Animals in the Friendly Zoo.* Why didn't the fucking Grab machinery brighten?

It was a relief of sorts to think bad words, so he said them again, this time aloud. "Why doesn't the fucking Grab machinery brighten?"

"Language, Pete," McAllister said. She smiled at him from the doorway, walked heavily to his side, and braced one hand on the wall to lower herself beside him. Pete blushed, then scowled, conscious of the forbidden knife under his shirt. He had sounded out the words on its sheath: CAUTION: *Carlton Hunting Knife. Very Sharp.*

"I came to keep you company," McAllister said. "Are you very bored?"

"Yes."

"You're doing a good job. You always do."

Pete looked away. He used to love McAllister's praise, used to practically live for it. Now, however, he wondered if she really meant it, or if she just wanted him to keep on doing what she wished. Did she praise all the Six the same way? And the older Grab kids, too?

McAllister watched him carefully. Finally she said, "You're growing up, Pete."

"I am grown up! I'm fifteen!"

"So you are."

Silence, which lengthened until Pete felt he had to say something. "How is the fetus?"

To his surprise, McAllister smiled, and the smile had a tinge of sadness in it. "Doing fine. Do you know how odd it would have been for a fifteen-year-old to utter that sentence, in Before?"

He didn't know. He said belligerently, "I don't see why. That fetus is important to us."

"You're right. And you Six have all grown up knowing that. Language follows need. It was your father who taught me that, you know. He was studying to be a linguist."

Startlement shook Pete out of his belligerence. McAllister—none of the Survivors—talked much about the ones who had died, or about their own lives Before. When he'd been a child, Pete and the other Six had asked hundreds of questions, which always received the same answer: "Now is what counts, now and the future." Caity had pointed out, years ago, that the Survivors must have made a pact to say that. Gradually everyone had stopped asking.

Now Pete said carefully (CAUTION: *Very Sharp*), "My father?"

"Yes. Richard had been a student at the same university I was, although we didn't know each other then."

"Where was that?" This flow of information was unprecedented. Pete didn't want to ask anything complicated that might interrupt it.

"The name of the university wouldn't mean anything to you, and there's no reason why it should. That's all gone, and what matters is now and the future."

"Yes, of course, but how did my father get here, McAllister? How did you?"

She sighed and shifted uncomfortably on the floor. Pete tried to imagine carrying something the size of a bucket inside you. McAllister said, "I was home from university for summer vacation when the Tesslie destruction began. They caused a megatsunami. That's a . . . You've seen waves in the ocean when you've been on a Grab, right? A tsunami is a wave so huge it was higher than the whole Shell, and could wash it right away. Wash away whole cities. The Tesslies started the tsunami with an earthquake in the Canary Islands off the coast of Europe and it rolled west across the Atlantic."

Her face had changed. Pete thought: *She's talking to herself now, not me*, but he didn't mind as long as she kept talking. He'd never seen McAllister like this. Was it because she was pregnant? It had been a while since anyone in the Shell had been pregnant: at least six years, when Bridget had miscarried that last time. The Survivors were too old (or so everyone had thought) and the Grab kids too young. The Shell was awash in babies, but in the last years no pregnancies. Until now.

McAllister kept talking, her back resting against the Grab room wall, her hands resting lightly on the mound of her belly. "We lived, my family and I, in the countryside of southern Maryland. Honeysuckle and mosquitoes. Dad had a little tobacco farm that had been in the family for generations. Ten acres, two barns, a house built by my great-grandfather. It wasn't very profitable but he liked the life. We had no close neighbors. That day my parents drove my little brother to Baltimore for a doctor's appointment, a specialist. Jimmy had had leukemia but he was recovering well. I woke up late and turned on the little TV in my room while I was getting dressed and I learned that by then the tsunami was forty-five minutes away. My parents might have been trying to call me but I'd forgotten to plug in my cell and the battery was dead."

The words made no sense to Pete but he didn't interrupt her.

"Mom and Dad had taken our only car—we didn't have much money and I was at university on a merit scholarship. They were so proud of that. I ran out of the house and climbed the hill behind the barns. The hill wasn't very high, not in coastal Virginia, but it was high enough to see the water coming. A huge wall of it, smashing everything, trees and houses and tobacco barns. *Our* house. I knew it was going to smash me."

Pete blurted, despite himself, "What did you do?"

To his surprise, she chuckled. "I prayed. For the first time in a decade—I was a smart-ass college kid who thought she had outgrown all that hooey—I prayed to a god, any god, to save me. And then a Tesslie did. It materialized out of the air beside me in what looked like a shower of golden sparks—that's why we called them Tesslies, you know. Ted Mgambe came up with the name. He said when they materialized through whatever unthinkable machinery they had, it looked just like the shower of sparks from Tesla's famous experiments."

She had gone beyond Pete again. He didn't interrupt.

"The materializing was quite a trick, but the Tesslie was solid enough, a hard-shelled space suit, or perhaps a robot, with flexible long tentacles. It wrapped one around me but it really didn't have to. The tsunami was almost on me, a wall of dirty raging water with trees and boards and pieces of cars and even a dead *cow* in it. I saw that cow and I clutched the Tesslie with every ounce of strength I had."

Silence. Pete said, "And then what? What?"

McAllister shrugged. "I woke up in the Shell, along with twenty-five other people. All about my age, all intelligent, all healthy. You know their names. Everything was here except the Grab machinery, which just *appeared* twenty years later when it became evident that we were not going to be able to produce enough children to restart the human race. Too much genetic damage, Xiaobo thought, although nobody knew from what. All of us Survivors came from Maryland and Virginia, although we represented genetic diversity. Xiaobo was a Chinese exchange student, Eduardo was Hispanic, Ted was black, Darlene was plucked from up-country Piedmont. The diversity was probably deliberate. And we all happened to be in the open, high up, and alone when the tsunami hit.

"When each of us regained consciousness, we explored the Shell, and we saw what Earth had become through the clear patch of wall in the unused maze—no, Pete, you weren't the first to go there. And after the initial grief and rage, we made a pact that we would do whatever it took to restart humanity. Anything, anything at all, putting the good of the whole first and our individual selves second, if at all."

"Didn't you hate them? The Tesslies, I mean?"

"Of course we did. They wrecked the world. Even the brief hysterical newscast I saw that last day said that the tsunami wasn't natural. It came from something—a quake, a volcano, I don't remember exactly—that couldn't have happened in that way by itself. And then the Tesslies saved us, like lab rats. We expected biological experimentation on us, those first years. It didn't happen. The Tesslies left us alone until they gave us the Grab machinery, although no one saw them do it. Until you went Outside, I thought they'd probably left Earth for good. But they hadn't, and I think now that they're here for whatever happens next. Because something *is* happening, Pete. The grass is growing Outside. You breathed the air, even if it isn't completely right yet. The Grabs have accelerated enormously. It's possible more Tesslies will return soon."

"Before, did you—"

She held out her hand. "Give me the knife, Pete. Or the gun, or whatever you've got."

He jerked his head to face her. His body shifted away. "No."

"Please. You can't do any good with it."

All at once fury swamped him in a big wave, like the tsunami she had spoken about but evidently didn't understand. None of them understood anything, the wimpy Survivors! He shouted, "What's wrong with you, McAllister? What? The Tesslies wrecked my future! Everybody's future! And you want to just welcome them back because they gave us the Shell and the Grabs and—when the Grab machinery appeared it didn't even have any learning circle to teach you that adults can't go through and so we lost Robert and Seth until that day Ravi jumped on it during a game and it happened to brighten and he came back whole! And still you never blame the Tesslies, you never blame anybody for anything, you just talk about the good of the whole but to not blame the Tesslies—Fuck, fuck, fuck! Do you hear me? Fuck! We're not . . . not gerbils!"

"No. But you're not thinking clearly, either. Survival—"

"Blame the fucking Tesslies! Hate them! Kill them if you can!"

"Pete—"

The platform brightened.

Pete pulled his knife, glared at the pregnant woman on the floor, and jumped into the Grab.

JULY 2014

The Yellowstone Caldera lifted upwards.

For several years the surface land had been rising as much three inches a year, but a few years ago the uplift had slowed and stopped. Now the ground inched upward again. A swarm of minor earthquakes followed, barely detectable at the surface. Tourists went on admiring the geysers and the bubbling, mud-laden hot springs. Rumbling at low sonic frequencies set off alarms at the Yellowstone Volcano Observatory and the White Lake GPS station.

Jacob Kahn rushed to his monitor. "Oh my God," he said. It was not a prayer.

JULY 2014

Two more nights in cheap motels, one without AC in a sweltering July. Two more days on library Internet connections. On her own laptop Julie had run and rerun algorithms as new data became available. Her driving had taken her steadily north, along the coast. Now she was in Massachusetts north of Salem. She knew where she was going. She had accumulated enough data points to be sure.

The Eve's Garden break-in in Connecticut.

The baby snatched on the Massachusetts coast while her teenage sister slept in the same room.

The Loving Pets burglary in New Hampshire.

Thefts at REI in southern Maine and Whole Foods in Vermont.

She was running out of money, and not all her news-watching had turned up the slightest hint that anyone was looking for her. On the other hand, neither had she turned up any more information on Dr. Fanshaw or mutated plant-killing bacteria. Both the glory hound and the deadly mutation seemed to have vanished, which was in itself scary. Still, she would have to go home soon. Or go somewhere.

Alicia had a cold, probably from exposure to all the germs in all the libraries. Julie had a massive headache. Was she just being stupid, imagining herself some dramatic fugitive from a third-rate action movie? Maybe she was just as narcissistic as Geoffrey Fanshaw. The sensible thing was to make the observation, alert Gordon, and go home.

At a K-Mart she bought a camcorder. Alicia sneezed and fussed. Julie got them both back in the hot car and drove north on Route 1. The algorithm pinpointed a Maine town, Port Allington, for the next incident. Also a time: between 5:30 and 5:45 tomorrow afternoon. Which was odd, since all the other incidents had occurred in the middle of the night or in early morning. Google Earth showed the location to be in a retail area centered on a large Costco.

She spent nearly the last of her money at a Ramada Inn, several steps up from the places she'd been staying. "You're lucky to get a room at all," the desk clerk told her. "It's high season for tourists, you know. But we had a cancellation."

"Oh," Julie said. She was tired, headachy, frightened. Alicia fussed in her car seat.

"Tomorrow the Azalea Festival begins over in Cochranton. You here for the festival?"

"No."

"You should go. My niece Meg is going to be crowned Miss Cochranton Azalea."

"Congratulations."

"You should give the festival a look-see."

It took Julie a long time to get to sleep. Her theory—*fanciful, dumb, insane*—kept spinning around in her head. When she finally slept, she dreamed that Miss Cochranton Azalea, dressed in a pink prom dress covered with blossoms, said, "That's the stupidest idea I ever heard. I thought you were supposed to be a scientist!"

The next morning she felt even worse. But today would end it. She fed Alicia, bathed her, had an overcooked breakfast at a Howard Johnson's. It was after noon when she got on the road. Another sweltering day. During just the short walk from restaurant to car, sweat sprang out on Julie's forehead and her sundress clung to her skin. Alicia, in just a diaper and thin yellow shirt, cried while Julie strapped her into her car seat. Julie turned on the AC and powered down the windows to flush the hot air from the car.

Only a few hours to drive, and it would be over.

All at once loneliness overtook her. She hadn't talked to anyone but motel clerks, librarians, and waitresses in days, and you couldn't call any of those things conversations. She felt near to tears. Ordinarily she despised weakness—she and Gordon had had that in common—but the way she'd been living wasn't human. And what did it matter if she turned on her cell? In a few hours the camcorder would have her proof, and she doubted that the FBI or CIA or whoever—even if they were looking for her—could locate her that fast if she were on the road. She needed to talk to somebody. Not Linda, who would ask too many questions. She would call her brother. Not to say anything personal—she and Jake seldom did that—but just to hear his voice.

The phone had nine voice mails waiting.

Sitting in the Howard Johnson parking lot, the AC finally making the car bearable, Julie stared at the blinking "9." Very few people had this number; she'd conducted her professional life on the more secure landline. Gordon? Had the investigation re-opened?

Her fingers shook as she keyed to voice mail.

"Julie, this is Jake. Listen, are you due for vacation? If so, don't travel out west. Nowhere near Yellowstone, do you hear me? I'll call and explain more when I have a minute to think clearly."

A mechanical voice informed her that the message was dated days ago, the day Julie had left D.C. The next message was also from Jake, a day later: "Sorry to alarm you, Sis, but my warning still holds. Some weird shit is happening here, signs that the Yellowstone Caldera could blow. You remember, don't you, I told you that for years now it's been ranked 'high threat'? Well, I guess it'll rank that way a while longer since nothing seems to be happening even though there's enough magma down there to blow up the entire state. Well, several states, actually. But as I said, it seems to have settled down. But don't come out here until you hear from me."

The next message alternated between jocularity and exasperation. "Still no supervolcano at Yellowstone. Just call us at the U.S. Geological Survey a bunch of Cassandras. But why haven't you phoned me? This is my third message."

Five of the other messages were from Linda, one from the hairdresser announcing that Julie had missed her appointment. Linda, calling first from home and then from Winnipeg, sounded increasingly frantic: "Where *are* you? It's not like you to not call me back." Her last message said she was calling the police.

Julie keyed in Linda's number, but it went to voice mail. Were the police already looking for her as a missing person? No, that last message was only an hour ago. Julie left Linda a voice mail saying she was fine, Alicia was fine, tell the police it was all a mistake, Julie would explain later.

Almost she smiled, imagining that explanation.

She pulled out and drove toward Port Allington.

JULY 2014

The alarms came from the Canary Islands station, simultaneously sounding at the Cosejo Superior de Investigaciones Cientificas offices in Madrid and Barcelona, and then around the world.

"La Palma!" a graduate student in Barcelona exclaimed. "It's breaking off!"

"Not possible," her superior said sharply. "That old computer model was disproved—you should know that! You mean El Teide!" He raced to the monitors.

It was not El Teide, the world's third-largest volcano, which had been smoldering on Tenerife for decades. It was the island of La Palma. A massive landslide of rock from Cumbre Vieja, itself already split in half and fissured from a 1949 earthquake, broke off the mountain. One and a half million cubic feet of rock fell into the Atlantic as the earth shook and split. The resulting tsunami crested at nearly 2,000 feet, engulfing the islands. The landslide continued underwater and a second quake followed. More crests and troughs were generated, creating a wave train.

"Not possible," the volcanologist choked out again. "The model—"

The ground shook in Barcelona.

The wave train sped west out to sea.

JULY 2014

It wasn't dark, and it wasn't light, until it was. Pete blinked. No Grab before had gone like this.

He stood in a vast store, bigger than any he'd ever seen. WELCOME TO COSTCO! Said a huge red sign. The lights were full on. The big doors just behind him stood wide open. But there were no people in the store, and none of the Before cars in what he could see of the parking lot. Everything was completely silent. A few tables had been tipped over, and half-full shopping carts stood everywhere.

"Hello?" Pete said, but very softly. He held Ravi's knife straight out in front of him. No one answered.

Cold slid down Pete, from his crooked shoulder on down his spine right to the tops of his legs. But he wasn't here to give in to fear, or to start conversations with weirdly absent people. He was here to Grab. He took one of the half-filled shopping carts—part of his job already done!—and pushed it past a display of round black tires. Not useful. Behind it were tables and tables of clothes, and behind those he could see furniture and food. What would McAllister want most?

As he pushed a shopping cart forward, something miraculous came into view: an entire wall of DIGITAL FOTO FRAMES. But these were enormous, and the pictures on them *moved*. In each DIGITAL FOTO FRAME a beautiful girl, more beautiful even than Susie's red-haired older sister, ran along a white beach and into blue sparkling water. The girl wore almost no clothes, just strips of bright cloth around her hips and breasts. The breasts bounced. Mouth open, Pete stared at the incredible sight. Could he maybe unfasten one from the wall and—

He heard a clatter behind him and he turned.

JULY 2014

Something was wrong. Suddenly cars jammed the exits to Route 1, as if everyone was trying to leave the highway at once. Julie would have guessed a massive accident blocking traffic, except that the cars were leaving the freeway in both directions. Could a wreck ahead be sprawled across all six lanes? Or maybe a fire? She didn't see smoke in the hot blue sky. She turned on the radio.

"—as high as 150 feet when it reaches the coast of the United States! Citizens are urged not to panic. Turn your radio to the National Emergency Alert System and follow orderly evacuation procedures. The tsunami will not hit for another four hours. Repeat, the Canary Islands tsunami will not hit the eastern seaboard of the United States for another four hours. Turn to the National Emergency Alert System—"

Tsunami. Waves 150 feet high hitting the coast of the United States.

For a moment Julie's vision blurred. The car wavered slightly, but only slightly. She recovered herself—Alicia was with her. She had to save Alicia. Drive inland—

She couldn't get off the highway. Traffic had slowed to a crawl, fighting for the exit ramps. An SUV left the highway and drove fast and hard into the fence separating the wide shoulder from a row of suburban houses. The fence broke. A blue Ford followed the SUV.

She knew about the "Canary Islands tsunami"—it had been the subject of a melodramatic TV show. Jake had discussed with her just why the program was wrong. "It couldn't happen that way, Sis. The fault isn't big enough, it was exaggerated for the computer model. And the model was based on algorithms— you'll appreciate this—used for undersea linear quakes, not single-point events. It's pure and inaccurate sensationalism. You would need a major sea-bed reconfiguration to get that megatsunami. Or an atomic bomb set off underwater."

Hands shaking on the wheel, Julie pulled her car off the highway and followed the blue Ford toward the fence. She had to drive down a slight incline and through a watery ditch, but her wheels didn't get stuck in the mud and the ground past the ditch was firm and hard, although covered with weeds. Her door handles and fenders tore off the tallest of these. Festooned with Queen Anne's lace, the car drove through the fence hole and across somebody's back yard. It was an old-fashioned 1950s house with a separate garage. Julie followed the two cars around the garage, down the driveway, and onto a road.

Everybody here was driving west, away from the ocean. But Julie had had time to think. Inland was not the answer. Not to the whole picture.

Her hands shook on the wheel as, guided by the compass on her dash display, she turned east. For several blocks she had to fight cars dashing out of driveways, the people glimpsed through windshields looking frantic and shocked. Cars jumped lanes, blocking her way. A woman stuck her head out of the window and screamed at Julie, "Hey! You're going the wrong way!"

By the edge of town, however, she had the road nearly to herself. No one else was heading toward the sea.

How far inland would the evacuees have to go to escape the tsunami? Jake had once told her that 8,000 years ago in the Norwegian sea, an ancient rockslide had left sediment fifty miles into Scotland.

With one hand she fiddled with the radio, searching for more information. A Canadian station broke off its broadcast to say something about the Yellowstone Caldera, then abruptly went off the air.

In her car seat, Alicia slept fitfully.

In Washington, in Brasilia, in Delhi, in London, in Pyongyang, in Moscow, in Beijing, the Canary Islands earthslide was perceived as unnatural. Too large, too sudden, in the wrong place, not the result of natural plate tectonics. Every single country had received the data on the quake and resulting tsunami. Every single country had a classified file describing the feasibility and techniques for using nuclear blasts at Cumbre Vieja as a weapon. Every single country came to the same conclusion.

In Washington the president, his family, and senior staff were airlifted to an undisclosed location. From the chopper he could see the Beltway with its murderous fight to get out of D.C. Most would not make it. He could see the dome of Capitol Hill, the Washington Monument, the Smithsonian with its treasures, the gleaming terraces of the Kennedy Center and mellow rosy brick of Georgetown. All would be gone in a few more hours.

"I need more information," he said to his chief of staff.

"Sir, retaliation scenarios are in place for——"

"I need more information."

A woman stood in the doorway of the store, carrying a sort of padded bucket with a handle, curved to hold a baby. The baby was asleep. The woman and Pete stared at each other. She spoke first.

"You're the one who has been stealing children, aren't you?"

"Not stealing," Pete said. "Rescuing."

"From the tsunami."

It was the second time Pete had heard that word today. He scowled to cover his confusion. "No. From the Tesslies."

"What are Tesslies?" She moved closer, just one step. It was as if she were pulled closer, jerked on some string Pete couldn't see, like the puppets Bridget had made for the Six when they were kids. The woman looked about McAllister's age, although not so pretty. Her hair matted to her scalp and her clothing was wet over her breasts, which made Pete look away. He started throwing bundles of towels into a shopping cart.

"You're taking things from this store, the way you did from the others. A sporting-goods store in Maine. A pet store in New Hampshire. A garden shop in Connecticut. A supermarket in Vermont. Ambler's Family Department Store in Connecticut . . ."

She recited the whole list of store Grabs, his and Caity's and Ravi's and Terrell's and Paolo's and even way back to Jenna's famous Wal-Mart Grab. Pete stopped hurling towels into the cart and stared at her, astonished. "How do you know all that? Who told you?"

"Nobody told me, or at least not all of it. A law-enforcement joint task force that . . . No, it would take too long to explain. You aren't here for long, are you? How much longer?"

Automatically Pete glanced at the wrister. "Sixteen more minutes."

"I've been waiting outside for you."

More astonishment. "You have? Why? Don't try to stop me!"

"I won't stop you. At first I came to video you, to get photographic proof that. . . . It doesn't matter. That's not why I'm here now. Listen to me, please—what's your name?"

"Pete." He yanked at another shopping cart and started emptying a table of clothing into it. So much clothing! And most of it big enough for Ravi and the Survivors. Eduardo's pants had a hole in them.

"My name is Julie. Listen to me, Pete. The tsunami will be here within the hour. It will smash everything on the eastern coast of the United States. Almost no one will survive—"

"McAllister will. She told me." Pants, tops, jackets, more pants but softer. "All the Survivors will live."

"Yes? Where will they go?"

"The Tesslies will take them to the Shell."

"That's where you live, the Shell? Where is it?"

"After." A third shopping cart. If he could tie them together, they would all come back with him—a lot more than Ravi had Grabbed! Better stuff, too. He yanked free a towel to lash the carts together.

"But the Shell is a safe place, isn't it? Is it some sort of space ship or underground colony? Are you from the future? It—oh my God!"

At her voice, Pete jumped. She stared at the wall behind him. He whirled around to look, knife at the ready. If it was a Tesslie—

JULY 2014

The front wave of the megatsunami loomed 300 feet high when it crashed into northwest Africa. When it reached the low-lying south coast England, the trough of the wave hit first. The sea retreated in a long, eerie drawback before rushing back to land. It breached England's sea defenses, roaring a mile inland, destroying everything it touched.

The main body of the wave train sped over the Atlantic at hundreds of miles per hour. When eventually it reached Brazil, the Caribbean, Florida, and the eastern coast of the United States, it would crest to a maximum of 120 feet.

Long before that, the missiles had been launched. Retaliation for the act of terrorism aimed at smashing the way of life of the Western world. The counter-response was not far behind.

The far wall of huge DIGITAL FOTO FRAMES had stopped showing the moving pictures of the beautiful girl running on the beach. Instead, they all showed fire spurting into the sky. At the same moment the ground shook beneath Pete's feet and he nearly fell. The woman staggered sideways against a table of rugs, righted herself, stared again at the row of DIGITAL FOTO FRAMES, which were screaming loud enough now to wake the baby. Something about a yellow stone.

Julie said, in a voice Pete recognized: "There goes the West. To match the East." The words made no sense, but the voice was the one Bridget had used when her last baby miscarried. Quiet, toneless, dead.

Pete stared at this baby, now awake in its padded bucket and peering curiously around. Was it a girl? How hard would Julie fight for it?

She said, "Take us with you."

He gaped at her. She didn't give him a chance to speak.

"You can, I know you can. You've taken twelve children, starting—"

"Thirteen," he corrected, without thinking.

"—with Tommy Candless over a year ago, and you can take us. Don't you understand, Pete? Everything here is dying, the Earth itself is dying! Tsunamis, earthquakes, a mutated bacteria that is killing every plant above tide level. Governments will collapse, and as they collapse they'll fight back, there will be nuclear retaliation with radiation that will—"

"Radiation, yes." She had used a word he knew. "It damages babies. It damaged me. But it's mostly gone now."

"Is it? Then take—"

"Everything you said, the destroying of the whole Earth—the *Tesslies* did that. But McAllister is leading us to restart humanity. And Ravi and I will kill the fucking alien Tesslies!"

"The —"

Suddenly all the DIGITAL FOTO FRAMES went black at once. The silence somehow felt loud. Into it Julie said, "No aliens wrecked the Earth. We did. Humans."

"That's a lie!"

"No, Pete, it's not. We poisoned the Earth and raped her and denuded her. We ruined the oceans and air and forests, and now she is fighting back."

"The Tesslies destroyed the world!"

"I don't think so. Tell me this: Are there any plants where you live? Growing wild outside the Shell, I mean?"

"There are now. Grasses and bushes and red flowers."

Julie closed her eyes, and her lips moved soundlessly. When she opened her eyes again, they were wet. "Thank God. Or Gaia. The microbial mutation reversed."

"What?"

"Take us with you, Pete. I can help your McAllister start over. I'm strong and a good worker and I know a lot of different things. I can be really useful to . . . to the Shell."

She took a step forward and looked at him with such beseeching eyes that all at once Pete *saw* her. She was a real person, as real as McAllister or Petra or Ravi, a person who was going to die in McAllister's tsunami. The first person in Before who had ever been real to him.

"Take us with you!"

He choked out, "I can't!"

"Yes, you can! You've done it twelve times already!"

"Only kids," Pete said. "If adults go through a Grab, they die." Robert, Seth, the thing that had come back with him and Kara and Petra. The thing that had been their father. "The Tesslies made the Grab that way. They didn't want the Survivors to just get everybody on the platform and lead them all back to Before."

Julie went so still and so sick-looking that for a crazy moment Pete thought she had turned into the "yellow stone" the wall had been screaming about. *Robert, Seth, the thing that had been Petra's father . . .* He started to babble. "But I can take that baby, yes I can, kids can go through a Grab so I can take the baby! Give it to me!"

Julie didn't move.

"Give me the baby! I've only got—" a quick glance at his wrister "—another two and a half minutes!"

The number brought her alive. She shoved the baby bucket into his arms. "Her name is Alicia. Tell her—oh, tell her about me!"

"Okay." He couldn't do that; it was important that the Grab kids belong to the Shell, not to Before. McAllister insisted on it. But he didn't have to tell Julie that.

She began to cry. Pete hated it when people cried. But she had a good reason, and anyway there were only three or four sobs before she got hold of herself and began to talk. "Listen, Pete, it *was* us, not any aliens. Have you ever heard of Gaia?"

"No."

"Is your McAllister an educated man?"

"She knows everything."

"Then tell her this: *We did it.* We wrecked the Earth, and now the Earth is fighting back. The planet is full of self-regulating mechanisms—remember those exact words!—to keep life intact. We've violated them, and Gaia—remember that word!—is cleansing herself of us. It's not mysticism, it's Darwinian self-preservation. Maybe Gaia will start over. Maybe you in the Shell are part of that! But tell McAllister that, tell everyone! Say it!"

She was hysterical, the way Petra's mother had got hysterical when Pete Grabbed Petra. But she was also real. So Pete repeated the words after her, and then repeated them again, all the while hurling more things into shopping carts. "Gaia. Darwinian self-preservation." Blankets, socks, a tableful of flimsy books. "Self-regulating planetary mechanisms." Three folding chairs, all he had room for. "Identical deadly plant mutations in widely separated places. Gaia." Now he'd reached the start of the food section. Loaves of bread! Boxes of something else!

The ground shook again. The baby started to whimper. Pete tied the huge shopping carts together with towels. He clutched one of the handles in one hand, the baby bucket in the other. Fifteen seconds.

"Bye, Julie. I'm sorry about the tsunami."

"Alicia!" Julie cried. Then, stopping herself in mid-lunge: "It was us."

"It was the Tesslies."

"No, no—don't you see? We humans always blame the wrong ones! The—"

Pete never heard the rest. He was Grabbed.

2035

"I'm back!" Pete cried from the platform. "Look! Look!" No one was in the Grab room.

That made no sense. McAllister had seen him go. She knew he would be back in twenty-two minutes, and his wrister said that he was. She, at least, should be waiting here. Disappointment lurched through him—he had a baby girl to show her! And all this great stuff! And all those words to tell her that Julie had said . . . If he could remember them.

He found he remembered them perfectly.

Pete's belly churned. The excitement of the Grab, the disappointment at no one seeing his triumphant return, his deep disturbance at Julie's statements, going deeper every moment. Where was McAllister? Where was everybody?

"Hello?" he said, but not loud. No answer.

He hopped off the platform, leaving his Grabbed prizes, still carrying Alicia in her baby-bucket. Cautiously he peered into the corridor.

No one. But through the wide arched entrance to the farm, he glimpsed a movement behind the wide white bulk of the fertilizer machine. A second later Ravi appeared, gestured wildly for Pete to come, then ducked again out of sight. Was it a game of some sort?

He knew it wasn't. He set the baby-bucket down in the middle of the corridor and sprinted toward Ravi.

"We don't have much time," Ravi gasped. "They'll find out it's missing."

My knife doesn't work at all on its bucket-case. But you have the laser on your wrister. Quick, kill it!"

Lying on the ground at Ravi's feet was a Tesslie.

JULY 2014

Julie walked calmly to a deep faux-leather chair in the Costco furniture display. Calmly she sat down. The calm, she knew with the part of her brain that was still rational, would not last. It was shock. Also several other things, including a preternaturally heightened ability to simultaneously comprehend everything around her, instead of in the linear shards that the human mind was usually stuck with.

Alicia was gone.

The megatsunami was on its way.

Washington D.C., including her life there, would soon no longer exist.

Her country would not allow that to go by without a military reaction.

Pete had left behind a pile of objects that must have slid off one of his shopping carts before he . . . left.

Jake was dead in whatever was happening at the Yellowstone Caldera.

The TVs on the wall had stopped broadcasting.

The Tokyo earthquake and tsunami had been a rehearsal for what would come, once the biologists had detected and contained the plant mutations. Or, alternatively, once Gaia had changed its tactics.

The chair she sat in was on sale for $179.99.

Linda and her family were in Winnipeg, far from the coast. Would that save them? For how long? Gordon and his kids, all the people Julie knew at Georgetown and in D.C.—all gone, or soon to be gone. And then incongruously: *The motel clerk's niece will never be crowned Miss Cochranton Azalea.*

Julie drew the snub-nosed .38 from her pocket. She would not wait for the tsunami. This was better. And Alicia—her baby, her treasure, the miracle she had given up hoping to have—was safe. Safe someplace that might, with any luck, become the future.

JULY 2014

Beneath the Yellowstone Caldera, the geothermal system exploded from pressure from below. A magma pool twenty miles by forty miles blew into the sky, greater than the supervolcano in Indonesia that, 75,000 years ago, had killed fifty percent of the human race. More than 250 cubic miles of magma erupted into the air. For hundreds of miles everything burned, and ash choked the air. Burning, suffocating night spread over the land.

The explosion triggered earthquakes in the San Andreas Fault and on into the Pacific Rim. As convergent tectonic plate boundaries lifted or subducted, more tsunamis were generated in the Pacific, and then in the Indian Ocean. Even in the deep sea life was affected as thermal vents opened—but not affected very much. Most of the ocean life was hardy, adapted, and innocent.

2035

Pete gaped at the Tesslie lying at Ravi's feet. Or . . . was it lying? The thing was the squarish metal can he remembered, without clear head or feet or *anything*. He said, inanely, "How do you know it isn't standing up instead of lying down?"

"Because I knocked it over!"

"Did it come out of the air in a bunch of golden sparks?"

"Yes!"

"It's not moving. How do you know it's still alive?"

"It won't be if you fucking laser it!"

Pete didn't move. Ravi leaped forward, grabbed Pete's arm with both hands, and fumbled with the buckle on the wrister.

Ideas surged and eddied in Pete's mind, even as he kept his eyes on the Tesslie. It lay still now, but Pete knew it wasn't helpless. It was watching. Without eyes or anything, it was still watching to see what he and Ravi would do. And it was not helpless. The Tesslies had built this whole Shell! They had made Grab machinery to send the Six back to get kids and stuff! They had come from someplace else through the sky! One of them was not going to let a human laser him open. Ravi was crazy.

But even more, Julie's words swirled in his brain. "Self-regulating planetary mechanisms." "Darwinian self-preservation." "Gaia." "We did it. We wrecked the Earth." And "We humans always blame the wrong ones."

Pete pushed Ravi away. Ravi said, "What the fuck? Give me the laser."

"I can't."

"You mean you can't laser the bastard? I can! Give it to me, you wimp!"

"I don't know . . . maybe the Tesslies . . . I don't know!" It was a cry of anguish. *We humans always blame the wrong ones.*

Ravi, much stronger than Pete, knocked him to the ground and sat on him. Pete stuck his arm with the wrister behind his back. Ravi easily got it out, but he couldn't unbuckle the wrister and also keep both Pete's arms pinned. Pete flailed, wrenching his bad shoulder, hitting Ravi's face, shoulder, anywhere he could reach. Ravi snarled at him, exposing the crooked stumps of the teeth that Pete had knocked out.

The Tesslie turned itself so it stood on a different side of its bucket-case, and waited quietly.

"Give it to me, you wimp!"

"No! McAllister said—"

"It took McAllister! It took them all, you fucking idiot! They're prisoners! That's why I—give it to me!" He smashed a fist into Pete's face.

"Prisoners?" He could barely get the word out for pain, even though he'd turned his head in time for Ravi's blow to hit him on the side of the jaw instead of on the mouth.

"Yes! The bastards took them all!"

"Petra?"

"Give it to me!"

"Took where?"

Ravi flipped Pete over and wrenched his arm behind his head. The pain was astonishing. Ravi got the wrister unbuckled, sprang off Pete, and aimed the laser at the Tesslie. Ravi fired.

Nothing happened.

Pete, gasping on the floor, saw the laser beam hit the Tesslie's bucket-case. The red beam vanished. The Tesslie stood stolid and silent.

Ravi gave a low moan. Pete got to his feet. His vision blurred during the process, but he did it. He faced the Tesslie.

"Don't hurt him, please. He doesn't know. He thinks *you* destroyed everything."

The Tesslie said and did nothing.

Pete blurted, "Did you?"

Nothing.

"Or was it really—" All of a sudden he couldn't remember the weird name Julie had said. Gouda? Or was that the cheese Caity had once brought back from a Grab? Guide-a? Gaga? Gina?

"—us?"

The Tesslie rose a few inches into the air and moved past Pete, floating on nothing at all toward the corridor. A long rope-like metal arm shot out of its tin can, startling Pete. The arm flicked toward him, then pointed to the corridor. The Tesslie floated on, and Pete followed.

"I'm not going!" Ravi shouted. "I'm not!"

"Wimp," Pete said.

In the corridor he picked up Alicia's baby-bucket. She had started to fuss, working up to a full wail. The Tesslie floated on, toward the maze at the far end and then through its small rooms. Pete trailed behind because he needed McAllister and anyway he couldn't think what else to do. What if they were all dead? What if he and this baby were going to their deaths?

That made no sense.

But, then, neither did anything else.

He heard Darlene first. She was singing at the top of her lungs, belting out a desperate stupid song in her scratchy voice: "Onward, Christian soldiers! Marching as to war . . ."

McAllister had told Darlene not to sing that song because wars were all over. Darlene had never listened. Now Pete could hear a baby wailing. Then McAllister's voice, sharp and uncharacteristically angry: "Darlene, stop that!"

Darlene didn't. The Tesslie and Pete rounded a corner in the maze and faced an open door.

They were all crowded into one small room. McAllister and Darlene and Eduardo stood in the front. Behind them huddled Caity, Paolo, Jenna, Terrell.

The Grab children were penned in the corner, the babies lying on the bare metal floor. Two more Tesslies guarded the doorway. Pete ran past them to McAllister. "Are you hurt? Is anybody hurt? What happened?"

Caity said, "They brought us here! Like . . . like gerbils!"

Where *were* the gerbils? Then Pete saw them, trying to get out of a large bucket. They couldn't. Tommy held the squirming Fuzz Ball. Tommy's eyes were big as bucket bottoms.

McAllister said, "You Grabbed another child? Where's Ravi?"

"He—"

The edges of the room began to shimmer with golden sparks.

McAllister ran forward, her big belly swaying. "No, please, not without Ravi—please!"

No response from any of the three Tesslies.

"Please! Listen, we're so grateful for all you've done but if you're really helping us again, we need everyone! We need Ravi!"

"That angel ain't going to listen to you!" Darlene said, with all the bitterness of her bitter self. "Them cherubim are flaming swords! Don't you know nothing?"

"Please," McAllister said to the Tesslie. And then, "Ravi is fertile!"

The golden sparks stopped.

"Ueeuuggthhhg," Caity said, which might have meant anything.

"Flaming swords!" Darlene shouted, and several children began to cry. McAllister whirled around and slapped Darlene. Pete gaped at McAllister; Darlene put her hand to her red cheek; Caity looked scared in a way that Caity never did; more children screamed.

A fourth Tesslie dragged Ravi into the room, its ropy metal arm wrapped around Ravi's neck. Released, Ravi stumbled forward as if pushed. He fell into Jenna, who also went down with a cry of pain. Jenna's fragile bones—

Pete had no time to pull Ravi off Jenna, or to pick up the crying Alicia, or to clutch at McAllister. The sparks enveloped all of them in a shower of gold, and then there was nothing.

It wasn't dark, and it wasn't light. It wasn't anything except cold. *I'm dead*, Pete thought, but of course he wasn't.

He lay on something hard in places and soft in others. The air felt warm and thick. Something gray shifted above him, far above him. Some noise, faint and rhythmic, sounded over and over in his ears. Something stirred behind him.

The cold retreated abruptly and Pete returned fully to himself. He sprawled Outside, beside Ravi and McAllister and, underneath Ravi, Jenna. He lay *Outside*, partly on rock and partly on some plant low and green and alive. Gray clouds blew overhead. Warm wind ruffled his hair. Dazed, he got to his feet, just as the others began to move.

They were all there, stirring on the ground. The Tesslies were gone. The Shell was gone. Piles of stuff lay on the ground in places where, he vaguely realized, it had all been lying when the Shell enclosed it: toys, blankets, food, tents, piles and piles of buckets. Pete turned around.

This was the view he'd had when he'd gone outside through the funeral slot and then had gone around to the far side of the Shell. He stood on a high ridge of black rock. Below him the land sloped down to the sea. The whole long slope was a mixture of bare rock, green plants, red flowery bushes. A brownish river gushed down the hillside. Beyond, along the shore, the land flattened and gold-and-green plants grew more thickly a long way out, until the water began.

It was quiet Eduardo who spoke first. "Regenerated from wind-blown seeds, maybe. From . . . wherever survived. And those lupines are nitrogen-fixers, enriching the soil."

McAllister said shakily, "There must still be ash in the air, it's so thick, but it's breathable . . . fresh water. . . ." She put her hands over her face, all at once reminding Pete of Julie, in the last-ever Grab.

He didn't want to remember Julie, not now. He wanted to shout, he wanted to cry, he wanted to run down the slope, he wanted to turn around and hit Ravi. He did none of those things. Instead he said, before he was going to do it, a single word. "Gaia."

McAllister jerked her hands away from her face and turned to him sharply. "What?"

"Gaia. It's a word the woman in the Grab said to me. Julie. Alicia's mother." He pointed at Alicia, who was now screaming with the full force of her lungs. Several other children also began to cry. Pete said some of

Julie's other words: "'Self-regulating mechanisms.' 'Planetary Darwinian self-preservation.' 'Cleansing.'"

Eduardo drew a sharp breath. Now the other children were shouting or screaming or whimpering. Fuzz Ball barked and raced around in circles. Darlene started to sing something about Earth abiding. Jenna began to cry. Into the din Pete said, "*We* did it. Not the Tesslies. Us. That's what Julie said."

McAllister didn't answer. She stared out at the water, which wasn't all that bright but still hurt Pete's eyes to look at. He could tell McAllister was thinking, but he couldn't tell what. All at once she turned to look at him, and in her dark eyes he saw something he couldn't name, except that he knew she felt it deeply.

Eduardo said to her, "The Gaia theory . . . It posited a self-regulating planet to keep conditions optimum for life. A planet that corrects any conditions that might threaten . . ." He didn't finish.

McAllister said to Pete, "Thank you."

"For what?"

"We'll do better this time."

"Better at what?" Why didn't he ever understand her?

But McAllister turned her beseeching look on Eduardo. "Our chances—"

"I don't know," he said quietly. "Maybe we can. If the seeds take. If any of those grasses are domesticable grains. If enough marine life survived. If we're in a tropical climate. I don't know. Maybe we can."

Can *what*? Before Pete could ask, McAllister's face changed and she was herself again, issuing orders. "Ravi, you and Terrell and Caity and Pete start lugging all that stuff down to that flat, sheltered place by the river—do you see where I mean? Bring the tents first, it's going to rain. And the food, all the food. Darlene, I'm sorry I slapped you. We can discuss it later. For now, try to get rations organized until Eduardo can determine which plants are edible. Eduardo, can you walk enough to find the best spot to put the soy into the ground? Paolo, you and Jenna are going to have to look after all the kids once we get them into tents—I'm sorry, but we can't spare anyone else. Tommy, you help move the food to under cover, and after that I'm going to want you to bring Eduardo some different plants from farther down the slope. Do you think you can do that?"

"Yes!" Tommy beamed at Pete. "You did make a big adventure!"

Pete clutched McAllister's arm. "But I have to finish telling you what Julie—"

"Later," McAllister said. "They'll be time. There will be lots of time."

Pete nodded. He raced with the others to where the Shell had been. The fertilizer machine was gone, the disinfectant and clean-water streams were gone, the Grab machinery was gone. Terrell and Pete each grabbed a rolled-up tent and staggered with it back down the slope. Darlene and Caity lugged buckets of soy stew from what had been the hot part of the farm. Over armfuls of canvas Pete spied Eduardo halfway down the incline to the sea, stooping to examine some low bushy plants.

"Abide with me," Darlene howled. "The darkness deepens—" until Caity told her to shut the fuck up.

For just a moment, Pete felt afraid. The Shell was all he'd ever known except for the Grabs, those terrifying jolts into places he didn't belong. The Shell had been ugly and boring, but it had been home. Sort of. A cage-sort-of-home. And now—

Had the Tesslies really captured the Survivors, caged them, and twenty years later let them out because the Tesslies wanted to *help*? And what were they, anyway? Robots, aliens, Darlene's angels, rescuers—maybe not even McAllister would ever know.

The moment of fear passed. The Tesslies were gone. This was now. He was here.

A bird swooped overhead, and on the wind came the sweet smell of warm rain.

NEBULA AWARD, BEST NOVEL

EXCERPT FROM *2312*

KIM STANLEY ROBINSON

Robinson's fiction has also won two Hugo Awards, the World Fantasy Award, the British Science Fiction Association's Award, and the John W. Campbell Memorial Award, and two other Nebula Awards. 2312 was published by Orbit Books.

PROLOGUE

The sun is always just about to rise. Mercury rotates so slowly that you can walk fast enough over its rocky surface to stay ahead of the dawn; and so many people do. Many have made this a way of life. They walk roughly westward, staying always ahead of the stupendous day. Some of them hurry from location to location, pausing to look in cracks they earlier inoculated with bioleaching metallophytes, quickly scraping free any accumulated residues of gold or tungsten or uranium. But most of them are out there to catch glimpses of the sun.

Mercury's ancient face is so battered and irregular that the planet's terminator, the zone of the breaking dawn, is a broad chiaroscuro of black and white—charcoal hollows pricked here and there by brilliant white high points, which grow and grow until all the land is as bright as molten glass, and the long day begun. This mixed zone of sun and shadow is often as much as thirty kilometers wide, even though on a level plain the horizon is only a few kilometers off. But so little of Mercury is level. All the old bangs are still there, and some long cliffs from when the planet first cooled and shrank. In a landscape so rumpled the light can suddenly jump the eastern horizon and leap west to strike some distant prominence. Everyone walking the land has to attend to this possibility, know when and where the longest sunreaches occur—and where they can run for shade, if they happen to be caught out.

Or if they stay on purpose. Because many of them pause in their walk-abouts on certain cliffs and crater rims, at places marked by stupas, cairns, petrogylphs, inuksuit, mirrors, walls, goldsworthies. The sunwalkers stand by these, facing east, waiting.

The horizon they watch is black space over black rock. The superthin neon-argon atmosphere, created by sunlight smashing rock, holds only the faintest pre-dawn glow. But the sunwalkers know the time, and so they wait and watch—until—a flick of orange fire dolphins over the horizon and their blood leaps inside them. More brief banners follow, flicking up, arcing in loops, breaking off and floating free in the sky. Star oh star, about to break on them! Already their faceplates have darkened and polarized to protect their eyes.

The orange banners diverge left and right from the point of first appear-ance, as if a fire set just over the horizon is spreading north and south. Then a paring of the photosphere, the actual surface of the sun, blinks and stays, spills slowly north and south. Depending on the filters deployed in one's faceplate, the star's actual surface can appear as anything from a blue maelstrom to an orange pulsing mass to a simple white circle. The spill to left and right keeps spreading, farther than seems possible, until it is very obvious one stands on a pebble next to a star.

Time to turn and run! But by the time some of the sunwalkers manage to jerk themselves free, they are stunned—trip and fall—get up and dash west, in a panic like no other.

Before that—one last look at sunrise on Mercury. In the ultraviolet it's a perpetual blue snarl of hot and hotter. With the disk of the photosphere blacked out, the fantastic dance of the corona becomes clearer, all the mag-netized arcs and short circuits, the masses of burning hydrogen pitched out at the night. Alternatively you can block the corona, and look only at the sun's photosphere, and even magnify your view of it, until the burning tops of the convection cells are revealed in their squiggling thousands, each a thunderhead of fire burning furiously, all together torching five million tons of hydrogen a second—at which rate the star will burn another four billion years. All these long spicules of flame dance in circular patterns around the little black pools that are the sunspots—shifting whirlpools in the storms of burning. Masses of spicules flow together like kelp beds threshed by a tide. There are non-biological explanations for all this convoluted motion—different gases moving at different speeds, magnetic fields fluxing constantly, shaping the endless whirlpools of fire—all mere physics, nothing more—but in fact it looks *alive*, more alive than many a living thing. Looking at it in the apocalypse of the Mercurial dawn, it's impossible to believe it's *not* alive. It roars in your ears, it *speaks* to you.

Most of the sunwalkers over time try all the various viewing filters, and then make choices to suit themselves. Particular filters or sequences of filters become forms of worship, rituals either personal or shared. It's very easy to get lost in these rituals; as the sunwalkers stand on their points and watch, it's not uncommon for devotees to become entranced by something in the sight, some pattern never seen before, something in the pulse and flow which snags the mind; suddenly the sizzle of the fiery cilia becomes audible, a turbulent roaring—that's your own blood, rushing through your ears, but in those moments it sounds just like the sun burning. And so people stay too long. Some have their retinas burned; some are blinded; others are killed outright, betrayed by an overwhelmed spacesuit. Some are cooked in groups of a dozen or more.

Do you imagine they must have been fools? Do you think you would never make such a mistake? Don't be so sure. Really you have no idea. It's like nothing you've ever seen. You may think you are inured, that nothing outside the mind can really interest you any more, as sophisticated and knowledgeable as you are. But you would be wrong. You are a creature of the sun. The beauty and terror of it seen from so close can empty any mind, thrust anyone into a trance. It's like seeing the face of God, some people say, and it is true that the sun powers all living creatures in the solar system, and in that sense *is* our god. The sight of it can strike thought clean out of your head. People seek it out precisely for that.

*   *   *

So there is reason to worry about Swan Er Hong, a person more inclined than most to try things just to see. She often goes sunwalking, and when she does she skirts the edge of safety, and sometimes stays too long in the light. The immense Jacob's ladders, the granulated pulsing, the spicules flowing . . . she has fallen in love with the sun. She worships it; she keeps a shrine to Sol Invictus in her room, performs the *pratahsamdhya* ceremony, the salute to the sun, every morning when she wakes in town. Much of her landscape and performance art is devoted to it, and these days she spends most of her time making goldsworthies and abramovics on the land and her body. So the sun is part of her art.

Now it is her solace too, for she is out there grieving. Now, if one were standing on the promenade topping the city Terminator's great Dawn Wall, one would spot her there to the south, out near the horizon. She needs to hurry. The city is gliding on its tracks across the bottom of a giant dimple between Hesiod and Kurasawa, and a flood of sunlight will soon pour far to the west. Swan needs to get into town before that happens, yet she still stands there. From the top of the Dawn Wall she looks like a silver toy. Her space-suit has a big round clear helmet. Her boots look big, and are black with dust. A little booted silver ant, standing there grieving when she should be hustling back to the boarding platform west of town. The other sunwalkers out there are already hustling back to town. Some pull little carts or wheeled travoix, hauling their supplies or even their sleeping companions. They've timed their returns closely, as the city is very predictable. It cannot deviate from its schedule; the heat of coming day expands the tracks, and the city's undercarriage is tightly sleeved over them; so sunlight drives the city west.

The returning sunwalkers crowd onto the loading platform as the city nears it. Some have been out for weeks, or even the months it would take to make a full circumambulation. When the city slides by, its lock doors will open and they will step right in.

That is soon to occur, and Swan should be there too. Yet still she stands on her promontory. More than once she has required retinal repair, and often she has been forced to run like a rabbit or die. Now it will have to happen again. She is directly south of the city, and fully lit by horizontal rays, like a silver flaw in one's vision. One can't help shouting at such rashness, useless though it is. Swan, you fool! Alex is dead—nothing to be done about it! Run for your life!

And then she does. Life over death—the urge to live—she turns and flies. Mercury's gravity, almost exactly the same as Mars', is often called the perfect g for speed, because people who are used to it can career across the land in giant leaps, flailing their arms for balance as they bound along. In just that way Swan leaps and flails—once catches a boot and falls flat on her face— jumps up and leaps forward again. She needs to get to the platform while the city is still next to it; the next platform is ten kilometers farther west.

She reaches the platform stairs, grabs the rail and vaults up, leaps from the far edge of the platform, forward and into the lock as it is halfway closed.

SWAN AND ALEX

Alex's memorial ceremony began as Swan was straggling up Terminator's great central staircase. The city's population had come out into the boulevards and plazas and were standing in silence. There were a lot of visitors in town as well; a conference had been about to begin, one that had been convened by Alex. She had welcomed them on Friday; now on the following Friday they were holding her funeral. A sudden collapse, and they hadn't been able to revive her. And so now the townspeople, the diplomat visitors: all Alex's people, all grieving.

Swan stopped halfway up the Dawn Wall, unable to go on. Below her rooftops, terrace patios, balconies. Lemon trees in giant ceramic pots. A curved slope like a little Marseilles, with white four-story apartment blocks, black iron-railed balconies, broad boulevards and narrow alleys, dropping to a promenade overlooking the park. All crowded with humanity, speciating right before her eyes, each face intensely itself, while also a type—Olmec spheroid, hatchet, shovel. On a railing stood three smalls, each about a meter tall, all dressed in black. Down at the foot of the stairs clustered the sun- walkers who had just arrived, looking burnt and dusty. The sight of them pierced Swan—even the sunwalkers had come in for this.

She turned on the stairs and descended again, wandered by herself. The moment she had heard the news she had dashed out of the city onto the land, driven by a need to be alone. Now she couldn't bear to be seen when Alex's ashes were scattered, and she didn't want to see Mqaret, Alex's partner, at that moment. Out into the park, therefore, to wander in the crowd. All of them standing still, looking up, looking distraught. Holding each other up. There were so many people who had relied on Alex. The Lion of Mercury, the heart of the city. The soul of the system. The one who helped and protected you.

Some people recognized Swan, but they left her alone; this was more moving to her than condolences would have been, and her face was wet with tears, she wiped her face with her fingers repeatedly. Then someone stopped her: "You are Swan Er Hong? Alex was your grandmother?"

"She was my everything." Swan turned and walked off. She thought the farm might be emptier, so she left the park and drifted through the trees forward. The city speakers were playing a funeral march. Under a bush a deer nuzzled fallen leaves.

She was not quite to the farm when the Great Gates of the Dawn Wall opened, and sunlight cut through the air under the dome, creating the usual horizontal pair of yellow translucent bars. She focused on the swirls within the bars, the talcum they tossed up there when they opened the gates, colored fines floating on updrafts and dispersing. Then a balloon rose from the high terraces under the wall, drifting west, the little basket swaying under it: Alex; how could it be. A surge of defiance in the music rumbled up out of the basses. When the balloon entered one of the yellow bars of light the basket blew apart in a poof, and Alex's ashes floated down and out of the light, into the air of the city, growing invisible as they descended, like a shower of virga in the desert. There was a roar from the park, the sound of applause. Briefly some young men somewhere chanted "A-lex! A-lex! A-lex!" The applause lasted for a couple of minutes, and arranged itself as a rhythmic beat that went on for a long time. People didn't want to give it up; somehow that would be the end, they would at that very moment lose her. Eventually they did give it up, and lived on into the post-Alex phase of their lives.

*   *   *

She needed to go up and join the rest of Alex's family. She groaned at the thought, wandered the farm. Finally she walked up the Great Staircase, stiffly, blindly, pausing once to say "No, no, no," for a time. But that was pointless. Suddenly she saw: anything she did now would be pointless. She wondered how long that would last—seemed like it could be forever, and she felt a bolt of fear. What would change to change it?

Eventually she pulled herself together and made her way up to the private memorial on the Dawn Wall. She had to greet all those who had been closest to Alex, and give Mqaret a brief rough hug, and withstand the look on his face. But she could see he was not home. This was not like him, but she could fully understand why he might depart. Indeed it was a relief to see it. When she considered how bad she felt, and then how much closer Mqaret had been to Alex than she had been, how much more of his time he spent with her—how long they had been partners—she couldn't imagine what it would feel like. Or maybe she could. So, now Mqaret stared at some other reality, from some other reality—as if extending a courtesy to her. So she could hug him, and promise to visit him later, and then go mingle with the others on the highest terrace of the Dawn Wall, and later make her way to a railing and look down at the city, and out its clear bubble to the black landscape outside it. They were rolling through the Kuiper quadrant, and she saw to the right Hiroshige Crater. Once long ago she had taken Alex out there to the apron of Hiroshige to help with one of her goldsworthies, a stone wave that referenced one of the Japanese artist's most famous images. Balancing the rock that would be the crest of the breaking wave had taken them a great number of unsuccessful efforts, and as so often with Alex, Swan had ended up laughing so hard her stomach hurt. Now she spotted the rock wave, still out there—it was just visible from the city. The rocks that had formed the crest of the wave were gone, however—knocked down by the vibration of the passing city, perhaps, or simply by the impact of sunlight. Or fallen at the news.

*   *   *

A few days later she visited Mqaret in his lab. He was one of the leading synthetic biologists in the system, and the lab was filled with machines, tanks, flasks, screens bursting with gnarled colorful diagrams—life in all its sprawling complexity, constructed base pair by base pair. In here they had started life from scratch, they had built many of the bacteria now transforming Venus, Titan, Triton—everywhere.

Now none of that mattered. Mqaret was in his office, sitting in his chair, staring through the wall at nothing.

He roused himself and looked up at her. "Oh Swan—good to see you. Thanks for coming by."

"That's all right. How are you doing?"

"Not so well. How about you?"

"Terrible," Swan confessed, feeling guilty; the last thing she wanted was to add to Mqaret's load somehow. But there was no point in lying at a time like this. And he merely nodded anyway, distracted by his own thoughts. He was just barely there, she saw. The cubes on his desk contained representations of proteins, the bright false colors tangled beyond all hope of untangling. He had been trying to work.

"It must be hard to work," she said.

"Yes, well."

After a blank silence, she said, "Do you know what happened to her?"

He shook his head quickly, as if this was an irrelevance. "She was a hundred and ninety-one."

"I know, but still. . . ."

"Still what? We break, Swan. Sooner or later, at some point we break."

"I just wondered why."

"No. There is no why."

"Or how, then. . . ."

He shook his head again. "It can be anything. In this case, an aneurysm in a crucial part of the brain. But there are so many ways. The amazing thing is that we stay alive in the first place."

Swan sat on the edge of the desk. "I know. But, so. . . . What will you do now?"

"Work."

"But you just said. . . ."

He glanced at her from out of his cave. "I didn't say it wasn't any use. That wouldn't be right. First of all, Alex and I had seventy years together. And we met when I was a hundred and thirty. So there's that. And then also, the work is interesting to me, just as a puzzle. It's a very big puzzle. Too big, in fact." And then he stopped and couldn't go on for a while. Swan put a hand to his shoulder. He put his face in his hands. Swan sat there beside him and kept her mouth shut. He rubbed his eyes hard, held her hand.

"There'll be no conquering death," he said at last. "It's too big. Too much the natural course of things. The second law of thermodynamics, basically. We can only hope to forestall it. Push it back. That should be enough. I don't know why it isn't."

"Because it only makes it worse!" Swan complained. "The longer you live, the worse it gets!"

He shook his head, wiped his eyes again. "I don't think that's right." He blew out a long breath. "It's always bad. It's the people still alive who feel it, though, and so. . . ." He shrugged. "I think what you're saying is that now it seems like some kind of mistake. Someone dies, we say why. Shouldn't there have been a way to stop it. And sometimes there is. But. . . ."

"It *is* some kind of mistake!" Swan declared, reaching out to hold his shoulder. "Reality made a mistake, and now you're fixing it!" She gestured at the screens and cubes. "Right?"

He laughed and cried at the same time. "Right!" he said, sniffing and wiping his face. "It's stupid. What hubris. I mean, fixing reality."

"But it's good," Swan said. "You know it is. It got you seventy years with Alex. And it passes the time."

"It's true." He heaved a big sigh, looked up at her. "But—things won't be the same without her."

Swan felt the desolation of this truth wash through her. Alex had been her friend, protector, teacher, step-grandmother, surrogate mother, all that—but also, a way to laugh. A source of joy. Now her absence created a cold feeling, a killer of emotions, leaving only the blankness that was desolation. Sheer dumb sentience. Here I am. This is reality. No one escapes it. Can't go on, must go on; they never got past that moment.

So on they went.

There was a knock at the lab's outer door. "Come in," Mqaret called a little sharply.

The door opened, and in the entry stood a small—very attractive in the way smalls often were—aged, slender, with a neat blond ponytail and a casual blue jacket—about waist high to Swan or Mqaret, and looking up at them like a langur or marmoset.

"Hello Jean," Mqaret said. "Swan, this is Jean Genette, from the asteroids, who was here as part of the conference. Jean was a close friend of Alex's, and is an investigator for the league out there, and as such has some questions for us. I said you might be dropping by."

The small nodded to Swan, hand on heart. "My most sincere condolences on your loss. I've come not only to say that, but to tell you that quite a few of us are worried, because Alex was central to some of our most important projects, and her death so unexpected. We want to make sure these projects go forward, and to be frank, some of us are anxious to be sure that her death was a matter of natural causes."

"I assured Jean that it was," Mqaret told Swan, seeing the look on her face.

Genette did not look completely convinced by this reassurance. "Did Alex ever mention anything to you concerning enemies, threats—danger of any kind?" the small asked Swan.

"No," Swan said, trying to remember. "She wasn't that kind of person. I mean, she was always very positive. Confident that things were going to work out."

"I know. It's so true. But that's why you might remember if she had ever said anything out of keeping with her usual optimism."

"No. I can't remember anything like that."

"Did she leave you any kind of will or trust? Or a message? Something to be opened in the event of her death?"

"No."

"We did have a trust," Mqaret said, shaking his head. "It doesn't have anything unusual in it."

"Would you mind if I had a look around her study?"

Alex had kept her study in a room at the far end of Mqaret's lab, and now Mqaret nodded and led the little inspector down the hall to it. Swan trailed behind them, surprised that Genette had known of Alex's study, surprised Mqaret would be so quick to show it; surprised and upset by this notion of enemies, of "natural causes" and its implied opposite. Alex's death, investigated by some kind of police person? She couldn't grasp it.

While she sat in the doorway trying to figure out what it could mean, trying to come to grips with it, Genette made a thorough search of Alex's office, opening drawers, downloading files, sweeping a fat wand over every surface and object. Mqaret watched it all impassively.

Finally the little inspector was done, and stood before Swan regarding her with a curious look. As Swan was sitting on the floor, they were at about eye level. The inspector appeared on the verge of another question, but in the end did not say it. Finally: "If you recall anything you think might help me, I would appreciate you telling me."

"Of course," Swan said uneasily.

The inspector then thanked them and left.

"What was that about?" Swan asked Mqaret.

"I don't know," Mqaret said. He too was upset, Swan saw. "I know that Alex had a hand in a lot of things. She's been one of the leaders in the Mondragon Accord from the beginning, and they have a lot of enemies out there. I know she's been worried about some system problems, but she didn't give me any details." He gestured at the lab. "She knew I wouldn't be that interested." A hard grimace. "That I had my own problems. We didn't talk about our work all that much."

"But—" Swan started, and didn't know how to go on. "I mean—enemies? Alex?"

Mqaret sighed. "I don't know. The stakes could be considered high, in some of these matters. There are forces opposed to the Mondragon, you know that."

"But still."

"I know." After a pause: "*Did* she leave you anything?"

"No! Why should she? I mean, she wasn't expecting to die."

"Few people are. But if she had concerns about secrecy, or the safety of certain information, I can see how she might think you would be a kind of refuge."

"What do you mean?"

"Well—couldn't she have put something into your qube without telling you?"

"No. Pauline is a closed system." Swan tapped behind her right ear. "I mostly keep her turned off these days. And Alex wouldn't do that anyway. She wouldn't talk to Pauline without asking me first, I'm sure of it."

Mqaret heaved another sigh. "Well, I don't know. She didn't leave me anything either, as far as I know. I mean—it would be like Alex to tuck something away without telling us. But nothing has popped up. So I just don't know."

Swan said, "So there wasn't anything unusual in the autopsy?"

"No!" Mqaret said; but he was thinking it over. "A cerebral aneurysm, probably congenital, burst and caused an interaparenchymal hemorrhage. It happens."

Swan said, "If someone had done something to—to cause a hemorrhage—would you necessarily be able to tell?"

Mqaret stared at her, frowning.

Then they heard another tap at the lab's outer door. They looked at each other, sharing a little frisson. Mqaret shrugged; he had not been expecting anyone.

"Come in!" he called again.

The door opened to reveal something like the opposite of Inspector Genette: a very big man. Prognathous, callipygous, steatopygous, exophthalmos—toad, newt, frog—even the very words were ugly. Briefly it occurred to Swan that onomatopeia might be more common than people recognized, their languages echoing the world like birdsong. Swan had a bit of lark in her brain. *Toad.* Once she had seen a toad in an amazonia, sitting at the edge of a pond, its warty wet skin all bronze and gold. She had liked the look of it.

"Ah," Mqaret said. "Wahram. Welcome to our lab. Swan, this is Fitz Wahram, from Titan. He was one of Alex's closest associates, and really one of her favorite people."

Swan, somewhat surprised that Alex could have such a person in her life and Swan never hear of it, frowned at the man.

Wahram dipped his head in a kind of autistic bow. He put his hand over his heart. "I am so sorry," he said. A froggy croak. "Alex meant a great deal to me, and to a lot of us. I loved her, and in our work together she was the crucial figure, the leader. I don't know how we will get along without her. When I think of how I feel, I can scarcely grasp how you must feel."

"Thank you," Mqaret said. So strange the words people said at these moments. Swan could not speak any of them.

A person Alex had liked. Swan tapped the skin behind her right ear, activating her qube, which she had turned off as a punishment. Now Pauline would fill her in on things, all by way of a quiet voice in Swan's right ear. Swan was very irritated with Pauline these days, but suddenly she wanted information.

Mqaret said, "So what will happen to the conference?"

"There is complete agreement to postpone it and reschedule. No one has the heart for it now. We will disperse and reconvene later, probably on Vesta."

Ah yes: without Alex, Mercury would no longer be a meeting place. Mqaret nodded at this, unsurprised. "So you will return to Saturn."

"Yes. But before I go, I am curious to know whether Alex left anything for me. Any information or data, in any form."

Mqaret and Swan shared a look. "No," they both said at once. Mqaret gestured: "We were just asked that by Inspector Genette."

"Ah." The toad person regarded them with a pop-eyed stare. Then one of Mqaret's assistants came into the room and asked for his help. Mqaret excused himself, and then Swan was alone with their visitor and his questions.

Very big, this toad person: big shoulders, big chest, big belly. Short legs. People were strange. Now he shook his head, and said in a deep gravelly voice—a beautiful voice, she had to admit—froggy, yes, but relaxed, deep, thick with timbre, something like a bassoon or a bass saxophone—"So sorry to bother you at a time like this. I wish we could have met under different circumstances. I am an admirer of your landscape installations. When I heard that you were related to Alex, I asked her if it might be possible to meet you. I wanted to say how much I like your piece at Rilke Crater. It's really very beautiful."

Swan was taken aback to hear this. At Rilke she had erected a circle of Göbekli T stones, which looked very contemporary even though they were based on something over ten thousand years old. "Thank you," she said. A cultured toad, it seemed. "Tell me, why did you think Alex might have left a message for you?"

"We were working together on a couple of things," he said evasively, his fixed gaze shifting away. He didn't want to discuss it, she saw. And yet he had come to ask about it. "And, well, she always spoke so highly of you. It was clear you two were close. So . . . she didn't like to put things in the cloud or in any digital form—really, to keep records of our activities in any media at all. She preferred word of mouth."

"I know," Swan said, feeling a stab. She could hear Alex say it: *We have to talk! It's a face world!* With her intense blue eyes, her laugh. All gone.

The big man saw the change in her and extended a hand. "I'm so sorry," he said again.

"I know," Swan said. Then: "Thank you."

She sat down in one of Mqaret's chairs and tried to think about something else.

After a while the big man said in a gentle rumble, "What will you do now?"

Swan shrugged. "I don't know. I suppose I'll go out back on the surface again. That's my place to . . . to pull myself together."

"Will you show it to me?"

"What?" Swan said.

"I would be very grateful if you were to take me out there. Maybe show me one of your installations. Or, if you don't mind—I noticed that the city is approaching Tintoretto Crater. My shuttle doesn't leave for a few days, and I would love to see the museum there. I have some questions that can't be resolved on Earth."

"Questions about Tintoretto?"

"Yes."

"Well. . . ." Swan hesitated, unsure what to say.

"It would be a way to pass the time," the man suggested.

"Yes." This was presumptuous enough to irritate her, but on the other hand, she had in fact been searching for something to distract her, something to do in the aftermath; and nothing had come to her. "Well, I suppose."

"Thank you very much."

LISTS (1)

Ibsen and Imhotep; Mahler, Matisse; Murasaki, Milton, Mark Twain;
Homer and Holbein, touching rims;
Ovid starring the rim of the much larger Pushkin;
Goya overlapping Sophocles.
Van Gogh touching Cervantes, next to Dickens. Stravinsky and Vyasa.
    Lysippus. Equiano, a west African slave writer, not located near the
    equator.
Chopin and Wagner right next to each other, equal size.
Chekhov and Michelangelo both double craters.
Shakespeare and Beethoven, giant basins.
Van Gogh a small ring between Cervantes and Bernini.
Al-Jahiz, Al-Akhtal. Aristoxenus, Asvaghosa. Kurosawa, Lu Hsun, Ma
    Chih-Yuan. Proust and Purcell. Thoreau and Li Po, Rumi and Shelley,
    Snorri and Pigalle. Valmiki, Whitman. Brueghel and Ives. Hawthorne
    and Melville.

It's said the naming committee of the International Astronomical Union got hilariously drunk one night at their annual meeting, took out a mosaic of the first photos of Mercury, recently received, and used it as a dartboard— calling out to each other the names of famous painters, sculptors, composers, writers—naming the darts—then throwing them at the map.

There is an escarpment named Pourquoi Pas.

TERMINATOR

Terminator rolls around Mercury just like its sunwalkers, moving at the speed of the planet's rotation, gliding over twenty gigantic elevated tracks, which together hold aloft and push west a town bigger than Venice. The twelve tracks run around Mercury like a narrow wedding band, keeping near the forty-fifth latitude south, but with wide detours to south and north to avoid the worst of the planet's long escarpments. The city moves at an average of five kilometers an hour. The sleeves on the underside of the city are fitted over the track at a tolerance so fine that the thermal expansion of the tracks' austenite stainless steel is always pushing the city west, onto the narrower tracks still in the shade. A little bit of resistance to this movement creates a great deal of the city's electricity.

From the top of the Dawn Wall, which is a silvery cliff forming the eastern edge of the city, one can see the whole town stretching out to the west, green under its clear dome. The city illuminates the dark landscape around it like a passing lamp; the illumination is very noticeable except at those time when high cliffs west of the city reflect horizontal sunlight back into town. Even these mere pinpricks of the dawn more than equal the artificial lights inside the dome. During these cliffblinks nothing has a shadow, space turns strange; then the mirrors are passed, that light fades. These shifts in illumination are a significant part of the sensation of movement one has in Terminator, for the glide over the tracks is very smooth. Changes in light, slight tilts in pitch, these make it seem as if the town were a ship, sailing over a black ocean with waves so large that when in their troughs the ship drops into the night, then on high points crests back into day.

The city sliding at its stately pace completes a revolution every 177 days. Round after round, nothing changing but the land itself; and the land only changes because the sunwalkers include landscape artists, who are out there polishing mirror cliffs, carving petroglyphs, erecting cairns and dolmens and inuksuit, and arranging blocks and lines of metal to expose to the melt of day. Thus Terminator's citizens continuously glide and walk over their world, remaking it day by day into something more expressive of their thoughts. All cities, and all their citizens, move in just such a way.

EXTRACTS (1)

Take an asteroid at least thirty kilometers on its long axis. Any type will do—solid rock, rock and ice, metallic, even iceballs, although each presents different problems.

Attach a self-replicating excavator assembly to one end of the asteroid, and with it hollow out your asteroid along its long axis. Leave the wall at least two kilometers thick at all points except for your entry hole. Assure the interior integrity of the wall by coating it with a dura of suitable strength.

As your assembly hollows the interior, be aware that ejection of the excavated material (best aimed toward a Lagrange salvage point, to collect the salvage fee) will represent your best chance to reposition your terrarium, if you want it in a different orbit. Store excess ejecta on the surface for later use.

When the interior is hollowed out, leaving an empty cylinder of at least five kilometers in diameter and ten kilometers long (but bigger is better!), your excavator assembly will return to the access hole and there reconfigure itself into your terrarium's propulsion unit. Depending on the mass of your new world, you may want to install a mass driver, an anti-matter "lightning push" engine, or an Orion pusher plate.

Beyond the forward end of the cylinder, on the bow of your new terrarium, attach a forward unit at the point of the long axis. Eventually your terrarium will be spinning at a rotational rate calculated to create the effect of gravity on the inner surface of the interior cylinder, so that when you are inside you will be pulled to the floor as if in a gravity field. This is the g equivalent, or gequivalent. The forward unit will then be connected to the bow of the terrarium by a geared axle, to allow the forward unit not to spin but instead to stay fixed. It will be nearly weightless in this bowsprit chamber, but many functions of the terrarium will go better without the spinning, including docking, viewing, navigating, etc.

It is possible to build an interior cylinder that spins freely inside an asteroid that does not spin—the so-called "prayer wheel" configuration—and this does give you both an interior with g effect and a non-spinning exterior, but it is expensive and finicky. Not recommended, though we have seen some good ones.

When stern and bow are properly installed and configured, and the asteroid is set spinning, the interior is ready to be terraformed.

Begin with a light dusting of heavy metals and rare earths, as specified for the biome you are trying to create. Be aware that no Terran biome ever began with the simple ingredients you will be starting with on an asteroid. Biospheres need their vitamins right from the start, so be sure to arrange for the importation of the mix that you want, usually including molybdenum, selenium, and phosphorus. These are often applied in "puff bombs" set off along the axis of the cylindrical space. Don't poison yourself when you do this!

After that, string the axis of the cylinder with your terrarium's sunline. This is a lighting element, on which the lit portion moves at whatever speed you choose. The lit portion of the sunline usually starts the day in the stern of the cylinder, after a suitable period of darkness (during which any streetlights overhead will serve as stars). The lit portion of the line, appropriately bright, then traverses the sunline from stern to bow (or east to west, as some describe it), taking usually the same time as a Terran day, as measured by the latitude of your biome on Earth. Seasons inside your terrarium will be rendered accordingly.

Now you can aerate the interior to the gas mix and pressure you desire, typically somewhere between 500 and 1100 millibars of pressure, in something like the Terran mix of gases, with perhaps a dash more oxygen, though the fire risk quickly rises there.

After that, you need biomass. Naturally you will have in your spice rack the complete genetic codes of all the creatures you intend to introduce into your biome. Generally you will either be recreating some Terran biome, or else mixing up something new, which hybrid biomes most people call "Ascensions," after Ascension Island on Earth, the site of the first such hybrid (started inadvertently by Darwin himself!) All the genomes for all the species of your particular biome will be available for print on demand, except for the bacteria involved, which are simply too numerous and too genetically labile to categorize. For them you will have to apply the appropriate inoculant, usually a muck or goo made of a few tons of the bacterial suite that you want.

Luckily bacteria grow very fast in an empty ecological niche, which is what you now have. To make it even more welcoming, scrape the interior wall of your cylinder, then crumble the rock of the scrapings finely, to a consistency ranging from large gravel to sand. Mixed with an edible aerogel, this then becomes the matrix for your soil. Put all of the ice gathered in your scraping aside, except for enough when melted to make your crumbled rock matrix moist. Then add your bacterial inoculant, and turn up the heat to around 300 K. The matrix will rise like yeasted dough as it becomes that most delicious and rare substance, soil. (Those wanting a fuller explanation of how to make soil are referred to my bestselling *All About Dirt*.)

With a soil base cooked up, your biome is well on its way. Succession regimes at this point will vary, depending on what you are looking for at climax. But it's true to say that a lot of terraria designers start out with a marsh of some kind, because it's the fastest way to bulk up your soil and your overall biomass. So if you are in a hurry to occupy, this is often a good way to start.

When you've got a warm marsh going, either fresh water or salt, you are already cooking good. Smells will rise in your cylinder, also hydrological problems. Fish, amphibian, animal, and bird populations can be introduced at this point, and should be if you want maximum biomass growth. But here you have to watch out for a potential danger: once you get your marsh going, you may fall in love with it. Fine for you, but it happens a bit too often. We have too many estuarine biomes now, and not enough of the other biomes we are hoping to cook out here.

So try to keep your distance at this point; keep a depopulate marsh, or stay away from it during this part of the process. Or join a trading scheme in which you trade asteroids when they are at the marsh point, so that you come into a new one wanting to change things, unattached to what's already there.

With the hefty biomass created by a marsh, you can then build up land using some of your excavated materials, saved on the surface of the asteroid for this moment. Hills and mountains look great and add texture, so be bold! This process will redirect your water into new hydrologies, and this is the best time to introduce new species, also to export species you no longer want, giving them to newer terraria that might need them.

Thus over time you can transform the interior of your terrarium to any of

NEBULA AWARDS SHOWCASE 2014

the 832 identified Terran biomes, or design an Ascension of your own making. (Be warned that many Ascensions fall as flat as bad soufflés. The keys to a successful Ascension are so many that I have had to pen another volume, *How To Mix and Match Biomes!* now available.)

Ultimately you will need to make many temperature, landscape, and species adjustments, to get to the kind of stable climax community you want. Any possible landscape is achievable; sometimes the results are simply stunning. Always the entire landscape will be curving up around you, rising on both sides and meeting overhead, so that the look of the land will envelope you like a work of art—a goldsworthy inscribed on the inside of a rock, like a geode or a Fabergé egg.

Obviously it is also possible to make interiors that are all liquid. Some of these aquaria or oceanaria include island archipelagoes; others are entirely water, even their walls, which are sometimes refrozen transparently so that in the end when you approach them they look like diamonds or water droplets floating in space. Some aquaria have no air space in their middles.

As for aviaries, every terrarium and most aquaria are also aviaries, stuffed with birds to their maximum carrying capacity. There are fifty billion birds on Earth, twenty billion on Mars; we in the terraria could outmatch them both combined.

Each terrarium functions as an island park for the animals inside it. Ascensions cause hybridization and ultimately new species. The more traditional biomes conserve species that on Earth are radically endangered or extinct in the wild. Some terraria even look like zoos; more are purely wilderness refugia; and most mix parkland and human spaces in patterned habitat corridors that maximize the life of the biome as a whole. As such these spaces are already crucial to humanity and the Earth. And there are also the heavily agricultural terraria, farmworlds devoted to producing what has become a very large percentage of the food feeding the people of Earth.

These facts are worth noting and enjoying. We cook up our little bubble worlds for our own pleasure, the way you would cook a meal, or build something, or grow a garden—but it's also a new thing in history, and the heart of the Accelerando. I can't recommend it too highly! The initial investment is non-trivial, but there are still many unclaimed asteroids out there.

"THE BOOKMAKING HABITS OF SELECT SPECIES"

KEN LIU

Ken Liu has won a Nebula Award, a World Fantasy Award, and two Hugos.

There is no definitive census of all the intelligent species in the universe. Not only are there perennial arguments about what qualifies as intelligence, but each moment and everywhere, civilizations rise and fall, much as the stars are born and die.

Time devours all.

Yet every species has its unique way of passing on its wisdom through the ages, its way of making thoughts visible, tangible, frozen for a moment like a bulwark against the irresistible tide of time.

Everyone makes books.

It is said by some that writing is just visible speech. But we know such views are parochial.

A musical people, the Allatians write by scratching their thin, hard proboscis across an impressionable surface, such as a metal tablet covered by a thin layer of wax or hardened clay. (Wealthy Allatians sometimes wear a nib made of precious metals on the tip of the nose.) The writer speaks his thoughts as he writes, causing the proboscis to vibrate up and down as it etches a groove in the surface.

To read a book inscribed this way, an Allatian places his nose into the groove and drags it through. The delicate proboscis vibrates in sympathy with the waveform of the groove, and a hollow chamber in the Allatian skull magnifies the sound. In this manner, the voice of the writer is re-created.

The Allatians believe that they have a writing system superior to all others. Unlike books written in alphabets, syllabaries, or logograms, an Allatian book captures not only words, but also the writer's tone, voice, inflection, emphasis, intonation, rhythm. It is simultaneously a score and recording. A speech sounds like a speech, a lament a lament, and a story re-creates perfectly the teller's breathless excitement. For the Allatians, reading is literally hearing the voice of the past.

But there is a cost to the beauty of the Allatian book. Because the act of reading requires physical contact with the soft, malleable surface, each time a text is read, it is also damaged and some aspects of the original irretrievably lost. Copies made of more durable materials inevitably fail to capture all the subtleties of the writer's voice, and are thus shunned.

In order to preserve their literary heritage, the Allatians have to lock away their most precious manuscripts in forbidding libraries where few are granted access. Ironically, the most important and beautiful works of Allatian writers are rarely read, but are known only through interpretations made by scribes who attempt to reconstruct the original in new books after hearing the source read at special ceremonies.

For the most influential works, hundreds, thousands of interpretations exist in circulation, and they, in turn, are interpreted and proliferate through new copies. The Allatian scholars spend much of their time debating the relative authority of competing versions, and inferring, based on the multiplicity of imperfect copies, the imagined voice of their antecedent, an ideal book uncorrupted by readers.

The Quatzoli do not believe that thinking and writing are different things at all.

They are a race of mechanical beings. It is not known if they began as mechanical creations of another (older) species, if they are shells hosting the souls of a once-organic race, or if they evolved on their own from inert matter.

A Quatzoli's body is made out of copper and shaped like an hourglass. Their planet, tracing out a complicated orbit between three stars, is subjected to immense tidal forces that churn and melt its metal core, radiating heat to the surface in the form of steamy geysers and lakes of lava. A Quatzoli ingests water into its bottom chamber a few times a day, where it slowly boils and turns into steam as the Quatzoli periodically dips itself into the bubbling lava lakes. The steam passes through a regulating valve—the narrow part of the hourglass—into the upper chamber, where it powers the various gears and levers that animate the mechanical creature.

At the end of the work cycle, the steam cools and condenses against the inner surface of the upper chamber. The droplets of water flow along grooves etched into the copper until they are collected into a steady stream, and this stream then passes through a porous stone rich in carbonate minerals before being disposed of outside the body.

This stone is the seat of the Quatzoli mind. The stone organ is filled with thousands, millions of intricate channels, forming a maze that divides the water into countless tiny, parallel flows that drip, trickle, wind around each other to represent simple values which, together, coalesce into streams of consciousness and emerge as currents of thought.

Over time, the pattern of water flowing through the stone changes. Older channels are worn down and disappear or become blocked and closed off—and so some memories are forgotten. New channels are created, connecting previously separated flows—an epiphany—and the departing water deposits new mineral growths at the far, youngest end of the stone, where the tentative, fragile miniature stalactites are the newest, freshest thoughts.

When a Quatzoli parent creates a child in the forge, its final act is to gift the child with a sliver of its own stone mind, a package of received wisdom and ready thoughts that allow the child to begin its life. As the child accumulates experiences, its stone brain grows around that core, becoming ever more intricate and elaborate, until it can, in turn, divide its mind for the use of its children.

And so the Quatzoli *are* themselves books. Each carries within its stone brain a written record of the accumulated wisdom of all its ancestors: the most durable thoughts that have survived millions of years of erosion. Each mind grows from a seed inherited through the millennia, and every thought leaves a mark that can be read and seen.

Some of the more violent races of the universe, such as the Hesperoe, once delighted in extracting and collecting the stone brains of the Quatzoli. Still displayed in their museums and libraries, the stones—often labeled simply "ancient books"—no longer mean much to most visitors.

Because they could separate thought from writing, the conquering races were able to leave a record that is free of blemishes and thoughts that would have made their descendants shudder.

But the stone brains remain in their glass cases, waiting for water to flow through the dry channels so that once again they can be read and live.

The Hesperoe once wrote with strings of symbols that represented sounds in their speech, but now no longer write at all.

They have always had a complicated relationship with writing, the Hesperoe. Their great philosophers distrusted writing. A book, they thought, was not a living mind yet pretended to be one. It gave sententious pronouncements, made moral judgments, described purported historical facts, or told exciting stories . . . yet it could not be interrogated like a real person, could not answer its critics or justify its accounts.

The Hesperoe wrote down their thoughts reluctantly, only when they could not trust the vagaries of memory. They far preferred to live with the transience of speech, oratory, debate.

At one time, the Hesperoe were a fierce and cruel people. As much as they delighted in debates, they loved even more the glories of war. Their philosophers justified their conquests and slaughter in the name of forward motion: war was the only way to animate the ideals embedded in the static text passed down through the ages, to ensure that they remained true, and to refine them for the future. An idea was worth keeping only if it led to victory.

When they finally discovered the secret of mind storage and mapping, the Hesperoe stopped writing altogether.

In the moments before the deaths of great kings, generals, philosophers, their minds are harvested from the failing bodies. The paths of every charged ion, every fleeting electron, every strange and charming quark, are captured and cast in crystalline matrices. These minds are frozen forever in that moment of separation from their owners.

At this point, the process of mapping begins. Carefully, meticulously, a team of master cartographers, assisted by numerous apprentices trace out each of the countless minuscule tributaries, impressions and hunches that commingle into the flow and ebb of thought, until they gather into the tidal forces, the ideas that made their originators so great.

Once the mapping is done, they begin the calculations to project the continuing trajectories of the traced out paths so as to simulate the next thought. The charting of the courses taken by the great, frozen minds into the vast, dark terra incognita of the future consumes the efforts of the most brilliant scholars of the Hesperoe. They devote the best years of their lives to it, and when they die, their minds, in turn, are charted indefinitely into the future as well.

In this way, the great minds of the Hesperoe do not die. To converse with them, the Hesperoe only have to find the answers on the mind maps. They thus no longer have a need for books as they used to make them—which were merely dead symbols—for the wisdom of the past is always with them, still thinking, still guiding, still exploring.

And as more and more of their time and resources are devoted to the simulation of ancient minds, the Hesperoe have also grown less warlike, much to the relief of their neighbors. Perhaps it is true that some books do have a civilizing influence.

The Tull-Toks read books they did not write.

They are creatures of energy. Ethereal, flickering patterns of shifting field potentials, the Tull-Toks are strung out among the stars like ghostly ribbons. When the starships of the other species pass through, the ships barely feel a gentle tug.

The Tull-Toks claim that everything in the universe can be read. Each star is a living text, where the massive convection currents of superheated gas tell an epic drama, with the starspots serving as punctuation, the coronal loops extended figures of speech, and the flares emphatic passages that ring true in the deep silence of cold space. Each planet contains a poem, written out in the bleak, jagged, staccato rhythm of bare rocky cores or the lyrical, lingering, rich rhymes—both masculine and feminine—of swirling gas giants. And then there are the planets with life, constructed like intricate jeweled clockwork, containing a multitude of self-referential literary devices that echo and re-echo without end.

But it is the event horizon around a black hole where the Tull-Toks claim the greatest books are to be found. When a Tull-Tok is tired of browsing through the endless universal library, she drifts toward a black hole. As she accelerates toward the point of no return, the streaming gamma rays and x-rays unveil more and more of the ultimate mystery for which all the other books are but glosses. The book reveals itself to be ever more complex, more nuanced, and just as she is about to be overwhelmed by the immensity of the book she is reading, she realizes with a start that time has slowed down to standstill, and she will have eternity to read it as she falls forever towards a center that she will never reach.

Finally, a book has triumphed over time.

Of course, no Tull-Tok has ever returned from such a journey, and many dismiss their discussion of reading black holes as pure myth. Indeed, many consider the Tull-Toks to be nothing more than illiterate frauds who rely on mysticism to disguise their ignorance.

Still, some continue to seek out the Tull-Toks as interpreters of the books of nature they claim to see all around us. The interpretations thus produced are numerous and conflicting, and lead to endless debates over the books' content and—especially—authorship.

In contrast to the Tull-Toks, who read books at the grandest scale, the Caru'ee are readers and writers of the minuscule.

Small in stature, the Caru'ee each measure no larger than the period at the end of this sentence. In their travels, they seek from others only to acquire books that have lost all meaning and could no longer be read by the descendants of the authors.

Due to their unimpressive size, few races perceive the Caru'ee as threats, and they are able to obtain what they want with little trouble. For instance, at the Caru'ee's request, the people of Earth gave them tablets and vases incised with Linear A, bundles of knotted strings called *quipu*s, as well as an assortment of ancient magnetic discs and cubes that they no longer knew how to decipher. The Hesperoe, after they had ceased their wars of conquest, gave the Caru'ee some ancient stones that they believed to be books looted from the Quatzoli. And even the reclusive Untou, who write with fragrances and flavors, allowed them to have some old bland books whose scents were too faint to be read.

The Caru'ee make no effort at deciphering their acquisitions. They seek only to use the old books, now devoid of meaning, as a blank space upon which to construct their sophisticated, baroque cities.

The incised lines on the vases and tablets were turned into thoroughfares whose walls were packed with honeycombed rooms that elaborate on the pre-existing outlines with fractal beauty. The fibers in the knotted ropes were teased apart, re-woven and re-tied at the microscopic level, until each original knot had been turned into a Byzantine complex of thousands of smaller knots, each a kiosk suitable for a Caru'ee merchant just starting out or a warren of rooms for a young Caru'ee family. The magnetic discs, on the other hand, were used as arenas of entertainment, where the young and adventurous careened across their surface during the day, delighting in the shifting push and pull of local magnetic potential. At night, the place was lit up by tiny lights that followed the flow of magnetic forces, and long-dead data illuminated the dance of thousands of young people searching for love, seeking to connect.

Yet it is not accurate to say that the Caru'ee do no interpretation at all. When members of the species that had given these artifacts to the Caru'ee come to visit, inevitably they feel a sense of familiarity with the Caru'ee's new construction.

For example, when representatives from Earth were given a tour of the Great Market built in a *quipu*, they observed—via the use of a microscope—bustling activity, thriving trade, and an incessant murmur of numbers, accounts, values, currency. One of the Earth representatives, a descendant of the people who had once knotted the string books, was astounded. Though he could not read them, he knew that the *quipu*s had been made to keep track of accounts and numbers, to tally up taxes and ledgers.

Or take the example of the Quatzoli, who found the Caru'ee repurposing one of the lost Quatzoli stone brains as a research complex. The tiny chambers and channels, where ancient, watery thoughts once flowed were now laboratories, libraries, teaching rooms, and lecture halls echoing with new ideas. The Quatzoli delegation had come to recover the mind of their ancestor, but left convinced that all was as it should be.

It is as if the Caru'ee were able to perceive an echo of the past, and unconsciously, as they built upon a palimpsest of books written long ago and long forgotten, chanced to stumble upon an essence of meaning that could not be lost, no matter how much time had passed.

They read without knowing they are reading.

Pockets of sentience glow in the cold, deep void of the universe like bubbles in a vast, dark sea. Tumbling, shifting, joining and breaking, they leave behind spiraling phosphorescent trails, each as unique as a signature, as they push and rise towards an unseen surface.

Everyone makes books.

ANDRE NORTON AWARD FOR YOUNG ADULT SCIENCE FICTION AND FANTASY

EXCERPT FROM *FAIR COIN*

E. C. MYERS

The Andre Norton Award for Young Adult Science Fiction and Fantasy is presented to the best young adult science fiction or fantasy book, in parallel with the annual Nebula Awards. Fair Coin was first published by Pyr Books.

Ephraim found his mother slumped over the kitchen table, her right hand curled around a half-empty bottle of vodka. A cigarette smoldered in the ashtray beside her; it had burned into a gray cylinder up to its lipstick-smeared filter. He ground the butt in the tray forcefully and waved wisps of smoke away from his face.

"I suppose this is *my* fault," he said to her still form. She'd drunk herself into a stupor, but she'd probably blame him for not rushing home from school to wake her for her late shift at the supermarket. He picked up the vodka bottle. Even if he woke her now, she wouldn't be in any condition for work. Besides, she was already an hour late.

"Mr. Slovsky's gonna dock your pay again," he muttered. Ephraim slipped the vodka out of her hand and took it to the sink. He filled a quarter of the bottle with tap water and swirled it around, diluting the alcohol. It stretched out the liquor supply; they already couldn't afford her two-bottle a week habit. Of course, it would be better for both of them if she didn't drink their money away at all. He screwed the cap on tight and thumped it onto the table where he'd found it. She didn't even stir.

"Mom?" Normally she'd be coming to by now, slurring incoherent curses while reaching for another drink. But there was no motion at all. Everything seemed to still around him, the sound of the humming refrigerator and the ceiling fan dropping away. Something was very wrong.

He touched her on the shoulder and leaned over her face to check her breathing.

"Mom."

There was something clutched in his mother's left hand. An amber pill bottle. A few purple capsules littered the scratched Formica around it. Ephraim's chest tightened as he realized that he'd never seen her take any kind of prescription medication.

"Mom!"

Ephraim shook her shoulders gently, then more roughly when she didn't respond. More of the candy-colored pills flew from the bottle and skittered across the table to the floor. The soft capsules popped under his sneakers as he stepped around her and took the bottle from her limp hand. The long, chemical name on the pharmacy label meant nothing to him.

Ephraim eased his mother to a sitting position. Her head lolled forward. "Mom." He patted her cheek gently. "Wake up. Wake up!" He felt her breath against the back of his hand—that was something, at least. "Please, wake up."

"Mmmm . . ." she murmured. Her head twitched.

"Mom!"

Her eyes fluttered open and she stared at him glassily. "Ephraim, where are you?"

"Right here, Mom. Look at me."

She blinked a couple of times, trying to focus on his face. "Honey?"

"Yes, it's me." She was really out of it. "What happened to you?"

She shook her head and tried to push him away. He held her shoulders tighter, worried that she would hurt herself. "No!" she said. "No!"

"What's wrong?"

She scrambled out of her chair and struggled when he tried to grab her arms. The chair fell between them and he bumped his hip painfully against the side of the kitchen table. She was stronger than she looked.

"You're dead!" She jerked away, more awake now. "Ephraim's gone!"

"Calm down, Mom. I'm right here."

"Ephraim's dead."

She sobbed.

"You just imagined it. Mom, look at me. Look at me! I'm fine."

She stumbled toward the stove and grabbed onto the side, then leaned over and retched. Clear liquid splashed onto the faded linoleum, along with some of the pills she had taken.

"Jeez!" he said. She wobbled, and he rushed over to catch her if she fell.

She collapsed to her knees, head bowed. She coughed a couple of times and stared down at her own mess. Finally she looked up, and this time he knew she recognized him. She was crying; eyeliner was smeared under her eyes like bruises. "Ephraim? But . . . I saw your body." A thin trail of saliva dangled from her chin.

"Do I look dead to you?" he snapped.

"A bus, it hit you, and—" She rubbed her face. "But you're here. You're alive? Are you really my Ephraim?"

"Why'd you do this, Mom?"

"You were so young." She closed her eyes. "My poor baby . . ."

"Mom, stay with me. You have to stay awake," Ephraim said.

"Stay . . ." she echoed.

"Mom!"

Her lips moved, murmuring something too low for him to hear. As he leaned closer to listen, she slumped back against the oven door and stopped moving.

Ephraim snatched the phone and dialed 911. While the line rang he lowered his mother gently down on the floor, using her purse as a pillow. His hands shook and hot tears blurred his vision.

A calm voice spoke from the phone. "911, what is your emergency?"

"My mother took some pills," he said.

If one more doctor or nurse came by to tell him he'd saved his mother's life, or tell him how lucky it was that he found her when he did, Ephraim thought *he* would be sick.

It was still sinking in, what his mother had done. What she had tried to do.

During the ambulance ride to Summerside General, she had drifted in and out of consciousness. Each time she awoke, she'd stared at him as though she couldn't believe he was there. She'd thought he was dead, she said.

He looked up and saw a nurse at the open door with curly brown hair and a kind smile. She seemed familiar, though he'd never met her before. The badge on her chest identified her as Julia Morales.

"Ephraim Scott?" She pronounced his name "Eff-ra-heem" with a rolling R, the way his dad did, instead of "Eff-rum," the way everyone else said it. He liked the exotic sound of her Spanish accent.

"Yes. How's my mother?" he said.

"She's still in Intensive Care, but resting comfortably. Thank God you found her when you did."

Ephraim winced.

Her expression softened and she sat down next to him, placing her hand on his arm. "Your mother will be okay now. Dr. Dixon doesn't think there'll be any permanent damage, but we have to hold her overnight." She frowned. "Possibly longer."

"Longer?"

"We can't send her home until we evaluate her. To make sure she won't try this again."

"It was an accident," he said. "She mixed up her medications. She had a little too much to drink, that's all."

"Sweetie—"

"She's never done this before. She didn't mean to!" The loudness of his voice in the small room shocked him into silence.

"Okay," the nurse said. "How are you doing?"

"How am *I*?"

"With all of this. It's a lot for someone your age. If you want to talk—"

"I'm just worried about her. So . . . What happens now?"

"A psychologist is going to talk to her. Try to understand what was going on when she—" She left the sentence hanging, her eyes darting heavenward.

He noticed a silver cross dangling from a slim chain around her neck. "Child Protective Services will want to talk to her too. And you," she said.

Ephraim clenched his jaw. "But she's fine normally, she really is." Aside from the alcoholism and depression.

"It's hospital policy."

Ephraim took a deep breath.

"She kept saying that I was . . . dead. Like she really believed it," he said.

Her hand jerked up then to the side in a quick motion, a bit like the blessing the priest gave at church, a cross drawn in the air.

"Someone made a terrible mistake," Mrs. Morales said.

"What do you mean?"

"We did have an accident victim earlier this afternoon. A boy, about your age and height, same hair color. His face was badly scraped, but honestly . . . I could see why someone might think he was you." She studied him carefully.

He tried to maintain a neutral expression, though his feelings were jumbled in a mixture of shock and anger. This was important, though—his mother wasn't crazy. She'd been fooled just like everyone else.

"He was hit by a bus?" Ephraim asked.

Mrs. Morales nodded, her lips pressed together. "Just outside the library. He was killed instantly, they said, a small blessing."

"So if you couldn't even identify him, how did my mother find out? Why didn't someone check with the school first? I was there all afternoon." Ephraim had stayed late, hoping for a chance to talk to Jena Kim, the hottest geek girl in his class, while his mother nearly killed herself.

"We had reason to think he was you. Your library card was in his wallet."

Ephraim's hand went to the bulge of his wallet in the right-hand pocket of his jeans. He'd used his card only the day before, and he remembered sliding it back into its usual place. Hadn't he?

"It was enough to make the identification, but we called in your mother to confirm it. I guess that poor kid must have picked it up somewhere. We all thought you were dead until you walked in here tonight." She pursed her lips. "On paper, you still are. I'd better fix that."

"Can I have my card back?"

"We gave all your—*his*—things to your mother when she came in." She shook her head. "I'm sorry your mother had to suffer through that. If one of my girls . . . Such a tragedy. Now we still have to find his family—" She stood up.

Ephraim leaned forward as she moved to the door. "Is the . . . uh, the body still here?"

She gave him a puzzled look. "You wouldn't want to see it." She paused in the doorway. "I'm off shift in an hour. Do you have anywhere to go? Anyone you can call?"

Ephraim didn't want to return to his apartment. He would have to wipe up his mother's vomit, crawl around and pick up every one of those purple pills from the kitchen floor.

"Not really. Can't I just stay here?" he asked.

"You've done enough for her tonight, no? We have a spare room. My oldest son is working at his university this summer."

Ephraim almost smiled at the thought of telling Nathan he'd slept at Mary and Shelley's house. But he wanted to be close to his mother in case she woke up. She might need reassurance that he was still all right. He should have been there for her today, and he wasn't going to risk leaving her alone while she still needed him.

"No thanks," he said. "I want to stay here."

"Then I'll ask the other nurses to let you know if anything changes. At least you won't miss anything important at school tomorrow."

Ephraim didn't need the reminder. He'd been dreading the last day of school more than anything—until he'd discovered his mother at the kitchen table.

Mrs. Morales left to finish her rounds and Ephraim sat still in the waiting room until his stomach gurgled loudly. He had missed dinner, of course. He didn't have much of an appetite, but felt he should eat something. The hospital cafeteria was closed now, but he'd seen a vending machine down the hall. Unfortunately he didn't have any money for it.

Ephraim picked up his mother's purse. He'd grabbed it when the paramedics came, in case they needed her ID or credit cards or something at the hospital. He looked for change, rifling through balled-up Kleenexes smeared with mascara, tubes of lipstick, and an empty two-ounce plastic bottle of rum. He threw the bottle across the room; it clattered hollowly behind a row of seats.

Shoved down to the bottom of the purse was a clear plastic bag with "Summerside General" printed on it. He fingered the wrapped contents and felt a prickle along the back of his neck. The bag contained a wallet, a key ring, a black digital watch, and a single quarter.

Ephraim dumped the bag out on the orange plastic seat beside him. He counted the keys on the ring. There were exactly five, matching the ones in his pocket: one for the lobby door, two for the apartment, one for the AV Club storage space at school, and a little circular key for a bicycle lock.

The watch was a cheap Casio like the one around his left wrist, but the plastic face was cracked. Faded pixels danced across the shattered LCD screen when he pressed his thumb against it.

He hesitated before prying open the Velcro of the gray canvas wallet. It felt comfortable in his hands, well-worn and familiar, just like his own. If he'd closed his eyes, he would have thought it was his. He flipped through a few pieces of paper that looked like foreign bills or Monopoly money in assorted colors, faded receipts, and business cards from comic book shops he'd never heard of. It also contained a membership card to a new video game store; a ticket stub from the multiplex cinema for something called *Neuromancer*; an expired coupon for a free ice cream; three fortune cookie fortunes; and, in the zipped inner pocket, a sealed condom.

Ephraim's library card was tucked into the plastic sleeve, exactly where he would have put it himself. He tugged out his own wallet—similar but made of black canvas—from his jeans and looked inside. The card wasn't there. He hurriedly checked through all the sleeves and compartments, but his library card was definitely missing. He'd lost it after all.

Ephraim let out a breath. His palms were cold with sweat. He had really worked himself up, had halfway expected to find another library card. But it was all just an amazing, terrible coincidence.

Just one item left in the bag. The quarter gave him a static shock when he pulled it out. It was one of those commemorative U.S. quarters: the back of it said "Puerto Rico 1998" at the top, with the mint date of 2008 at the bottom. The picture showed a little frog in front of an island with a palm tree.

He had a jar of those state and territory quarters back in his room, but he'd never come across one for Puerto Rico. They'd been released in limited quantities, making them rarer than the rest of the series. But the territory coins had all been minted in 2009, which meant this one could be a prototype that somehow had made it into circulation. Guiltily, he slipped it into his back pocket, reasoning that it was better off with someone who knew its value so it didn't end up in a parking meter or vending machine. He imagined if the hospital managed to contact the other boy's family, he could return it to them and explain why he'd held onto it.

Ephraim retrieved his library card, too, and dropped the rest of the things back into the plastic bag. He stuffed the bag back into his mom's purse and tucked it under his arm as he walked down the hall.

His mother only had a few dollars tucked into the plastic wrapping of a carton of cigarettes, so he picked out a bag of chips, Twinkies, and a can of soda. On his way back to the waiting room, he spotted someone rounding the corner ahead of him. It looked like Nathan.

"Nathan? Nathan, wait up!" Ephraim ran to the corner but his friend wasn't anywhere in sight. A nurse at the station looked up at Ephraim and frowned. "Sorry. Thought I saw someone I know," he said.

It couldn't have been Nathan anyway. Ephraim hadn't told him he was going to the hospital.

Maybe the stress was finally getting to him. Ephraim turned around and noticed a door near the corner. He wandered over and read the small sign mounted above it: MORGUE. That was where they had the body that supposedly looked like Ephraim. He actually reached for the handle before he stopped himself. He wasn't really going in there, was he? He glanced back at the nurse's station. She wasn't paying attention to him anymore.

It was probably locked anyway. But when he nudged it slightly, it opened. It would just take a second to slip through.

No, he wasn't going to sneak into a hospital morgue. As morbidly curious as he was, he couldn't see himself doing something like that. He pulled the door shut and went back to the waiting room. He dropped his mother's purse on the seat beside him with the chips and Twinkies.

Ephraim popped open the soda can, and it fizzed all over his right leg before he could move it to arm's length over the floor. He'd shaken it too much when he ran down the hall.

"Perfect," he muttered. The dark wet patch on his jeans quickly grew cold and sticky against his skin in the air conditioned room. At least that would keep him up for a while. He had a long night ahead of him.

The last day of school was just one long assembly where they handed out awards and gave drawn-out speeches. Ephraim had never had much school spirit. As soon as it was obvious there wouldn't be news about a local teen dying in an accident, he tuned out the rest of the announcements. He kept falling asleep and Nathan would jab him in the ribs to wake him up.

When Ephraim wasn't drifting off, his mind wandered. He pictured his mother unconscious in the kitchen. He wondered who had been killed by that bus; he could understand if the administration didn't want to make a statement before the student was identified, but it was strange that none of his classmates were gossiping about it either. *Someone* must have known the victim, even if he went to another school.

After the assembly, Ephraim and Nathan ran into Jena and the twins outside the physics classroom. The halls were emptying quickly.

"Hi, Ephraim," Jena said. The twins simply nodded. Few people could tell the willowy girls apart, so they were jointly called "Mary Shelley" most of the time, which didn't seem to faze them. They practically encouraged it, usually wearing matching outfits the way they had in junior high, though it was more sexy than cutesy now.

"Hey," Ephraim said. He swallowed, his mouth suddenly dry. "Congratulations on all your awards, Jena. I think you collected them all."

"All but one." She pointed at the rolled-up paper in his hand. "How much you want for it?"

Ephraim grinned.

The twin on Jena's right spoke. "Sorry to hear about your mother, Ephraim."

"Thanks," he said, worrying over how much they had been told. Wasn't there some kind of doctor-patient confidentiality?

The one on Jena's left nodded. "Our mother's dropping us at the train station on her way to work. I'm sure you could ride with her to the hospital if you're going back there for visiting hours."

"Um, yeah. That would be great." Ephraim still hadn't told Nathan about his mother. His friend was uncharacteristically silent, as if the conversation didn't register. He looked dazed and his hands were locked tightly around his camera. Ephraim knew what was affecting him: the identical brunettes had the best figures in school, and they weren't shy about flaunting them.

"Where are you guys going?" Ephraim asked.

"Dinner and dancing in the city," Jena said. "To celebrate."

"A girls' night out," Mary and Shelley said quickly.

"Will your mother be all right?" Jena asked.

"She's fine now." Ephraim was embarrassed, even as he was pleased at her show of concern. "No big deal."

"Oh! Before I forget," Jena said. "I have something for you."

"You do?" Ephraim's heart started pounding and he felt something quiver in his gut.

She rummaged in her bag then held out a white plastic card.

His library card.

He closed his hand over it, the hard edges pressing against his palm and fingers. Blood rushed in his ears.

"Where did you get this?" he asked.

"You left it at the circulation desk the other day. What's wrong?"

"Nothing. Thanks . . . I didn't know I'd lost it." He pulled out his wallet and snuck a glance at the one he'd recovered at the hospital. They were identical. He tucked the two of them inside together, then snapped his wallet shut and squeezed it tightly.

"I figured you'd need it, since I see you at the library a lot," Jena said. "I'll be working there again this summer, so I guess I'll run into you."

He nodded. Was that an invitation? Did she actually want to see him there or was she just being polite?

"Coming, Ephraim?" said the twin on Jena's right.

"I need to empty out my locker," he said. "Meet you outside?"

"Don't be long." The twins spoke in chorus. How did they do that?

"I'll be right out," he said.

The three girls split around Ephraim and Nathan as they passed, and then smoothly merged back into a row as they walked down the hall. Nathan turned and stared after them as they left, then he joined Ephraim at his locker.

"What was that about Madeline?" Nathan said.

Ephraim didn't know when it had started, but Nathan called Ephraim's mother by her first name. She actually enjoyed it.

"She's in the hospital. Nothing serious." He couldn't bear to go into the details right now.

"Shit, no wonder you're such a mess. Sorry to hear it. I'll drive you over there. I'd like to see her, too."

"No no, that's okay. Mrs. Morales is taking me, and I think my mom doesn't want a lot of attention at the moment. Thanks, though."

"Hey, I bet this'll take your mind off your troubles!" Nathan said. He showed Ephraim a picture of the three girls on his camera. They were cut off just below the shoulders and above their thighs.

"Your framing's off," Ephraim said.

"No, it isn't." Nathan grinned and pointed out Mary and Shelley's impressive cleavage in their blue summer dresses. "It's a shame Jena doesn't have much up there, but she isn't bad. Especially when she isn't wearing those frumpy shirts she usually has on."

Ephraim had to agree. It was nice to see Jena in a skirt. The growth spurt she'd had the summer before their freshman year of high school had distracted Ephraim into almost failing Algebra, the one class they'd shared that first semester. A lot of guys paid more attention to her that year, until she began covering herself up. Now they all wondered what she was hiding.

"She's hot the way she is," Ephraim said. "How did you sneak that picture anyway?" Ephraim was unable to tear his eyes from it.

"I turned off the shutter sound. But wait, there's more."

Nathan clicked over to the next picture, a shot of Mary, Shelley, and Jena from behind.

"Pervert," Ephraim said. "You should be ashamed of yourself. Make sure you e-mail me a copy of that as soon as you get home."

"I could charge for these!" Nathan leaned his wiry body against a locker and gazed blissfully at the camera screen. His long blond hair fell over his eyes. "Listen, when you get in their car, try to sit between them—"

"I'm not going to cop a feel. Their mother will be in the car." Not to mention Jena. He wondered if he could sit close to her, though he supposed he'd be forced to ride shotgun.

"That's what makes it extra naughty. They probably won't say anything in front of her. Come on, look at those calves!" Nathan exclaimed. Ephraim rolled his eyes.

When he opened his locker, a piece of paper fluttered out. He bent to retrieve it from the floor.

"Make a wish and flip the coin to make it come true," he read. It looked like Nathan's handwriting. "What the hell is that supposed to mean?" He tossed it to his friend.

Nathan read it. "Weird. I don't know."

"That isn't your handwriting?" Ephraim was sure of it.

"I did not leave a note in your locker. That's so elementary school." Nathan scrunched up his eyes as he looked at it again. "It does look like my hand-writing. A little. But I don't know what it's supposed to mean. What coin? It doesn't make any sense."

He handed the note back to Ephraim.

Ephraim stared at it. Could it be referring to the quarter he'd found last night? He hadn't even mentioned that to Nathan yet. This was as unsettling as the duplicate library card and the idea of another kid who looked like him. But what did it mean? And who had written the note?

He pulled the quarter from his back pocket and reread the note one more time.

"You're actually going to try it?" Nathan snorted.

Ephraim shrugged. "No harm in it." He held the coin flat on his palm and cleared his throat.

"I wish . . ." He glanced at Nathan. "I wish my mom wasn't in the hospital."
Nothing happened, of course.

"Flip it," Nathan said. "Like the note said."

"Never mind. This is silly," Ephraim said. He moved to put it back in his
pocket and felt a jolt in his palm, as if someone had stabbed it with a pin. He
dropped the coin, and it rolled away on the uneven gray tiles.

"Ow," he muttered.

"What happened?"

"It . . . *shocked* me," Ephraim said, glancing around. The coin had landed
under the locker across from him. He crouched and picked it up, shaking off
clumps of dust. It had come up heads. The metal felt hot for a second, but it
quickly cooled in his hand. His vision swam and he suddenly felt nauseous.
He clutched his stomach.

"Ephraim?" Nathan said. "What are you doing on the floor?"

He had to get to the bathroom. "I—" He wasn't going to make it.

Ephraim turned and stuck his head into his locker.

"Dude!" Nathan said. He moved to the other side of the hall while
Ephraim vomited.

Ephraim wiped his mouth with the back of his hand. "Sorry," he said. He
held his breath and closed the door of his locker, deciding he didn't really need
the papers and comic books that had accumulated at the bottom throughout
the year. He walked to the water fountain at the end of the hall to rinse out his
mouth. The water was warm and tasted metallic.

"Are you all right? The nurse might still be here," Nathan said.

"I feel fine now." It was as though nothing had happened. Ephraim stuffed the
quarter and the note in his pocket and grabbed his backpack. He suddenly realized how lucky he was. If that had happened while he'd been talking to Jena . . .

"But you just barfed in your locker. I mean, at least tell the janitor."
Nathan turned his camera so Ephraim could see the screen. It was a blurry
shot of Ephraim with his head tucked into his locker. It was enough to make
him feel queasy again. He pushed the camera away.

"I'm so glad I have you around to document my greatest moments,"
Ephraim said.

"The camera doesn't lie," Nathan said. "You really are that much of a tool. You sure you're okay?"

"Maybe I caught a bug at the hospital," Ephraim said. He'd been sitting there all night, after all. But who'd ever heard of a twenty-four-second stomach flu?

"When were you in the hospital?" Nathan asked.

"I just told you, my mom went in last night."

"Oh no!" Nathan's eyes widened. "Is it serious? How's Madeline?"

"Did we not just have this conversation?" Nathan must have been more distracted by the twins than he'd thought. "She'll recover. I'm catching a ride with Mary and Shelley to the hospital now," Ephraim said slowly. "Remember?"

Nathan seemed even more surprised by that. "You're kidding. I'd love to share a back seat with them. Man, I wish *my* mom were in the hospital."

"Careful what you wish for," Ephraim said.

Wait a minute. Wish?

He'd just made a wish that his mother wasn't in the hospital. Now Nathan didn't remember it . . .

"FIVE WAYS TO FALL IN LOVE ON PLANET PORCELAIN"

CAT RAMBO

This is Cat Rambo's first nomination for the Nebula Award; she has also been nominated for the World Fantasy Award.

Over the years, Tikka's job as a Minor Propagandist for the planet Porcelain's Bureau of Tourism had shaped her way of thinking. She dealt primarily in quintets of attractions, lists of five which were distributed through the Bureau's publications and information dollops: Five Major China Factories Where the Population of Porcelain Can Be Seen Being Created; Five Views of Porcelain's Clay Fields; Five Restaurants Serving Native Cuisine at Its Most Natural.

Today she was composing Five Signs of Spring in Eletak, her native city.

Here along the waterfront, she added chimmerees to her list as she watched the native creatures, cross between fish and flower, surface. Each chimmeree spreading its white petals as it rose, white clusters holding amber centers, tendrils of golden thread sending their scent into the air along with the most delicate whisper of sound, barely audible over the lapping of the water.

The urge towards love beat along every energy vein of her silica body, even down to her missing toes, but she resisted it. She would remain alone this spring, as she had every spring since she had made her vow and inscribed it in the notebook where she kept her personal lists, under "Life Resolutions," 4th under "Keep myself clean in thought and mind," "Devote myself to promoting Porcelain's tourism," and "Fall in love." The third item had been crossed off at the same time, in vehement black pen strokes.

Her first sign of spring had been the singing of the tree frogs, which had awoken her three nights ago, in the small hours when most of the citizens cracked, gave way to despair, and crumbled in the manner of the elderly.

She was afraid of cracking, examined herself with obsessive care in the sluice for any sign that her surface was giving in, allowing the forces of time to work at her. She'd lain awake in the darkness, checking her mind with the same care. Were there any sorrows, any passions that might lead her thoughts along the same groove till it gave, eroded into madness?

She knew of one, and she kept her thoughts away from it as though it were made of thorns. Pain surrounded its edges and she could not avoid brushing against them even as she avoided it, but she kept herself from touching its tender heart, when silica melted in emotion and loss. She clicked her eyelids shut and contemplated what the morning would bring: ablutions and prayers, and a walk to the stop where the balloon-tram would take her to work. The sides would be hung with flower-colored silks in honor of the season. That would be her second sign of spring.

At work, there was jostling going on over a corner, windowed office. A writer had given way to cracking, premature, as sometimes happened with those who lived carelessly. Tikka was keeping back; she liked to do her work outside, and didn't think herself enough in the offices to merit such a coveted space. Not that she would have been first in line for it; of the three Minor Propagandists, she was the most junior, with only six years to the others' respective ten and fifteen.

Attle met her with a list in hand.

"Not again," Tikka said. "I like doing my own, you know that."

Attle shrugged. She was tall and willowy to Tikka's squatter lines. "He says they're only suggestions."

Tikka took the list and studied it. "Suggestions that are heavily encouraged," she said. "If I don't take at least half of them, it'll affect my next review."

"No one really worries about reviews," Attle said. It was true; the small

Bureau's turnover rate was glacial. Like most government jobs, it was steady and guaranteed work in a place where poverty was rampant.

"I do," Tikka retorted. She was all too conscious that she didn't resemble most of the other citizens in the office. She had won her post through a scholarship, was one of the tokens allowed positions so they could be held up to the lesser advantaged as what they could be if they kept their mouths shut and worked hard.

More tourists meant more money for everyone, even if it did have to trickle through the layer of upper citizens at first. She didn't think many of the topics were designed to attract tourists.

"'Five spots celebrated in the works of the poet Xochiti'? Who reads him? We need things that tourists are looking for, new experiences and new trinkets to buy. Five places where they serve fin in the manner of the Brutists is not going to do it."

"He believes in niches," Attle murmured in habitual response.

"Some niches are so small that no tourist would fit in them!" Tikka waved Attle off when she would have spoken again. "I know, I know, it's none of your doing."

She went to her desk, situated in a paper-walled cubicle. The patterns were from several years ago; the department's budget had been shrinking of late and even the plants that hung here and there were desiccated but unreplaced, delicate arrangements of withered ferns draped with dust that no one wanted to touch, lest they be mistaken for a lower-class servitor of the kind the Bureau could no longer afford.

Her fingers danced across the transparent surface of her data-pad, which dimpled beneath her touch. She pulled up a master document and transferred the least objectionable of the Master Propagandist's "suggestions" into it, scoffing under her breath.

A clink of drummed fingers behind her snatched her attention. She turned so quickly she nearly collided with the author of the suggestions himself. "Sir!" She stepped back to a safer, more polite distance.

"Am I to believe you feel you have worthier candidates for your time than those I have advanced?" he said. Master Propagandist Blikik was made of smooth white clay, a material so fine that it gleamed under the office lights in a way Tikka's coarser, low-class surface could never match, even with disguising cosmetics. His colors would never fade, while hers would eventually succumb to the sun, give way to pale, unfashionable hues.

She dropped her gaze to the felted carpet beneath his feet. "No, sir."

He waited.

"I'm sorry, sir." She met his eyes. "I thought perhaps we might consider some alternative ways of attracting tourists."

Clatter of halted movement behind her as others stopped to listen. She could feel the shockwave reverberate through the office as whispers of her boldness were hissed to outliers who hadn't heard.

Blikik's robes, swirled with gold and crimson, a style as outdated as the cubicle walls, rustled as indignation drew him upwards, made him tower over Tikka.

"You will do as you are told," he barked, so crisp his teeth snapped together with an unpleasant, brittle sound. "You are not paid to think. If you wish to think, other accommodations can be made for your employment. Is that what you wish?"

"No, sir, not at all, sir," she rushed to supply into the shocked void his words had left.

He nodded once, turned on his heel, and walked away.

After she'd drafted a couple of lists, Tikka escaped outside to the terraced gardens overlooking the sound garden (one of Eletak's five most impressive sites). Its massive steel structures were strung with cabling and wire that sang whenever the wind stopped sweeping across the water and came to investigate the inland. Shapes huddled on the sculptures, the winged monkeys that made them their nesting grounds, where they raised their thumb-sized offspring and lived the lives of one of Eletak's five most distinctive native species.

The air smelled of monkey shit, which, combined with the unpleasant sensation of the vibrations from the sound garden, drove most visitors away. Rumor held that the sound garden could set off interior echoes that might leave someone dust on a pathway, but she had never believed it. Childhood prittle prattle, don't do this or that or you'll fall afoul of unseen forces. Meaningless superstition.

She leaned on the wooden railing, using her jacket to cushion her arms. The wires sang a song she'd heard years ago, *love love careless love.*

She could give way to it. She could go find a mate and the two of them could pose, take on the shape of love and freeze together in the most intimate contortion. She hated the helpless feeling afterward, where you were caught still mingled with the other person until the rigidity that came with orgasm, lasting hours, seeped away and you were your own unique person, rather than part of the larger construction, again.

How freakish, the ways of love on this planet, or anywhere else. The illusion that you had become something other than you were. The illusion that you could be something other than alone.

She would not succumb.

Love, love careless love, the wires complained. It was unseasonably cold. Two monkeys huddled together for warmth in a metal Y only a few feet down from her. Pathetic.

She would not love again.

Too many memories were in the way.

It had happened the second spring that she had been working for the Bureau. She had traveled a lot the first year, taking pictures and conducting interviews of tourists in various areas to find out what had brought them there. She had written a private list: Five Things Tourists Dislike about Porcelain.

The standoffish nature of its people.

The unabashed attitude of greed towards tourist money.

The slowness of the balloon transit center.

The number of political uprisings.

The number of native species prone to throwing shit at tourists.

The man had been trying to clean monkey shit off himself near the sound garden. She'd intervened, led him to a public sluice.

"No wonder all your people seem so clean," he'd said, washing himself off in the stream of heated water.

"Down here," she said. She didn't know why she said it. It was forbidden to speak to tourists with anything other than pleasantries. She'd had to go through weeks of training to do it.

"Other areas don't have these?" he said.

"Other areas don't have running water," she said. "Why waste technology on lesser clay?"

A monkey screamed behind him and he flinched. His eyes checked the badge on her chest. "You can deal with tourists, can't you? Not like most of these, forbidden to talk to us. Come and have lunch with me."

So few restaurants catered to both kinds, but she took him to a place near the Bureau, disks of aetheric energy which she slotted into her mouth, a salad for him, odd grainy lumps scattered through it.

Humans. The richest of all the multi-verse dwellers, at least many of their branches were. Was he from one? She rather thought so, given the cut of his clothing, the insouciant ease with which he leaned back to survey her and the restaurant. His was not a species accustomed to scraping or scrabbling.

He said, "I've never understood why more people don't come here. A world peopled by china figurines."

There were more interesting worlds in the multi-verse, she knew. Paper dolls, and talking purple griffons. Intelligent rainbows and everyone's favorite, the Chocolate Universe. She shrugged.

"I want you for my tour guide," he said, staring at her. "Can we do that?"

It was unorthodox. But he had unexpected pull. Blikik had been forced to allow it, although he heaped her with instructions and imprecations. Porcelain must preserve its public face for tourism, he had said. No talk of politics, no talk of clays or those who did not live in the cities.

She nodded until she thought her neck would give way from the motion.

Places to take tourists on Planet Porcelain:

A birthing factory, where the citizenry are mass produced. The list is short; tourists are only taken to the upper class factories, where citizens are made of the highest quality porcelain, rather than one of the more sordid working class manufactories.

The bridges of Etekeli, which run from building to building in a city more vertical than horizontal. There is a daring glee to the citizenry here; the ground is littered with the remains of those who came to this place, which has a suicide rate twenty times that of elsewhere on the planet.

The Dedicatorium.

The first sight of the Dedicatorium awed him. She understood how it must look: from afar a wall of thorny white. Then as one approached, it resolved itself into a pattern made of feet and hands, arms and legs.

"People leave these here?" he half-whispered, his voice roughened by the silence.

"They do it for several reasons," she told him. "Some in gratitude for some answered prayer. Others to leave a piece of themselves behind."

As they watched, a woman approached. She carried a bundle in her only hand. When she got close to the wall, she fumbled away the coverings to reveal the other hand. She searched along the wall until she found a place to fold it into a niche. It curled there, its fingers clustered as though to form a hollow where a secret might be whispered.

His face was flushed, but she could not read the emotion. "Your people can detach their own limbs?"

"It is easier to get someone else to do it," she said. "It is not without pain. The joints must be detached, and it usually breaks them to do so."

"I have seen no amputees on your streets," he said. His eyes searched the wall, taking in the delicate point of a toe, the rugged line of a calf's stilled muscles.

"It is an injury that often leads to cracking," she said. "Few survive unless they take great care of the point where the limb was severed."

"It's barbaric," he said, but she heard only love and appreciation in his voice.

"You spend too much time with him," Blikik complained.

She let his complaints wash over her like water, eroding irritation. Through his eyes, she was learning to craft lists tailored to humans, their petty desires for restrooms and food that tasted like the food they had at home. And their greed, which must be fed with lists of the cheapest markets, the most inexpensive hostelries, free performances.

Tourism had increased a very small percentage, but it was due to her efforts. She could not spend enough time with him. He was too full of valuable information, conversation, insight.

He was such good company, so interesting to listen to, so fascinating in his different viewpoint. She wrote lists specifically for him, five restaurants that served his favorite condiment, five places to view a sunset shaded with indigo and longing.

Five places to be alone with your native guide.

Ways to fall in love on Planet Porcelain:

Slowly, so slowly. At first just a hint of delight at his face when he heard the chimmeree singing.

Like a revelation, a book opening as he told stories of his childhood, life under a different sun, where different songs held sway. He never talked of taking her there, but she was content. This was his story now, its happy ending on Planet Porcelain.

Knowing that it was wrong, unheard of. And knowing that its forbidden nature gave it extra savor, gave it the allure of something that shouldn't be, overlying the touch of the exotic that it held for them both.

In snatches and glances, moments seized outside the monitors. In a corridor, his fingers touched hers, warm against cool, and she felt a liquid warmth pervading her brain until she could barely think. Apart from him, she dreamed of him, and totted up list after list of the things she loved: the hairs on the back of his wrists, the way his teeth fit into the gum, the shape of his ankle, the burr his voice took on when tired or irritated, the flush that mounted to his cheek when he felt aroused.

Verbally. Word after word, opening secrets. He asked her about coupling and she told him how it was, how the urge drove you together, touch and caress until the moment where you froze and fused, knowing yourself a single part of a larger thing. And how, afterwards, that feeling faded, until you could see the body that had been part of yours and think it something entirely different.

"Can we go to bed together, you think?" he asked her. At first she didn't understand what he meant. There was no reason they could not share a bed. But his words, the heat in his face, made her realize her mistake.

Could they? Lovemaking was mental as much as physical, she had always been told. As long as they took care, could they not touch each other to arousal and beyond?

She could find nothing about such moments in her research. Unthinkable that they could have invented a perversion new to the multi-verse. And yet perhaps they had.

He circled the topic, over and over. She could feel her resistance wearing away.

Wearing away.

It was the only flaw in their affair, his curiosity about her body. Everything else was so perfect.

Asked again. And again.

At some point she realized she would give in eventually. Her determination crumbled beneath that assault.

In his hotel room, she removed her clothes, let him stroke her.

"How would we do this, if we were the same?" he demanded.

"As we become aroused, our flesh softens," she said. "Can you feel how mine has changed?"

He touched it cautiously, as though afraid he might leave finger marks. "It's closer to my own now," he said.

"We soften and we come together, and merge," she said. "It is a very intimate and secret thing."

"And you harden again, together." His breath quickened as his fingers dragged across her skin.

"When the moment of the most pleasure comes and peaks, we harden," she said. "We become a single thing, melding where our skin touches."

"And you stay that way for hours?"

"Till the state gives way, and we can separate," she said. "Hours, yes."

"And you think I can bring you to the point where you come like that?" he asked.

Everyone made their own experiments in self-delight as a child. It was not the same, but it was similar, and hard to hide, although the motionless state was shorter. He could do that for her, at least.

She reached for him.

He entered her arms without hesitation.

He played with her as he would have a human woman, licking, spreading, opening. He did not penetrate her—they had both agreed it was too dangerous.

This was the only time most people could touch without fear of chipping, of breaking each other. Was that the draw he'd had for her all along, that she could touch him like that and know there was no danger of breaking him?

Her breath filled her, energy rushed along her like swallows fluttering in the wind, trying to break free of its grasp. Pleasure drowned her and she succumbed, feeling her flesh shudder and stiffen, frozen in the moment.

Where a Porcelain lover would have stayed with her, he drew away. She was aware of him circling her, his fingers straying over and over her surface.

Touching.

Testing.

He began with a toe. Pain surged through her as he broke it off. If she had been able to move, she would have screamed. As it was, all she could do was let it shine in her eyes. What sort of mistake was this? An accident, surely.

But then he began to detach the joints in her knee. He intended to take her foot. Anger and pain and agony surged through her and she fell unconscious, carrying with her the vision of him sitting on the side of the bed, examining the foot in his lap with an expression she'd never seen before on his face.

Tikka had never seen him again. She had never been able to guess if the moment had been there in his head all along or if the desire had seized him somewhere along the way, perhaps when she showed him the Dedicatorium.

In time, she did learn that the perversion was not new. In some channels, the severed limbs sold very well, particularly those unmarred in any other way.

She padded the stump with soft plastics, a cap that fit over the protrusion, the jagged bits of joint that had not fallen away. She limped, but not much, grown accustomed to the way she moved.

She paused to watch the sky. Clusters of limentia, like jellyfish floating on the wind, translucent tendrils tinting the light. They filled the air with their mating dance, drifted around her till she stood in the center of a candy-colored cloud. Love surrounded her in a web of tendrils, unthinking action and reaction that drove life, all life, even hers.

She made a mental note of their presence, of the way they shone in the sunlight, of the acrid smell of their lovemaking, filing details away with clinical precision.

They were only another sign of spring on Planet Porcelain.

ABOUT THE DAMON KNIGHT MEMORIAL GRAND MASTER AWARD

In addition to giving the Nebula Awards each year, SFWA also may present the Damon Knight Memorial Grand Master Award to a living author for a lifetime of achievement in science fiction and/or fantasy. In accordance with SFWA's bylaws, the president shall have the power, at his or her discretion, to call for the presentation of the Grand Master Award. Nominations for the Damon Knight Memorial Grand Master Award are solicited from the officers, with the advice of participating past presidents, who vote with the officers to determine the recipient.

There have been twenty-nine Grand Masters since the award was founded in 1975. Gene Wolfe is the most recent.

1975	Robert A. Heinlein (1907–1988)
1976	Jack Williamson (1908–2006)
1977	Clifford D. Simak (1904–1988)
1979	L. Sprague de Camp (1907–2000)
1981	Fritz Leiber (1910–1992)
1984	Andre Norton (1912–2005)
1986	Arthur C. Clarke (1917–2008)
1987	Isaac Asimov (1920–1992)
1988	Alfred Bester (1913–1987)
1989	Ray Bradbury (1920–2012)
1991	Lester del Rey (1915–1993)
1993	Frederik Pohl (1919–2013)
1995	Damon Knight (1922–2002)
1996	A. E. van Vogt (1912–2000)
1997	Jack Vance (1916–2013)
1998	Poul Anderson (1926–2001)

1999 Hal Clement (Harry Stubbs) (1922–2003)
2000 Brian W. Aldiss (1925–)
2001 Philip José Farmer (1918–2009)
2003 Ursula K. Le Guin (1929–)
2004 Robert Silverberg (1935–)
2005 Anne McCaffrey (1926–2011)
2006 Harlan Ellison (1934–)
2007 James Gunn (1923–)
2008 Michael Moorcock (1939–)
2009 Harry Harrison (1925–2012)
2010 Joe Haldeman (1943–)
2011 Connie Willis (1945–)
2012 Gene Wolfe (1931–)

"GENE WOLFE"

MICHAEL DIRDA

Many years ago, around 1980, I began to hear about an extraordinary writer named Gene Wolfe. I was then working as an editor at *The Washington Post Book World*, responsible for the literary side of things, and had just recently inaugurated a monthly science fiction and fantasy column. When the proofs of *The Shadow of the Torturer* landed on my desk, I sent it out for review to James Gunn, who was doing that month's round-up. A year or so later Thomas M. Disch wrote about *The Claw of the Conciliator*, followed by Peter Nicholls on *The Sword of the Lictor*. Both these were standalone reviews. When Wolfe reached the conclusion to *The Book of the New Sun* I persuaded my colleagues that John Clute's essay-review of *The Citadel of the Autarch* should be given the front page.

What's more, I decided that we needed a short interview with the author to accompany the jump of Clute's piece. So one morning I spent an hour or so talking to Wolfe on the phone, then produced the following profile. It's certainly dated now, but readers might enjoy this glimpse of Gene Wolfe when he was still a part-time writer and not yet, to use the Japanese term, a Living National Treasure.

Every morning between 5 and 5:30 Gene Wolfe sits down at one of his two IBM typewriters. Before he goes to bed that day he will have written five pages. "Usually it takes between an hour and a half and three hours," he explains over the phone, but sometimes he's still working at midnight.

In itself this may sound like a lot of work—even before you realize that Wolfe also puts in a full day as a senior editor at *Plant Engineering* magazine in Barrington, Illinois, a Chicago suburb. There he edits, buys some 25 free-lanced articles a year, and writes a major cover story every few months. "The latest," he says, "is the first in a series on industrial robots."

Such disciplined energy recalls that of the great but often slapdash Victorian novelists or of many writers of pulp science fiction. In fact, Wolfe is nothing if not an artist, a perfectionist. Every one of his carefully wrought stories and novels undergoes at least three drafts, occasionally as many as ten. "I write to please myself. I try to write what I myself think a good book, one that satisfies me. Until I mail a manuscript out I'm never sure that I'm through with it."

In *The Book of the New Sun* Wolfe has certainly written a book that many people will be satisfied with. "It's gotten a greater readership than I anticipated. And I'm happy about that." Wolfe is as modest as he is painstaking, for his four-part novel about the adventures of the torturer Severian on far-future Urth has been called "one of the two or three best-written books in the field of science fiction ever" and "a major landmark of contemporary American literature."

Born in 1931, Gene Wolfe grew up in Texas, where his father was a restaurateur and small businessman. After attending Texas A&M and dropping out because of poor grades, Wolfe found himself drafted into the Korean War. He served as a private, earning the Combat Infantry Badge. After the service, Wolfe returned to Texas A&M on the GI Bill, received a bachelor's degree in mechanical engineering, and soon married a childhood friend. While working in research and development for Procter & Gamble in Ohio, the young engineer thought he might write some stories.

"If you have a wife and four children, as I do, you tend to be scraping around for ways to make a bit of additional income. I started trying to write in late 1956 or early 1957, hoping to earn enough to buy some furniture—but it was about 1963 before I got anything published. Most of those early stories were pretty bad. I just hadn't learned how to write fiction. I had to start by trying to figure out which end of the fiddle you stick under your chin. And eventually how to play it." In 1967 Damon Knight—a mentor to many contemporary science fiction writers—published Wolfe's third story and the engineer realized with a sense of epiphany that he'd become a writer. "That's what I meant when I dedicated *The Fifth Head of Cerberus* to Damon in memory of when he grew me from a bean." Since then, Wolfe says quietly, "I've sold about a hundred stories." They range from technological science fiction to complex psychological studies, and include the comic, sentimental, and macabre.

"You don't in my experience have an idea for a story. You have several different ideas you are nurturing or trying to shove out of your consciousness. Eventually out of the crowd of a dozen or so perhaps three or four seem as though they might work together in one book. That's the way it was with *The Book of the New Sun*. I wanted to do the grave-robbing scene that kicks off *The Shadow of the Torturer*, that scene in the cemetery with the people pulling the corpse up out of the ground. I also wanted to do a book about a torturer, the kind who is running the dungeon in all those old cartoons, to put myself in his shoes. I enjoy writing about people who are generally considered bad guys. That is, I take heroes who are villains and try to show things from their standpoint." (One of Wolfe's best-known tales, included in his collection *The Island of Doctor Death and Other Stories and Other Stories*, carries the title "The Hero as Werewolf.")

As for the tetralogy's setting—a future earth, spinning beneath a red sun, mingling science, mystery, and the medieval—Wolfe says forthrightly, "I don't think there's any question that I've been influenced by Jack Vance." At the beginning of a collection of essays, *The Castle of the Otter*, Wolfe recalls that at one period in his life Vance's elegiac, marvel- filled novel *The Dying Earth* was for him "the finest book in the world."

Still, there are other influences. "A friend of mine told me that the tone of The Book of the New Sun reminded him of Robert Graves' *I, Claudius* and *Claudius the God*, and immediately I saw that he was right." Severian's voice—measured, serene, precise—contrasts with his story's complex twistings back and forth through memory and with the ornate, not quite familiar words of his society: cacogen, psychopomp, fricatrice, fuligin. None of these is made up.

"A lot of them I'd come across here or there, just noticed them. I went through lexicons, dictionaries, and whatnot, and traced down leads when I thought I needed an odd word. When I started the book I remembered Jim Blish"—one of science fiction's best writers and critics—"having said that on too many planets you find a rabbit and it's called a smeat. And it's obvious that the author is thinking of a rabbit—just as Lorne Greene on *Battlestar Galactica* used to think of a space ship as an aircraft carrier. You could tell. Anyway it occurred to me that earth really had enough odd words to describe odd things and I didn't have to make up any. As for the names, I largely looked for real names with sounds that seemed appropriate to a character I had in mind. Severian suggests both sever and severe."

Surprisingly, the now-pervasive religious theme developed later in the book's seven years' writing. "Sometimes you start with a small idea and it grows," remembers Wolfe. "I put religion into *The Book of the New Sun* because I tried to put it in just about everything I thought important in human life. You know the story about Leo Tolstoy the night after he sent the manuscript of *War and Peace* to his publisher? He is supposed to have sat up in bed, slapped himself on the forehead and said: 'My God, I forgot the yacht race.' I don't have a yacht race in *The Book of the New Sun*, but I tried to talk about children, war, love and death, God, heaven and hell and all these things that are really pivotal to the human condition. I would like to have put in a lot more that I couldn't manage. Music for instance."

The Book of the New Sun may not have music or a yacht race, but it seems to contain everything else: myths, folktales, poems, a miracle play, marching songs. Severian encounters figures from every class of society, including various partly human characters. At one time he journeys, unsuspectingly, with a robot, a giant, a bionic woman, a homunculus, and a revived corpse—all of whom readers come to care about deeply.

Such exuberant invention explains why Wolfe admits "my favorite author is Dickens. I also like Kipling. *Moby-Dick*. And Oscar Wilde's fairy tales—no pun intended. Once Damon Knight asked about writers or books that had influenced me and I said J. R. R. Tolkien, the much neglected G. K. Chesterton, and the standard handbook of mechanical engineering." Engineering? "I think engineers have a better feel than most writers for the difficulty of developing new machines, new devices, and for the rate of speed at which such technological advances occur."

Wolfe's attention to style, his employment of demanding formal structures—"I love obliquity"—and his psychological acumen also link him to some of the contemporary science fiction writers he most admires: Ursula K. Le Guin, Thomas M. Disch, R.A. Lafferty. All of them shuffle uneasily under the science fiction rubric.

"I don't hold much with categories, really," says Wolfe. "They're for publishers and booksellers. I simply try to write the best story I can. People who condemn a particular genre, whether science fiction or mysteries, really can't know what they're talking about. It's as though I were to say all movies are bad. . . . I know that science fiction is dismissed by a lot of people, but I don't believe its dismissed by very many readers."

At the moment Wolfe is hard at work as usual. "After I finished the first draft of *The Urth of the New Sun*, a kind of coda to Severian's story, it seemed a good time to work on a couple short stories that I'd promised people. That was what I was doing this morning. In fact, I was working on both of them."

Will there be any more novels about Severian's world after *The Urth of the New Sun*? "I don't know," answers Gene Wolfe, "but I suspect that will be it. I don't like to repeat myself."

That little profile/appreciation ran more than thirty years ago, and Wolfe has gone on to write about Long Suns and Short Suns, as well as amnesiac soldiers and wizard-knights and much else. There are scores of short stories as well, featuring dream detectives and toy theaters and automatons and fairy tales, including some, like "The Map" and "The Cat," set on Severian's Urth.

When I reviewed *The Knight* back in 2004 I stressed that Gene Wolfe "should enjoy the same rapt attention we afford to Thomas Pynchon, Toni Morrison and Cormac McCarthy." After all, he possesses comparable range, ambition and achievement, and his best books will last. That's not too shabby for a former engineer who—for good or ill—helped invent the machine that manufactures those utterly addictive Pringles potato chips.

"HOW TO READ GENE WOLFE"

NEIL GAIMAN

I wrote this in 2002, for the World Horror Convention, when Gene and I were guests of honor. The numbers have changed—you can add ten years to every date I mention in it—but my affection for, respect for, and love of Gene Wolfe, the man and his work, has only grown in that time. And the reading advice I give is as pertinent now as it was then. We in the strange half-worlds of science fiction and fantasy and horror and whatever the hell else it is that we do have always known how good Gene was and is. It is peculiarly satisfying to see it acknowledged by the wider world as well.

—Neil Gaiman, January 2012.

Look at Gene: a genial smile (the one they named for him), pixie-twinkle in his eyes, a reassuring moustache. Listen to that chuckle. Do not be lulled. He holds all the cards: he has five aces in his hand, and several more up his sleeve.

I once read him an account of a baffling murder, committed ninety years ago. "Oh," he said, "well, that's obvious," and proceeded off-handedly to offer a simple and likely explanation for both the murder and the clues the police were at a loss to explain. He has an engineer's mind that takes things apart to see how they work and then puts them back together.

I have known Gene for almost twenty years. (I was, I just realized, with a certain amount of alarm, only 22 when I first met Gene and Rosemary in Birmingham, England; I am 41 now.) Knowing Gene Wolfe has made the last twenty years better and richer and more interesting than they would have been otherwise.

Before I knew him, I thought of Gene Wolfe as a ferocious intellect, vast and cool and serious, who created books and stories that were of genre but never limited by it. An explorer, who set out for uncharted territory and brought back maps, and if he said Here There Be Dragons, by God, you knew that was where the dragons were.

And that is all true, of course. It may be more true than the embodied Wolfe I met twenty years ago, and have come to know, with enormous pleasure ever since: a man of politeness and kindness and knowledge; a lover of fine conversation, erudite and informative, blessed with a puckish sense of humor and an infectious chuckle.

I cannot tell you how to meet Gene Wolfe. I can, however, suggest a few ways to read his work. These are useful tips, like suggesting you take a blanket, a flashlight and some candy when planning to drive a long way in the cold, and should not be taken lightly. I hope they are of some use to you. There are nine of them. Nine is a very good number.

HOW TO READ GENE WOLFE

(1) Trust the text implicitly. The answers are in there.

(2) Do not trust the text farther than you can throw it, if that far. It's tricky and desperate stuff, and it may go off in your hand at any time.

(3) Reread. It's better the second time. It will be even better the third time. And anyway, the books will subtly reshape themselves while you are away from them. *Peace* really was a gentle Midwestern memoir the first time I read it. It only became a horror novel on the second or the third reading.

(4) There are wolves in there, prowling behind the words. Sometimes they come out in the pages. Sometimes they wait until you close the book. The musky wolf-smell can sometimes be masked by the aromatic scent of rosemary. Understand, these are not today-wolves, slinking greyly in packs through deserted places. These are the dire-wolves of old, huge and solitary wolves that could stand their ground against grizzlies.

(5) Reading Gene Wolfe is dangerous work. It's a knife-throwing act, and like all good knife-throwing acts, you may lose fingers, toes, earlobes or eyes in the process. Gene doesn't mind. Gene is throwing the knives.

(6) Make yourself comfortable. Pour a pot of tea. Hang up a Do Not Disturb sign. Start at Page One.

(7) There are two kinds of clever writer. The ones that point out how clever they are, and the ones who see no need to point out how clever they are. Gene Wolfe is of the second kind, and the intelligence is less important than the tale. He is not smart to make you feel stupid. He is smart to make you smart, as well.

(8) He was there. He saw it happen. He knows whose reflection they saw in the mirror that night.

(9) Be willing to learn.

DAMON KNIGHT MEMORIAL GRAND MASTER: GENE WOLFE

"CHRISTMAS INN"

Gene Wolfe has won four World Fantasy Awards, a British Science Fiction Association Award, a British Fantasy Award, a John W. Campbell Memorial Award, and two Nebulas. In 2007, he was inducted into the World Science Fiction Hall of Fame. He selected "Christmas Inn" to represent his work in this anthology. The novelette was first published as a stand-alone book by PS Publishing in 2006.

I'm June Christmas. My husband Julius and I own the Christmas Inn, an old hotel out in the country that we keep modernizing as we get the money. That Christmas, it didn't look like we were going to get any, just deeper in debt. I kept telling myself it was good, because of breakfast.

Felix is our cook and he handles lunch and dinner, usually without any help from me. But I do breakfast. When we have twenty or more guests, that's a buffet, with lots of scrambled eggs, bacon, and sausage. Milk and coffee, and hot water for tea. Cold cereal. Bread and bagels for toast. You know.

Before she was married, our daughter Mary would help. Then after the divorce, she helped again; but Mary had been taken from us a year ago. She was dead and gone, Julius said. Sometimes our son helped, mostly at the waffle iron. It's hard to get him to do much.

That Christmas, before the five of them came (the five who looked to all of us so much like four), it seemed the only breakfasts would be for Julius, Wyatt, and me.

Hi. My name's Wyatt Christmas. Go ahead and laugh. People call me Whitey, mostly. Mom calls me Darlin', like she can't think of my name. Dad calls me The Snide Brat. Or Pimples. I get that sometimes, too. You can call me anythin'. Don't matter to me.

It started a couple days before Christmas. We were snowed in, and I mean snowed in good. There wasn't one guest in the whole fuckin' place. I liked it 'cause there wasn't as much for me to do, only Dad kept pissin' and moanin' about no money comin' in.

As if much ever did.

He told me to get out there and shovel the drive, and he didn't give a damn whether it was snowin' or not, by God get out there and shovel. He's got a big, loud voice for such a little guy. So I got my coat and boots and the shovel, and out I went. With Dad yellin' at me, it took about fifteen minutes.

Was it snowin'? Jack, you never seen so much fuckin' snow in your life. It was snowin' so hard I was down off the porch and about to turn around and shovel the steps before it got through to me that there was a place in the drive that looked darker than it should have. Naturally, any dark was darker than it should've been. Everythin' else was blind white. So I went to see, wadin' through three feet of snow. That was my first big mistake.

It was a big SUV, just sittin' there. I've been tryin' to remember if there were tire tracks behind it. I don't think so, so either it had been there a while or somethin' else. I know what else, only I'm not goin' to say. You want to guess? Give it a shot.

I went up to the driver's side window and rapped it with the handle of my shovel, and said very polite, "Can I help you folks?" when he rolled it down. I'm the politest bastard you ever saw as long as there's a chance of a tip.

The big, square-faced guy behind the wheels said, "We are looking for Christmas."

"You're here," I told him. "Clean rooms and good food. Hikin', cross-country skiin', and huntin' and fishin' in season."

There was a dark lady in back that looked like she had a fever. She leaned up and touched my arm and said, "Have we come to the place? For Christmas?"

If I'd known what was comin', I'd have hit her with the shovel. But I said, "You bet. This's the Christmas Inn. We've got Christmas decorations and all sorts of stuff you can send for presents. We'll have carol singin' and games, and the biggest tree in the county." Dad couldn't have done it better.

"Dendrolatry?" That was the other woman, the big blonde.

I thought it sounded good, so I said, "Sure." Then I said, "If you folks'll just pull up another hundred feet, I can help you up the steps—they'll be slippery—and bring in your bags."

Even a big SUV ought to have trouble in three feet of snow, but that one didn't. It rolled right up to the front door, practically floatin' on the snow. I never did hear the engine start.

J. R. Christmas heard voices and the stamping of feet, and got behind the long desk between the fireplace and the grandfather clock as the doors opened.

Andril and Dondel came in shoulder to shoulder; Andril was tall and stooped, with burning eyes. Dondel was tall, too, but wide. Red-faced in the cold, a big man who looked as if he might have played football in college.

Erennide followed them, brushing snow from her green parka with rose-red gloves. (All four wore green parkas.) Erennide's face seemed all big blue eyes and plump pink cheeks. Golden hair strayed from under her knit cap.

After her, Nranda—smaller than Erennide, darker than Andril, and ready to solo on her first broom.

The child came last. No one paid much attention to the child.

Julius R. Christmas is my name. June and I own this place. We've owned and run it for eight years, and have felt, both of us, that it would eventually be a highly profitable operation, one that would make us rich. I don't for one moment doubt we're right, but we're right only if we can keep it. There's a mortgage, a big one. People say (correctly, I believe) that banks never foreclose at Christmas, biding their time until January. I don't know that I've ever dreaded anything quite as much as I dreaded January that day.

We're out-of-the-way, you see. To reach us, you exit the Interstate and drive a bit over three miles along back roads. Snow had made those roads almost impassible.

Let me be frank. There are a lot of lonely men and women at Christmas. Good people, many of them. They have no families, or their families are far away. Some are alienated by long-standing quarrels. I could give details; some confide in me, but it's better not to repeat those confidences. What are they to do for Christmas? Where can they go? Should they sit alone in some apartment, cut off from humanity, drinking and watching television? It's a recipe for suicide.

Our place offers a solution. They come by dozens, each alone in his or her car. They sit around the fires (we've seven fireplaces), drink hot buttered rum, and talk like old friends.

Which they soon are. Don't get me wrong. They're good people for the most part. Lonely women who never found a man, and lonely men who never found the right woman. In a day or two they're very good friends indeed. Let me put it like this. For eleven months of the year, we just get by. It's at Christmas each year that we start making real money.

That was how it'd been for the first seven. Not this one. The cancellations came in waves; when a wave slacked and I'd begun to think it was over, a new one began. It was the snowiest winter in the history of the state, the weathermen bleated, and more snow on the way.

I'd been counting on Christmas to bail us out, to let us make up all the past-due payments. Christmas had come, and there was nobody. We've forty-two rooms; not a one was reserved. Not even one.

So when Andril and Dondel came to the desk, I thought, "Thank God! This is two rooms anyway." I supposed they were married couples, you see.

Andril asked how much. He didn't have a good voice; it was thin and hard, an accountant's voice. I smiled and told him, "Only fifty dollars per night, sir, and that includes a good big breakfast."

Dondel produced his wallet and got out a fifty. "This is fifty dollars?"

"Certainly, sir, and it will cover your room for the first night." I reached for it.

He took it back, returned it to his wallet and counted five one-hundred dollar bills onto the desk. "This is ten times as much?" As soon as I'd heard him, I'd decided he was in sales. He had the big, hearty voice that tells the client, lunch is on me.

I said, "Yes, sir. It'll take care of your room for ten nights."

"We shall remain," he said, "until the morning after Christmas."

"In that case," I told him, "I'll owe you money when you leave, even if you and your wife eat all your meals with us and charge them."

The thin, dark one butted in. "For the room? How much?"

"Fifty dollars a night," I told him again, "but you needn't pay cash. We take credit cards."

Dondel pointed to the five bills on our registration desk. "Two rooms," he asked, "to the day after Christmas?"

I said yes, it would more than cover them both.

Dondel got out his wallet again and laid another five hundred on the desk. "Four rooms?"

That was when I realized that they were four singles carpooling, not two couples. I said, yes, of course, and got out four keys.

Dondel pulled five fifties from his wallet; he laid those on the desk, too. "Five rooms," he told me. I had no idea why four guests would need five rooms, but it was over twelve hundred dollars and we needed it badly. I took it, put it in the register under the tray, and gave him five keys.

When they had checked in, Wyatt offered to move their vehicle into the parking lot. Dondel said he would take care of it and went into the bar. He gave four keys to Nranda first, and asked her to see that Wyatt distributed the luggage correctly.

I was vacuuming the hall when they came, and I stopped to look. My first impression was that they were ghosts, which was what Julius said at the seance. You'll laugh, but was how I felt, just the same. He says I'm irrational. He laughs about it and is nice, but he believes I'm wrong. I feel I'm right. What we feel is what makes us do things, not what we think. It's what we feel that's true.

I see it again and again. Mary's with me often—her spirit, I mean. Dead and gone? I know that though Mary's dead, she's not gone. Julius thinks, so he thought we'd lost her. I feel and knew she was with us still.

Where was I?

I felt they were all spirits, then I saw the child. If they were spirits, what was the child? (I can't say *he* or *she* because I don't know. It was like seeing an old, cracked photo of a child, taken when all small children wore dresses. You don't know, unless you read the name.) I wondered whether Mary could see it, whether she knew.

When they'd gone, Julius said they'd want dinner. He wanted me in the kitchen, getting ready. I felt I could not cook well when I knew all the snow they'd tracked in—Wyatt, too—was melting into the carpet in the lobby. I swept out as much as I could while Julius built a fire in the bar.

I'm tellin' you, Jack, their luggage was everyplace in that SUV. In front, in back, behind the back seat, and tied to the roof. There were no names on the bags, and no initials. No company name on the SUV, either.

I carried everything upstairs and knocked on a door lookin' for help. It was the dark one. She pointed to a big hard-sided bag and said, "That is mine. Carry it into the room."

So I did, and she said, "You must open this for me."

"Guests usually do that for themselves," I told her. "I got to see about the rest."

"Open it!"

It wasn't locked, and her underwear was right on top. So I figured I could put an end to this quick. I picked up a lacy number and said she must look good in it.

"You wish to see?"

She was startin' to undress, and that's when I sat on the bed. I'm not goin' to tell everythin' we did—it was a lot—or everythin' we said. But when I couldn't anymore and she shoved me out, with me carryin' half my clothes and my hair a mess, I felt like shit. Those dumb fuckers at school say there's good sex and bad sex but even bad sex is pretty good. That wasn't how I felt. They never did it with Nranda.

Probably not with anybody.

*   *   *

Dondel, Andril, Nranda, and Erennide sat in the big dining room at a table for four, served by Wyatt, who answered their questions in a monotone and would meet no one's eyes. Dondel had roast beef, Andril chicken potpie, Nranda a vegetarian plate, and Erennide lasagna, at Dondel's suggestion. She and Dondel ate dessert—plum pudding and strawberry shortcake.

Dondel signed for all four; when Wyatt muttered that he could add a tip to the bill if he chose, he said, "Yes, I had forgotten. And carrying our sacks?" The tip was a hundred dollars.

I fixed all the food. We'd told Felix not come in (the same with both maids), because of the snow and the cancellations. I know all the cooking sounds hard, but it wasn't. Everything was frozen except for salads and desserts. I just put it in the microwave and unwrapped it afterward for Wyatt.

He was depressed. I don't like that, but I see a lot of it and I thought Julius had tied into him for something. I asked him to help with dishes afterward, so I could talk to him; but he just cleared and stacked for me. He didn't even scrape them like you have to for the dishwasher. He looked so blue I didn't have the heart to say anything.

Mary had won Julius from the beginning. Me, too. She was the daughter everybody wants, so clean and pretty and kind and even tempered. And smart! When she married that teacher, I knew she was making a mistake. I should've said so. It was the first big mistake she'd ever made, and she didn't know how to handle them. She divorced him, but . . .

Oh, I don't want to talk about it!

The child came in and asked for something, mostly by signs. I peeked out into the dining room, and there they were at a table for four. They didn't even have a place for the child.

I said, "Do you speak English?" The child shrugged and didn't want to look at me, just like Wyatt.

So I tried a cookie and glass of milk, then a bowl of strawberries, with milk and little sugar on them. "How old are you?" That got seven fingers held up, but when I said, "You don't look that old," the child only shrugged.

"Are you a boy or a girl?"

"Soon I must choose."

It was the most I had heard the child say, so I felt encouraged. I was a friend, and it saw I was. That was how I felt. Pretty soon it would be my friend, too. I said, "I'm June. What's your name?"

"Soon I must choose one."

"You get to choose?"

A tiny nod.

"What's your mommy's name?"

The child shrugged, and as soon as the strawberries were finished there was no child. I looked all around to see if it was hiding, but I couldn't find it.

We ate as a family when they'd gone. It means a lot to me, but Julius and Wyatt don't care.

Wyatt wanted his hundred dollars immediately, but his father refused to give it to him until Dondel had settled. "All right," Wyatt said. "I got somethin' real important, and I'm not goin' to tell you."

Almost nothing was said after that, until the desk phone rang.

When Julius was in the next room, June said, "What's your important news, Darling?"

"If I tell you, you'll tell him."

"I won't. That's a promise." June crossed her heart.

"No matter what it is?"

She nodded. "No matter what it is."

"Well, I wanted to take their SUV and park it. The big guy said he would, only he didn't. Only it's gone. It's not out front, and it's not in the lot."

"He parked it somewhere else," June said. "You can find it tomorrow, if you want to."

It was the big blonde. I was looking in the book—we're old-fashioned here—for her name while I was talking to her. I found her writing pretty easily, a big florid hand for a woman, and green ink. Big curves and curlicues I could no more read than Chinese. Her name's Erennide. I got it a lot later. Which was not until I had my coveralls and had found my tools. My coveralls are pretty warm. I ought to say that. So I took off my tie and the dress shirt I had been wearing, and my wool slacks.

I don't know what another woman would have called that lacy thing, but it looked like she'd been sewed into it. I said, "Have you gotten it to flush?"

She just smiled and shook her head. She'd the best smile I ever saw. I've never seen another like it. It made me feel we were kids, a boy and a girl, and we were into mischief. It was good mischief, and we'd never be caught.

I went into her bathroom and there was nothing in the toilet. I said, "You flushed it with water from the tap, I guess. I understand, believe me, and I wouldn't want to embarrass you."

That got the smile again. "Nor would I wish to embarrass you, my Jule. I have locked the door."

From here, I don't know what to say or what not to say. It was wrong and I knew it.

But every time I looked at her it seemed her breasts got bigger. I knew it couldn't be true, but that was how it seemed. Bigger breasts and a warmer smile. Every time I touched her, a little more of the lacy thing fell off.

Afterward, when we lay in bed panting and sweating, me on my back feeling wonderful and she on her side facing me, I could see each breast was bigger than her head. You'd think a woman with breasts like that and hips like hers would be thick at the waist.

That night when things had quieted down, I got a flashlight and went out lookin' for the SUV, mushin' through the snow like a fuckin' sled dog. There wasn't any. Not anyplace. When I got back inside and got my coat and sweater off, I went down to the kitchen, made coffee, and thought about it.

There was only one way it could've happened. There'd been somebody else in there with them. Somebody I'd never seen. When they got out and I got all the bags out, he'd driven it away. That was how it had to be.

Only how could there have been? I'd been all over it grabbin' their luggage. If there'd been somebody else in it, I'd have seen him for sure.

That reminded me of what my mom had said at dinner, about a little kid with them. I'd never seen any kid and neither had Dad, but he'd said they took five rooms. He thought they were expectin' somebody else.

So I went to the front desk and got the room numbers. Nranda was in two-twenty, at the top of the stairs. I knew because I'd been in there and I'd never forget it as long as I lived. There were names for the next three, and what looked like grown-up writin'. Two-twenty-four had a little wavy line where the name should've been.

I'm not supposed to have a master key, but I know where Dad keeps his. I went upstairs for a look at Two-twenty-four. The door wasn't locked, that was the first surprise. The lights didn't work. That was number two.

Okay, in a way they did. When I hit the switch, they came on dim and faded out. No power, right? Only the hall lights were fine. I still had my flashlight, so I looked around. It got dimmer and dimmer. The bed was made, and I couldn't see anybody.

"What is it?" That was a kid's voice. Score one for Mom.

I said, "I wanted to see if there was anybody in here. Your door wasn't locked."

He didn't say anythin'.

"Is everythin' okay? It seems like your lights don't work."

They came on as soon as I said that. There was nobody there. Nobody at all. I looked in the bathroom and under the bed. My flashlight was fine again. Our closets don't have doors anymore. If there'd been a kid in the closet, I'd have seen him. "If you'd like to move to another room or anythin', just let me know," I said.

He didn't answer, and by then I just wanted to split. The light went off as soon as I was out in the hall. I heard the switch click, but I never touched it. I thought of lockin' the door from outside, but I never even shut it. I heard it close when I was on the stairs.

That's it, only when I woke up next mornin' I kept hopin' it'd been a dream. I knew it hadn't been but kept tellin' myself it had.

"Your hair's wet," June Christmas told her husband.

"I showered up in her room," he said. "I had to. I was filthy."

"I'll have to wash your coveralls separately, I suppose."

"They're not so bad. I rinsed them in her tub before I put them back on."

Brenda and Gisele checked in the next day. Brenda had a jeep with big tires. That was kind of girl Brenda was. It had made it through the snow of the back roads. Brenda was small and energetic, like her jeep. Gisele was taller and wore her hair in two long braids; she was the kind of girl who is blond in the summer.

Dondel was in the lobby when they came in. Julius, who had been at the desk looking for his master key, had not known he was there until the doors opened, but there he was. "You are very brave," he told the girls. Then, "Let me take your coats." Brenda gave Gisele a look that said, *See? I told you there'd be guys here.*

Julius called, "Boy!" and Wyatt put on his coat and boots and went out for their luggage.

"If you have not eaten," Dondel was saying, "we would think it a privilege to buy your lunches."

Gisele looked around, and Brenda said pointedly, "We?" As soon as she spoke, Andril rose from a wing-back chair that had looked empty. He was younger and better-looking than Julius remembered. So was Dondel, for that matter.

Wyatt was busy, so I took their orders. The taller girl had our Christmas Inn sandwich, bacon, lettuce, tomato, and smoked turkey breast on a croissant. So did the dark handsome man. The smaller girl and the big man had the Cobb Salad. I think the girls must've asked the men what was good here; so those were what the men had told them. I'd brought menus but nobody looked at them.

"Have you been here before?"

Dondel shook his head. "We got here yesterday. Have you?"

"Brenda has."

Andril smiled at her. His smile was small and showed no teeth; but it was a good, warm smile anyway. "You must have liked it."

Brenda nodded. "It's okay. I didn't come last year because I had a steady and we went to his parents' for Christmas. I dumped him after that."

"There are two women with us," Dondel said. "You shall meet them. But—"

That was when June Christmas came to take their orders.

"Why not?" Brenda asked.

Andril smiled again. "Perhaps we know them too well."

Dondel laughed. "Or they know us too well."

Gisele whispered, "This is an old place. I feel it." She was talking to everyone and no one.

"Very old." Dondel nodded. "Old and full of ghosts."

Brenda said, "Don't tell me you've seen a ghost!"

"Then I will not." Dondel's smile was much larger than Andril's. "I sense them, as our lovely Gisele does."

Brenda turned to Gisele, grinning. "He's trying to get next to you."

Gisele blushed and studied the tablecloth.

Andril asked, "Would you like to see ghosts? Are you curious?"

Brenda seconded him. "Ghosts at Christmas are an old tradition. Remember Scrooge? Ghosts and ghost stories."

Dondel nodded. "You are quite correct. Furthermore, there are many ghosts in this house, ghosts Gisele senses."

"Fine! Tell us a ghost story."

"I cannot," he said. "I am no storyteller. But we have a lady with us who might show you several."

Gisele looked up. "A medium?"

"You, I believe, would call her a size six."

Not long after that, their food came.

The new guests had gone into the dining room with the men, and I knew June would be busy with them. My son would disappear so I couldn't put him to work; it was something I could count on. I went up to her room and tapped on the door.

She opened it, as lush and blond as ever. The lacy thing was gone, replaced by a dark green robe that didn't look exactly like terrycloth. "Again?" She was smiling. "So soon?"

I shouldn't have coughed, but I couldn't help it. I said, "I noticed you hadn't come down for lunch, and I wanted to tell you that you could have it brought to your room if you prefer. We don't have a room service menu, but I can tell you everything we have, if you're interested."

"This is very fine of you. I take it my telephone no longer operates?"

She was onto me, and I knew it. I said, "It does, I'm sure. Might I come in for a moment?"

She shut the door behind me and locked it, just like before.

I said, "There's no need for that, Miss . . . ?"

"We have been so close and you do not know, my Jule? I am Erennide. So you must speak of me." Here I got the smile. It was as good as ever. "When we are alone, you may speak endearments as you wish. Shall I take this off?"

All my willpower was needed to tell her to leave it on, but I did. "What we did was wrong." I know I sounded as if I were choking. "I want you to promise you won't tell my wife. That you won't tell anyone."

"She will leave you? I will tell no one."

"It isn't that. That would be what I deserve, and I wouldn't whine about it. But it would hurt her terribly, and I don't want her hurt."

That was when Erennide grabbed me and kissed me.

"You do not want me to go with you," Nranda said as she was strappin' on the skis I got her.

"You're a guest," I told her. "If you want to come, you can do it. What I want or don't want doesn't matter."

"I must come. Erennide is my friend. She will wish to know, to see many times what I will record for her. She would try, but she is too fat." Nranda laughed. It made me think of The Vampire Hour on TV. "Deep into your snow she sinks, Wyatt. We walk in these?"

"In here we do. You mustn't ever let them cross." I showed her how. "You push with the poles, okay? I'm out of here, and if you want to come you can. If you can't keep up, I'll wait. When you want to go back, I'll take you and see that you get back okay."

Her smile said I'm goin' to fix you. "Such devotion I never found in all my time!"

"Right." I was headin' out. I pretended to think she meant it.

"We will bite down this tree?" If I'd had any luck, she'd have fallen. She didn't.

"I got a hatchet in my backpack. We're not goin' to cut a real big one."

Outside, she was faster than I'd expected. It took her five minutes to catch on, and after that she kept up with no trouble. "Should I speed down hills on these? Strike hard a tree at the bottom?"

"There aren't any steep hills where we're goin', and the hills have trees all over them. What we're wearin' are cross-country skis. You could go down a mountain pretty fast on them, but it's not what they're for."

Could I have picked a closer tree? Shit, yes. But I wanted to wear her out, and Dad had jumped all over me for cuttin' a tree too close last year. I don't think we went five miles, but it must have been almost that. Then I saw a really pretty tree about eight feet high. That's perfect for us.

I got out my hatchet and cut it down while she waved a wand all around us. Catchin' pictures, she said. When she had enough, I got out my nylon rope. Tyin' it eight inches above the cut guaranteed it wouldn't slip off. "We've got to drag it back," I told her. "Both of us. I'd have done it alone if you hadn't come, but since you're here you might as well help. Grab hold and put your back into it."

I'd figured she'd give up after a hundred yards. It was more like a quarter mile. Then she said, "We cannot do this, my Wyatt. You have taken too big a one. I will go back for Dondel and Andril. Dondel's so strong! You must see him with no clothes."

That was supposed to hurt. I asked whether she could get back okay on her own. She pointed to our tracks and said she'd follow them. "Fine," I told her. "Just sit tight if somethin' goes wrong. I'll be along with the tree in an hour or so."

After that, I waited for her to get out of sight before I took out my block. It's a little plastic one like you'd use to pull up a small boat, but plenty big enough for that tree. I threaded my rope through it and tied it to a good big hemlock. There's a four-to-one ratio, and when I hauled her in that little tree just scooted along.

* * *

They set up the tree that afternoon and trimmed it that evening, while Erennide waved a wand of her own at globes of red and gold glass, Santas, gingerbread men, teddy bears, and tinsel icicles. Urged by Julius, Brenda, and Gisele, four of the five guests who had come in the black SUV learned and sang "Deck the Halls," "God Rest Ye," "Rudolf the Red-Nosed Reindeer," "Jingle Bells," and a dozen more. They played Scrabble, blind-man's-buff, and other games. Four of the five women wandered by purest accident beneath the mistletoe—each of them at least once, and Nranda three times.

And at last, when it seemed the rest had gone to bed, June got out the old wooden crib set her mother had given her when she was a child and set it up beneath the tree. Not the elephant, the camel, and the wise men—those would come later at Epiphany. But Mary and Joseph, the stable, the manger in which the blessed child would lie, the ox and ass, and the angels and shepherds.

When it was complete, she rose with a little hum of satisfaction and found Andril bending over it and her, his thin, handsome face rapt.

"What are they doing?" he whispered.

"Worshipping." The word stuck in her throat.

"The tree?"

She shook her head.

"The trough? The trough is empty."

"This is Christmas Eve," she explained. "Tomorrow I'll lay the child Jesus there and they'll be worshipping him. Until I do, there's nothing for them to worship."

"I see. . . ." From Andril's tone, it was clear that he did not.

"The star up there." She pointed. "The whole tree. It's for him, really. For God and God's son, who's God."

To her utter astonishment, Andril kissed her.

When they separated (after a kiss that seemed to her very long) and she had caught her breath, she said, "I'm not under the mistletoe."

Smiling, Andril told her, "My mistake."

*　　*　　*

The question isn't whether it was wrong. I know it was wrong. The question is how I feel about it, and why. Those are the things I have so much trouble grasping.

Something passed between my husband and the blonde. I know that. I know him and know when he's done something wrong. I saw the way she looked at him, and I knew.

I love him, and I've been faithful to him up until that night. He loved me, and I believe he was faithful to me. So is it her fault?

Yes, it is. So what? It's his fault, too. And it's my fault, and so what again? It doesn't matter whose fault it is. What matters is how she feels about it, and him. How he feels about it, and her. How I feel about it, and them.

How I feel about that night, and how Andril feels. Those feelings matter because they'll make us act the way we will.

I keep telling myself I would not have done what I did if Julius had not done what he did. That's a lie. I know it's a lie because it was never how I felt. I got up, and when I came back Andril was sitting on our bed, silent in his silky black pajamas. And Julius was still asleep.

That was when I saw the child again, standing in the lobby and staring at the tree—at all the lights. I didn't say anything, and neither did Andril. We just went up the stairs to his room holding hands. When we got there, I washed the creme off my face and took my hair out of the curlers.

Christmas is always a magical day, but that Christmas Day . . . Well, I'll never forget it. For one thing, my son was happy and smiling. It was the first time I'd seen him smile since he was a little fellow. For another, June was radiant. It had been years since I'd seen her so happy or looking so beautiful. As for me . . . Well, Santa and his elves would've been proud of me, I'm sure.

I can tell you what happened that day. I can't make you believe it or understand it, and I'm not sure I do either.

They came. Felix and Clemente were the first. Felix is our cook and Clemente's his helper, and they came on Clemente's snowmobile. I hadn't even known he owned one, but I was so happy to see them I hugged them both. June gave each of them a kiss. They presented us with their gifts, and we gave them the things we'd picked out and wrapped for them before the snow started, and introduced them to everybody: "Folks, these bold snowmobilers are our friends and employees Felix and Celemente. Boys, I want you to meet our lovely lady guests—Erennide, Nranda, Brenda, and Gisele. And these gentlemen are Dondel and Andril."

Then Dinah and Maria, the maids. To say nothing of Maria's boyfriend Maximo. With a name like *Maximo* he ought to be a little guy like me, but he's the size of a small truck. What's more he owns a great big truck, a rusty monster with big wheels and a real good diesel engine. More presents, more hugs and kisses, more introductions and Happy Holidays.

We'd almost got settled when we heard the bells, silvery bells a long way down road. A long way, but maybe (just maybe, we told each other) coming closer and closer. That's when Gisele started to sing; she isn't a pretty girl, but she has a lovely voice. After a minute or two, June joined in. Then Dinah and Brenda. Erennide and Nranda were next, and after that I started singing myself and lost track. Wyatt gave us a shaky tenor, and Maximo an earth-shaking bass with a strong Hispanic flavor.

> *"I heard the bells on Christmas Day*
> *Their old, familiar carols play,*
> *And wild and sweet the words repeat*
> *Of peace on earth, good will to men!"*

After that we sang "Jingle Bells."

And not longer after that, the sleigh came. It was an open one pulled by horses all right, just like you see on Christmas cards; but there were two horses, not just one. Two horses trotting along the tracks left by Maximo's big truck. It turned out the whole thing had been organized by Katie Bates, who's been here for Christmas every year for the past five. She'd found the sleigh at a riding stable in town and lined up seven others to chip in on the price.

There wasn't room for all of us in the sleigh, but we all took sleigh rides. I've forgotten just who was in my bunch, but I can swear to June, Wyatt, Maria, and Maximo. I think Nranda and Brenda were with us, too. The driver was a kid named Ron.

None of the sleigh people stayed overnight, but all of them ate with us and paid for their dinners. They chipped in and bought one for Ron, too, so that was nine for the Christmas Inn. The rest of us ate after they'd finished, and no charge for any of those. That's been my policy ever since we opened—employees eat free. I stretched a point and included Maximo as an employee even though he would have paid, and paid for Maria's dinner, too.

The sleigh people left at ten thirty or eleven, after a whole lot of good-byes and enough business at the bar to keep all three of us hopping.

And that's when we had the seance. It's where we had it, too.

"Spirits calling to spirits," J. R. Christmas said as they prepared.

Brenda giggled nervously.

Gisele told her, "The best ghost stories I've ever read were by M. R. James. He only wrote one a year, a story that he read to his family at Christmas."

"You do not fear the dead?" Nranda asked. "That is well, though some are dangerous."

She sat at a small table in the middle of the bar. They had moved the other tables to one side and stacked some of them. The curtains on all three windows had been drawn wide and the shades pulled up. Every window looked out at the snow and the freezing night, out at the dark and the countless stars.

"Those who wish to remain must form a circle," Nranda announced. "Those who wish to go must go at once and shut the door. Do not look in until we have finished." She pointed first to J. R. Christmas, then to her right. "You. Here I wish you."

He moved his chair to the place she had indicated.

"You do not leave, my Wyatt. Remain."

"You said those who wanted to go—"

"Not you." Nranda shook her head. "You are to assist me. The rest, I do not care."

Grumbling, Wyatt sat on her left.

"Next to my Wyatt's father, Erennide," ordered Nranda. "Next to Erennide, the big man. Next to the big man, you I will have."

Maximo and Maria took their seats.

"We shall have Dondel next. After him, the girl with braids."

Gisele said, "I'm not sure I'm going to stay."

Dondel said, "You will have my protection," and she settled into her chair.

"Andril beside her. The mother of Wyatt must sit beside him."

They complied and Nranda pointed to Wyatt. "You must put a chair there, and we must find another man. We have a woman over still."

"Me," Brenda said, "and I'm not leaving. I'm paying for my room just like you are."

Nranda turned to Wyatt. "You see? Had you gone, so much the worse. What more men have we?"

J. R. Christmas put in, "Our cook and his helper. They left with Dinah. I'd take Felix, if it were up to me."

Wyatt brought him and dialed down the lights.

"You may join hands if you wish. It does not matter. Minds, you must join. Each is to touch the mind to the left."

What a fuckin' farce, I thought. Only then I felt her thoughts coming in through the right side of my head. It was like we were some kind of twins, only I'd never known about it. What she was tellin' me mainly was how to touch Ms. Pepper. So I did, and it felt good. I told her what Nranda had told me, and I said, "You and me, anytime. I can't promise you'll like it, but I'll try. Hard."

It felt better than I'd ever have imagined when Felix touched me. I'd always known he was a good man, cheerful and hard-working, a man who cared about what he did and had his own quiet pride. I'd liked him, and never known that he liked me, and respected me, too. He told me how to touch Andril. That was what I thought, anyway, but when I tried, it wasn't Andril.

It was the child, small and pure. Simple as water and as deep as the sea.

Not good or bad, because the child didn't know those things, didn't know what they were and had never done anything because it was a good thing. Or because it was a bad thing, either.

"I love you," I thought. "I'll take care of you. Don't worry."

I was still trying to figure out how you were supposed to hold minds instead of hands, when Erennide's snuggled up against mine. It was a little bit apologetic and a little bit passionate. Most of all, it was friendly. She kept saying over and over that she was my friend whether I was her friend or not.

After a second or two of that, I wanted say, "I'm your friend, Erennide. I always will be, but I don't deserve a friend like you."

The problem was that it wasn't Erennide's mind my thoughts were going into. It was Nranda's, and that was when I found out about her and my son. I was glad then that June was not sitting where I was.

There was a little table in front of Nranda. I don't think I said that. It was one of ours, draped in a white tablecloth from the dining room, a table just big enough for two people with drinks. There were twelve of us in the circle, so you can see that our circle was a lot bigger than the table. The middle had been empty, but all of a sudden, right after I got through learning about Nranda and my son, there were people in there and a funny kind of light. It didn't come down from the ceiling or up from the floor. It was as if every person had swallowed a light bulb, and the light was shining through them.

"Don't let it burn," a man said to me. "Don't let it burn, don't ever let it burn." The third time he said it, I realized that he was talking about our place, about the Christmas Inn. I wanted to say I wouldn't, but I kept thinking that he was dead, I was trying to talk to a dead man, and I couldn't open my mouth.

One was talking to Maximo. I heard him say something in Spanish. I didn't understand it, but I saw Maximo's face. There were others, but I don't want to talk about them. One may have been Gisele's mother. Something like that.

What I want to talk about is my grandsons, Adam and Mark, because they were there, too. I waved to them—waved hard. Adam didn't see me, or perhaps he didn't want to. I was pretty strict with them when they were here with Mary. He went over to the other side of the circle, and I thought at first he was going to see Grandma June.

He wasn't. There was another kid there, one I hadn't seen before, sitting between June and Andril. They came together, and after that they were gone. I guess I took my eyes off them for a moment to look at Mark. When I looked back, it was like neither had ever been there.

Mark came straight over to me. He said, "I'm dead, Grandpa. Our plane came down in the water and I got my hand back, but I'm dead. Can you help us?"

I said, "I can't, sport. I wish I could. But pretty soon I'll be dead myself. Then we can be dead together."

Then my Mary said, "Hi, Pops." I'd loved Mary since she was a baby, and I'd never heard that deep, deep sorrow in her voice before.

"Mary! Mary . . ." I wanted to jump up and throw my arms around her, but I knew I couldn't do it. It would have been like hugging a soap bubble. As soon as I tried, she'd be gone and I'd never see her again. I put my head in my hands, and I cried.

I felt her touch and looked up. I don't know what I expected to see, but it certainly wasn't what I saw. What I saw was the most beautiful sunlit landscape imaginable: gentle hills with blue mountains in the distance, lovely green grass with wildflowers all through it and groves of trees here and there. Two brooks trickling down through the hills, one making a waterfall that might have been four feet high.

Mary was standing next to me with her hand on my shoulder, and I said, "Where are we, Mary? What is this? How did we get here."

"People who know about it call it Summerland, Pops. Have you ever heard that name?" She smiled as she spoke, and her sadness was mixed with something like joy.

I shook my head. "It looks like Heaven."

"It isn't. They say Heaven's a lot different and much nicer. What you see is our place of punishment."

"Hell?" I felt as if my legs had been kicked from under me. "You can't mean that."

"No," Mary said, and her voice made me want to cry all over again. "Hell's different again, and much worse. This is . . . Temporary. No one stays. Heaven is forever, and so is Hell. But until things change, this is where I am."

"You live here?"

"I don't live at all, Pops. I'm dead, remember? I know what they told you, and in a way it was true. This is where I stay when I'm not on earth with you and Mom. I can't rest where you two are, you see, so I get awfully, awfully tired, and then I come back here. It's not cruel, my punishment. Nobody's rubbing his hands and laughing. It's just the bad part of what I've earned, and I have to work my way through it. You see how beautiful this is? It's what Earth could be like. It's what we were supposed to do, and didn't. Its beauty hurts us because it reminds us, each and every time we see it, of the place we were given and what we did with it. It cheers, too, when things seem worst. We were thought worthy of this, and we could be worthy of it yet. Look at me, Pops? Look me in the face, please, just for a minute."

I did, and she said, "We're out of the game here. That's the thing that hurts the most. We can rest here, like I told you. We can rest and drink in all the beauty, but we can't eat and we can't sleep. We can't work or play, or even make friends. We can go back to your earth, sometimes. We can go back, but we can't do any of those things there, either. Or even rest. I told you that."

I nodded.

"We're out of it. I played soccer in high school and college. Do you remember how you and Mom tried to get to all my games?"

I did. I said, "Soccer and softball, Mary. You were good at both of them, the best one on the team."

That got me a sad little smile. "Thanks, pops. You were my biggest fan. I was yours, too. A bigger fan even than Mom. Did you know it?"

I had, and I nodded.

"You used to say that business was a game, too, and you were right as usual. Here we're out of all the games. Am I making this clear? All of life is a big, big game made up of little ones, with everybody playing on the same team. Do I have to explain who and what you living people are playing against? Entropy is one of their names."

I thought I knew, and I said so.

"That's good, because I'm getting terribly tired. We're out of it here. We can rest because we're on the sidelines, and the sidelines are where you get to rest. Only when you're on the sidelines you want to get back into the game. Eventually some of us move up. It means our playing careers are over. We're no longer undergrads and can't stay on the team, although we can cheer for it and do certain other things to help. The rest of us will go back after we've worked through all the things we have to work through. When we've remembered and repented all of the opportunities we missed, all the times we hotdogged when we should have helped a teammate. We go back and begin a fresh life fresh, somewhere else, some other time."

I wasn't sure I understood everything, but I nodded.

"You've been here before, Pops. Probably three or four times. Try hard and keep trying, and you may remember it. Or not."

"I'll try," I said, "and I'll keep on praying for you."

"That's good. I'm almost through. But I want you to remember this, too, and I know you will. I loved you as much as any girl's ever loved her father. So long, Pops."

She took her hand off my shoulder, and I realized that my face was in my hands and wet all over with tears.

Nranda smiled at the stunned expressions around the circle. The clock in the lobby was striking; she waited until the echoes of the twelfth and final stroke had died before she spoke. "The time is midnight. Your great holiday is done. You have entertained us with your farce for several days. We thought it only just that we should entertain you with our tragedy before we go. Both plays are at the final line. We, the players, drop our masks. We, the audience, rise and think of home and friends once more."

"There is an epilogue," Andril said.

"Exactly. You are eight, an inconvenient number. Therefore, those who have seen least are to go. Big man." Nranda pointed to Maximo. "Go! Take your woman with you. The cook, also."

Maximo rose and glowered at her but did as he had been told.

"Five remain, and this is what we wish." There was silence as she looked from Wyatt on her left to Brenda, from Brenda to June, from June to Gisele, and from Gisele to J. R. Christmas on her right. "You may choose, but one must choose for the group. Is that understood? You may remember us, and all that has taken place in this, the Christmas of us. Or you may forget—if that is what the chooser wishes."

No one spoke until Dondel caught the eye of J. R. Christmas. "You will be concerned for your profit," Dondel said. "You have great need of it, I believe."

J. R. Christmas nodded. "We need it badly. You're right."

"Though you forget, it will not be gone. You will not remember how it came into your hands, but you will have it still." Dondel took a thick packet of bills from his coat. "Here is more. It is nothing to us. Do not count it until we have gone. And merry Christmas." He tossed it to Erennide.

"This is from Dondel," she said. "Some of you may receive other gifts from certain ones of us in the years to come. That might happen." She passed the packet—a stack of fifty dollar bills—to J. R. Christmas.

Nranda said, "You five who remain know not only the ghosts we have exhibited to you, but us. You have heard our words, and we have heard yours. Some of you have shared food with us, and there is not one of you who has not shared life with us. Who denies this?"

J. R. Christmas looked at June, and June at him. Gisele and Brenda exchanged glances. Wyatt looked at his shoes.

Andril coughed. "Very well. Quickly, please. Who are we? Whom have you kissed? To whom did you teach your songs? Are we your countrymen? You know we are not. If we are not, who are we?"

June said, "You're human beings. That's what I feel."

Wyatt whispered, "Not me." He had not meant it to be heard, but all of them heard him.

"You must be specific," Nranda snapped. "You. The waiter. What are we? Say it!"

"You're devils," Wyatt told her. "Mr. Dondel gave me a hundred bucks, but that doesn't change what I think, and I think you're a devil straight from Hell."

"The short woman next." Nranda pointed.

"I'm with this kid," Brenda said. Her hand found Wyatt's and clasped it. "With him or anyway close to him. Friendly or unfriendly, you're demons."

"Mrs. Christmas next. Speak."

June shook her head.

"You have no opinion? None?"

"I know what I believe you are," June said. Her voice carried no emotion. "I don't want to be the one to choose, so I won't say."

"You must!"

June shook her head.

Andril smiled at her. "I understand, although I am not certain Nranda does. We will take you last. If either of the others arrives at the answer, we will not take you at all."

June smiled; she was not pretty even when she smiled, yet there was something better and more lasting in her eyes.

Andril turned to his left. "You are called Gisele, are you not? You must share your wisdom with us, Gisele. We insist."

"I saw a ghost," Gisele said.

Nranda snorted.

"I saw a ghost. He was—it doesn't matter. What he told me was meant to be terribly, terribly cruel. I know that. But it wasn't. Those were the words that unlocked my cage, and I spread my wings." She looked at Wyatt and seemed hardly older than he.

"You must tell us what you think," Nranda snapped. "Your most promising theory. Who are we? What are we?"

Gisele rose. For a moment she looked at Dondel.

And giggled.

He chuckled, a chuckle full of warmth and friendship, and she crossed the circle and tried to take Nranda's hands. "I think you're angels. You may be fallen angels, like the waiter said. You're angels just the same."

"Please return to your seat," Nranda told her, and she did.

Erennide whispered, "You must try like the others, my Jule."

J. R. Christmas nodded. "I saw ghosts, too, just like Ms. Grantham. I saw ten or twelve, and three spoke to me." He himself could speak no more.

From the other side of the circle, June said softly, "Was it so bad, Julius?"

"It wasn't. It was good." He raised his voice. "I said I talked to three ghosts, and that's the truth. I think there's a bigger truth—that I've talked to seven. You're ghosts, if you ask me. The ghosts of what, I don't know. But ghosts. You wanted my guess. All right, you have it."

"And we," Andril murmured, "must have your wife's after all." He turned to June. "Had any of the other four been correct, I could have spared you this. They were not, by which you know that we are not devils, demons, angels, or ghosts. You called us human beings, and you were quite correct. We are. Be more specific."

June rose. Although she was not tall, she seemed tall in that moment. "You want a guess," she began. "You're going to get a speech instead. Last night, when most of you were in bed, I put up my old crib set under the tree. This man Andril," she gestured to her left, "watched me, and asked what Mary and Joseph, and all the shepherds and angels, were worshipping. I told him I'd put the child Jesus in the crib on Christmas morning—I've done it, though I doubt that anybody noticed."

"I did," Andril murmured.

"And I said that until I did, they were worshipping nothing. I thought about that later, and I've thought about it ever since. I feel it's the key, or maybe the key to the key. It's the key to what's wrong with Christmas. And it's the key to the key to what's happened to the five of us this Christmas."

She paused as if waiting for an interruption; none came.

"The trouble with Christmas is that we don't think of the child. Holiday means holy day. I suppose everybody knows. All right, there's nothing wrong with the things we think about, decorating the house, and getting presents for other people and giving them. There's nothing wrong with singing, or playing games, or kissing under the mistletoe. But mostly we don't think of the child at all, and as long as we don't, we're worshipping nothing."

"She knows," Erennide told Andril.

Very slightly, he nodded.

"There's a child with you," June said. "I gave that child milk and a cookie, and some strawberries I had. We didn't see it much, and when we did, we didn't pay much attention to it. The child's the key just the same." She pointed. "Anybody here who understands about the child understands Erennide there." She pointed again. "And Nranda, too. And both the men."

Dondel clapped. His hands came together softly, making no sound; but he continued clapping.

"You won't get a guess from me," June said. "I've told you why you won't get one. I've given the rest a clue, and any of them who want to decide can speak up and do it."

For a moment, no one spoke; then Brenda said, "I just wish I knew what the hell you're talking about."

"You must decide," Erennide told June. "You cannot escape this."

"It's whether we forget all this or remember it?"

Erennide nodded. So did J. R. Christmas, who was fingering the thick packet of bills in his coat pocket.

"I want a vote." June sighed. "I'll decide whichever way the vote goes."

Wyatt said, "Don't call on me first, Mom. I got to think."

"I'll go first," Brenda announced. "I want to forget. Is that plain enough?" June nodded.

Gisele's soft voice seemed to float in the silence. "I wish to recall everything. I must. I must remember."

J. R. Christmas cleared his throat. "Some of it was bad and some was good, June honey. I'd like to forget the bad and remember the good." He glanced at Erennide and stood a trifle straighter. "That's probably the way it is for everyone, but we don't get to pick and choose. So I'm with Ms. Grantham. I want to remember."

More loudly than necessary, Wyatt said, "So do I, Mom. Can I explain?" June nodded.

"Me and Nranda did things you wouldn't like, and it got me thinkin' about the kids at school and what jerks they are. Then I thought, oh shit, they're only kids, cut 'em some slack. After that it hit me that I was growin' up. I was growin' up, and you don't know how bad you need to till you start. I want to hang onto that."

Andril rose. "You are not bound by them or by what you have said, June.

You are to decide, not they. If you choose with Brenda Pepper, they will never know you chose to disregard their vote. And neither will you."

June looked at her husband and her son, at Brenda and at Gisele. Then at Erennide. Last of all, and longest, at Andril.

She shut her eyes and seemed to nibble her lower lip.

ABOUT THE RHYSLING AWARDS

The Rhysling Awards are given each year by the Science Fiction Poetry Association (SFPA) in recognition of the best science fiction, fantasy, or horror poems of the year. Each year, members of SFPA nominate works that are compiled into an annual anthology; members then vote to select winners from the anthology's contents. The award is given in two categories: works of fifty or more lines are eligible for Best Long Poem, and works shorter than that are eligible for Best Short Poem. Additionally, SFPA gives the Dwarf Stars Award to a poem of ten or fewer lines.

"THE LIBRARY, AFTER"

SHIRA LIPKIN

The library sat quietly for some time, keeping to itself. Years passed, and decades, and the library was alone—no hands on its card catalogs, no requests in its system, no books entering or leaving by any means. Static.

It was some intrepid teen-girl-detective book that ventured forth first, exploring the grounds and the records. She found no data. Actually, she found a profound lack of data, the cessation of data. All clues led to one conclusion:

The library had been abandoned.

There was a cacophony from the periodicals, quick-tempered as they were; a slow susurrus from Reference, with their heavy and ponderous minds. Encyclopedias yawned and woke from their long sleep of disuse. Fiction gathered close to itself with a complete lack of regard for genre classifications. History found no precedent. Philosophy had some theories, but no one listened.

And after the flurry, the panic, what?

Awakened, the library went feral.

The books opened—reference first, because reference had always thought that information ought to be free. Fantasy explored reference, found new information and new tangents that it shared with mystery and science fiction. Noir and romance touched hesitantly, losing their shyness quickly once exposed to new ideas.

New genres formed and split and reformed, tangents spilling out like capillaries. Freed of the responsibility to be useful and to fit human desires and expectations, Story explored itself in Mandelbrot swirls.

Results were mixed, but intriguing.

The children's books told each other their stories. Mischievous cats changed the fates of giving trees. The girl-detective books mapped points of interest. The periodicals flew like birds over the stacks and gathered intel.

The science-noir-unicorn genre was shortlived, but did spawn an actual theoretical quantum unicorn, who lurked in his trenchcoat and fedora behind the medical books, reading graphic novels and hoping for a dame to walk through the door.

The books found that when they agreed upon something enough, it became so. The unicorn soon had many companions, though none so long-lived as he. It is difficult for that many stories to reach consensus.

The humans never returned, but the books grew not to mind. They told each other to each other, and sent pages out into the world; the wind blows them onto abandoned buildings, gargoyles, doghouses and towers, and says *listen*.

Let me tell you a story.

"THE CURATOR SPEAKS IN THE DEPARTMENT OF DEAD LANGUAGES"

MEGAN ARKENBERG

Every year, there are people—not many,
but some—who send me charcoal rubbings,
etchings, transcriptions from old tombs
and ask me what they mean.
Some, I can translate; we reached
the language in time, or the phrase survives
idiomatically on other tongues,
or guesswork is enough to patch
the ragged edges of what we know.
But every year, there are some I cannot find,
some I cannot save.

Why do I hate it so much, writing
these letters, these terse apologies for failing
to satisfy a stranger's curiosity? That's all
it is; these tombs do not belong to
parents, old lovers, or even more distant relations.
Most have stood silent for centuries.

Yet there are people who care enough
to ask what they said, and I must admit
guilty ignorance.

When I was a very small girl,
I found a broken chickadee beneath
the oak that held its nest. I took it in,
washed it and fed it rice and built it
a nest of soft rags, but it lived only
one night. I cried hard at its death,
as long and hard as I would cry for my mother's
decades later. I think of that sometimes
while writing these letters: the awful risk
of caring for strangers.

We cannot save all of them.
Even the ones that survive have been
broken, lamed, their limbs amputated,
their features mangled past recognition.
Inevitably, some pieces are lost. Words
slip through the cracks, nuances are buried
in pauper's graves.

On the red moon of Tzevet'an,
a thief told me of the fourteen words
men cannot say to women,
but there were no other men
in the ice-bound prison where he died.
The words are lost, unguessable.
The last speaker of the Kao-Kling tongue
was a little girl, four years old, who knew
little more than the names of fruits
and the disease that killed her family.

Her mother had been a flower arranger
to the Lord of Fenkanpao; again and again
the child told me of a flower
as wide as her mother's hand, the blue of fresh milk
that had the most beautiful name.
She could not remember what it was, and
fever carried her off before
she could show me where it grew.

These are the mysteries
we know about. There are times
my frustration is so great,
my anger at time's merciless entropy
is so strong, that I give voice
to the most punishing thoughts.
How much is buried in the conquered lands,
not only of answers
but of the questions themselves?
How much more plentiful
are the dead without ghosts?

And yet I am trying.
Without funds, without time, sometimes
without love—but I am trying.
If not to save all of them, at least
to leave a marker above the graves.

"BLUE ROSE BUDDHA"

MARGE SIMON

Blue roses in her ears,
an embroidered hat to match
she sees beyond tomorrow,
her lips pursed in a smirk
that lasts a hundred lifetimes.

She awaits her tea in silence,
knowing that the end of the world
won't bother her routine.

Thrice she moves her hand
to swat the flies.

PAST NEBULA AWARD WINNERS

1965

Novel: *Dune* by Frank Herbert
Novella: "He Who Shapes" by Roger Zelazny and "The Saliva Tree" by Brian Aldiss (tie)
Novelette: "The Doors of His Face, the Lamps of His Mouth" by Roger Zelazny
Short Story: "'Repent, Harlequin!' Said the Ticktockman" by Harlan Ellison

1966

Novel: *Babel-17* by Samuel R. Delany and *Flowers for Algernon* by Daniel Keyes (tie)
Novella: "The Last Castle" by Jack Vance
Novelette: "Call Him Lord" by Gordon R. Dickson
Short Story: "The Secret Place" by Richard McKenna

1967

Novel: *The Einstein Intersection* by Samuel R. Delany
Novella: "Behold the Man" by Michael Moorcock
Novelette: "Gonna Roll the Bones" by Fritz Leiber
Short Story: "Aye, and Gomorrah" by Samuel R. Delany

1968

Novel: *Rite of Passage* by Alexei Panshin
Novella: "Dragonrider" by Anne McCaffrey
Novelette: "Mother to the World" by Richard Wilson
Short Story: "The Planners" by Kate Wilhelm

1969

Novel: *The Left Hand of Darkness* by Ursula K. Le Guin
Novella: "A Boy and His Dog" by Harlan Ellison
Novelette: "Time Considered as a Helix of Semi-Precious Stones" by Samuel R. Delany
Short Story: "Passengers" by Robert Silverberg

1970

Novel: *Ringworld* by Larry Niven
Novella: "Ill Met in Lankhmar" by Fritz Leiber
Novelette: "Slow Sculpture" by Theodore Sturgeon
Short Story: No Award

1971

Novel: *A Time of Changes* by Robert Silverberg
Novella: "The Missing Man" by Katherine MacLean
Novelette: "The Queen of Air and Darkness" by Poul Anderson
Short Story: "Good News from the Vatican" by Robert Silverberg

1972

Novel: *The Gods Themselves* by Isaac Asimov
Novella: "A Meeting with Medusa" by Arthur C. Clarke
Novelette: "Goat Song" by Poul Anderson
Short Story: "When It Changed" by Joanna Russ

1973

Novel: *Rendezvous with Rama* by Arthur C. Clarke
Novella: "The Death of Doctor Island" by Gene Wolfe
Novelette: "Of Mist, and Grass, and Sand" by Vonda N. McIntyre
Short Story: "Love Is the Plan, the Plan Is Death" by James Tiptree Jr.
Dramatic Presentation: *Soylent Green*

1974

Novel: *The Dispossessed* by Ursula K. Le Guin
Novella: "Born with the Dead" by Robert Silverberg
Novelette: "If the Stars Are Gods" by Gordon Eklund and Gregory Benford
Short Story: "The Day before the Revolution" by Ursula K. Le Guin
Dramatic Presentation: *Sleeper* by Woody Allen
Grand Master: Robert Heinlein

1975

Novel: *The Forever War* by Joe Haldeman
Novella: "Home Is the Hangman" by Roger Zelazny
Novelette: "San Diego Lightfoot Sue" by Tom Reamy
Short Story: "Catch That Zeppelin" by Fritz Leiber

Dramatic Presentation: *Young Frankenstein* by Mel Brooks and Gene Wilder
Grand Master: Jack Williamson

1976

Novel: *Man Plus* by Frederik Pohl
Novella: "Houston, Houston, Do You Read?" by James Tiptree Jr.
Novelette: "The Bicentennial Man" by Isaac Asimov
Short Story: "A Crowd of Shadows" by C. L. Grant
Grand Master: Clifford D. Simak

1977

Novel: *Gateway* by Frederik Pohl
Novella: "Stardance" by Spider and Jeanne Robinson
Novelette: "The Screwfly Solution" by Racoona Sheldon
Short Story: "Jeffty Is Five" by Harlan Ellison

1978

Novel: *Dreamsnake* by Vonda N. McIntyre
Novella: "The Persistence of Vision" by John Varley
Novelette: "A Glow of Candles, A Unicorn's Eye" by C. L. Grant
Short Story: "Stone" by Edward Bryant
Grand Master: L. Sprague de Camp

1979

Novel: *The Fountains of Paradise* by Arthur C. Clarke
Novella: "Enemy Mine" by Barry B. Longyear
Novelette: "Sandkings" by George R. R. Martin
Short Story: "GiANTS" by Edward Bryant

1980

Novel: *Timescape* by Gregory Benford
Novella: "Unicorn Tapestry" by Suzy McKee Charnas
Novelette: "The Ugly Chickens" by Howard Waldrop
Short Story: "Grotto of the Dancing Deer" by Clifford D. Simak
Grand Master: Fritz Leiber

1981

Novel: *The Claw of the Conciliator* by Gene Wolfe
Novella: "The Saturn Game" by Poul Anderson
Novelette: "The Quickening" by Michael Bishop
Short Story: "The Bone Flute" by Lisa Tuttle [declined by author]

1982

Novel: *No Enemy but Time* by Michael Bishop
Novella: "Another Orphan" by John Kessel
Novelette: "Fire Watch" by Connie Willis
Short Story: "A Letter from the Clearys" by Connie Willis

1983

Novel: *Startide Rising* by David Brin
Novella: "Hardfought" by Greg Bear
Novelette: "Blood Music" by Greg Bear
Short Story: "The Peacemaker" by Gardner Dozois
Grand Master: Andre Norton

1984

Novel: *Neuromancer* by William Gibson
Novella: "Press Enter [ ]" by John Varley
Novelette: "Blood Child" by Octavia Butler
Short Story: "Morning Child" by Gardner Dozois

1985

Novel: *Ender's Game* by Orson Scott Card
Novella: "Sailing to Byzantium" by Robert Silverberg
Novelette: "Portraits of His Children" by George R. R. Martin
Short Story: "Out of All Them Bright Stars" by Nancy Kress
Grand Master: Arthur C. Clarke

1986

Novel: *Speaker for the Dead* by Orson Scott Card
Novella: "R&R" by Lucius Shepard
Novelette: "The Girl Who Fell into the Sky" by Kate Wilhelm
Short Story: "Tangents" by Greg Bear
Grand Master: Isaac Asimov

1987

Novel: *The Falling Woman* by Pat Murphy
Novella: "The Blind Geometer" by Kim Stanley Robinson
Novelette: "Rachel in Love" by Pat Murphy
Short Story: "Forever Yours, Anna" by Kate Wilhelm
Grand Master: Alfred Bester

1988

Novel: *Falling Free* by Lois McMaster Bujold
Novella: "The Last of the Winnebagos" by Connie Willis
Novelette: "Schrödinger's Kitten" by George Alec Effinger
Short Story: "Bible Stories for Adults, No. 17: The Deluge" by James Morrow
Grand Master: Ray Bradbury

1989

Novel: *The Healer's War* by Elizabeth Ann Scarborough
Novella: "The Mountains of Mourning" by Lois McMaster Bujold
Novelette: "At the Rialto" by Connie Willis
Short Story: "Ripples in the Dirac Sea" by Geoffrey A. Landis

1990

Novel: *Tehanu: The Last Book of Earthsea* by Ursula K. Le Guin
Novella: "The Hemingway Hoax" by Joe Haldeman
Novelette: "Tower of Babylon" by Ted Chiang
Short Story: "Bears Discover Fire" by Terry Bisson
Grand Master: Lester del Rey

1991

Novel: *Stations of the Tide* by Michael Swanwick
Novella: "Beggars in Spain" by Nancy Kress
Novelette: "Guide Dog" by Mike Conner
Short Story: "Ma Qui" by Alan Brennert

1992

Novel: *Doomsday Book* by Connie Willis
Novella: "City of Truth" by James Morrow
Novelette: "Danny Goes to Mars" by Pamela Sargent
Short Story: "Even the Queen" by Connie Willis
Grand Master: Frederick Pohl

1993

Novel: *Red Mars* by Kim Stanley Robinson
Novella: "The Night We Buried Road Dog" by Jack Cady
Novelette: "Georgia on My Mind" by Charles Sheffield
Short Story: "Graves" by Joe Haldeman

1994

Novel: *Moving Mars* by Greg Bear
Novella: "Seven Views of Olduvai Gorge" by Mike Resnick
Novelette: "The Martian Child" by David Gerrold
Short Story: "A Defense of the Social Contracts" by Martha Soukup
Grand Master: Damon Knight
Author Emeritus: Emil Petaja

1995

Novel: *The Terminal Experiment* by Robert J. Sawyer
Novella: "Last Summer at Mars Hill" by Elizabeth Hand
Novelette: "Solitude" by Ursula K. Le Guin
Short Story: "Death and the Librarian" by Esther M. Friesner
Grand Master: A. E. van Vogt
Author Emeritus: Wilson "Bob" Tucker

1996

Novel: *Slow River* by Nicola Griffith
Novella: "Da Vinci Rising" by Jack Dann
Novelette: "Lifeboat on a Burning Sea" by Bruce Holland Rogers
Short Story: "A Birthday" by Esther M. Friesner
Grand Master: Jack Vance
Author Emeritus: Judith Merril

1997

Novel: *The Moon and the Sun* by Vonda N. McIntyre
Novella: "Abandon in Place" by Jerry Oltion
Novelette: "Flowers of Aulit Prison" by Nancy Kress
Short Story: "Sister Emily's Lightship" by Jane Yolen
Grand Master: Poul Anderson
Author Emeritus: Nelson Slade Bond

1998

Novel: *Forever Peace* by Joe Haldeman
Novella: "Reading the Bones" by Sheila Finch
Novelette: "Lost Girls" by Jane Yolen
Short Story: "Thirteen Ways to Water" by Bruce Holland Rogers
Grand Master: Hal Clement (Harry Stubbs)
Author Emeritus: William Tenn (Philip Klass)

1999

Novel: *Parable of the Talents* by Octavia E. Butler
Novella: "Story of Your Life" by Ted Chiang
Novelette: "Mars Is No Place for Children" by Mary A. Turzillo
Short Story: "The Cost of Doing Business" by Leslie What
Script: *The Sixth Sense* by M. Night Shyamalan
Grand Master: Brian W. Aldiss
Author Emeritus: Daniel Keyes

2000

Novel: *Darwin's Radio* by Greg Bear
Novella: "Goddesses" by Linda Nagata
Novelette: "Daddy's World" by Walter Jon Williams
Short Story: "macs" by Terry Bisson
Script: *Galaxy Quest* by Robert Gordon and David Howard
Ray Bradbury Award: Yuri Rasovsky and Harlan Ellison
Grand Master: Philip José Farmer
Author Emeritus: Robert Sheckley

2001

Novel: *The Quantum Rose* by Catherine Asaro
Novella: "The Ultimate Earth" by Jack Williamson
Novelette: "Louise's Ghost" by Kelly Link
Short Story: "The Cure for Everything" by Severna Park
Script: *Crouching Tiger, Hidden Dragon* by James Schamus, Kuo Jung Tsai, and Hui-Ling Wang
President's Award: Betty Ballantine

2002

Novel: *American Gods* by Neil Gaiman
Novella: "Bronte's Egg" by Richard Chwedyk
Novelette: "Hell Is the Absence of God" by Ted Chiang
Short Story: "Creature" by Carol Emshwiller
Script: *The Lord of the Rings: The Fellowship of the Ring* by Frances Walsh, Phillipa Boyens, and Peter Jackson
Grand Master: Ursula K. Le Guin
Author Emeritus: Katherine MacLean

2003

Novel: *Speed of Dark* by Elizabeth Moon
Novella: "Coraline" by Neil Gaiman
Novelette: "The Empire of Ice Cream" by Jeffrey Ford
Short Story: "What I Didn't See" by Karen Joy Fowler
Script: *The Lord of the Rings: The Two Towers* by Frances Walsh, Phillipa Boyens, Stephen Sinclair, and Peter Jackson
Grand Master: Robert Silverberg
Author Emeritus: Charles L. Harness

2004

Novel: *Paladin of Souls* by Lois McMaster Bujold
Novella: "The Green Leopard Plague" by Walter Jon Williams
Novelette: "Basement Magic" by Ellen Klages
Short Story: "Coming to Terms" by Eileen Gunn
Script: *The Lord of the Rings: The Return of the King* by Frances Walsh, Phillipa
    Boyens, and Peter Jackson
Grand Master: Anne McCaffrey

2005

Novel: *Camouflage* by Joe Haldeman
Novella: "Magic for Beginners" by Kelly Link
Novelette: "The Faery Handbag" by Kelly Link
Short Story: "I Live with You" by Carol Emshwiller
Script: *Serenity* by Joss Whedon
Grand Master: Harlan Ellison
Author Emeritus: William F. Nolan

2006

Novel: *Seeker* by Jack McDevitt
Novella: "Burn" by James Patrick Kelly
Novelette: "Two Hearts" by Peter S. Beagle
Short Story: "Echo" by Elizabeth Hand
Script: *Howl's Moving Castle* by Hayao Miyazaki, Cindy Davis Hewitt, and
    Donald H. Hewitt
Andre Norton Award for Young Adult Science Fiction and Fantasy:
    Magic or Madness by Justine Larbalestier
Grand Master: James Gunn
Author Emeritus: D. G. Compton

2007

Novel: *The Yiddish Policemen's Union* by Michael Chabon
Novella: "Fountain of Age" by Nancy Kress
Novelette: "The Merchant and the Alchemist's Gate" by Ted Chiang
Short Story: "Always" by Karen Joy Fowler
Script: *Pan's Labyrinth* by Guillermo del Toro
Andre Norton Award for Young Adult Science Fiction and Fantasy: *Harry Potter and the Deathly Hallows* by J. K. Rowling
Grand Master: Michael Moorcock
Author Emeritus: Ardath Mayhar
SFWA Service Awards: Melisa Michaels and Graham P. Collins

2008

Novel: *Powers* by Ursula K. Le Guin
Novella: "The Spacetime Pool" by Catherine Asaro
Novelette: "Pride and Prometheus" by John Kessel
Short Story: "Trophy Wives" by Nina Kiriki Hoffman
Script: *WALL-E* by Andrew Stanton and Jim Reardon. Original story by Andrew Stanton and Pete Docter
Andre Norton Award for Young Adult Science Fiction and Fantasy: *Flora's Dare: How a Girl of Spirit Gambles All to Expand Her Vocabulary, Confront a Bouncing Boy Terror, and Try to Save Califa from a Shaky Doom (Despite Being Confined to Her Room)* by Ysabeau S. Wilce
Grand Master: Harry Harrison
Author Emeritus: M. J. Engh
Solstice Awards: Kate Wilhelm, Martin H. Greenberg, and Algis Budrys (posthumous)
SFWA Service Award: Victoria Strauss

2009

Novel: *The Windup Girl* by Paolo Bacigalupi

Novella: "The Women of Nell Gwynne's" by Kage Baker

Novelette: "Sinner, Baker, Fabulist, Priest; Red Mask, Black Mask, Gentleman, Beast" by Eugie Foster

Short Story: "Spar" by Kij Johnson

Ray Bradbury Award: *District 9* by Neill Blomkamp and Terri Tatchell

Andre Norton Award for Young Adult Science Fiction and Fantasy: *The Girl Who Circumnavigated Fairyland in a Ship of Her Own Making* by Catherynne M. Valente

Grand Master: Joe Haldeman

Author Emeritus: Neal Barrett Jr.

Solstice Awards: Tom Doherty, Terri Windling, and Donald A. Wollheim (posthumous)

SFWA Service Awards: Vonda N. McIntyre and Keith Stokes

2010

Novel: *Blackout/All Clear* by Connie Willis

Novella: "The Lady Who Plucked Red Flowers beneath the Queen's Window" by Rachel Swirsky

Novelette: "That Leviathan Whom Thou Hast Made" by Eric James Stone

Short Story: "Ponies" by Kij Johnson and "How Interesting: A Tiny Man" by Harlan Ellison (tie)

Ray Bradbury Award: *Inception* by Christopher Nolan

Andre Norton Award for Young Adult Science Fiction and Fantasy: *I Shall Wear Midnight* by Terry Pratchett

2011

Novel: *Among Others* by Jo Walton
Novella: "The Man Who Bridged the Mist" by Kij Johnson
Novelette: "What We Found" by Geoff Ryman
Short Story: "The Paper Menagerie" by Ken Liu
Ray Bradbury Award: *Doctor Who*: "The Doctor's Wife" by Neil Gaiman (writer), Richard Clark (director)
Andre Norton Award for Young Adult Science Fiction and Fantasy: *The Freedom Maze* by Delia Sherman
Damon Knight Memorial Grand Master Award: Connie Willis
Solstice Awards: Octavia Butler (posthumous) and John Clute
SFWA Service Award: Bud Webster

2012

Novel: *2312* by Kim Stanley Robinson
Novella: "After the Fall, Before the Fall, During the Fall" by Nancy Kress
Novelette: "Close Encounters" by Andy Duncan
Short Story: "Immersion" by Aliette de Bodard
Ray Bradbury Award: *Beasts of the Southern Wild* by Benh Zeitlin (director), Benh Zeitlin, and Lucy Abilar (writers)
Andre Norton Award for Young Adult Science Fiction and Fantasy: *Fair Coin* by E. C. Myers

ACKNOWLEDGMENTS

I'd like to thank James Gunn, Vaughne Hansen, Jim Kelly, John Kessel, and Gary K. Wolfe.

ABOUT THE EDITOR

Photo © Beth Gwinn.

Kij Johnson is an American writer of fantasy. She has worked extensively in publishing as managing editor for Tor Books and TSR, collections editor for Dark Horse Comics, and content manager working on the Microsoft Reader. While working at Wizards of the Coast, she was also continuity manager for Magic: The Gathering and creative director for AD&D settings Greyhawk and Forgotten Realms. She teaches creative writing and fantasy literature at the University of Kansas, where she is associate director for the Center for the Study of Science Fiction and serves as a final judge for the Theodore Sturgeon Memorial Award. Johnson is the author of three novels and more than thirty short works of fiction and is a winner of the Nebula, Hugo, World Fantasy, Sturgeon, and Crawford Awards.

Visit Kij at www.kijjohnson.com.